Steel & Thunder

Steel & Thunder

DOMINIC N. ASHEN

4 Horsemen
Publications, Inc.

4 Horsemen
Publications, Inc.

4 Horsemen Publications, Inc.
1497 Main St. Suite 169
Dunedin, FL 34698
4horsemenpublications.com
info@4horsemenpublications.com

Edited by Tilda M. Cooke
Cover by Oxford and VW
Typeset By Sarah Casagrande

Library of Congress Control Number: 2021933897

Hardcover ISBN-13: 978-1-64450-269-3
Audiobook ISBN-13: 978-1-64450-268-6
Paperback ISBN-13: 978-1-64450-195-5
Ebook ISBN-13: 978-1-64450-163-4

Table of Contents

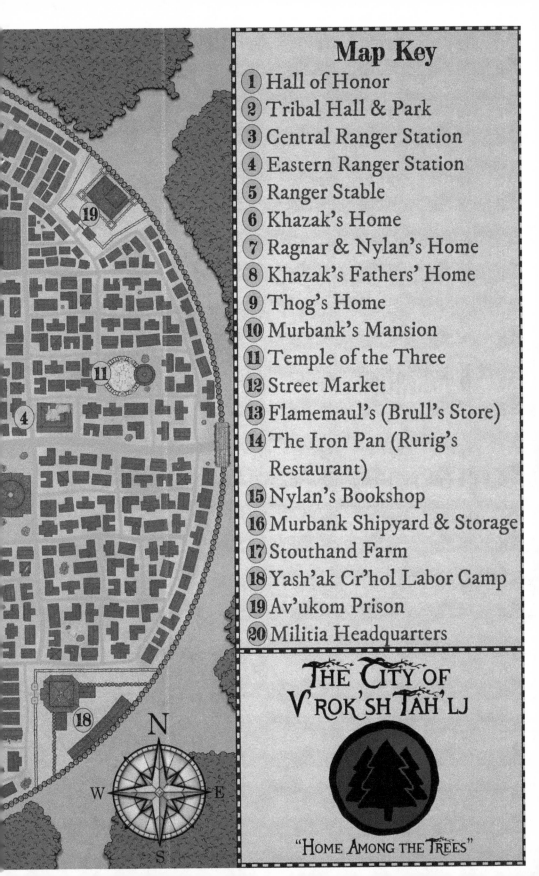

Map Key

1. Hall of Honor
2. Tribal Hall & Park
3. Central Ranger Station
4. Eastern Ranger Station
5. Ranger Stable
6. Khazak's Home
7. Ragnar & Nylan's Home
8. Khazak's Fathers' Home
9. Thog's Home
10. Murbank's Mansion
11. Temple of the Three
12. Street Market
13. Flamemaul's (Brull's Store)
14. The Iron Pan (Rurig's Restaurant)
15. Nylan's Bookshop
16. Murbank Shipyard & Storage
17. Stouthand Farm
18. Yash'ak Cr'hol Labor Camp
19. Av'ukom Prison
20. Militia Headquarters

The City of V'rok'sh Tah'lj

"Home Among the Trees"

Dedication

To Erik for always supporting me, to Frank for always believing in me, and to Mike for always taking care of me. I couldn't have done this without you.

Chapter One

"**A**re we there yet?" I hear Nathaniel ask for the hundredth time since we started walking this morning.

"*No*," Elisabeth growls from the front of the group. "Now *stop asking*."

"Yes, dear," Nate sighs.

Corrine and I share a look, no doubt thinking the same thing: What does she see in him?

"We're almost there," Adam says from his position in front next to Liss (short for Elisabeth). "We should have just made it past the orc camps." The people in the last town told us the orcs in the area were mostly peaceful, but we still wanted to play it safe and steer clear. I've also never actually met an orc before, so I'm not entirely sure I believe them.

Where we come from, there aren't any orcs. Or many non-humans at all. Growing up, I learned there were orcs on the mainland in the south and east, but everything I knew came from the stories I heard. They didn't exactly paint a pretty picture: lots of fighting, blood, and death. Sometimes they were a race obsessed with honor, other times creatures who would invade your land and raze your fields. So yeah, holding my breath on that one.

The current marching order has become our default travel formation. Adam, Liss, and I are the muscle, though those two have me beat in that department lately. They stay on guard in front while I take the rear, with our two squishy magic users sandwiched in the middle. I don't mind—Corrine is surprisingly fun to talk to—but sometimes Nate is just so fucking irritating. I swear he does it on purpose. That's what happens when you agree to travel halfway around the world with someone you barely know.

The five of us have been traveling together for a month now (two if you count that godsawful boat ride), and even rang in the new year together just a few weeks ago, making all sorts of plans as a group. Our goals as exploring adventurers are still a little undefined at this point, but after wandering up and down the coast taking odd jobs for weeks, we *finally* got a lead on something good in Holbrooke, the last town we stayed in. Apparently, a few years back, an earthquake uncovered some elven ruins in the mountains. Most people stayed away because of the orcs, but the rumors of there being something magical and powerful inside were enough to sway us. The desperation to do *anything* besides making a delivery or killing a giant rat may have contributed as well. That was four days ago.

I'm not sure what awaits us once we get to the ruins, but I trust my team to be able to handle it. Well, most of them at least. I've known Adam forever: tall, blonde, muscular, your classic golden boy who was nearly always the top of our class. I say nearly because the two of us were usually engaged in a friendly competition over...everything—sports, archery, sword fighting. Once, in the middle of a school day, we both jumped in a lake just to see who could hold their breath the longest. We met Liss when we entered the knight academy after finishing school. She's maybe an inch or two shorter than Adam with fiery red hair that she normally dyes brown and cuts short. Since that's not really possible out in the forest, she's taken to wearing a hood over it. I'm just a couple of inches shorter than she is, clocking in at around 5'10" last time I checked. My black hair is currently shaggier than I like it, and I've got the beginnings of a beard from the three days we've been out here.

Corrine and Nathaniel joined us only a few days before we got on the boat. I was the one who noticed Corrine in the tavern, not that it was hard to spot the tall blonde pigtailed woman dressed like a nun. After asking me not to call her that, she told me she was looking for a group to make the journey across the ocean with for her "missionary work." She seemed a little weird, but there was a healthy amount of fear and disgust over the establishment we were sitting in, so I knew she wasn't totally out of her mind. Other than some Bible-study and group prayers, I haven't seen her do much missionary-ing, but she says that "helping out anyone in the name of God is good work."

We met Nate the following night in the same tavern after he answered an ad Adam posted. We were getting desperate for a magic user, but I still told Adam we might want to rethink going with the obvious mage-school dropout. His robe is dirty, his brown hair messy, and he seems to have perpetual stubble, even after spending days in the forest. He's also *just* a little taller than I am, which wouldn't be something I'd ever pay attention to if he didn't point it out *over* and *over* and *over*.

At some point during the boat ride, Liss and Nate started fucking. A month on the water with only your hand is no fun, and it's not like I have any experience myself to speak of, so I didn't blame her for taking care of what she needed to. I was just surprised it continued once we were back on solid land, and there were more viable candidates around. A lot more viable. I mean, he's been a *fine* wizard, I guess.

"Are you sure we didn't pass it?" He's just so fucking annoying.

"I think I see it." Liss points as we pass a hill to reveal the base of the mountain. A few more paces and I'm able to see what she means, spotting a cave in the distance. Large boulders sit on either side of it, huge cracks split the ground and mountainside, but there's still a clear path—as if the rocks have been moved intentionally.

As we get closer, the details get less fuzzy, and I can make out some of the stonework carved around the entrance. I've never actually *seen* elven ruins before, so I don't know if this is what they usually look like. There's a smooth column along each side of the cave, but they've got to be purely decorative.

We stop just outside the entrance. The cave is dark—duh, it's a cave—but that's not an issue since Adam is already grabbing a torch and flint from his pack. There are letters along the top of the entrance—Corrine calls them runes—but I can't read them. I swear it feels like I've seen them before, which is weird because, again, this is a first for me. For all of us, actually.

"Okay, I'm taking point," Adam tells the rest of us. He's technically the leader of our group. I'm second in command, though Liss might argue differently. "Once we're inside, Nate and Corrine will start checking for magic. Elf ruins aren't known for their traps, but David and Liss, keep your eyes peeled for anything I might miss." He reaches in his pack for another torch, handing it to me once it's lit. "Ready?"

"Ready," we agree in unison. Adam draws his sword and in we go.

The walls of the cave are smooth, like the floor and ceiling. They're plain at first, but as we move deeper inside, I see carvings along them. At first, it's just more of the oddly familiar script I saw outside, but soon there are small figures, and then full-on faces, very detailed and obviously elven.

I don't get much info on who they are, mostly because I still can't read any of this. I'm trying to take in the details on the walls but also *everything else* since you never know when there might be a trap or a secret passage. These places have those, right? But so far, it's just been one long hallway. I look back periodically and watch the cave entrance growing smaller behind us. I also hear some kind of ringing or buzzing in my ear.

"Hold." Adam slows down. It looks like we've reached the end of the hallway and the entrance to a larger room. Adam and Elisabeth enter first, the orange-yellow light from the torch illuminating the room around them. "I think we're good."

The rest of us enter the room carefully. It's pretty big. You could probably fit three or four dozen people in here. I count one, two...eight walls, including the one we entered from. They go very high, each one carved from floor to ceiling in intricate designs. I see words, figures, entire scenes depicted, the light making the details harder to see as they vanish into the darkness above. But what *really* pulls focus is across from us, facing the entrance. Without being prompted, Adam steps closer and holds up his torch.

In the center of the wall is a large, very detailed sculpture of a man. I guess I'm not sure sculpture is the right word. *Is it a relief?* I didn't really pay that much attention in art class. It's a part of the wall, but it also seems to be coming *off* the wall. He's tall, though I guess I'm not sure if he's meant to be life-sized or not. He's in a robe, arms at his side, with short slightly curled hair and a full beard. He's also got pointed ears, so not a human, but an elf.

"Do you guys hear that?" I rub my ear in irritation. The ringing worsened when we walked inside, and it's making it hard to focus.

"David, get over here so we can get a better look at this." Liss points next to Adam.

"Hold on." Somehow, my ear and the wall aren't the only things grabbing my attention in the room.

In the center of the room is a raised platform with a large pedestal, a brazier on the floor on either side. As I step forward, the buzzing in my ear grows, but it's not so bad that I can't light the two with my torch. As soon as the second one is lit, eight smaller braziers along the wall light up by themselves. The sudden illumination makes everyone jump, Liss even drawing her sword. No one says anything, waiting to see if we just sprang a trap.

"Shouldn't you be telling us about things like magical lights?" Liss gripes, sheathing her weapon.

"Sorry," Nate sighs before muttering a spell.

"I think that's Zeus." Corrine's voice echoes through the chamber, startling herself. We all stare at her and then back at the wall.

The elf is flanked on either side up and down by clouds, each of them thundering with lightning. Strewn among the clouds and lightning are dozens of eagles, each carved so intricately I can make out the individual feathers from here. I've heard the name Zeus, but my family has never been terribly religious and wasn't exactly interested in learning about someone else's. But I'll take Corrine's word for it—she is the "missionary" after all. And if we're looking at a god, I guess he might be life-sized after all.

"He's not usually depicted as an elf though." She steps past me, looking confused.

"The only other magical thing in the room is inside that box," Nathaniel announces to the rest of us and points to the pedestal in the center of the room.

"Fuck, I think that's where that sound is coming from too." It hurts a little to even look at it.

"What are you talking about?" Adam uses the floor to put out his torch now that the room is lit.

"Seriously, does no one else hear that?" I put my own torch out and rub at my ears again.

"No." Elisabeth moves forward. "What are you hearing?"

"I dunno, like a really high-pitched screech?" I shut one eye and rub my ear as if that'll help block out the sound. The rest of the group converges on the pedestal while I stay put. Getting closer to that box makes my head hurt.

"Looks like it's made of lead," Nate says before tapping the box with his staff. "It's pretty rusted and banged up. Probably meant to block out whatever magic thing David is hearing."

"What happens if we open it?" *It's not gonna make my head explode, is it?*

"Dunno. Wanna find out?" Nate grins and lifts his staff high to strike the box.

"Hold on. Maybe we should—" Adam cuts himself off when he hears the same thing I do: footsteps. Heavy ones, coming down the hall toward us. *Shit.* "David, on my right; Cor, Nate, get behind us."

I move to stand in formation, ignoring the throbbing pain in my head as I get closer to the lead box. I drop my pack and bedroll from my back and kick it to the side of the chamber, the others doing the same with their heavier gear. Corrine starts to speak the words to a spell, and a second later, my body tingles as the magic bolsters my strength. We all pull out our weapons as the footsteps quickly get loud enough for *everyone* to hear, and they're moving toward us fast.

I can feel everyone around me tense up as a group of orcs bursts into the room, swords drawn. A total of seven pour in, all green skin and leather armor, weapons aimed steadily in our direction. After a tense moment of both groups eyeing the other warily, the leader (*I mean, he's the one in front at least*) shouts something at us. Unfortunately, since none of us speak Orcish, it just sounds like a lot of growls and grunts.

Adam and I share a confused look, and he turns back to the leader. "We can't... Are you able to speak Common?"

The orc narrows his eyes at us and huffs, looking *very* displeased. He opens his mouth to respond. "Who—"

And that's when all hell breaks loose.

"IGNI!" A fireball the size of my fist flies over my left shoulder, landing near three orcs on our right who leap out of the way as it explodes.

"Dammit!" Adam shouts, annoyed but having no real choice but to leap toward the enemy leader while he's distracted.

Liss and I are right behind him, each taking on a group of orcs on either side. Nate's little stunt, while stupid, did manage to take out at least one of my group, who looks to be out cold with some nasty burns. The other two might be a little singed, but mostly they just look pissed off. I hear the sounds of grunts and metal on metal to my left, and I've got to hope that my team is able to handle things themselves for now.

I grip the sword tightly in my hand, ignoring the constant ringing in my ears and waiting for one or both of them to attack me. I really wish I'd brought that second sword. These two are big muscle-y motherfuckers: a man and a woman. Strong doesn't mean graceful though, and when one of them runs at me, it isn't too difficult to dodge and send him flying to the floor with a well-placed kick.

Just as it looks like his friend is going to lunge at me, a high-pitched scream has us both turning our heads. I find the source, Corrine, running around the back of the room with an orc in pursuit. The rest of the team fares no better, with Liss pinned to the wall by one orc and Nate being *literally* pinned to the floor by another. Adam himself is being wrestled to the ground by the leader who is growling something at him that I can't make out from here.

"Hey!" I shout at the orc on Adam and rush him, and *fuck* is he big. Taller than Adam and with shoulders wider than I've ever seen on a human. I attempt to tackle him, but he doesn't even stumble as I bounce into his side. *Ugh, have I lost that much weight?*

I pick myself up and grab my sword, ready to try again, but the orc doesn't give me the chance. Dropping Adam, he barrels into me, shoulder checking me across the room and right into the pedestal. As searing pain shoots through my head, I look up to see a blurry green figure looking down at me, and then everything goes black.

I dream that I'm flying over an endless ocean. Dark clouds fill the sky above me, stretching on forever. The seas and winds are calm, at least until the rain begins to fall. It starts slowly, barely a trickle, but soon it's torrential with lighting streaking across the skies and thunder so loud my body shakes. The lightning begins to strike faster, moving closer and closer, until with a loud crack, my vision is blinded by white.

"I think he's waking up." *That sounds like Corrine.*

"Mmmmff." I slowly open my eyes, the blurry world coming back into focus. I wipe a hand down my face and sit up. "What happened? Where are we?"

"A jail cell," Nate answers. "The orcs took us back to their city."

"City? I thought it was just a small camp?" I rub my head. Feels like I've got a nasty bruise.

"Nope, it's a whole-ass city." Nate shrugs.

"Pretty impressive, actually," Corrine adds.

"Where are Adam and Liss?" I look around the cell, realizing they aren't with us. We're in a small cell with no furniture to speak of, the three of us sitting on the ground. The walls are all made of solid stone except one. Instead, it has a set of metal bars with a door.

"After you went down, Adam and Liss kept fighting," Corrine explains. "They... got pretty banged up. The guards said they were taking them to a healer."

"Yeah, right," Nate scoffs.

"Fuck." For once, I agree with Nate. We need to get out of here and find them—*now.* "What about you guys? Are you okay? Can you cast something and get us outta here? And what did they do with all our stuff?" Not just my sword, but my armor and pack are gone too.

"Not at the moment." Corrine frowns and holds up her shackled wrists.

"Anti-magic bracers." Nate shows me his matching pair. "Neither of us can cast anything as long as these are on."

"Shit." *How the hell are we going to get out of here?* I'm the only one whose hands are free. "What do we do? What happens now?"

"They said someone would be back to talk to us." Corrine frowns again. "But that was over an hour ago."

"We're never getting out of here." Nate slumps down.

Like hell we aren't. I stand up and dust myself off. My clothes are in surprisingly good condition considering our situation. I wouldn't have expected our captors to be gentle with my unconscious body. I'm missing my leather armor though, and Corrine and Nate don't have their robes, just the shirt and pants they wear underneath. I think it's safe to assume they took all our weapons and other belongings. First thing to do is to find out what they intend to do with us.

I stand and walk to the cell bars, too close together to stick more than an arm out. We're outside, and the sun is behind us, our cell casting a shadow into the empty cell opposite us. I can't see anything else, though I do hear the telltale sounds of people in the distance, so it seems we *are* in a city. Then I hear heavy footsteps not far from us.

"Hello?" I call out, hoping it's one of the guards.

"What are you doing?" Nate questions behind me.

"Finding out what's going on." I hold my face near the bars and shout again. "Hello? Is someone there?"

Sure enough, the footsteps get louder, and I almost jump back in surprise when someone with vibrant green skin comes into view. *Right. Orcs.* He's a big guy too, with a shaved head, full beard, and a pair of tusks that go nearly up to his nose. I straighten up, feeling dwarfed by his size. The two of us just stare at each other for a minute before I finally have to break the silence.

"Where are our friends?" I don't hide the resentment in my voice.

"Healer." The orc narrows his eyes when he answers me.

"When will they be *back*?" The orc only shrugs in response. *Real helpful, this guy.* "Fine, do you know how long you're planning on keeping us in this—" I stop and gesture at the cell around me. "—wonderful place?"

"Sorry," the orc responds flatly. "Other cells being fixed."

I roll my eyes at the bad joke. Either this guy doesn't want to say much or isn't smart enough to know how. Common isn't his first language. "Is there someone else I can talk to, buddy?"

The orc sighs, looking annoyed before stomping off. Hopefully to get someone capable of saying words with more than two syllables. I hear what sounds like a door, so he must have gone inside.

"Well, that was helpful," Nate mocks.

I ignore him, verbally at least, turning around to lean against the bars and flip him off. *I'm doing more than you are, dick.* It's about ten minutes before I hear the door again followed by more footsteps. Expecting to see my new friend, I'm surprised by the sight of a different orc. He's not as tall and certainly not as muscular, the skinniest orc I've seen so far. His skin tone is a little darker than I've seen so far, and he's got short, slicked back, dark red hair and no beard. He's also wearing clothes way nicer than I would have expected for anyone around these parts, the kind you'd see on stuck up rich people back home.

"It is good to see you are awake, Mister..." He speaks Common a lot better than I would have expected too, but the way he's precise with his pronunciation tells me it's still not his first language. *Does he have an accent?* He's waiting for me to finish for him.

"David."

"David...?"

"Just David." No reason this guy needs to know my full name.

"I see. Mr. David." He adjusts his glasses before his dark green eyes settle on me. "I am terribly sorry for the delay; we do not get many situations of this nature, and it took me longer to prepare than I expected. I am Naruk Redwish, and I will be acting as your legal advocate. In a few days, once your companions are healed, the five of you will be brought before a member of the tribal council for a hearing on your crimes. Given the circumstances and evidence against you, I am going to recommend presenting a signed an admission of guilt, then we—"

"Hold the fuck on—guilty of *what*? Why the hell are we even being held here? What gives you the authority? What did we even *do*?" The words spill out of my mouth like a petulant child.

"Are you being serious?" Any cheerfulness in his tone has vanished. "Trespassing, destruction of property, attacking a group of *seven* rangers. From what I understand, you barely even attempted to *speak* with them, just drew your swords and blasted fire everywhere." I turn to glare at Nate, who sheepishly ignores my eyes. "Three of our best officers are currently at the same healer as your friends being treated for burns and other injuries. Now, I am not quite sure what your group *thought* you were doing, but I can tell you that your options on what you do next are *very* limited."

My mind starts reeling at his words. What the fuck have we gotten into? "What... What happens after the hearing?"

"Well, no matter what I think you can expect to do some time behind bars." I hear Corrine gasp behind me. "Most likely, *if* you accept your guilt, you can expect imprisonment for no more than six months. However, if you decide to argue a defense—and I *would not recommend it*—you may be looking at a few *years* at minimum if you were to lose." Naruk speaks plainly as he lays everything on the table.

"Six *months*?!" Corrine sounds like she's near tears.

"Holy shit," Nate barely whispers.

"Those are our only options? Months or years in jail? That's not... Please, it was just a misunderstanding." *Okay, that sounded a little pathetic.*

"Misunderstandings do not typically end with someone having their arms and torso covered in serious burns, Mister *David*." He says my name with a hint of disdain.

"There *has* to be something else." Six months in an orc prison? Would we even survive that? I mean, look at where they're keeping us now. I'm pretty sure that puddle in the corner is Nate's piss.

"I am not sure what you would have me do." He looks put out.

"Aren't you guys supposed to be all about fighting and battle? Survival of the fittest? Isn't there some other way we can resolve this?" I am *totally* just pulling stuff out of my ass now.

"Do you not feel that being knocked unconscious and waking up in a jail cell already did that?" *Good to see sarcasm is a universal language.*

"That was hardly a fair fight. Too many people in one room, and it's not like either side was prepared for it." Not to mention the loud piercing sound shooting through my head. "We certainly didn't go in there expecting to fight a bunch of fucking orcs. I just want a rematch." He flinches at the word fucking. I really need to learn to watch my mouth sometimes. But orcs love a fight, right? I'm trying to mentally comb through every story about orcs I've ever been told. Even the fairy tales. There's something on the tip of my tongue...

He looks even *more* annoyed now. "What exactly do you think we—"

"Trial by combat!" That's the term I was looking for! Maybe it was a bard singing in a tavern or a story one of the old generals at the academy told...I just remember a story about an orc king ordering two of his subjects to fight to the death to resolve something. Strength and honor and blood and blah blah.

"Trial by..." He sighs and pinches the bridge of his nose. "Why would you think we—" He cuts himself off, suddenly lost in thought. "Actually, there may be...something. The *Nagul Uzu'gor.* I think in your language it would be called..." He pauses, looking for the words. "The Ritual of Steel and Thunder."

"What is it?" Those words may as well be gibberish to me.

"A trial by combat, as requested." His tone is... I'm not sure. It's not annoyed, but it also isn't friendly. "The captive fights his captor, in this case the captain of the group you attacked. He would first have to accept the challenge—which he is *not* required to do—and if he did and you won, you and the rest of your party would go free. However, if you lost…" He smiles at me darkly, letting the unspoken answer hang in the air. *Death. It's a fight to the death.* "Your friends would also still be brought before the council."

I squeeze the cell bars, thinking. Six months versus a fight to the death? The two hardly seem equal. But could we even make it that long in an orc prison? No one knows we're here or where here is, exactly. Hell, most people don't even know I'm on this side of the world. "But if I win, that's it? All five of us are free? We get all our stuff back too?"

"Likely minus some fines, but ritual or no, you would receive your belongings back once you and your friends are released." He nods his head.

I wish I had Adam and Liss here to talk to. I could use some advice. They'd probably fight better than me too. *If they're even still alive right now.* No, I can't… I *won't* let us die in here. I can do this. I may not be as strong as I used to be, but I'm still a good fighter. Hell, I was handling those orcs in the ruins better than anyone else before I got knocked out, and there won't be a stupid magic box giving me a headache this time either. "I'll do it." Another gasp from Corrine.

"Are you sure?" Naruk eyes me up and down. "There is no backing out once it has begun."

"I'm sure." My voice is confident because I'm confident. I got this.

"Very well. I will let the rangers know. If the captain accepts your challenge, someone will be out to collect you to begin preparations. Good luck." His tone is less creepy and back to friendly, and he gives me a smile and a small bow before turning to leave.

I exhale once he is out of earshot, running my hand through my hair.

"Are you sure you know what you're doing?" Nate asks, worry evident in his voice.

I take another breath, mustering up my most confident smile before nodding at Nate and Corrine. "Yeah. I'm getting us out of here."

Chapter Two

Nathaniel, Corrine, and I sit silently in our cell, the tension thick in the air. No one has tried to talk me out of it though. Just an awkward silence—they want to get out of here as bad as I do. For my part, I do my best not to overthink things. The more I think about it, the more I might try to talk *myself* out of it, and I'm determined to get us out of here. True to Naruk's word, the orc guard returns about an hour later.

"Captain Ironstorm accept challenge." Well, if that isn't an incredibly intimidating name, even in broken-sounding Common. He unlocks the door with a key, cuffing me in manacles before leading me out.

"If Adam and Liss get back here before I do, let 'em know that I'm getting us outta here." I do my best to make my final words to my team sound confident and not so...final.

"Good luck, David." Corrine gives me a sad smile from her side of the bars.

"Yeah, kick his ass, man." Nate does his best to not look quite so unconvinced.

"We'll be out of here in no time." I try not to think about how our freedom—and my life—is on the line.

Leading me from behind, the orc pushes me past a few more empty cells until we reach the door I assume I heard earlier. It's heavy and made of metal, though I don't see a lock. He presses his wrist to the door, above the handle, and a second later I hear a click. *Huh?* Before I have a chance to ask anything, I'm pushed through it.

As I'm led through the building, I do my best to take in my surroundings. We pass a few more doors before we end up in a larger room with a few other orcs. Some are conversing, but most are seated at desks and looking at papers. A few watch with amusement as we make our way through the room before we exit a final set of double doors to the outside.

Wow.

We are definitely in a city. Buildings line the road on either side. The streets aren't packed, but there's plenty of people—orcs—going about their business. A hand on my neck has me moving again, my warden apparently tired of my gawking. We turn right, and then right again down the next street so we are facing behind the jail, and I see where we are heading.

What looks like a large arena over two stories tall is situated just a few blocks down from us. The bottom half seems to be made of wood while the top half is stone. We're doing this with an audience then. I suppose I did ask for that. We pass several orcs along the way, some doing a double take when they notice the metal cuffs on my wrists. A few even run off to the arena ahead of us, I guess to get a good seat.

Once we reach the open-air building, I see that the wooden walls outside are actually just panels laid over more stone. Several have been carved with intricate depictions of orcs engaged in different activities. They're mostly battle scenes, but I also see what I think might be some kind of game or sport being played, and occasionally just some orcs standing around talking. Before I can look in more detail, I'm pushed through *another* series of doors, past more orcs I don't know—who all look at me funny. The guard finally slows down when we reach what seems to be the final door, knocking when we approach.

A woman opens the door, her skin, tusks, and large pointed ears a match for my jailer, though her hair is long and black. She says something in Orcish and the guard grunts in response before pushing me to her.

"Come with me, sweetheart." Another orc who knows her Common, and also one who is a lot less pushy; she's content to let me follow at my own pace into the room.

It's a large room, not at all what I expected. In one corner is a wooden bathtub, the water within hot enough for me to see the steam rising from the surface. There's also a table filled with food, and along one wall is a large mirror situated above a shelf covered with all sorts of bottles. There's a couch against another wall with a second female orc currently sitting on it. About the only thing in the room I do expect is the *huge* amount of weapons lining one of the walls.

I follow my new guard over to the mirror. I'm only just realizing I don't think I've ever seen a female orc before today, not even in artwork. I mean, I guess I knew they had to exist, but I've only ever thought of orcs as male. They don't look any different than a human woman does from a man. I just never pictured them before for some reason. I've seen more than a dozen in the last twenty minutes, including the two in front of me now, both dressed in simple black robes.

"Did he leave the keys?" the other orc, whose dark hair is pulled into a bun, asks.

"Damn, I forgot," the first orc sighs.

"It's fine. Come here sweetie." The other orc signals for me, and I step forward. She takes a hold of my cuffs, placing her hand over the lock before muttering something to herself. The lock on my cuffs clicks, the manacles easily sliding off. "Much better."

"Now, do you need help getting ready?" the first orc asks. Both these orcs sound a lot more natural when they speak.

"Um, no thanks. I think I'm okay." *Get ready with what exactly? It's a fight. Are they gonna spar with me or something?*

"Alright. You should have about thirty minutes. Once the ritual begins, you'll hear a bell chime. Select your weapon from the wall—only one—and then walk through that door there." She smiles warmly as she explains, pointing at a door set in the same wall as all the weapons.

"Feel free to use any of the oils or perfumes along the mirror. Just one more thing." The second orc leans forward and places her hand on my lower stomach, muttering to herself again.

Ooooooohhh boy. Whatever she just did, it felt weird. Kinda like I'm... I dunno...lighter or something? The hell did she do that for?

"Alright, good luck." The second orc winks at me, both women smiling before turning and leaving the room through a separate third door.

That was weird, but at least I'm alone for a little and can think. I make an immediate beeline to the table of food. It's simple things like fruits and cheese, but still better than anything I've had in a *long* time. I haven't exactly been eating great since we started traveling. I've lost a *lot* of weight, almost thirty pounds, and most of it was muscle.

I used to hold my own against Adam or Liss in a one-on-one fight, but now I can't so much as arm wrestle them. It's not like I'm starving or anything; I just never knew how much I needed to eat to maintain my size. You don't really fill up on meals when you spend most nights sleeping outside. Still, what I lost in strength has been gained back in agility. I move quickly, precisely, using my opponent's strength against them. I've even practiced picking a few pockets here and there.

Which is why I'm not too worried about my chances here. But I do need to eat something. I help myself to some of the food, stopping when I feel like my stomach is full, though not so full that it'll hinder my movement. Then I look over the rest of the room. The mirror I really don't see the use for, but the bath... I haven't felt hot water in ages. I pull off my clothes and toss them on the couch. They're nothing fancy, just a shirt, some pants, and a loincloth, all cotton.

I use the stepladder next to the large wooden tub to lower myself in slowly. *Fuck* does that feel good. For a few minutes, I just lay there with my eyes closed, content to mindlessly soak. Only for a few minutes though—I've got a death match to win after all. I spot a bar of soap and a washcloth on a small table next to the tub, and I am happy to scrub all the days of being outside off of my skin. I'm not sure how long I'm in there exactly, but the water never seems to go cold. These orcs certainly know their magic.

After a rinse and a few more minutes of soaking, I grudgingly pull myself from the tub. After weeks of nothing but cold river baths, that was heaven. I grab the towel laid out for me nearby, tossing it to the floor once I'm dry. I leave off my clothes, content to wander the room naked for now, something else I haven't been able to do for a while.

I ponder the wall of weapons. There's a lot: swords, staves, maces, bows, and quivers—just about any weapon I could think of and a few I don't even know the names for. My weapon of choice used to be a broad-sword, but after all the weight loss, I switched over to something smaller, usually a short sword. They're lighter, and at the moment, easier to wield. I've been practicing using a second one in my offhand lately so it sucks that she said I could only take one.

I reach for a sword that looks to be a good size, removing it from its perch. Steel, I think, the blade sharp and well balanced. I practice swinging it a few times before adding in a few jumps and dodges. It feels a little silly to be doing this naked, but I want to get a good feel for this thing before I head out there. I wish I could use my own sword. It's nothing special, but I'm used to it.

I continue to practice with my weapon of choice, taking the time to warm myself up. I don't wanna go out there totally unprepared. I'm in the middle of doing some stretches when I hear a loud bell ring coming from somewhere behind the weapon wall. I guess it's time. I pull on my clothes, grab my sword, and head through the door.

Another hallway, though I can see the gate on the opposite end is open to the outside. The arena. I make my way toward it, suddenly feeling like I'm walking to my doom.

Which I guess I might be.

Nope, not gonna think like that. I'll kick this orc's ass and win us our freedom. Maybe I won't even have to kill the guy. Maybe I can convince him to yield instead. Everyone wins!

Yeah, right.

The sun is blinding as I walk into the open air. The stands look near packed, the gathered crowd erupting in applause at my appearance. A much more positive reception than I would have expected for a human who's about to try and kill one of their own. I'm tempted to wave, but opt to remain stoic. This isn't exactly fun, and the more the crowd cheers, the more I realize how fucked up this all is. Did I make a mistake?

My opponent, Captain Ironstorm, is already on the field. The closer I get, the more I recognize him from the "incident." He's got short, cropped black hair, and if it weren't for the green-olive complexion, he'd almost remind me of my dad. Unlike Dad though, he's got a full beard, and well maintained at that. His tusks are at least an inch long, maybe an inch and a half, and he has deep, intense looking chocolate-brown eyes. *Not sure why I added that last part.*

He's not wearing much in the way of armor, at least not compared to the leathers I remember him in earlier. He's got at least half a foot of height on me, maybe a little more, and *holy shit* is he built. No wonder Adam had problems taking him down. Fuck, I remember how he knocked me halfway across the room. If I try to jump at him like I did last time, he'll wipe the floor with me. I leave some distance between us when I approach, matching my relaxed stance to his.

"Come here often?" Cracking jokes at inappropriate times is a nervous habit. He looks...amused? He gives me a curt nod of acknowledgment but says nothing. I nod in return, but the only thing on my face is determination. This won't be easy, and... I really don't want to hurt anyone. But I'm going to do what I have to.

The bell chimes again, and I think it's to signal the start of the fight. Ironstorm shifts into a more combative stance, though his expression is only slightly more serious. I follow suit, and as the audience shouts, the two of us begin to slowly circle each other. He chose a sword as well, but his weapon is much bigger than mine. Definitely a two-hander.

He makes the first move, leaping at me with a horizontal slash, and I move backward to dodge before jumping forward myself. My own sword is deflected easily, but it doesn't feel like we're really fighting yet. Just sizing each other up. He comes at me again, this time with a series of steady over the shoulder swipes. I don't so much deflect them as I knock them out of the way. He's got biceps the size of my head, and it's all I can do to meet his attacks head-on.

Gotta think smarter, David.

He tries to leap at me again, and this time, I not only knock his sword away but deliver a swift kick to the gut too. He's pushed back slightly, holding his free hand to his stomach for only a moment. Gonna have to use my sword if I stand a chance.

We continue to toy with each other like this for some time. I'm not sure how long, but I'm starting to get tired, and frankly, the people watching seem like they're getting bored. Time to stop screwing around, I guess. I think back to the fight in the ruins, the way that first orc came at me but totally biffed it and hit the ground. I don't think my opponent here is quite that stupid, but maybe there's a way I can still provoke him and use his reaction to my advantage.

I switch tactics, going entirely evasive, making sure I am consistently out of his reach while doing my best to land quick kicks and jabs where I can. Nothing more than small annoyances to him, but that's the idea. I can tell he's starting to get riled up when the smirk on his face shifts to a scowl, and then to outright anger. Here we go.

He lunges at me again, much harder and faster than he has before. But instead of jumping back and using his recovery to land a punch, I twist to the side, letting him pass me entirely and putting *all* my strength into delivering a hard kick to the back of his knee. His leg gives out and down he goes, his sword clattering to the ground just out of reach. *This is it.* He's face down on the ground, his neck and back exposed. I raise my sword, ready to land the final blow, his body prone before me to take out.

But I hesitate.

And that's all it takes.

He pushes off the ground quickly and comes at me, spinning around and delivering his own kick right to my stomach. The wind is knocked out of me, and I am launched backward before hitting the ground. My sword goes flying, to where I don't know since I'm too focused on trying to breathe again. Before I have the chance to move, I feel a leather boot on my stomach again, though not pressing to hold me down.

In victory.

Once I can breathe again, I look up, seeing his muscular green form standing over me, the sun behind him, his sword pointed down at me. I'm brought back to the ruins, the last time I passed out with him above me. As sounds begin to filter back into my ears, I can hear the crowd roaring, and I can only imagine the sight we are.

Why is he drawing this out? To humiliate me? Just get it over with.

"Do it," I say once I can find my ability to speak.

"Do what?" His voice is deep, gruff even.

"Kill me." Fuck, is he going to make me beg to die?

"What? Why would I... Why would I kill you?" He lets his sword arm drop to his side, and though the sun makes it hard to read his expression, he sounds genuinely confused.

"Because that's what we're doing? Trying to kill each other?" What the hell is happening right now?

"You were trying to *kill* me?" Okay, now he's less confused and maybe a little angry.

"Y-Yes? Weren't you trying to kill *me*?" I get a really bad feeling in the pit of my stomach, beyond the boot-shaped bruise I have growing. "Isn't that what we were supposed to be doing?"

"**NO!**" he roars down at me.

"O-oh." I don't know what to say to that. I don't know what's going on right now. What was all this then? What happens now? "I don't understand. What were we supposed to be...? What are you going to do now?"

There's a beat of silence. "Why don't I *show* you?" I don't need to see his face to hear the venom in his voice. If he's not going to kill me, it sounds like I may wish he had.

He tosses his sword to the side, and I see it land some distance from us. When I look back up, he's pulling his shirt off next, tossing it away as well. Shit, I can't believe I actually almost beat this guy. He's a hairy motherfucker, and I'm not sure Adam, myself, or any other knight back at the academy could get a body like his, even if we hit the gym every day.

He moves down, his boot no longer on my stomach. Instead, he kneels over me, and I can finally see his face clearly. Yeah, he looks none too happy right now. I probably wouldn't be either if I found out someone was trying to kill me. But what is he doing, and why did he take off his shirt? There's some roundness to his stomach but even that has a fuck-ton of muscle underneath it.

He reaches into his pocket and pulls out a small pocket knife. I thought we were only allowed one weapon? I guess it doesn't really count, not like he used it. And just as I think that, he grabs my shirt in his other hand and uses the knife to rip it in half. The spectators around us cheer.

"What the hell!" *That's my fucking shirt!* I don't have a lot of those!

"Quiet, or I'll gag you." The order is delivered the way my old drill instructors used to give them, the kind not to be defied or questioned. He finishes tearing my shirt, removing it from me entirely before he drops the knife and grabs my wrists to position my hands above my head. Then, using the tatters of my now ruined shirt, he ties them together. *Is he taking me back to jail?* "Do *not* move these."

I make no attempt to move them. He searches my face for a moment, but all he finds is confusion. "You truly have no idea what is to happen here?"

"I told you... I thought we were supposed to be trying to kill each other." Can't say I pictured ever having to say that to someone. This is more humiliating than I could have ever imagined.

"Hmmph. Humans." He pauses before picking up his pocket knife again. "You really should learn to think before rushing to action." Then he grabs my pants by the waist and rips the knife down one of the legs.

"Would you stop that!?" I need my pants! I have even less of those than shirts! "Can you just tell me what you're doing!?"

"Taking my prize for winning." His expression changes from anger to hunger. *What?* He then rips through my other pant leg, the crowd erupting as he yanks the torn fabric out from under me. That leaves me lying on the floor of the arena in nothing but my loincloth, hands bound above my head. Then I notice his own pants, or at least the prominent bulge sticking out from them. *Oh gods, why is he...* Remember when I said this was more humiliating than I could have imagined?

I'm too scared to ask if my assumptions are right. My whole body flushes red and thanks to that fucking pocket knife, it's all on display. Everything except for the thin layer of fabric I call my underwear. Ironstorm, looking confident even when shuffling on his knees, leaves my side. When I realize it's to move between my legs, I snap them shut in a futile attempt to keep him away.

He only smirks, grabbing my ankles and swiftly removing my shoes before taking my knees in both hands and easily parting my thighs. As he moves forward, his eyes rake down my torso before stopping on the only area I still have covered, his eyebrows quirking up in amusement. "It seems you may have figured it out."

What is he...? Oh no. In my humiliation and fear-induced state, I didn't notice Little David deciding to wake up and join the party. Why here? Why now?

It's not like I'm enjoying any of this! I did not wake up today and think, "Oh boy I sure would like to get manhandled and tied up by a hot muscular half-naked orc." I don't even like men! Even if I did just refer to him as hot. I've never been with anyone, okay? And traveling in close quarters for two months with four other people doesn't exactly give you a lot of alone time either. I'm just pent up, *that's all.*

"I think I will keep these as a trophy," Ironstorm jokes as he reaches for my underwear, apparently not intending to shred them. Instinctively, my bound hands shoot down in an attempt to hold onto my dignity, but they're caught before they reach their target. My captor looks none too amused with my stunt. "What did I say about moving these?" he growls before slamming my wrists back into the dirt above my head, his entire body looming over mine.

"Please." Not entirely sure what I'm asking for here. He's practically on top of me, his arm stretched over my head as he holds me down. His underarm is as hairy as the rest of him, and the scent of his musk hits me full-on. I can even feel his erection poking against mine. "I... I've never..." Aaaaaand I'm turning red again. *Please don't make me say it out loud.*

He looks at me curiously, but I can tell he doesn't quite believe me. "Do *not* move them again," he grumbles before moving back to his earlier position, kneeling between my thighs. He takes both my legs in his hands again, this time bringing them together, sticking them straight up and bending them over his left shoulder. Then, lifting me with one strong arm, he slips the loincloth off my ass and up my legs. You know, like when you diaper a baby.

Why can't he just kill me?

He lays my legs down once again, spread wide and leaving me fully exposed to him and everyone else in the audience, who are once again raucous with glee at my debasement. My hands are balled into fists as I fight every urge to cover myself, too fearful of the wrath of the giant man currently ogling my naked body. It's not like I have anything to be ashamed of. My dick is a nice seven inches when hard. It's more the being-forced-to-do-this-in-front-of-a-bunch-of-people of it all that is getting to me.

He moves forward and uses his knees to spread my thighs farther, exposing more than just my dick. He grabs my left leg and lifts it, placing it on his shoulder. He then reaches into the pocket of his leather pants, pulling out a small glass vial. I watch suspiciously as he uncorks the top and dribbles a clear liquid onto his fingers. By the time he recorks the vial and I realize what he's doing, his index finger is pushing into my ass.

I can't help but hiss and squirm, half in pain and half in surprise. I can't tell how much he's got in me, but it feels like a lot, and I know his hands are fucking huge. My eyes water as I futilely try to push him out, but he only pushes farther inside in response.

Fuckfuckfuckfuck. I've never done anything like this before. *Maybe* I've thought about it once or twice, but I've never *actually* had something in my ass before!

"Breathe." My eyes snap open at the order, and I take a breath as requested. I didn't realize I was holding it. That's the only bit of kindness I get though, as he continues to drive his large green digit in and out of my hole. I try to focus on breathing, but it's difficult, *especially* after he adds finger number two. My eyes scrunch up in pain, and I turn my head to whine into my arm, earning me a small chuckle from above. It's about the only thing I can do. His free arm is wrapped around my leg, holding it tightly to his chest.

The initial entry may have been fast, but now that he's in, he seems perfectly happy to take his time. His fingers stretch me as they slide in and out of my body, sometimes in sync, sometimes in a rhythm, and when he scissors them apart, it feels like I'm at my limit, like I might split in two. And once or twice he does this thing where he hooks his fingers upward and has me arching off the ground.

I'm not entirely sure when this switched from pain to pleasure, but now instead of fighting to push him out, I have to fight myself not to start pushing back on him. *Especially* when he hits that one spot. I don't even realize it's me making the noise when I start hearing the whimpering and moaning. I try to use my arm to muffle myself, but I know he's already heard me. Not to mention my dick, which wilted slightly after the first intrusion, and has stiffened back up to full hardness. *Traitor.*

More gently than I would have expected, Ironstorm pulls his fingers from my hole, chuckling when I whimper at their loss. It just feels weird, okay? I guess I haven't really considered the next logical step in all this, only realizing when he stands and begins undoing his pants what comes next. Panicking, I look at the entrance I came through, hoping for a chance to escape. But no, the gates have already been shut. Would I have even made it that far if they weren't?

When I look back up, he's once again towering over me, only this time he's fully naked. The sun once again blocks the details of his features, but his outline is clear. His cock is *massive* and as green as the rest of him. Even at my decent size, I'd probably develop a complex growing up next to that. He's got the vial out again, pouring more of the viscous liquid into his hand before discarding it with his pants. I'm mesmerized as he runs his slick hand up and down his shaft. *Out of fear!*

He kneels back down between my legs, and I shiver when his skin touches mine. The closer he gets, the more my anxiety grows, and when he lifts one and then the other of my legs to his shoulders, my body starts to quake. When he's this close, I can read the desire on his face. This is really happening. He's really going to do this.

Why aren't I fighting to get away?

I feel the brush of his slick cockhead against my ass, and my breath hitches. I don't know if everyone has gone silent, or if I just can't hear anything over the pounding in my chest. Why did I agree to do this? Why did Nate have to cast that fucking fireball spell? Why did I even get on that fucking boat?

A hand on my face brings me back to myself. It's gentle, just cupping my cheek, making me look up at who it's attached to. The face looking back at me is softer than I've seen it all afternoon. The anger, or at least most of it, has faded away. In its place is...concern? I look up at him questioningly but before I can figure it out, he's leaning down to me, closer and closer, until...

Oh.

I gasp a little, certainly not expecting a kiss in the middle of all this. I mean, I guess it shouldn't be entirely unexpected. People tend to kiss when they fu—*aaaand his tongue is in my mouth.*

I groan, mostly in surprise but also because, and I hate to admit this, he's a pretty good kisser. I've kissed my fair share of girls, but none of them were like this. I was also usually the initiator of those kisses, though I guess I can see why some girls like the guy to take the lead.

Against my better judgment, I relax into the kiss. His tongue, larger than my own, slowly maps the inside of my mouth. It's so different from kissing a girl. His beard scratches softly against my face, his tongue thicker and more demanding. He even tastes different. I run my tongue along his, letting myself moan a little. Something about my pride is making me want to prove that I'm a good kisser too. I feel a rumble of approval in response.

And then he starts pushing his cock into my ass.

I shriek—that's really the only word for it—into Ironstorm's mouth at the sudden invasion, though I'm not sure even *I* hear it as the crowd explodes into cheers at the same time. Anything resembling a moan of pleasure warps into a whimper of pain. I start breathing heavily again, and I can't help but move my arms from where I'm supposed to keep them. I know I can't push him off, so I wrap them around his neck and squeeze. I just need something to hold on to.

For his part, Ironstorm continues to kiss me as he pushes into me farther, stopping before I take the whole thing, his hips still some distance from my ass. I'm struggling to stop panting as my hands scrabble feebly at his back. I'm still whimpering, unable to stop them or the rest of my body from pleading with my abuser for some comfort. The tongue in my mouth continues its gentle mapping, and I don't know if orcs *purr* exactly, but there's that same gentle rumble from before as if he's trying to calm me.

I should point out that during all of this I am essentially being *bent in half*. I've always been pretty flexible, but this is not a position I've been in before. My knees are being pushed almost to my shoulders, and I can feel the full weight of the captain on top of me. I'm actually thankful for it because it means I can just relax my limbs and let him do the work at keeping me in place. Maybe thankful isn't the word to use there…

Eventually, somehow, most of the pain subsides, and I'm able to relax, leaving me mostly with a feeling of fullness. But no sooner do I do this than the orc currently occupying space in my guts pulls back—both his cock and his face. My arms are pulled back over my head and what greets me is some of the same softness from before, but this time with an underlying lust that is clear as day. Lust that only grows as he pushes himself forward again.

He doesn't so much force the air out of me as he does a groan, an act he repeats a number of times at a steady pace. There's a slight burning sensation each time his cock is dragged in and out of my hole, but it's not nearly as bad as the first time. I find that I have to actually concentrate on relaxing because tightening up only makes things harder. The orc's face is on mine, no less hungry but watching me closely, I *hope* for signs of pain.

But…the more he does it, the less pain there is. My own cock lies against my stomach, having gone completely soft when Ironstorm first speared me open, but starting to wake up again. Because of the size that my "friend" is working with, he has no problem hitting that spot inside me that he used his fingers to toy with earlier. And it's starting to feel pretty good.

The first moan is involuntary. As is the second, and the third. I try to hold them in at first, but as he picks up the pace of his thrusts, I realize I'm fighting a losing battle. I didn't notice before, but the captain has actually been ever so slightly fucking more of himself inside me with each thrust. I look down at my cock again, fattened up slightly but not by much. However, a small puddle of my own sticky juices is pooling on my stomach, each pass inside seeming to push more out.

A glance up reveals my captor grinning down, knowing without a doubt that I've begun to enjoy this. And I'll be honest with you: at this point, I don't really care anymore. After all the humiliation and pain, I'm surprised I'm able to enjoy this at all. It's a little late to start fighting again now, so I'm done.

Two green hands grab me by the backs of my knees, pushing my thighs down and once again folding me in two. Leaning his weight on his upper body, the captain starts to speed up while also changing the angle of his thrusts. The people in the stands shout at the change of pace and position, and I nearly join them, the incessant prodding making me see stars.

I look up to watch him as he works, his hairy muscular form shining as the sweat from his exertion starts to drip down his chest. Some of it falls onto me, and it's only when the cool drops hit my skin that I notice just how hot I am. Even though I've done little more than lay here, I'm sweating like crazy.

That's not the only thing happening. With each slam of his cock, I feel that little burst of bliss. But I also feel a pressure growing, somewhere in my lower regions. I can't tell where exactly, or why, but the more it grows, the harder it is to concentrate on staying relaxed.

I look down, as if that'll give me any answers, but all I find is my still mostly soft cock leaking more than I have ever seen, even by my own hand. Thanks to my amazing flexibility, I can also watch his cock pistoning in and out of my ass. It's mesmerizing, the green skin disappearing between the pink and tan, only to be pulled back out, dragging some of the skin with it. I almost forget I'm looking at myself. But that pressure keeps building and building, and I still have no idea what it means. Only that I feel full, so very full.

"Fuck." I don't know what's happening, but my eyes roll back in my head. It feels like I'm going to explode, my eyes squeezing shut, my toes curling. Every single muscle in my body is tight, and I can't help but cry out when after one, two, three more thrusts, I suddenly let go of *everything* I'm holding. More than that, I can feel all my muscles *pushing* outward. I groan loudly as the tension is literally fucked out of me.

My head lolls back, and I struggle to catch my breath. *What was that? How do I do it again?* Once I can see straight, I look down, my cock still only half-hard and sitting in a pool of my precum. *Did I cum? It felt like I came.* Even though I'm still *really fucking horny*. I look up at the captain, a look of triumph on his face, his body covered in sweat from his head to his waist. *Holy shit.* I am absolutely going to regret and probably repress all of this later, but this is one of the hottest things I've ever experienced. The sweat-drenched fur matted to his chest, the ripple of his muscles as he moves, the look of determination on his face—hell, I don't think I've ever *smelled* someone like him before and been so turned on.

The pressure starts to build again, and this time I'm looking forward to what I know is on the horizon. I bite my lip as it continues, closing my eyes in anticipation before I notice that the captain's thrusts are starting to get a little...erratic. Just as the pressure reaches its apex, I open my eyes to watch him looking even more determined than before, slamming forward and burying himself completely with a growl.

After a few more short and fast thrusts, his full weight is on me again as his tongue seeks entry to my mouth. It feels like his cock is growing bigger inside me, and as he cries into my mouth, I understand what's happening. I can feel the hot jets of his cum volley into my ass, the thick pillar of meat pulsing with each shot. Ironstorm still tries to thrust himself deeper inside me, as if he isn't already buried to the hilt.

All of this is of course more than enough to push me over my own edge, the climax rolling through my body, if that's even what it is. I let my arms once again wrap around his neck as my body releases, some deep part of me (that I will likely *also* repress) finding the idea that I came with his load buried inside me intoxicating. I can't exactly see it, but once again it feels like my cock hasn't actually shot anything, but if that *wasn't* an orgasm, I'm not sure I know what is.

All the while our captive audience roars with applause in the background, hoots and wolf-whistles abound. Eventually, his cock stops pulsing and my body relaxes. My arms back on the ground, he raises himself on his hands, a thin line of drool connecting his tongue to mine for a moment. I almost try to follow him, but I'm spent. I'm not even sure I can walk right now.

His hand cups my cheek again, the lust in his eyes sated. I grip his wrist for a moment, fighting and losing the urge to kiss the inside of his palm. He smiles, and it's only as he pulls his hand back and very gingerly pulls himself from my surely-wrecked ass that our surroundings start coming back into focus. I hiss once he's free, blushing at the wet feeling that follows. I reflexively try to tighten my hole, cursing at the sudden sharp pain when I do so. As my legs are lowered to the ground and the passion dies down, reality rears its ugly head and the realization of what I've just done begins to weigh on me.

Captain Ironstorm, after giving me one last look, stands, turning to face our crowd of onlookers. As he roars in victory to the sky, they explode once more, yelling and cheering for their captain and his conquered. He turns back to me and bends down, at first I think to help me up. Instead, his arm goes under my waist, and I'm lifted and tossed over his shoulder, like a prize. Which I guess I am. I want to protest, to fight further indignities, but I've got nothing left in me. I'm exhausted.

Looking down, all I am met with is a hairy, muscular, green ass. I dare not look any higher unless I make eye contact with someone in crowd who just watched me nearly get the life fucked out of me. As the crowd applauds, the captain moves, taking me along with him. I still have no idea what comes next. I was expecting to either win this fight or die trying. My friends are going to sit in that jail cell for the next six months, and after the brutal fucking I just received, I'm not sure if what I ended up with is better or worse.

Chapter Three

A shadow moves overhead as Captain Ironstorm walks us inside, the roof of the arena providing cover. At least that's what I assume because the only things in my eye line are the ground, my bound wrists, and a green orc butt. I'm too exhausted to struggle or look around for more. There's a pause and what sounds like a door opening, the dirt floor giving away to stone as we go inside.

Once the door closes behind us, two voices begin speaking. They're both in Orcish, so I have no idea what they're saying or what Ironstorm's response is. But it sounds like it could be the two women from earlier, before the match. My body flushes, seeing as they're probably just at eye level with my ass. My ass which currently feels like a sloppy mess. I feel what I think is his cum (*god, I hope it's just his cum*) start to leak out and by reflex tighten my hole, hissing at the sudden pain. Oh yeah, I'm also *really fucking sore*.

There's more talking and then he's chuckling about something and patting my ass, making me blush more. Can he just put me down so I can curl up and die somewhere, please? Thankfully there are only a few more exchanges, the two of them say something in unison that Ironstorm repeats back, and then I hear feet shuffling, a door closing, and we are alone. I hope.

Ironstorm walks farther into the room with me before I feel his arm coming across my back, holding and lifting me as he lowers himself to the ground and sets me on my own feet. My knees buckle when I try to stand, and I stumble forward, bound wrists grabbing onto his still-naked form to steady myself. *Fuck, my legs are like jelly.* I immediately try to correct myself only to fall *again*, making the orc chuckle as I cling to him.

"Easy." His voice is soft as he puts a hand on the small of my back to steady me.

" 'm fine," I mumble. I'm not even sure I believed that. I mean I'm as fine as I can be after... My face heats up again as I remember what happened out in the arena.

He doesn't respond, only helps to keep me from falling. There's a stone ledge I can lean against, and once he sees that I can balance on my own, he leaves me and I finally have a chance to see the rest of the room. It's dark, not pitch black, but the only lighting seems to be candles, a lot of them grouped together on a few different surfaces in the room. Other than that, though, it actually looks pretty similar to the room I was in earlier. Maybe this is where he got ready? There are a few differences. No couch, just a few chairs, and instead of a large mirror taking up one of the walls, there's only a single standing one.

There's also not a bath, but a shower, and the ledge I'm against divides it from the rest of the room. Well, it's really a small indoor waterfall, but I assume it serves the same purpose. We have one at home, but it was always such a pain in the ass to heat up the water first, and it always ran out before I was done. I jump—and almost fall again—when I feel a hand on my waist. Ironstorm has finished whatever it was he was doing. It hits me again that I have no idea what's supposed to happen next.

Following closely behind, the orc guides me to the falling stream of water, and given the state of my lower body, I have little choice but to move with him. He's slow and careful, especially once we step onto the wet stone sunken into the floor a bit deeper than the rest. The water is warm as it splashes onto our legs. Moving in front of me, he pulls my body flush with his and turns us both directly under the water.

I struggle to hold onto him but manage not to shout in surprise, mostly because the water isn't cold. After a few seconds, he turns us again and sets me back down. I try, very carefully, to stand on my own again, tentatively balancing on my own two feet. Ironstorm is still. I can feel his eyes on me but can't bring myself to look at him.

After seeing that I'm steady, he leaves me again. I shiver a little in the cold air, but nearly jump again a second later when I feel his warm hand on my back holding a soapy sponge. Thinking he's going to hand it to me, I lift my hand only to have him run the sponge along my chest himself, his other arm wrapping around my back as he steps closer to support me. That finally has me looking up at his face, and I am surprised by the warmth I find looking back at me.

In the flickering lights of the room, I watch the wet, furred outline of his muscles ripple as he slowly runs the sponge along my chest, arms, and stomach, occasionally switching to his own. He has a leg on either side of my body, his cock pressing against my lower stomach. His body feels hot, even under the warm water, and I can feel his breath against the side of my face.

He moves closer in front of me, pulling our soapy bodies together and running the sponge along my back. Our chests slide together, his coarse body hair scratching against my own. His hands move farther down until he reaches my ass, rubbing slow circles along each glute. Then, dropping the sponge on the stone ledge, he brings his still-soapy hand to my rear. His slippery digits roam up and down my ass for a moment before moving to the center, delving between my cheeks. I whimper as a finger strokes over my sore hole, hearing another chuckle and feeling a soft kiss on the top of my head.

The fingers return to my hole, gently washing away the stickiness gathered there. I bite my tongue rather than make more noises, but my cock is already betraying me. There's no way he can't feel me pressing against him. He bends to reach down farther, cleaning the rest of his sticky spend from the backs of my thighs, our bodies continuing to slide against each other. He runs his hands up my back slowly as he straightens himself, still keeping me pressed against him.

Grabbing the sponge again, he moves to stand behind me, wrapping an arm around my stomach. He moves down as he scrubs along my thighs and waist, slowly inching closer to but never actually touching my cock, which is more than half-hard and pointing down at an angle. His own hardening length presses against my soapy ass, and I fight the urge to grind back against him. When the sponge-filled hand finally reaches my shaft, it's another fight not to hump forward.

He soaps up my cock almost methodically, grabbing me with his free hand and spreading the soap up and down my shaft and sack. I say nothing as my cock grows to full hardness under his touch, biting my lip when he kneads my balls slowly, taking the sponge to my inner thighs. I can feel his heartbeat when we're pressed together like this, his breath hot against my ear.

What... What is this? I have been in a grand total of zero relationships in my life, but I'm pretty sure this isn't how they normally start.

Why is he treating me like a lover? Is that what we are now, after...that? After he knocked me to the ground, stripped me, and... I wince again as my hole clenches in pain, remembering the violation in vivid detail. Vivid enough that my cock twitches when I recall some of the more pleasurable moments. I shut my eyes, trying to will away my erection, suddenly not sure I want him aware that I enjoyed my earlier treatment.

The sponge is gone, replaced with something I can't quite make out in the dark. The arm around my waist moves to grab my bound hands, bringing them up to my chest. As the object is brought closer, I catch a glint of it in the candlelight—a knife. I go still, holding my breath as the blade slices through the wet cloth tying my wrists together. As it falls to the ground with a wet thud, the knife is gone, green hands already soothing my irritated skin.

I'm spun around and a hand under my chin lifts my gaze to his. Even in the dim light of the room, I can make out the soft brown of his irises. I can feel myself panting. I can feel a lot of things right now: his warmth, his muscles, his hard cock grinding into me. But not anger, or even desire really. Just that same strange tenderness peeking through. I close my eyes without thinking as he leans down and his lips touch mine, returning his gentle kiss slowly. He turns us together once more under the stream, rinsing the soap from us as the water cascades down our bodies.

One of his hands drifts down to the swell of my ass, cupping it gently before squeezing it tightly. At the same time, he deepens our kiss, his tongue swiping forward into my slightly parted mouth. I whimper and open my mouth farther, wordlessly asking for more. He doesn't disappoint, the thick muscle of his tongue plunging into my mouth. My hands move to wrap around his neck, and I finally allow my weight to relax into him.

I lose track of time as we kiss under the water, his beard scratching against my own as my nose makes the occasional bump into his tusks. It's a lot easier to kiss with those than I would have guessed, but he's probably had some practice. The fur on his stomach rubs gently against mine, his hands roaming up and down my ass and back. I am openly rutting my hard cock against his. The warm water feels like it's washing away all the soreness from my muscles.

When he finally pulls away, I actually *whine*, like a puppy. That earns me another chuckle and a short, chaste kiss before he moves to disentangle us. I'm steadier than I was a few minutes ago but still not sure what I should be doing. I follow him to the edge of the shower area where he grabs a very large towel from a nearby table. It looks like the rest of our clothes are there too. Well, his clothes, my underwear, and the ripped-up rags of my shirt and pants. Someone must have brought them in when we were... Well I guess I'm just letting everyone see everything today. You know, I'm not even sure I have any shame left in me.

I don't know why I'm surprised when the orc starts to dry me rather than hand me the towel to do it myself. Once he's done with me—and he's very thorough—he uses the same towel to dry himself. I stand there, unsure of what to do with myself while he sits and begins to redress. There are small torches on this end of the room, and with the distance between us, I'm able to make out the various tattoos covering his body. Dark bands wrap around his upper arms while smaller symbols dot his shoulders. Across the left side of his chest is the shape of a large, solid black sword, crossing down from his shoulder, the blade jagged in the middle. He catches me staring at him, and I quickly turn away, looking for my own clothing. Seeing as I only have the one thing to wear, I reach for my underwear and—

"What are you doing?"

I freeze at the question. "Getting dressed?" *Right?*

"I told you—those are mine now." He nods at the thin layer of cotton that is my underclothes.

Is he serious? "What am I supposed to wear, then?"

"Hmm. I suppose we will need to buy you some new clothes." To replace the ones he ripped up?

"What do I wear until then?" Am I supposed to wait here while he goes shopping? "What... What is this? What's happening right now?"

He considers me for a moment. "I apologize. I was not sure if your ignorance was authentic or not. You will be coming with me."

"For the night?" I cross my arms, becoming more aware of my nudity the more he gets dressed.

"Yes, but you misunderstand. You are coming with me indefinitely. You now belong to me." *The fuck?*

"What are you talking about?" *Belong* to him? "Do you mean what happened out...there? That was—"

"It is simple," he cuts me off as he reaches down to tie his boots. "You lost the battle and are now mine. I own you."

"The hell you do!" *What the fuck is this orc talking about!?* "That is *not* what I signed up for!"

"No, apparently you signed up for a death match." He stands, instantly towering over me. "Is that what you would prefer?" The threat is empty, but it does the trick.

"I—"

He steps even closer. "I know I was rough," he cuts me off again, hand reaching out to stroke my cheek. "But surely you found it more enjoyable than dying."

"That's not—"

"Here. This should be large enough for the time being." He turns and grabs his leather tunic, practically forcing it over my head. I struggle in vain but quickly relent, sticking my arms through the holes in the shoulders so I'm not helpless. It's fairly large on my frame and just long enough to keep me decent, though I wouldn't trust any strong winds.

"Can't I at least wear my—"

"No." He stuffs my former underwear in his pocket like it's the final word on the subject. "Come now. You can have your shoes, and then we'll get this on you." He turns to reach for an item on the far side of the table I somehow missed earlier.

"What the hell is *that*?" I ask, knowing full well what it is.

"A collar. Are you not famil—"

"*I know what it is!*" I snap. I know I asked—*shut up.* "I am *not* wearing that!" A sudden realization comes over me. He wasn't showering with me like a lover. He was *bathing* me, like I'm some kind of— "And I'm not your fucking pet!"

"Call it what you like, but you are *mine*." He walks toward me, collar in hand, the amusement quickly draining from his face.

I take a step back as he comes near me, and I start thinking about potential exits. I can make out a door behind him, and there's the way we came in on my right. There was also a third door in my room, the one the ladies exited through, but I don't want to chance looking behind me for it. *Arena it is.* Dammit, this is gonna suck without my boots but... I make a break for the door.

I hear a sound of confusion behind me, but I don't look back, throwing open the large wooden door and bolting through. I can see freedom at the end of the tunnel in front of me, sunlight streaming in through the archway. The doors of the gate are open, and I can use the crisscrossing beams on inside of them to climb out of the arena. Piece of cake! Now I just need to—

The bolas wrap around my ankles in an instant and send me flying face-first to the ground. I skid along the dirt, my arms taking the brunt of the damage as I come to a stop. I try to lift myself up, but I can already hear the footsteps behind me. Flipping onto my back, I watch the orc captain draw closer before he squats over my prone body.

"That was very stupid." He holds me by my elbow as he inspects the damage from my fall. "Nothing too bad. I can take care of these when we get home. Come."

I only glare in response. Expecting to be helped up, I squawk indignantly when I'm thrown over his shoulder again. Once we're back in the room, he sits me on the clothing table, cords still wrapped around my feet. The first thing he does is bind my wrists again, this time behind my back with leather bracers attached by a ring. I'd like to fight him, but I'm not sure how I would. After that comes the collar. I glare daggers straight in his eyes as he buckles the leather around my neck. Finally, he untangles my feet, replacing the throwing weapon on the wall he grabbed them from. I didn't consider those when I made a break for it.

"Alright, one last thing." He stands after lacing my boots, grabbing a final item on the table.

"Oh, *fuck off*." It's a leash. *The collar is one thing but a leash?!* I try to wriggle out of his grasp.

"Quite the mouth on you." He grabs the back of my neck and quickly attaches the leash to the collar. "I cannot exactly trust you not to run off, can I?"

He stands in front of me, leash in hand, looking way too satisfied with himself. He is of course shirtless, and if it weren't for the collar and leash, it might not be blatantly obvious that I'm the one wearing his shirt. The lower half of my thighs are exposed, as are most of my arms. I look ridiculous. And I can't stop glaring at that fucking leash.

"Okay. Let us get you home." Ironstorm ruffles my hair like a fucking kid before helping me off the table. Leash still tight in his hand, he pulls me to the door and leads the way through it.

We're back inside the arena, same as when I was brought in. There are a few orcs milling about, and when they see us exiting the room, we get some cheers. Self-conscious, I try to use my bound hands to pull the tunic down farther, but after giving his audience a wave, Ironstorm is already walking away. Not wanting to risk being dragged, I try to keep pace, though once we are outside, the distraction of the city makes that difficult.

We're getting plenty of stares, but I do my best to ignore them, instead focusing on the city around me. The buildings that line either side of the street are all made of wood and stone, the architecture a lot less crude than I would have expected. I mean, you hear the words "orc camp," and you picture everyone living in tents. But this isn't that unlike the last town we stayed in. The style is different: the lots aren't packed together, and I don't see a building taller than two stories, but I don't know how you could possibly mistake this place for anything other than civilization.

I notice a familiar building on my left—the jail—before Ironstorm turns right at the next road, looking back to make sure I'm following.

He's been occasionally glancing back at me the whole time but for the most part seems content to lead in silence. *Fine by me.* I don't wanna talk to him anyway. Even though I have a million questions about where we are and what we're doing.

Like how big is this city anyway? I haven't seen a lot of it yet, but I can probably figure it out. The arena is the largest building I can see, which *probably* means it's toward the center of town. There's a tree line along the city's outskirts, meaning we're in the middle of a fairly thick forest. I think it's maybe a mile away from us? Maybe less. It's kind of hard to tell because those trees look...really big. Like, tall, taller than trees normally grow. I swivel my head around, and in the spots I can peak through between buildings, the trees look just as large. They're like that almost all the way around. I can see a mountain range far in the distance ahead of us, so I'm pretty sure we're facing north.

Alright, if the arena is in the center, and we've walked about four blocks so far—

I slam into the body in front of me, which has come to a stop without my noticing. I bounce off, shouting in both surprise and distress as I struggle to keep my balance. I shut my eyes as I tumble to the ground, unable to brace for the impact with my immobilized wrists. *This is gonna suck.*

Imagine my surprise when a thick, muscled arm catches me behind my shoulders.

"You really should be more careful." I cautiously open one eye, though I already know who's going to be looking down at me. "Do you not think you have spent enough time lying on the ground for one day?"

I huff in anger but say nothing as he helps me stand. Just another glare. If he thinks I'm gonna thank him for that, he can go fuck himself. Still, we've stopped in front of a house to our right, so I guess that means...

"We are here," the orc announces. It's a modest-sized house, single-story just like rest I see in the area. A single wooden door adorns the front with two square windows peering out on either side of it. He walks to the front door, leaving me little choice but to follow him past the wooden fence into the yard. He reaches into his pocket to pull out a ring of keys, unlocking the door and ushering me inside.

"Welcome to my home." He shuts the door behind me, placing his key ring in a drawer. "I suppose it is now your home too."

I'm not sure what I expected, but it's as nice as any other home I've been in. To the right of the entrance is what I'd guess is the living room.

It's sunken into the floor, a few steps on either side of a couch leading down into it. There's a fireplace along the wall and in one corner an armchair nestled between a pair of bookcases. In the other corner lies… a large pile of pillows and blankets?

Directly across from the entrance is a kitchen, a small wood-burning stove in the corner with a series of stone counters and shelves to its left. On one of the counters, closest to the living room and door, is a small wooden clock. In the opposite corner is a small wooden table that could sit four people if you really squeezed. I see a few doors that could lead to other rooms or maybe just a closet or pantry.

The difference that sticks out the most to me between this place and a human's home is the furniture. It's not that I don't recognize it; it's just constructed differently. The tabletops look like tabletops, but when you get to the legs, instead of wood that's been cut and sanded, it's like it was bent into place, bark and all. Same with the chairs and the couch. It makes for a very interesting look.

"Come, I will show you around." Leash still in hand, he starts his tour. "Can you read?" He points to the bookcases in the living room.

"Of course." I'm not a child.

"I have met many humans who cannot read." He actually looks a little impressed. "Most of those are not in your language, but I do have a few you might enjoy when you are bored. I visit the bookshop quite frequently."

"…Thanks." Who cares if their slave gets bored?

"That is the kitchen. I do a lot of cooking, so you can expect to spend some time there." He points out the kitchen as he walks past to a short hallway situated between the two open rooms. At the end of the hall are three closed doors.

"This is a spare room." Ironstorm lifts one hand and places it on the door to our left. "Right now, it is just a bed and some storage, so nothing you need to worry about. *This* door—" He actually opens the center door and steps aside to let me see in. "—is the lavatory. You are free to use this as you need, no permission needed."

Why the hell would I ask permission to use the bathroom? Although... *Is that an indoor toilet? How rich is this guy?* My family still uses an outhouse. *Most* families back home still use outhouses. I also notice a tall stone basin and a large wooden tub for washing. This is some relatively fancy shit.

"And finally, this—" He closes the bathroom door and moves to open the final door on the right side of the hall. "—is my bedroom."

I'm actually ushered inside this time, though Ironstorm only stands in the doorway. The obvious focal point of the room is the large bed raised on a wooden pallet against one wall. It's bigger than any bed I've ever slept in, and the head and footboard are made of the same bent natural wood as that of the rest of the furniture. The headboard even has leaves on it. Other than that, there are a couple of small tables, one next to the bed and the other in a corner alongside several large chests, one of which is open and stuffed with clothing.

I turn around facing him, uncertain of what he expects now, the fact that we're in a bedroom not lost on me. He's looking at me like he wants me to say something. "...You have a lovely home?" *Is that what you usually tell the person holding you captive?*

"Thank you." He smiles, and my stomach picks that exact moment to rumble. I've barely eaten today. "I guess I should start dinner then."

I follow him back into the living room, but as he enters the kitchen, I clear my throat. "Um. Do you think you could take off the...?" I face away from him and wiggle my tied wrists.

"Of course." He moves to stand behind me and unbuckles the straps on the cuffs. I rub the feeling back into my skin as he places them on the smooth stone countertop. "Here, let me take care of the scrapes on your arms."

I watch as he reaches onto a shelf above the counters and pulls out a small basket with some bottles and white cloth. Taking one of my arms, he opens one of the bottles and pours the liquid onto some cloth. I hiss at the sting as he dabs over the irritated and torn skin—alcohol to clean the wounds. He repeats the process on my other arm before releasing me.

"What about this?" I tug on the collar, but he's already walking away from me.

"I am not terribly fond of that collar, but I am afraid it stays on until we get a replacement." He places some firewood in the stove and uses some nearby flint to light it. "Probably tomorrow."

"Seriously?" I don't want a replacement. I want it off.

"Is it bothering you?" He closes the stove and watches me.

"Yes. I don't *like* it." Of course it's bothering me.

"Is it irritating your skin or making it difficult to breathe?" He rolls his eyes and turns back to pull things off shelves.

"I guess not?" Kinda wish this thing would *choke me.*

"Then you will be fine until we get your replacement." He places a few jars—spices or some kind of pickled vegetables—on the counter, turning away from me to open a large stone chest. I look down. Other than the collar, I'm still wearing his tunic and my boots.

And my hands are free.

I look back up at the orc as he stares down into the contents of the chest, deciding on what to do with whatever is inside. I look behind me to the front door. The front door that he did not lock after we came in.

I think you see what I'm getting at here.

Very quietly, I inch my way to the door, my eyes locked onto Ironstorm's form. He's bent down into the chest now, the sounds of whatever he's got in there scraping together as he moves it around. Once my hand is on the doorknob, I turn it ever so slowly, until...

click

Chapter Four

Ironstorm's form freezes at the sound of the open lock clicking, and I don't wait to see what comes next. I throw the door open and bolt outside. The arena and jail are to the left, so I go right, taking off with all the speed I can muster. First thing to do is get *far* away from here and find someplace to hide. And hopefully a pair of pants.

I start looking for an alley or back street I can turn down. There's a crossroad coming up ahead, but taking that seems too obvious. But if I can get behind or even on *top* of some of these buildings... *Oh shit, is that a cart coming down the road?* A big one with two huge black horses in front. Maybe I can jump on the back of it.

They're moving fast. Really fast. I'm not sure I can make that jump. Why are they moving so fast in the middle of a city? I hear someone yelling in the distance as they barrel through the intersection without so much as slowing down. They could kill someone driving like that.

I know Ironstorm has to be right behind me, so I have to move quickly. I start looking for alternate exits or even something I might be able to slow him down with, anything to put some extra distance between us while I make my escape. That's when I notice something in the road. Someone: a small green child tottering around, playing with a doll. And that cart is heading straight toward them.

Dammit.

I'm closer than the cart is, but those horses are way faster than I am. The kid isn't even looking up. Where the hell are their parents? *Aaarrrgggghhh.*

I put every last ounce of energy I have into my run. I've gotten faster in the last two months, but this is cutting it close. I shout a "hey!" to get them to move, but then the kid—a little girl it looks like—just starts staring at me instead, still not moving. I look up at the cart, but I can't even see the driver, the horses' reins being held from the inside.

Why did I even bother getting up today?

I dive at the little girl, who picks that exact moment to finally notice the horses about to trample her. I wrap my arms around her when we make contact, clutching her tightly to my chest. My ass hits the ground first as we roll, the thunderous stomps of the horses just missing us. We tumble a few times before I slam into a stone fence with my arm and side. *Oww, that's gonna bruise.*

I peek an eye open, having shut them tightly during the tuck-and-roll. The sight I'm greeted with is that of a slightly frightened and very confused orc child looking back at me. *Phew.* Afraid and confused is still alive. With her hair in pigtails, she kind of reminds me of my little sister. Then comes more shouting, and I see a panicked looking woman over the kid's shoulder coming toward us from inside the fence.

She immediately reaches down and scoops up her child, holding her tightly while planting kisses all over the kid's face and hair, muttering continuously. I hope she saw the cart and doesn't think I just tackled her kid for no reason. I'm about to stand up and dust myself off when I hear the plodding of a familiar pair of boots as Ironstorm's shadow falls over me. Fucking kid.

I pick myself up from the ground, but before I have the chance to say anything, the woman pulls me into a *very* strong hug. I can't really breathe, but at least I know she saw the cart. She's still saying things I can't understand, but I assume they're something along the lines of "Thank you for saving my child." I hear the captain behind me chiming in on his own, and they continue to talk after she releases me, saying one last thing before taking her child back inside. The smile I'm wearing is cut short when the shadow behind me looms over me once more.

I turn hesitantly, positive that what awaits me is a very pissed off orc. But no, when I actually venture to raise my head enough to look him in the eye, he seems fairly calm. He's giving me a look that is somewhere between confusion and consideration, the one he had on when he first held me to the ground in the arena. He doesn't say anything, just takes me by the arm, firmly but not enough to hurt. I don't argue, and we start the walk back to his home together.

The front door is open when we approach, and he pushes me inside. Keys are pulled out of the drawer to my left, and he grabs the discarded set of cuffs from the kitchen before turning us down the hallway to the bedroom. He pushes me to the bed, and I grab a seat with a sigh while he just...stares at me.

"Why did you do that?" He breaks the silence, his tone softer than I'm expecting for that question.

"Well don't take this the wrong way or anything, but becoming an orc's slave wasn't exactly on my bucket list," I deadpan.

"Not that." He shakes his head. "The little girl."

"What do you mean?" Is that what's bothering him? "I wasn't gonna let her get run over."

"You could have," he points out for some reason. "You were escaping. If anything, she slowed you down. You could have even used the accident to—"

"*Woah!*" I jump up from the bed, actually offended. "What the hell? I wasn't going to let a *child* get *trampled* to death."

"No, you were not." He's smiling now for some reason. "Still, you could have been hurt. You only *barely* missed those horses, and I saw how hard you hit the ground afterward. How could you possibly have known you would make a jump like that?"

"I didn't." I shrug. "I saw the kid in trouble and did something. Didn't really stop to think about it."

"Seems to be a recurring theme with you." He crosses his arms, but he's still smiling. "It was very brave. I am honestly impressed."

"Thanks?" I didn't think he brought me in here to pay me compliments, but I'll take it.

"It is a shame I have to punish you now." *Do what now?*

"Punish me?" I back up into the bed. "What? Why?!"

"You have made two escape attempts in less than an hour. Before I have even had the chance to go over any of the rules or guidelines you will be expected to follow." He takes a heavy step toward me.

"Then how about we just don't count those attempts and call it even?" I debate climbing onto the bed next, but I have a feeling he won't be too amused by that.

"Nonsense." He takes another step, crowding me in. "How can I expect you to learn if I do not teach you?"

"Teach me what, exactly?" I refuse to cower even if it does feel like he's twice my size. "Not to save children from certain death? Because if I hadn't run out at that exact moment, there'd be a little girl-shaped pancake on the road right now."

"What you did was commendable, truly." He doesn't move. "Something to be rewarded even. But that does not negate that you broke a rule—a fairly obvious and big one at that—and need to be corrected."

I glare at him—and then try to bolt around him and out of the room. It's no use though; he's got me by the arm as soon as I move. Then his other hand is at the bottom of my tunic, which he pulls up over my head. I struggle in the dark against the sudden restriction, but in the confusion, he sits on the bed and pulls me over his lap. He finishes pulling the tunic off me, grabbing both arms as soon as they are free. I do my best to fight, but the events of the day are finally catching up with me. All the walking, being knocked out, the fight and the...other stuff in the arena. I also still haven't really eaten since this morning. I'm exhausted, I'm hungry, and I don't have anything left in me. I cry out in frustration as my arms are pinned to my back.

"Clearly, it was a mistake to take these off of you," Ironstorm comments as he reattaches the cuffs to my wrist. I hear the *click* of a lock this time, twice.

"Oh my *god*, why do you even care so much?!" I struggle against my binds even though I know it's no use. "Will you just *let me go* already?"

"Why should I, exactly?" I detect no amusement in his voice. He suddenly squeezes me tightly by the hips as he reaches down to remove my shoes. "The first thing you did when I met you this morning was attack me. Then, the *second* you woke up, you challenged me to a fight—one in which you *apparently* intended to kill me or be killed yourself! Then when you *lost* that fight, rather than uphold your end of the bargain, you tried to run away from it. Twice."

"What I do *not* understand," he continues, "is why you insist on fighting me so much. By your own admission you thought you would be *dead* right now. Maybe this is a human issue, but to me, your current circumstances certainly seem better than *not being alive*. Not to mention that you hardly seem to be *minding* your treatment all that much."

"What is that supposed to mean?" I try to say with as much dignity as I can manage, naked with my face pressed to the sheets.

"This." I jump when a hand reaches under me and grabs my not-so-flaccid dick. Not sure when that happened.

"That's not... I don't—!" I get flustered and try to shake his hand off. "That's never happened before today!"

"Oh please." What the hell does he know?

"No! This...stuff only started happening after I got here." That is the *only* explanation. Never in my life would I have done any of this. "Maybe you did something to me when I was knocked out, or, or there's something in the water. Maybe they put something in that bath I took before we fought, or in the food, or—" A memory from earlier flashes in my mind. "That woman. She did this to me."

"What are you talking about?" He actually leans back so he can look me in the eye when he asks.

"Those two women from earlier. They were...older, I dunno." I pause, not knowing how else to describe them. "Before we fought, one of them put her hand on my stomach and cast some sort of spell. I didn't think it was anything then, but right after that you throw me to the ground and fuck me stupid! There is no other explanation. There's no way in hell I would ever want something like that. This is all because you people did something to me."

He looks at me confused while I rant but then something clicks. "I see. So, this woman, right before our match put her hand right here below your stomach, yes?" He reaches a hand underneath me again to demonstrate. "And she cast a spell?"

"Yes." I nod slowly. *This is a trap.*

"Sorry to say this, David, but 'that woman' was only making sure you were ready for your inevitable loss." He mocks me with his smile. "Really, you should be thanking her. All she did was empty your bowels with a little magic and added some lubricant."

"She...what?" I have no way of knowing if that's true or not. It's not like I'd know what that feels like.

"She was just helping make sure you were *prepared* for what would happen on the field." I don't believe his explanation, but even if I did, how do I know that's *all* she did?

"You're lying." He has to be.

"I am not sure I have much of a reason to, but if thinking that makes you feel better..." He pats my flank, still mocking.

"Fuck you," I spit out, starting to struggle again. "This wasn't supposed to happen! I thought I was helping my friends! I didn't fucking ask for this! None of it! This isn't what I—" I choke back a sob. "I was trying to help. None of this was supp—" The frustration builds and the dam breaks. I sob into the mattress, thrashing weakly against my bonds. The tears cut off my vision as they start to flow.

"I know," his voice is soft, losing the unkind edge from moments ago, his hand on my back. "But right now, this is what you have to deal with. I know you have no reason to trust me, but I promise that you will be well cared for."

"What am I supposed to do?" I almost whisper.

"Accept and submit." He strokes his thumb along my back. "I promise I will take care of you, David."

The first *smack* against my ass really throws me, and I cry out more in surprise than pain. He's *spanking* me?! The second *smack* quickly proves me right and my hands, tied as they are, are fruitless to block any further blows. I haven't been spanked since I was a kid! How is *this* supposed to make me stop trying to escape? The third, fourth, and fifth blows, all of which cause me to start crying out in *actual* pain, make me reconsider that.

I lose count after that. Around ten, he evidently gets tired of seeing my hands flailing around and pins them to my back, adding a little extra strength to keep the rest of my body from moving. His other hand, his right I think, continues to rain down on my already-abused ass. And his hands are fucking *huge*, able to cover each half of my poor butt in its entirety. The sting of each blow makes me cry out into the bed below. He changes up the force, the angle, able to seemingly pinpoint a different yet-to-be-touched spot with each strike.

There's no rhythm, no rhyme or reason to how he's hitting me. The only thing I know is that more is coming. Always more. I'm not even yelling anymore, barely able to grunt each time his hand connects with my ass. That doesn't mean I'm not still crying, just that I've got nothing left in me to yell about. The hand holding my own loosens its grip at some point after I stop struggling. The spanking stops altogether sometime after that, though I'm not really clear on when.

Too busy being a sobbing, blubbery mess.

Eventually the crying slows down, and I notice the hand stroking my hair as I catch my breath. My arms are still tied, and I'm still naked, still over his lap. Kinda lost myself there for a minute. My ass feels like it's on fire, so much that I'm afraid to look. Ironstorm says nothing, content to pet my hair and back as I return to the land of the living.

"Let us get you cleaned up and fed." He helps to ease me to the floor on my knees before helping me stand. Holding me by the cuffs behind my back, he ushers me out of the room and back to the kitchen. He walks me to the sink, turning it on and using a washcloth to wipe the tears and snot from my face.

"Wait here." He leaves me in the kitchen next to the table, heading back down the hallway. I don't have the energy to even think about escaping, so I just sort of numbly stare at my feet while I wait for him to get back. When he does, I hear a familiar metal rattling—he's holding a chain. He moves into the living room, lighting lanterns in the house as he goes. Didn't even notice it was getting dark. He grabs something out of the drawer he keeps his keys in and a very large pillow from the pile in the living room.

He throws the pillow on the floor when he returns to me in the kitchen. Then, after pulling me closer to the wall, I realize what he's doing. There's a metal ring on the wall I didn't notice earlier. He slips a padlock through one end of the chain and attaches it to the ring, then does the same with the other end and my collar. I'm being leashed again.

"Seriously?" I mutter. It's a long chain, nearly touching the floor when I stand, but that doesn't make it better. "Is this really necessary?"

"I am afraid so, pup." He tweaks my nose and I try to shake his hand off. "Until I can trust you not to run, you will be kept secured when I am unable to do so myself. You can earn your freedom of movement back the same way you can earn the privileges of wearing clothes or having your hands free."

"I don't get to wear clothes?" Well, that sounded whiny.

"I do not see why I should make it any easier on you to leave. Besides, nudity suits you." He winks and ruffles my hair, and I try to shake his hand away again. *Why is he being so friendly?* "Go ahead and rest while I make dinner."

I huff and think about continuing to stand just to spite him, but I really am exhausted. I gingerly lower myself onto the pillow, hissing as soon as the fabric makes contact with my ass. *Right, that.* It takes some effort to find a comfortable position, and I'm reminded of the way our old dog used to try and find a comfortable sleeping position on the floor. I'm even wearing a collar. I end up leaning on my side, able to keep my eyes on the orc while keeping the pressure off my poor butt.

I watch Captain Ironstorm as he moves about the kitchen. He places a large skillet above the still-lit stove before pulling a few vegetables from a basket on a shelf under the counter. I recognize the onion, but there's also some round and bumpy green things and something that sort of looks like an orange potato that I've never seen before. He opens the chest again, and now that I'm closer, I see there's frost on the inside of the lid. An icebox. He pulls out a slab of meat—more meat than I've seen in a long time— and closes the lid.

I actually like cooking, for the small amount I've been able to do it. I used to help my mom a lot back home, and I'd sign up to be on kitchen duty whenever I could at the academy. I don't know if I've done enough to say I was good, but I enjoyed it. It also usually meant getting extra food. Have I mentioned that I used to weigh a lot more?

The orc knows what he's doing, chopping the veggies and throwing them in the skillet followed by the cubed chunks of meat. I'm not sure what it is, but I know it's not fish. Given our location, I'd guess some kind of venison. It's a little more difficult to see from the floor after that, but a few of the other small jars are grabbed and added here and there. It starts to smell pretty good. I mean, I'm starving, but I'm actually looking forward to eating this. Also being able to use my own hands again will be nice.

I watch as the skillet's contents are emptied onto a single large plate. The stove is put out, hands are washed, and what appear to be a fork and a pitcher of water are grabbed. Everything is set on the table to my right before finally, the orc turns to me. I stand as he approaches and retrieves the keys from his pocket. Lifting my chin, he unlocks the padlock holding the chain to my neck, snapping it shut once it is clear and letting the chain dangle freely against the wall.

Ironstorm returns to the table, pulling out and taking a seat. I follow, aiming for my own chair when I am grabbed and pulled onto his lap. I try to buck off him immediately, both from the weirdness of being a grown man on another grown man's lap and the pain radiating from my ass. But no matter how I squirm, he's adamant about keeping me in place.

"Are you serious?!" Will the humiliations never end?

"Well, I suppose I *am* very curious to see how you intend to feed yourself with your arms behind your back." He loosens his grip as the words slow my struggle.

"Are... Are you going to make me eat it like a dog or something?" My stomach sinks, and I can barely even bring myself to ask.

"What? No." He sounds offended. "I am going to feed you myself."

"Uh, no thanks? I can feed myself." Now I sound offended.

"You can feed yourself when I know I can trust you." He grabs me by the waist and adjusts me so I'm sitting over one thigh, facing the table with him. "Now can we eat, or do you enjoy your food more when it is cold?"

I say nothing, content to wallow in my misery. Which is hard to do when someone is holding really good smelling food in front of your face. My mouth waters and my stomach groans as I take in the scent. I was wrong before—that's beef. Where the hell did he find a cow around here? Any remaining willpower I had has just left the building, and I open my mouth, nearly diving from my perch to grab it. *Holy shit* it's so good. I actually moan when the taste hits my tongue.

"Easy," Ironstorm chuckles before bringing me another forkful. "You can have as much as you would like. I made extra and can eat whatever is leftover tomorrow."

I take him at his word as he alternates bringing forkfuls of food to each of our mouths. Once I stop thinking about the specifics of how and why, I don't actually mind being fed all that much. I'd still rather do this on my own, but I don't know—he's not being a dick about it or anything. The food keeps coming and every now and then the water is brought to my lips. I do notice he's making sure I get a lot more of the vegetables than he is.

"You not big on veggies?" I nod at the next forkful as it's brought toward me. It's not like I mind; they taste just as good as the rest of it. The green things are just a little spicy, and the orange potatoes taste just like potatoes, only sweeter. Just curious.

"I enjoy them, but an orc's diet does not require as much as a human's." He grabs a bite for himself next. "I made most of them for you."

"Oh. Uh, thank you?" Back to feeling like a pet. I should probably be happy he's at least feeding me well, but I'm curious about why he knows the specifics of a human's dietary needs.

I don't ask any more questions, happy to fill my belly. I haven't eaten like this in a long time. I know I've got sauce and grease all over my face, and if I wasn't so hungry, I'd probably care more. Sadly, it doesn't take long for me to get full. I say sad only because I would *really* like to keep eating this. A side effect of having cut down on the size of my meals for so long is that my stomach shrank along with them.

" 'm full." I shake my head when the fork approaches again.

Ironstorm takes the food for himself, swallowing it down quickly. "You ate more than I anticipated. I apologize for not feeding you sooner."

I shrug as he continues to eat. It's not that big a deal; I've gone longer without eating, especially in the last two months. This might actually be the highlight of the day for me.

It has been a really fucked up day.

He eats the rest of the food fairly quickly. I guess I really did eat more than he expected seeing as he finishes off what's left. He helps me stand then wipes my face again with the washcloth. I watch as our cutlery, dish, and skillet are washed, only just realizing that like his bathroom, he has *running water* in his kitchen. The sink, like the countertops, is made up of very smooth, solid stone, even the faucet. Is this guy loaded or something?

As he dries the dishes, there's a split second where I think about running. Only for a second though. I am very naked, very tired, and very tied up. I can worry about how I'm getting out of here tomorrow. Besides, it's not like he's gonna make me sleep like this, right?

The lanterns are put out, and I'm led away from the kitchen to the bathroom where I'm stood in front of another sink and cleaned up. He washes and dries my face, and there's even a toothbrush. I don't think I've seen someone else use one of these besides my friends since we left the academy.

Still, the fact that he's not letting me do any of this myself is more than a little humiliating. But it beats washing in a river.

My hopes of possibly sleeping by myself in the spare room are dashed when I am steered into the main bedroom. I hear the familiar jingle of keys though and am relieved when I feel my wrists being freed. I eagerly bring them around to the front, only to have the cuffs *re*locked around my wrist immediately.

"I have to sleep like this too?" I grumble.

"Actually, thank you for reminding me." He steps around me to one of his chests that is already open and pulls out...another chain. *Motherfucker.*

He wraps the chain through the headboard and uses a lock to cinch it before pulling me close and attaching the other end to my cuffs. How many fucking padlocks does this dude have?

Content with his handiwork, he finishes getting himself ready for bed, which mostly just involves taking off his boots, pants, and underwear. He pulls back the sheets on the bed—ugh, of course it looks comfortable—and climbs in, staring at me. Waiting.

"Maybe I should sleep on the floor." I stare at the ground. It doesn't look *that* uncomfortable.

"If that is what you would prefer." He crosses his arms, looking amused. "I can assure you though, you will be safe in bed with me."

"...You'll stay on your side?" I would really like to sleep in a bed tonight.

He puts his hands up in a show of surrender, even inching away from me slightly. After a little more hesitation, I carefully climb into the bed. Once I'm in, Ironstorm pulls the sheets over us and turns out the final lantern. For a moment I'm tense, listening as the body next to me shuffles in the dark.

But once I hear him settle, I relax. I fumble a little myself as I try to find a comfortable position to sleep in with the chain attached to my hands, ending up on my side, facing Ironstorm. I don't want to keep my back to him for obvious reasons. For a moment, it's just me, the night air, and my thoughts. Plans for escaping, my friends in their cell, even my family back home all drift in and out of my mind, until sleep takes me, and I'm not thinking about anything at all.

Chapter Five

I wake up slowly, barely hanging on to the threads of a dream. Something about birds? I snuggle into my pillow. This bed is so warm. Haven't been this comfortable in months. *Maybe I can convince Adam that we should stay in town another night...*

Then I feel the arm around my waist tighten, and my eyes fly open when I remember that I'm not sleeping at an inn with my teammates. A glance down at the green, muscular limb confirms that, yep, I'm still in Captain Ironstorm's bed in the middle of...wherever here is. I should probably ask about that when he wakes up.

It would seem at some point in the night we both migrated to the center of the bed. Or, seeing as I'm still tied up, he probably grabbed me after I fell asleep and pulled me here himself. Whatever. The sun is up and so am I, and thanks to these cuffs, I can't exactly go anywhere. Some quiet time to think is nice.

I run through yesterday's events in my head. Everything started so normally. After a shitty breakfast of beans and jerky by the campfire, we packed up and started looking for that cave. Then everything went to hell. Getting knocked out, waking up in the jail cell, the fight in the arena... What happened right after the fight in the arena.

What was that? Not what we did—I know what sex is. I mean my reaction to it. Not only did I barely try to fight him off, I was hard before he even finished stripping me. Hell, once I was naked, there was no attempt to fight at all. Pretty much the exact opposite.

Look, maybe there's been a time or two in the past where I've looked at a guy a *little* differently than I'm supposed to, but never like that. I've never imagined getting tied up, or stripped, or...*fucked* out in the open. Certainly not by a stranger—an *orc*. But even thinking about it now is making me want to grind my morning wood into the mattress.

Some movement at my back reminds me why I won't be doing that. Ironstorm shifts in his sleep, his arm tightening around my waist again as he pushes his knee forward between my legs. His own hard cock grinds against me, and I bite my tongue to hold in a hiss at the contact with my sore ass. *Fuck.*

The spanking... That is something I wouldn't mind forgetting. I haven't been spanked since I was like nine years old. Maybe longer. And never that hard! He's like some ass-slapping expert. Fuck, if I had been spanked like that as a kid, I'm not sure I'd even be alive right now. Sitting down today is going to be a pain in the ass. *Heh.*

"Mmmf." Distracted by my own stupid joke, I fail to hold in a whimper when there's another shift behind me.

I go stone still, holding my breath before realizing that will be even more suspicious. There's more movement, then the arm around me goes slack. Things are still, at first, until I feel his hand drifting up and softly rubbing my stomach. Then he dips down, carding his fingers through my pubic hair before wrapping them lightly around my shaft.

I can't help but hump forward a little at the contact, biting my lip and hoping to pass it off as involuntary. If he notices, he doesn't say anything, his fingers still wrapped around my dick, stroking softly, slowly against the smooth skin. His touches are light, almost too light, bordering on ticklish. They probably would be if they were on any other part of my body. But he seems content to keep playtime relegated to my dick, and I'm finding myself surprisingly okay with that.

"You know, some people might consider it rude to make me do *all* the work." I jump when the voice whispers in my ear, immediately batting his hand away and rolling forward off the bed. I stand by the bedside, unable to do much more than glare thanks to the chain still connecting me to the headboard. None of that seems to faze him, lying there in all his glory with a shit-eating grin on his face. Stupid sexy orc.

No, not sexy! An asshole!

"I am hungry. Are you hungry?" He scoots across the mattress toward me and stands, acting like none of that just happened, like our dicks aren't pointing at each other right now. He reaches down to unlock the chain from my cuffs, ruffling my hair and walking out of the room.

What the hell was that?

I hear the telltale sounds of someone peeing, and when he doesn't come back to the room, I figure I should follow him...after I wait for my hard-on to go down. Which I had *before* he started touching my dick! Once my perfectly-normal-to-have-first-thing-in-the-morning erection goes away, I follow his lead and relieve myself before padding out to the living room. I think about wrapping myself in a sheet, but what would be the point? He clearly intends to keep me naked.

The stove is already lit, and I can see the captain standing over it, pouring something into a pot of water. It looks like ground oatmeal. Is porridge still a thing? I guess I'll find out. My stomach growls. I bet my teammates are hungry too. *What am I doing thinking about breakfast? I need to get out of here.* I look down at my still cuffed wrists. My last two escape attempts didn't exactly work out. I'll have to bide my time and wait for the opportunity to present itself. And in the meantime, I can try to learn more about where we are exactly.

"Can I... Can I ask you some questions?" My request has him poking his head up.

"I suppose that would be alright," he answers while stirring the contents of the pot.

"Where are we?" I'm mostly just curious; anyone I could write to for help is an ocean away. "Like, what's the name of the city?"

"*V'rok'sh Tah'lj,*" is what I think he says. "Though you may find that difficult to pronounce. It translates to 'home among the trees.'"

"Vorekish Talj?" I repeat back the best I can.

"Close enough," he responds without looking over.

"What about your name?" Ironstorm can't be his first name. At least I hope not.

"What about yours?" *Touché.*

"Cerano." It's not like holding onto it was doing me any good. "David Cerano."

"Cerano. I like that." My name rolls off his tongue easily. "I am Khazak Uzi'gar."

Yeah, I'm gonna butcher that. "Can I call you Zak instead?"

"No. *You* will refer to me as Sir or Captain." His tone leaves little room to argue.

"I thought your last name was Ironstorm?" *Gonna just blow past that sir nonsense for now.*

"A rough translation of *Uzi'gar.*" He looks over his shoulder at me. "Human tongues seem to have problems with our language, at least from your part of the world."

"Human tongues are just fine." I narrow my eyes at him. "Maybe your language is just overly complicated."

"Yes, perhaps." Sarcasm. "Anything else?"

"What happens now?" I wrap my arms around myself, feeling a sudden chill. "Like, is this it? Am I just yours forever?" Stuck in this town in the middle of nowhere for the rest of my life.

"More or less." He takes the pot off the stove while he speaks. "You are mine until I decide to release you."

"And I'm guessing you're not planning on doing that anytime soon," I sigh, mostly to myself.

"Do you have somewhere to be?" he jokes as he empties the pot into a shallow bowl. Just the one, again.

"My friends——"

"Are in jail." He moves to the table and takes the same seat he did last night, pushed away from the table, leaving his lap open. "Come. Eat."

"I'm not sitting on your lap again." I eye him warily.

"No, I suppose your ass is a little too tender for that right now." I hadn't actually thought about that until he just mentioned it.

"I more meant because I'm a *grown man*." Why can't I have my own seat?

"You are free to kneel on the floor instead." He spreads his legs and gestures to the spot between them.

"Seriously?" I grit my teeth. "Fuck off then. I'm not hungry."

He cocks an eyebrow and taps his fingers on the tabletop, reminding me a lot of my last drill sergeant. "I am fairly certain the entire city heard your stomach growl earlier, so I know that is a lie. I was happy to let us sleep in some today, but we do still have things to take care of before it gets too late. So you can either take a seat where I have told you, or you can spend another day with your arms bound. One that will start with you being force-fed a cold breakfast."

I squeeze my hands into fists and think about fighting him. Then my stomach growls again. With a sigh, I step into his space, lowering myself to my knees in front of him. I figure this will be less humiliating *and* save my sore ass from some pain. When Ironstorm adjusts his seat and I look up, I see I'm only half right.

The first thing I notice is my proximity to his dick. Is he always this naked at home, or is it because I'm here? His legs are spread wide, soft green cock against one of his thighs. It would be really easy for him to grab my head and... Maybe I should have gone with the lap. *Oh fuck, how long have I been staring at his dick?* My eyes shoot to the floor.

"Maybe I can feed you some of that later," the orc laughs and takes a bite while my face burns. Lifting my head to retort, I am greeted with my own spoonful of what might be oatmeal. With a sigh, I allow myself to be fed. I'm surprised when the flavor that hits my tongue is savory and not sweet. Not bad. More finely ground than oatmeal and a little creamy. He can cook. I wonder if he'll ever let me...

Stop thinking like you'll be here long enough to get comfortable, David.

The rest of breakfast is eaten in relative silence and finishes rather quickly since there's not much to it. He helps me to my feet and guides me by the shoulder to the bathroom to clean up. I'm still not over the fact that orcs actually brush their teeth, but I guess when you have tusks, dental care is pretty important. Before we exit, Ironstorm grabs a small jar and pushes me to the bedroom.

"Get on the bed and lay on your stomach." My hackles rise instantly.

"What? Why?" I turn to face him. He's not about to beat my ass again for not sitting on his lap or something, is he?

"Calm down." He holds both his hands up in front of them, one of them holding the jar. "I just want to put some of this salve on you. It will help with the soreness."

I eye the small container warily but allow myself to be turned around and bent over the bed. I prop myself up on my elbows, looking behind me as Ironstorm opens the lid and uses two fingers to scoop out a glob of white. I hiss at the coolness as it touches my inflamed skin then try not to whimper as he spreads it around with both hands. It seems like he's trying to be gentle at least.

"Lay there for a moment while it dries." He rubs his hands together as he steps around the bed.

"What are we doing today?" I ask as he starts rifling through one of his chests.

"First thing is getting you some clothes. I do not have much that will fit you." He pulls out a long-sleeved shirt and holds it aloft before mumbling to himself. "I think this belonged to my brother. Or maybe my sister?"

Good, he can replace what he tore off me yesterday. "Then what?"

"There is some paperwork we need to fill out in regard to our current situation and the ritual yesterday. Then we need to make one last stop at a shop run by a friend of mine." He holds up a pair of shorts big enough that my waist could fill one of the legs.

"You guys have a word for paperwork?" I'm pretty impressed with his Common.

"*Hr'klor.*" He tosses the clothes in front of me on the bed. "Which directly translated means 'sad wood.'"

I bark a laugh. "Sad wood?" I can't tell if he's joking, but I really hope he's not.

"Poetic, yes?" He deadpans and bends over, finally unlocking my cuffs and starting to dress himself. "I know these will not fit well, but it is only for the next hour."

I push myself up with a sigh, grabbing the shorts first and pulling them on. I'm swimming in them, and if it weren't for the rope belt around the waist, there's no way they would hold up on their own. The fabric is a little rough on my ass, though I'm not sure how I'd feel about wearing underwear right now to be honest. The shirt fits a little better, but the arms are too long, and I have to pull them up at my wrists to stop them from covering my hands.

"Probably need new shoes as well." He examines the worn-down sole of one of my boots before handing it to me with some oversized socks. Not gonna complain about new shoes, either.

"Do I get to use my hands today?" I ask, probably a little too smartly, while I tie my laces.

"Are you going to behave today?" he asks as he buttons his shirt.

"Yes." There's that eyebrow again. "Sir."

He smiles at the title. "As long as you do not give me a reason otherwise, your arms may remain free today." He grabs the discarded cuffs from the bed and puts them in a leather pouch slung over a corner of the bed. "These will be coming with us, so that can change at any time."

"...Yessir." I try not to glare daggers at the bag. The threat is clear enough.

I watch as he finishes straightening his clothes, and I attempt to do the same with mine. I look absolutely ridiculous in these. I really hope he's not lying when he says I'm getting new clothes. Satisfied, he grabs the bag and slings it over his shoulder as we head into the living room. I move to the door, but he aims for the kitchen counter—and the damn leash.

"Oh, come on," I whine as soon as he walks toward me with it in his hand. "Why do I have to wear that?"

"We are going to be walking around the city a lot today. I do not want you getting lost." To his credit, he doesn't *sound* like he's fucking with me.

"I'm not going to get lost." Why does he insist on treating me like a child? "Everyone will be staring at the human on a leash."

"*I* will feel better if you are wearing it." He crowds me against the door and clips the leash to my collar before I can fight him. "Besides, I think everyone will be staring at you for entirely different reasons." He steps back and looks over my "outfit" for emphasis.

I glare, seeing as the only reason I have to wear this oversized bull-shit is because of him. Then he pulls me away from the door so he can open it, and we walk outside. He takes a right once we hit the road. He's not moving fast, but I wish he was so I can hurry up and get out of this fucking get up. The rope belt is doing a really shitty job of keeping my shorts in place, and I have to pull them up more than once.

Between the distraction of my wardrobe and not wanting to make eye contact with any passersby, I don't do a great job of paying atten-tion to where we are or where we're going. I just focus on Ironstorm (*Khazak? Sir? Asshole?*) in front of me and making sure my lower half remains clothed.

At some point, I notice the amount of people around us growing and a quick look up reveals a street full of carts and stalls selling all sorts of things: clothes and fabric, what I'm pretty sure are fruits and vege-tables (from what I can recognize), and even weapons—it's an open-air market, same as we have back home. The stalls look different, fewer wagons and more tents, but it's basically the same thing. There's a lot of people around us talking, all of it Orcish, so I don't really notice when one orc in particular calls out Khazak's name.

He walks up and they greet each other loudly, like old friends. I can't understand a word of it. It's all smiles until the new orc notices me and what I'm wearing, and I wish the ground would just swallow me up right now. He says something—about me, I assume—to Ironstorm, who turns to look at me in response. I just stare at my feet. Did he have to run into a friend here?

I hear Ironstorm say something to his friend, then I'm being tugged along again. I look up and after passing a few more stalls, he enters a building with me right behind him. Standing in the entrance, I imme-diately notice two very detailed wooden mannequins to our left. I sigh in relief. *A clothing shop.*

"I apologize for that." He turns to face me and clasps my shoulder. "I did not expect to see anyone I knew here. I also apologize again for the clothing. I assure you—I did not choose it to intentionally humiliate you."

"...Thank you." I'm uncomfortable with the sincerity and eye con-tact, so I turn to look at the rest of the shop.

It's not too large; there are a few tables with folded clothing on top, some shelves with more of the same, and a few more mannequins. They're vaguely orc shaped, all of different builds and genders with the same level detail. It's not their faces; those are all blank. It's the rest of them—their bodies, the proportions, the musculature—it's all very lifelike. Either the result of a very talented carver or magic.

A clerk behind the counter notices our entrance, walking over and speaking animatedly at both of us. She does a double-take when she sees my outfit and then says something else.

"Do you speak Common?" Ironstorm asks before responding, gesturing to me as he does.

"Oh, yes. How may I help you?" she asks as if it isn't obvious.

"As you indicated, we are in need of some new clothing for this one." He clasps a hand on the back of my neck. "Some shirts and trousers."

"Is there anything in particular you are looking for?" She looks me over as she asks. "Any colors in mind?" She's speaking Common, but both questions are directed at the orc. I guess the collar and leash clued her in.

"Hmm." He turns to look me over. "I am rather fond of blue, but green would match your eyes." I shift uncomfortably at the comments about my appearance.

"I think I have some options you may like." She turns and walks toward some of the clothing and begins pulling various articles from different shelves. "Could you bring him over here?"

Ironstorm turns to me and unhooks the leash before walking me over to the clerk. She holds up a few different shirts in front of my body, each a shade of blue, green, or brown. The first few are oversized, but she seems to figure it out. She puts the shirts down and from a pocket on her hip pulls out what I'm guessing is measuring tape. She quickly wraps it around my waist before dropping down to measure the length of the outside of my leg. Thankfully she doesn't check the inseam, just turns to grab a few pairs of pants, mostly browns and tans. She stacks some of the shirts on top before handing me the pile.

"There is a changing area right over there." She points at a wooden divider against one wall, her voice still directed at Ironstorm and not me. "Please let me know if anything does not fit well."

"Thank you." He gives her a nod of appreciation before guiding me to where she pointed, clothes in hand. I am not surprised when he follows me behind the divider and takes the clothes from my hands. There's a large mirror against the wall.

"Go ahead and undress." He nods to me with his arms full.

"Come on. I can try—" A raised eyebrow cuts me off, and with a sigh, I pull my shirt over my head. I throw it over a chair to my right before kicking off my shoes and bending over to follow suit with my shorts. No reason to fight something I know I won't get out of anyway. Standing as nonchalant as I can, I hold one hand out for the first item, which ends up being a pair of pants.

"We, uh, didn't get any underwear," I point out, holding them in front of me but not stepping into them.

"We will be taking care of that later." He nods at me to continue. I feel kinda weird about my dick flopping around in pants that aren't technically mine yet, but I don't really have a say in the matter.

After the pants comes a dark green shirt with buttons down the center. I pull it on and start buttoning it up as Ironstorm sets the clothes down on the same chair. He looks me over while I finish adjusting, before I turn to check in the mirror for myself—not bad, honestly. Then I see his figure stepping behind me and I turn.

"It looks good on you." He reaches forward to fix a button I missed near my collar. "I was right about your eyes." He runs his thumb down the side of my face.

I'm blushing more now than when I was naked.

This process repeats with another five shirts and three pairs of pants, all in varying shades and cuts. There are even some shorts that actually fit me. I wouldn't mind if the shirts did more to hide the collar, though. Captain Ironstorm seems to like everything, or at least doesn't have anything negative to say. After I hand him the last set, he hands me back the first.

"Go ahead and change into those." He picks up the clown clothes I walked in here wearing and stuffs them into his bag. "I will not force you to wear these the rest of the day."

"Thanks." I give a genuine smile as I redress for the final time.

Gathering the clothes together, Ironstorm moves to the counter the shopkeeper has returned to, placing them all on top.

"Everything he tried on was perfect. We will take them all." He reaches into his leather pouch, producing an even smaller pouch.

"I would have to agree with you, sir. He looks wonderful." She looks me over and smiles brightly. Probably more at the news of a sale than how I look. She sorts through the clothes on the counter and makes note of what I'm wearing before she starts to fold everything neatly. "I can do twenty-five *gral* for everything."

"More than fair." I watch as he produces two golden coins and five silver ones and drops them in her hand. They are all inscribed with symbols I wouldn't understand even if I could make them out from here, but I can still tell what the coins are made of. It's the same kind of money the rest of the world uses and more proof that they aren't as primitive as we were led to believe.

"Thank you very much. Should you have any more clothing needs, I hope you will return." The shopkeeper happily deposits the coins in her own pouch.

Ironstorm gives a small bow after stuffing the folded clothes and his money back into his satchel. She must have been good at folding them since the bag doesn't seem to be bulging out like I would expect. Or at all, really. Throwing it over his shoulder, he makes his way toward the exit. I turn and give the woman an awkward wave before chasing after him.

I guess I have a sugar orc now.

Chapter Six

The leash is re-clipped to my collar as soon as we step outside. I sigh but don't argue—just follow. Even in nicer clothes, there are still enough people around that I'd rather not cause a scene. At least now I can look around with fewer people staring at me.

"Khazak!" Dammit, it's the orc from before. Now that I'm not embarrassed about meeting his eye, I get a better look at him. He's got the same height and build as Ironstorm, but his longer brown hair is pulled into a small bun. They greet each other again, much less boisterously this time. After exchanging a few words, the other orc looks me over again before turning to Ironstorm and saying...something. *What was that?* I roll my eyes, but keep to myself since it's apparent that they have no intention of including me. Instead, I'll do what I usually do when there's time to kill in a town: people-watch.

The market is still busy with orcs of all shades and sizes roaming between the different stalls. Thankfully none of them seem to be looking at me. I actually see a few non-orcs too. There are more than a few humans, a handful of elves, and even a green-haired gnome manning a wheeled cart full of mechanical knick-knacks. Almost all of them have skin tanner and darker than mine. I keep turning my head to look around and do a double-take when I spot someone else in a collar. An orc. No leash though, so maybe it's just a fashion statement?

But then I see another orc in a collar, this one *with* a leash that is being held by a different orc. They both seem to be happily looking over a display of...rugs. They're all smiles while they talk to each other, at least. I continue scanning the crowd and spot *another* collar and leash, this time on an elf. An elf who is making eye contact with me. He turns his head to the side, giving me a questioning look which I return until I am distracted by the sound of the two orcs next to me hugging, seemingly done with their conversation. The other orc says something to me I obviously don't catch before waving and turning into the crowd. After waving in return, Ironstorm turns to me and then leads us down the street and out of the market.

"That was an old friend of mine. We were schoolmates." Ironstorm slows to walk next to me as he explains. "His mother has been sick, but he wanted me to know that she is feeling much better."

"Oh. That's good." Again, I know that orc moms exist, but I've never really thought about one before.

"He also found you attractive," he adds.

I do another double-take. "Huh?"

"He thought you were cute. He liked the new clothing." He speaks like it's nothing.

"Should I have said thank you?" What is the etiquette here exactly?

"I told him for you. He would not have understood you." *Good point.*

We continue walking together in a comfortable silence, with him next to me instead of in front. He said we were doing *paperwork* next, something I have very little interest in learning about. Now that we're out of the market and I'm not tripping over myself, I'm able to take in more of my surroundings. There are fewer orcs here, all just going about their daily lives. I am happy that no one seems to be paying me any attention despite the leash. Looks like we're in a residential area, though I have no real way of telling a home from a business here.

The buildings are still made of wood and stone. I'm noticing now that a lot of them, especially the frames, are made of that same type of wood as Ironstorm's furniture. It looks like it's been bent into shape perfectly, bark and all. The walls are made of more traditional lumber on top of a stone base, but even the stones seem to be melded together with the surrounding materials just a *little* too well. Seems like the people here have found a lot of different uses for magic.

Ahead of us, just around the corner, I can see an open grassy field, and as we get closer and more of it peeks out from behind the buildings, I notice all of the people in it. Children run around, some older orcs wrestle and spar while others just sit and eat. There are trees and a small pond—it's a park. When we finally reach the corner and it comes into full view, I also see the large stone building on the other side of it.

It's not as big as the arena, but it's larger than any of the other structures I've seen. It's also made entirely of stone; if there's any wood, I'm not seeing it. There's a series of large statues out front, six that I can see. Each features a different orc, men and women, most holding some sort of weapon aloft. If I had to guess, I'd say that's where we're headed.

"The Tribal Hall," Ironstorm informs me when he sees me taking the building in.

We cut across the road and enter the park, walking a well-worn trail through the grass. A gaggle of orc children suddenly cut through our path, seemingly playing a game that I assume exists everywhere: tag. A few more meters and we pass a pond on our right and a man with a cart on the left. Whatever he's selling—some kind of meat on a stick—it smells *really* good.

"Are you hungry?" Ironstorm's question has me turning my head.

"Maybe a little?" We ate only a couple of hours ago, but it wasn't a lot. Not like dinner last night. *Shit, am I getting spoiled after one meal?* "I'm fine."

"No. Better to get something in your stomach now." He changes course to move toward the cart. "I am sorry to say this may take longer than I would like."

If he insists. I don't tend to argue when food is involved. He reaches into his bag again to pull out his coin pouch. He holds three fingers up to the orc working the cart, grabbing a few silver coins and exchanging them for three meat kabobs. As we continue walking, he separates one of the sticks from the others and takes a *large* bite out of it, sliding the top half of the meat off the stick and into his mouth. He hands me the remaining half along with one of the uneaten kabobs. I wanna complain, but it's not like I haven't had the man's tongue in my mouth already, *right?* So I take a bite.

Damn, that's good. A little chewy, but very juicy and tender. I can't help the small moan that escapes me.

"Sounds like you approve." I ignore the half-smirk on his face.

"What is it?" It's familiar, but I can't put my finger on it.

"Venison. Elk, I believe." He tears into the remaining meat-stick.

I follow suit, and the rest of our walk is quiet other than the sounds of our tearing and chewing. By the time we reach the statues, I've got one empty stick, and I'm polishing off the second. When I'm finished, both are taken from me and dropped into a waste bin, and I'm handed a handkerchief to wipe my mouth with. After stuffing it back in his pocket, Ironstorm walks us up the steps and into the building. The entryway is open, the large wooden double doors swung all the way inside.

There are more orcs in here than at the park. Some are lined up in front of a large table with more orcs behind it; others sit at desks looking over papers. A number of them look fairly well dressed, like that fancy orc lawyer from the jail. Whatever this place is, it feels very "official."

Ironstorm seems to know where he's going, leading us straight to a hallway on our left. Makes sense. He's basically this city's version of a knight or guard so he's probably been here a lot. I follow him down a few winding hallways, passing doors as we go, some closed, some open with people inside. Honestly, it's all pretty boring. Eventually we come to a stop in front of an office, and Ironstorm raps his knuckles against the open door.

"Khazak!" The orc behind the desk looks up from his papers and smiles before saying something in Orcish and waving us in.

"Khazak" sits in one of the chairs on this side of the desk, and I take the other one. The two of them begin to speak about something that doesn't seem terribly urgent. The new orc gives me an occasional glance, but the conversation stays between the two of them. Finally, after laughing at a joke I can't understand, he turns his attention to me fully.

"So this is your new *Avakesh*?" What did he just call me?

"This is him." A hand squeezes my shoulder.

"You and your friends have been the talk of the town since you arrived." The orc grabs a stack of papers and begins rifling through them. "And after your match yesterday, people have not stopped asking questions about you."

Really? Am I that interesting?

"Alright, here is the paperwork to finalize the outcome of the *Nagul Uzu'gor*, the official immigration papers, and the form to register him as your *avakesh*." The orc hands the stack of papers to Ironstorm. "Is that everything?"

"I believe so." Ironstorm flips through the papers. "We shall fill these out now, if that is alright?"

"Please, take your time," he stands as he speaks. "I have a meeting I must attend. If you finish before I return, just leave everything on my desk, and I will make sure it is submitted correctly."

"Thank you, Orduk." Captain Ironstorm clears some desk space in front of him. "*Rumk'r Avon.*"

"*Rumk'r Avon.*" The other orc—Orduk—repeats the words back and nods his head before exiting the room.

"What was the last thing you both said?" I wait until we're alone before asking. I'm pretty sure I heard him saying that yesterday before we…showered.

"I believe it translates to 'many blessings' in your language." He reaches for a small inkpot and a pen and begins to write on the top sheet of paper. Writing with a pen somehow makes it seem even more official.

"Whose blessings?" Who do orcs pray to, exactly?

"Hmm. Ancestors, nature, spirits." He continues looking down and writing as he speaks. "It is not tied to one particular thing."

"Do orcs follow a religion?" That's my third question while he's trying to fill out the stack of papers. "Sorry. Not trying to annoy you."

"It is alright. Ask whatever you would like. This first batch will take the longest. Normally this would have already been filled out by someone else, but as I am both responsible for the arrest *and* one of the ritual's participants, it falls to me." He flips through the top half of the paper stack. "As it is, I am writing the details of our initial confrontation and your arrest. This will act as a resolution to your charges."

"To answer your question," he continues to talk as he returns to writing, "I can only speak for the orcs in this city. We do not have a formal name for our religion, but we do have our own pantheon: Nargol the Sky-Father, Vol'tha the Earth-Mother, and Sha-mir the River-Guardian. However, I would say that only a third of the city is particularly devout. The rest of us still observe certain festivals and try to keep the teachings in mind but generally go about our normal lives. There are a few locations in the city devoted to certain ceremonies and rituals, but we only have a single temple of worship. We also have followers of a few other faiths in the city and a number of small shrines dedicated to the Olympians, the Aesir, and the Kami. I believe we even have a growing number of citizens who follow *your* god."

"My god?" That's news to me.

"Yes. Yahweh." He looks at me, tilting his head when I do not respond. "The god of Abram?"

"Oh, uh, count me among the un-devout." I think I've heard Corrine say the name Abram before, so I figure that's the god he's talking about. "Where I'm from isn't all that different from here, really. There are a few people who are in church almost daily, but most of us aren't religious at all. Everyone still tries to be a good person though." *Or at least that's what they claim.* "I haven't even been in a church since I was little and that was for my grandmother's funeral. Also, I think most of his followers just call him 'God.'"

"Of course they do," he sighs and grumbles. "I was under the impression that all humans from your part of the world were his followers." He dips the pen back in the ink and continues writing. "I am glad neither of us will have to worry about waking up early for prayers."

That makes two of us. Why would he care about his slave's religion anyway? Actually, thinking about the word *slave*... "What was the other thing he called me? Vakish?"

"*Avakesh?*" He moves the finished paper to the side and starts on the next. "Roughly translated it would be close to slave, servant, or pet. Though none of those words really capture the meaning."

"Oh." How handy, instead of humiliating me with three words, he can do it in one. "What about Nagleuzgore?" It sounded familiar.

"*Nagul Uzu'gor.*" He finishes another sheet. "That is the name for what we did: the ritual."

That's right. That's what the red-haired lawyer called it. I don't have another question right away, so I give him a moment while I think. "I'm impressed by how many of you speak Common. I really didn't expect that."

"It is not all that *uncommon* here." I can hear how pleased he is at his terrible joke. "My father insisted that my siblings and I learn when we were young, but many people working in the government or as merchants usually take the time to learn additional languages. Those of us who would interact with others outside of the city."

"Does that happen a lot?" I think I saw maybe four or five humans at the market earlier and that's it. "My friends and I didn't even know this place existed."

"No, not very often. We prefer our privacy and do what we can to keep *most* outsiders unaware of our location. Though as time goes on and the city grows, that has become increasingly difficult." More ink. "We have trade routes established with several cities in the west. Certain individuals in those cities have the knowledge and ability to travel here, but outside of that, most trades and deliveries are done outside the city. When new settlements began cropping up in the east, we attempted to establish the same trade relationships, and in return, those settlements sent missionaries in an attempt to 'convert' us. For the most part harmless, but there have been more than a few humans calling the lot of us *heathens.*"

"I'm sorry. That sucks." Seems like a waste of time to me. "Why would they care about which gods you follow?"

"One of your friends in jail is a missionary, are they not?" He looks up to cock an eyebrow at me.

"Uh." I don't have an answer for that. I know that's what Corrine calls herself, but I can't imagine that girl being rude to a mouse, let alone an entire race of people because of a difference in religion. I can't believe that those other people would either, especially since I think that's at least part of why they left their homelands in the first place.

"As I said, most of our interactions have been harmless." He finishes another page and adds it to the pile, straightening and ordering what he's completed so far. "There were a few violent clashes when they first landed. They tried to prevent us and others from using the coastline for fishing, something we have done for ages. We made sure to settle *those* issues some time ago."

I don't know all that much about the settlements he's talking about, except for how they relate to where I came from, Lutheria. Something like 200 years ago, the founders of Lutheria left the nation of Albion after the Albionian Church, which basically runs the country, started cracking down on people they felt were not "true believers." I'm not really sure what that means or how you enforce that, but they tried to and it got violent. After enough blood had been shed, the people had had enough and got on some boats and left. They only went one island over really, but it was enough of a distance to create their own home free of interference.

The island—Inisfalia—wasn't uninhabited, but the lives of the people there were chaotic. For centuries they had been on the receiving end of attacks from northern raiders who would regularly pillage their coastlines. Now, if there was one thing our people were good at, it was fighting tyrants—or at least that's what my dad always said—so they offered their aid in exchange for the chance at starting a new home. The two groups worked together, and after more than a year of repelling the attacks, the raids finally ceased. In that year, as Albion spread its influence eastward, other countries had similar exoduses, displaced outcasts in search of a new home. As more people immigrated, old cities were rebuilt and new cities were established and soon Lutheria was formed.

In the years that followed, many more people did the same, though they ended up traveling much farther—to the coasts here, across the ocean. I'm not sure what they call this continent here, but back home it was known as "Nova Mundus," eventually shortened to just "Nova" by most of the Common speaking population. In the time since, the settlements and Lutheria banded together in the name of "mutual cooperation" (that's a term I remember from class), which is how we were able to get from there to here so easily and without having to fill out any boring-ass paperwork like this.

When I come back from my personal history lesson, I see Ironstorm has finished another paper and is looking at me. "Next is your immigration paperwork, so now it is my turn to ask some questions."

"Why do I need immigration paperwork?" It's not like I'm moving he—*Shit.*

"Because you are an immigrant?" He looks a little bewildered by my answer, which, yeah, was kinda dumb. "The city is not large and likes to know who is within its borders. Your friends will have to fill out the same forms at some point."

"Got it." I just nod. *Let's do this.*

"Can you spell your name for me?" The pen is dipped in the ink again as he waits for my answer.

"D-A-V-I-D C-E-R-A-N-O."

"Thank you." He writes the name on the sheet of paper. "Date of birth?"

"The 13th of Geminus, 4021." I'll be twenty-two in two months!

"And you are originally from...?"

"Northlake, Lutheria." My good-old hometown.

"Hair: black. Eyes: green. How tall are you?"

"Five foot, ten inches," I respond mechanically.

"That is about 178 centimeters, correct?" *Uhhhhh.*

"I think?" He's better at math than I am if he pulled that number out of nowhere.

He chuckles but says nothing, just writes in the number. "Weight?"

"I'm not sure. Used to be like 220 pounds? A lot less now." I look down at my flat stomach and lack of muscles. Then I remember he asked me about centimeters, and I have no idea how that relates to pounds. "Honestly, I have no clue."

"That is alright. I will make an estimate." He looks me up and down for a moment before jotting something down. "Other than your clothes and weapons, were you carrying anything out of the ordinary? Any magical items or things like that?"

"Uh, no. Some granola bars and jerky? There was a bedroll too, I guess." I don't exactly have a ton to my name at the moment.

"Hmmph," he snorts a laugh. "Reason for visit. I suppose I could just write 'theft'..."

"We didn't come here to steal anything!" *Theft my ass.*

"Right." He looks thoroughly unmoved by my defense. "So we found the five of you in the ancient elven ruins on our lands...sightseeing?"

Good point. "...Sorta? We didn't know it was your land," I explain. "People in Holbrooke told us about it. They mentioned some 'orc camps' but nothing about this city, or that the ruins were yours. Honestly."

"Ah, Holbrooke." He starts writing something else down. "That town has sent more than one group of adventurers on a fruitless venture out here. Though most of *them* did not attack us without provocation."

"...Okay, the guy who attacked you with that fireball is a dick and *not* my friend." Seriously *fuck* Nate for getting us into this. "The rest of us aren't like that. *I'm* not like that."

He pauses his writing for my answer.

"Hmmm." He doesn't seem impressed with my explanation. I probably wouldn't be either, but I still had to try. "So then why did you all travel here?"

"Um, to see the world and explore?" Definitely not to run away from or avoid anything back home. Though I'm sure they'd all get a real kick seeing me on *this* side of the law.

He looks even less impressed with that explanation. "We will just leave the expected date of your departure blank for now." He scribbles something at the bottom—a signature?—and adds the paper to the pile of others that he's finished. "Only one form left."

I guess this is the form that officially marks me as his slave. It's surreal to watch this giant mountain of a man calmly filling out paperwork to turn me into his house pet.

"What does this do exactly?" I ask like I don't know, which I kinda don't.

"It is a declaration of ownership. Of you," he adds the unnecessary clarification. "It states that you are my property, that you are expected to obey my rules as if they were the laws of the city, and that you are to be returned to me in the event that we are separated."

"Great. Like a dog." I slump back in my chair.

"It is not entirely one-sided." He puts the paper down to look at me. "It also says that I am now responsible for you. That I will keep you fed and sheltered. Ensure you remain healthy. That I will not be cruel or inhumane."

"Wait, it actually uses the word *inhumane*?" Because there's no way it does.

"I am paraphrasing," he tells me flatly.

"...Still your slave." I sigh and he shrugs his shoulders in response.

"One final thing to do." He reaches down into his pocket and pulls out the knife he used yesterday during our match and in the shower afterward.

He brings the knife to his other hand and uses it to prick the very tip of his ring finger. I see a small droplet of blood well up immediately. He then brings his finger to the paper, tapping it against the lower-left corner. Suddenly and with a hiss, words in red burn their way onto the paper.

"What was that?" Blood and magic together freaks me out.

"The paper is enchanted." Well *duh*. "The blood acts as a signature. It is much harder to forge your blood than it is your name." He nods in my direction and holds up the knife, handle first. "Your turn."

"I have to sign that paper with *my* blood, too?" *Uh-uh, no way.*

"I am afraid so, pup." Same nickname from yesterday.

"What happens when my blood touches the paper?" I really wish I had Mikey here to ask about blood magic. "Does it, like, bind me to you?"

"What? No." He drops the knife, head tilted in confusion. "I told you. It is just a signature."

"Why does *this* paper need blood but not the other two?" I argue.

"This paper is more important," he counters.

"What happens if I don't sign it?" Because I'm really not sure I want to.

There's a beat of silence before he answers. "Nothing. I would still own you, you would still go home with me, and your friends would still be in jail. It would simply be an unfinished piece of paper."

I eye the form warily, his red signature flashing like a warning sign.

He sighs and fiddles with the knife in his hand. "I am not going to force you to do this, but it is something that will have to be done eventually, and I honestly would prefer to finish it now so we can get on with the rest of our day."

"So sorry that my aversion to being enslaved is inconveniencing you." He gives me a really unimpressed look at that. "...Fine." I sigh and hold out my hand.

He takes my hand, holding my finger steady between his thumb and forefinger as he brings the knife closer. There is just the *slightest* pinch of pain when the blade touches my skin. The pink is replaced by red, and my hand is released. The paper is pushed toward me and a blank spot on the bottom right pointed out. He's going to make me do this on my own. My hand hovers over that paper, my finger up, for one, two, three seconds. I know this form means nothing. I know he says it's just a signature. But it feels like I'm about to sign away my life to a demon.

I tip my hand and watch the drop of blood fall. It hits the paper below, and with a sizzle, my signature—my *actual* signature—is etched onto the page.

I hope my demon is a merciful one.

Chapter Seven

Our magical signatures are still sizzling when Orduk returns to the office, grumbling. "I swear the council gets off on dragging out point-less meetings."

"I feel your pain, brother. Two weeks ago, Councilman Murbank dragged a hearing on for *four* hours. Over stolen cheese." Ironstorm smiles a little wearily while handing him the completed paperwork. "We just completed the last of these."

"Excellent. Let me look them over, and I can send you on your way." He takes the stack of papers as he sits on the other side of the desk, flip-ping through them quickly. "As thorough as always, sir. I will get these filed right away." He and Ironstorm both stand and lean over the desk, clasping each other's forearms the same way I saw the orc at the market do. After a bow to me that I awkwardly return, my leash is grabbed, and we make our way out of the building.

The park has emptied somewhat, the sun no longer high in the sky. It'll be sunset in maybe half an hour. We walk back through the park, but when we cross the street after exiting, we don't seem to be following the path we took here. I know we have one more stop to make but don't know what for. Just that it may involve buying me underwear, which feels a lot more ominous than underwear has any right to.

We walk for a while, and if I wasn't so used to walking literally every day for the last month, *after* a month of being stuck on a boat, I'd com-plain. As it is, this is pretty nice. I don't usually get to walk around a city like this; we're usually in and out. You spend enough time in the woods—you start to miss the sounds of other people just existing around you.

We're in another commercial area now, multiple orcs moving in and out of buildings, most with the doors wide open. I see a lot of bars and taverns. Big surprise: orcs like beer as much as the rest of the world. There are a few inns as well and...*is that a brothel?* Two tall, lean, and scantily clad orcs, one male and one female, stand outside wearing little more than black leather straps placed precariously over their more sensitive bits. The male orc catches me looking and smirks when we make eye contact, forcing me to turn away. Why are we in this part of town? I try to push the knowledge that I will be getting underwear somewhere around here to the back of my mind.

We pass one more bar before entering the next building on our right. It's a little larger than the clothing shop was, though with fewer shelves. Instead, there are a lot of things hanging from the walls. Some of it is clothing—I think—and a lot of the other items look like they're made out of leather. There are tables in the corners, each holding a large, irregularly shaped rock that glows and illuminates the room. Before I can get a closer look at anything, yet another orc is coming toward us. This one matches the captain's height, though I'd say he's got a good 50-60 pounds on him, and not necessarily muscle. His large, dark brown beard includes a few braided strands adorned with small metallic rings, and he's got a large one made of gold hanging from his nose. His head is shaved, and he's got a number of markings tattooed on his arms.

"Khazak!" Another old buddy, maybe? "Been expecting you."

"Brull, it is good to see you friend." The two hug their hellos. "I apologize if we are early. I wanted to make sure we got here before your usual evening rush."

"Nonsense. Started working right after we talked yesterday. I've got almost everything you need ready." Brull turns to me. "So this is him up close. What's his name?"

"David." I answer for myself because I'm *right here*.

"Feisty." He chuckles before giving me a once over. "I bet taming him is gonna be a lot of fun."

"I have been up to the challenge so far." Khazak—*because he can't control what I call him in my head!*—jokes to my left. "I appreciate your fitting me in on such short notice."

"Always happy to help a brother." Brull waves off the concern. "Besides, it's not like we hadn't talked about your plans for this sort of thing before." *What plans?* "I still need to make a few adjustments. Let me get a measurement of his neck, then you can show him around the shop while I finish up. Can you take off the collar?"

Ironstorm moves over to me and pulls out his keys, unhooking the padlock on my collar and removing it. I move my neck around once it's free, rubbing the uncovered skin with my hand. That feels a *lot* better after having that thing on since yesterday. Brull steps forward, wrapping his thumb and forefinger on both hands around my neck, and again against my collarbone. It feels oddly less threatening than I'd expect.

"Perfect. Give me just a few minutes." The larger orc steps into a back-room, leaving the two of us alone in the front.

"He seems...nice." Not really sure what to make of the man who just wrapped his hands around my neck. Why do I even care?

"He is an interesting friend to have, to say the least." A hand grabs a hold of my shoulder. "Come. Let me show you around the store."

I'm steered toward a set of shelves. At first, I can't really tell what's on them. Sticks? Really thick wands? Then I see a few that have been carved a bit more intricately, the detailed veins making it apparent what they are. *Fake dicks.* This is a shelf of dildos. The sizes vary in both length and thickness. Most of them seem to be made of polished wood, but there are a few metal and stone ones as well. I almost reach up to touch one, because that's *gotta* be cold, right? But I stop myself. Where the fuck did this orc take me?

"Brull has always been very talented with his hands. Most people expected him to put his wood and metalworking skills to use in carpentry." Ironstorm reaches forward and picks up a thick, dark, and very detailed dick. "Personally, I find this much more interesting."

I open my mouth but immediately snap it shut, no idea what I could possibly say right now. My eyes go wide as the fake phallus is held aloft, almost like he's trying to find the balance on a new weapon. He regards it for a moment longer before placing it back on the shelf.

"Brull has made a few things to my personal specifications, but there are still others I would like to pick out. See anything you like?" I shake my head no at the question, eyes still wide. "No, I suppose we do not need any of these. At least not right now." What the fuck does *that* mean? "However, *these...*"

He takes a step around to the other side of the shelf to look over the rest of the stock, and I follow. These are... I'm not sure what these are. They're made of the same materials but aren't as detailed. Just weirdly shaped. One end is bulbous, sometimes rounded, sometimes more pointed, and is connected by a thinner piece of material to a flatter, flared base almost as wide as the rest of the object. I have no idea what they are, but the fact that they're made of the same things as the dildos has me connecting the dots.

The orc runs his hands over a few of the...whatever they are before settling on one and picking it up. It's made of dark wood, the larger end almost the size of my wrist. The top of it—is that the top?—is oblong-shaped, sort of resembling an egg. I hear Ironstorm hum appreciatively, looking from the toy to me. He moves it to his other hand before grabbing my shoulder and walking me to our next destination. He's buying that, isn't he?

As he walks me to the other end of the shop, the wall we pass to our left is covered floor to ceiling in clothing. Well, clothing is generous. They look more like costumes. Shirts and jackets, colorful tights, hats and hoods—including one that looks like a very funny looking dragon. There are a few corsets and even some wigs. I don't really need to imagine what these are for, but I'm glad we're not stopping to look closer.

The wall in front of us has more things hanging, all made of brown and black leather. They're connected with rings of metal, and from the shape, I'd say they look like harnesses, like for a horse or dog, but much smaller. To their right are different kinds of restraints, including a pair like I wore this morning. Most of them are leather, with varying numbers of rings, some connected, some with straps to adjust. Next to them are more restraints but in metal. Things like cuffs and manacles, some that don't look terribly nice or comfortable. I'm glad we've stuck with the leather.

Next to the leather and metal restraints are tied bundles of rope, dyed in different colors. Not sure on the fabric but probably something soft and cheap, not like the climbing rope I kept in my pack. Ironstorm stops and looks over the selection, even pulling a red-colored bundle from its post on the wall. He runs his thumb over the material and hums to himself but puts it back after a moment. I let out a sigh of relief, drawing his attention and making him chuckle as he pulls me over to see the rest of the wall's selection.

It's more clothing, specifically underwear. At least, most of it is. I see traditional loincloths and briefs, and then... I dunno. Some look like little more than pouches with strings attached. Some look like they're made of straps, offering little to no coverage of anything. Almost all of them are dyed, in even more colors than the rope. There are even patterns like stripes or dots or the markings of an animal's fur. Some of it has lace, some has leather. It's all very intricate.

"Does he sew too?" I wonder aloud, because who has the time to make all this stuff?

"No, he does not." I jump when the orc in question re-enters the room to answer. "What he has is a good friend that likes to make these and would prefer to remain anonymous given my clientele."

I don't have a response to that, but I notice what looks like measuring tape hanging from his hand.

"Time for some more measurements, kid." He turns to his friend, my owner. "Mind stripping him for me?" He nods to the wall behind us. "You can pick out a few pairs while I make the last few adjustments. He can try on everything together."

I start to protest, but Ironstorm is already moving toward me with a smirk on his face. "This is happening one way or another, puppy. We have had a fairly pleasant day so far." He takes another step in my direction. "I am hoping that can continue into the evening."

I don't open my mouth because I don't have an argument. It's not like I have experience with this. I'm not even clear on what I'm being measured for. But as they both move closer, I decide to save what little dignity I have and strip myself. I undo the top few buttons of the shirt, pulling it over my head. My actions stop the orcs in their tracks, and I untie the belt at my waist, letting my pants fall to my ankles and shaking them off in the corner behind me, dropping the shirt on top.

"Shoes too?" I ask, arms crossed at my chest like I'm not standing naked in a store where literally anyone could walk through the door at any moment.

"Yeah, I need to get those sizes too. Boots won't be ready for at least a week." The last part isn't said to me.

I kneel down to untie and remove my shoes and ratty excuses for socks, setting them next to my other clothes.

"Alright, c'mere." Brull crooks a finger at me.

With a sigh, I step forward. He gets right to work, holding the tape in one hand as he pulls my limbs in whichever direction he needs. My arms are pulled up and out as he notes the length of them and my torso. The tape is wrapped around my chest, stomach, and waist before he moves behind me and drops to one knee. There's a whistle, and I yelp when I receive a smack on my still-sore ass.

"Looks like someone got themselves in trouble. Not bad." The words are again directed at Ironstorm and not me, though my skin flushes at the compliment.

The outside of my leg is measured (why didn't we ask the lady at the clothing shop for any of this?) and then my legs are pushed apart. I feel his hand traveling up my inseam, but still jump when my balls are suddenly grabbed. They both laugh at that, and Brull takes his time holding my junk out of the way while he takes the measurement. After wrapping the cord around my thigh, he drops to one knee and has me lift one foot, allowing me to balance against him while he measures that too. When he's finished, he stands and delivers another *smack* to my ass.

"Didn't really need most of the stuff below the waist, but that was fun." Brull gives me a leer when he walks back around to my front. "Alright, just a few minutes. Be *right* back." He returns to his backroom once more.

"Go ahead and pick out some that you like." Ironstorm is looking at the wall of underwear again.

Given that he just stood there while his friend felt me up for apparently no real reason, I glare. *Fine.* I turn to the wall and find the only things that look like regular underwear—a white loincloth and some white briefs. Wow, these actually have elastic in the waistbands. It's a fairly recent invention, something a group of gnomes came up with like ten years ago. Very handy for holding things like underwear and socks up—I don't miss having to *actually* tie a loincloth around my waist.

That means the city does a lot more trading with the outside world than I thought. Did he downplay that when he was explaining it to me? I keep getting surprised by how much more advanced these orcs are than I expected. Than most of the world expected. They didn't just build a city; they've got an entire fucking system of government—complete with boring paperwork. Hell, they have things most of us back home don't even have, like indoor plumbing. Why are they underestimated so much?

I shake the thoughts from my head and return to the task at hand. I can worry about how smart these orcs are when I'm not standing naked in a sex shop. I grab the plain-white undergarments, holding them to my waist since I can't exactly tell the size. I hand him my picks and cross my arms in defiance.

"No fun at all, are you?" The orc looks down at my choices with amusement, stepping up to the wall himself.

He browses the wall's selection thoroughly, moreso than he did the rest of the shop. He must pick out nearly a dozen things in all sorts of colors and styles. I hold my breath when I see him stop at something pink and lacy but exhale in relief when he skips over it. Not that the rest of them will look any better.

"Done!" Brull rejoins us just as Ironstorm finishes. He's carrying a small chain in one hand, while his other arm has leathers hanging over it. He hands the chain over to Ironstorm. "If you would do the honors, sir."

Ironstorm holds the chain aloft, and I can see a padlock at one end. Another one. He takes a hold of the lock, looking at one side closely before flipping it and doing the same with the other, a smile on his face. "Excellent work as always, Brull." He then looks at me and moves closer.

"I trust this more agreeable than the strip of leather?" He holds the chain in his hand, lock on display for me to see. Strip of leather? *Oh.*

"I mean, it's *still* a collar," I say flatly, displeasure clear on my face.

"I thought you might say that, but I am afraid it cannot be helped." I look up at him, clearly about to ask why. "*Avakesh* are required by law to wear collars within the city." Of course they are.

"What does it say?" Now that it's closer, I can see the detail in the metalwork of the collar. The rings making up the chain are almost as small as chainmail, and they shine brightly in the shop's light. If it weren't a collar, I might actually like it. I can see something carved onto the lock, symbols or letters, but can't read them.

"That is my name and address, in the event you were to get...lost." It's a fucking pet tag.

"Let me guess: my name is on the other side?" I swear if he put some fucked up pet name on it...

"No, though I suppose we could have it added if you'd like." He flips the lock over in his hand to show me. It's not writing but a drawing. Or a symbol, I guess. It's a diagonal sword with a jagged blade, made to look like a bolt of lightning. The detail is nice, and I realize it's a match for his tattoo. It doesn't look bad, not really, but I still don't want to have this thing locked around my neck.

"What does it mean?" I'd like to know what I have chained around my neck at least.

"I think you would call it a family crest?" He runs his thumb over the lock. "It is the symbol of Clan Ironstorm."

"Is that what your family is called?" Are all orc families "clans"?

"A long time ago." He grabs hold of the lock in his hand, grabbing the free end of the chain collar with his other. "Ready?"

"Yes?" Not sure why he's asking permission now.

He steps forward, moving the collar over my head and laying it against the back of my neck. He meets the two ends in front, looping the lock through the chain and snapping it shut. I try to look down at it, but the short chain means I can only make out the bottom of the lock. I can certainly feel the weight around my neck, though.

"Perfect." The back of Ironstorm's hand is against my chest while he runs his thumb over the lock before moving back.

"Here's the key." Brull hands over a small key before he grabs the leather hanging over his arm. "Now for the harness. Arms up, pup."

Up close and hanging from his hands, I can see more clearly that it's like what I saw on the walls earlier. I lift my arms wordlessly; I have no real options here. I'm naked with two large orcs blocking any path of escape and have no hope of overpowering them. The sooner I do this, the sooner I can get dressed and we can leave.

The leather slips over my head, Brull making sure my arms are going where they should. He adjusts the straps resting on my shoulders before moving down, pulling the lock of my collar up so it's not laying under the strap across my chest. Moving around me to make sure my shoulders and back are good, he steps to the side so both orcs can admire his handiwork.

Brull pulls against the straps running under my arms. "Now, he's kinda scrawny…" *Hey!* "But I figure you'll fatten him up in no time, so you can adjust these here as he fills in."

"Your work is impeccable as always." Ironstorm runs his hands lightly along the harness and my skin, making me shiver. Then he grabs me by the chest strap, pulls me to him, and kisses me.

"Mmmf!" I half-mumble, half-yell, not thinking straight enough to protest when his tongue sweeps into my mouth. I forgot he was good at that.

He growls when he releases his hold on me and pulls away. I catch my breath, my eyes locked onto his hungry face. What was *that*?

A whistle to my right draws me back to my senses. I look between Brull and the open door behind him. At least this time there was only a crowd of one. "Alright, now I believe I said something about picking out underwear, did I not?" Brull grins lecherously.

"That you did my friend." Ironstorm holds the giant wad of clothing in one hand.

"Hold on, let me grab some chairs." Brull heads into the backroom as I am handed the pile of underwear. He returns with two stools in hand, setting them down a few feet away from me and the wall of underwear.

I sigh to myself, grabbing one of *my* choices and letting the others fall to the ground. At least I get to wear underwear. I bend over and step into them when a sudden "tch tch" from my audience freezes me in my tracks and draws my head up.

"Come on now. Give us a little show." Brull's request makes me stand up straight, my fist tightening around the briefs in my hand. I look from Brull to Ironstorm, clearly about to voice my displeasure.

"It is okay, David." Ironstorm gives a small smile, his hand waving away the order. "Just try on the underwear. No theatrics required."

"You going soft on me?" Brull cocks an eyebrow at his friend.

"It has been a long day, and considering it is only his second, he has performed admirably." Same small smile. "He has earned a reprieve."

My anger softens at his words, and I return to slipping on the first pair of underwear.

"Softy," Brull ribs his friend.

I pull the briefs up over my thighs. These are...comfy. Whoever sewed them sewed them well. They hug my butt nicely, which isn't something I usually think about when buying new underwear.

"Turn around." I glare at Brull. "Please." *That's better.*

I do as requested. It's not like I don't know why they're doing this. It feels like there's a little more dignity in doing it on my own rather than having one of them force it. I eye the front door warily. No one else has come in yet, but I figure it's only a matter of time. The faster I am, the less chance I have of showing off to more than just these two. I hear some mumbles of approval, and once it feels like they've ogled me enough, I slip the pair off and quickly grab my other choice: the loincloth.

"Not bad, if not a little basic," Brull notes as I adjust the ties at the waist. "Shows more skin than the last one."

I turn around again, doing my best to ignore the commentary. As I turn, I look down at the underwear that still awaits me. All things Ironstorm picked out. Maybe I should have left my selections for the end. I slip the loincloth off and toss it with the briefs, turning to the unworn pile and taking a breath before grabbing whatever is on top. Let's just get this over with. I pick up something black. There's a pouch, but the rest just seems to be a series of straps.

"I, uh... I'm not sure how to put this on," I admit somewhat sheepishly.

Both of the orcs make to stand, Ironstorm giving Brull a clear "what do you think you're doing?" with his eyes, which has the larger orc laughing and backing off. He moves into my space, taking the garment from my hands and adjusting it.

"I believe this is called a jockstrap." He holds it against my crotch so I can see which end is up. "Right, Brull?"

"Technically it's a 'jockey strap,' something horse riders from your part of the world wear for protection," Brull explains from his seat. "But that sounds stupid, and I figured out a much better use for 'em."

Ironstorm holds the underwear, showing me the waist and leg holes and letting me use his shoulder to balance myself as I step into it. He pulls the waistband up over my butt before bending over to do the same with the leg straps, settling them just under my ass. The fabric making up the straps has a nice stretch to it and my package fills the pouch in front rather nicely. That doesn't change the fact that this thing seems to be missing a few crucial parts.

"There's no ass on this." My head is swiveled around to look at my own exposed butt.

"That is the idea," Ironstorm comments as his eyes rake over my form.

"To not be underwear?" Why wear anything at all at this point?

"I wouldn't say they're not underwear," Brull chimes in. "Your cock and balls are covered and held in place. Very useful for when you're traveling, or fighting, or getting *fucked*." I almost choke on my own spit at the last word. "Which coincidentally is also why there's no back."

I look down again at the "jockstrap" I'm wearing. Didn't really consider that, but of course that's why he wants to put me in these. He hasn't...*fucked* me since yesterday, but it's only a matter of time, right? Hopefully the next time he won't throw me on the ground and tear my clothes off before... Fuck, I turn around, blushing at the memory and feeling my cock chub up. *Not now...*

Brull whistles at my on-display ass and Ironstorm returns to his seat, content that I now know what I'm doing. Thankfully the reality of the situation returns, and my cock stops trying to fill the damn pouch on this thing. I slip it off, swapping it for another in red with slightly thicker straps. It takes me a second, but I figure out how to get it on like that last one, and I quickly go through three more in green, blue, and white.

"The red looks good against his skin. That is definitely an ass made for a jock," Brull comments to my owner. "Good choices."

Ironstorm says nothing, though I can see him smiling at me, a combination of warmth and lust in his eyes. I remember that look when I was on my back in the arena, his weight on top of me, his skin against mine... *Dammit, David. Stop it.* Alright, what's left? Still in the jockstrap, I grab the next item for my little fashion show and it's...a dark green thong. I look down. They all are. *What the hell?*

"These are for women." I can remember seeing a few server girls in taverns wearing these. And a few in *other* professions, if you catch my meaning.

"That pouch look like it's for a woman?" Brull crosses his arms.

He's got a point; it certainly looks like it's meant to hold a dick. That's not a thought I ever expected to have. But the rest of this is just... "I..."

"Need help with that one too?" Brull cracks wise, pulling another chuckle from Ironstorm and a glare from me.

I hate this. I can feel my face—and the rest of my body—getting hot as I slip the *thong* up my legs. I have to adjust myself in the pouch in front, my balls completely missing the target on their own. I can't pull the back up without that thin strip of fabric slipping *right* up my ass, which feels fucking *weird*. I feel even more exposed than I did in the thing that intentionally has no ass by design. I stand, eyes staring at the floor in front of me while they get their looks in.

"Hold on." Ironstorm stands and walks over, reaching down to adjust the waistband on my side where it's been twisted. His hand still on my hip, he ushers me to turn around in front of him. "Though I can tell you do not, I think you look incredible in this." He speaks softly as his hand slides over my hip to my ass, mumbling something to himself in Orcish.

I don't respond, not sure I have anything positive to say about something I hate. The orc returns to his seat, and I grab my next piece of poison, this one purple. At least he skipped the lace. Though there is something *pink*... Just not thinking about that right now. Pulling off the green, I pull on the second thong, checking the waist straps on my own this time. The strap up my ass *still* feels weird.

"Very nice. Think I prefer the jocks, but the fact that you can tell he hates it makes it a little hotter." I'm just getting heckled now.

The next two are blue and red respectively, none of the styles really differing all that much. I'm just as exposed in each of them. But finally, we're down to the last. I really should have saved one of the boring white ones, the pink fabric mocking me from its spot on the floor.

"Heh, figures after that woman comment he'd have a problem with pink." I'm getting real fuckin' sick of the peanut gallery.

I'll show you who has a fucking problem. Incensed at the comment, I snatch the thong off the floor. Then, after locking eyes with Brull, I pull off the blue one I'm wearing, step into the pink one and pull it up, never breaking eye contact. When I'm finished, I strike a pose, sarcasm dripping off my face. I even throw my hands up.

And of course, that's the *exact* moment someone decides to walk into the store.

My arms fall to my sides, hands shooting forward to cover my clearly-visible-through-this-fabric dick. My whole body turns bright red, which only manages to bring out the pink of this thong even more. I can't bring myself to look up, but I don't hear anyone moving so I'm sure all eyes—especially the new ones—are on me. I just *had* to leave the pink for last.

"See? Feisty." Brull laughs at his own callback.

"Quite." In the corner of my eye, I see Ironstorm stand. "Now if you are finished riling my puppy up, it looks like you have some business to conduct." I hear voices break into Orcish as Ironstorm moves over to me.

"You did very well." He speaks low into my ear. "Thank you."

"Can I get dressed, please?" I sound pathetic.

"Of course. Change into whichever you would prefer." He takes a step back.

"Thank you." I don't exactly want to get naked again in front of another stranger, but I want to be wearing this pink thong even less. I grab the white briefs from the bottom of the pile and quickly swap them. While I grab my pants, Ironstorm picks up the pile of discarded underwear, and once I'm finished zipping up, helps pull the harness off over my head. As I sit down to pull my socks back on, he turns to me once more.

"I will go pay for these and the other things, then we can walk home." He looks down at my feet. "I will get you some new socks as well."

I nod silently as I tie my shoes. The new boots will be nice. I stand and dust myself off, watching him walk to the counter where he places the harness, the underwear, and everything else he's buying. Including the thing made out of polished wood. *Two* of them. When did he even grab a second one? He sets them down with the rest as Brull talks to his other customer. The customer who is staring right at me with an all-too-familiar look in his eye, the same one Brull wore not two minutes ago.

I guess that's why I'm here now, isn't it? To give people a show. Or more. The anxiety in my chest builds. This is my life now, ordered around and used at the whims of my owner. Today it's getting naked in public. What's tomorrow: public fucking? OH WAIT, that was *yesterday*. My hands are shaking as I pull my shirt over my head, barely able to button it when my hands bump into the collar around my neck. It feels ten times heavier than it did a moment ago. I watch Ironstorm join the conversation, saying something and patting the heap of my humiliation next to him, making all three of them laugh.

I can't do this.

The three of them continue talking and laughing, likely at my expense, but none of them are actually watching me. I look at the open door to my left. I can hear people, see the bodies moving outside, more than doubled from when we walked in here. I look down. I can still feel the collar, but visually, it's tucked underneath my shirt. I look just like a regular person. I'm even wearing clothes from inside the city.

No one would have any idea.

There's another round of laughter to my right, and I take that as my cue. Making sure no one is watching—Brull even has them all looking at the same sheet of paper—I slip outside and into the crowd.

Chapter Eight

It's easy enough to blend in with the people around me once I'm outside, even if most of them are orcs. The cool night air helps calm me after the small freak-out I had in the shop. The city's streets are lit from above with torches and more glowing stones, each sitting atop a long wooden pole. They're not that bright, but the fact that I'm human *and* wearing this blue shirt might make me a little easy to spot. I need to get off the street.

Lucky for me, there's an alley entrance on my left. Seedy parts of towns *always* have alleys you can hide in. I maneuver myself through some gaps in the crowd and slip into the dark unnoticed. Alright, first thing I need to do is get somewhere far away from here, the jail, and Ironstorm's place. Then I need to find some new clothes because this shirt stands out too much, and I need to figure out some way to get this collar off me. Probably won't be able to convince anyone to do it willingly, but maybe I can steal some bolt cutters or—

"Hello, David." Captain Ironstorm stands before me in the middle of the alley.

I freeze in place, mouth agape. *How... How did he get here?*

"Well, I'll be damned, you were right." Brull's voice and footsteps ring down the alley behind me. "Alright, I'll knock five gral off your—"

A raised hand cuts him off, Ironstorm's eyes still locked on me. "David," he repeats my name. "Are you alright?"

I can't hold back a snort of laughter at that. *Am I alright?* Is he seriously asking me that?

"No." I'm not sure I can unpack just how *not* alright I am.

"I know the last two days have been very trying, David." Oh good, he's patronizing me. *Just gonna stomp all that baggage down.* "You have been forced into a lot of unfamiliar situations. I know you are learning things about yourself, things you may not have been fully aware of before." Oh, fuck *off.*

"I haven't learned a fucking thing!" I snap. Who the fuck does he think he is? Acting like he knows me better than myself. *He just met me two days ago!*

"Seeing as this is escape attempt number three, I would be inclined to agree with you."

For some dark, fucked up reason, the joke actually makes me laugh. I clamp my hand over my mouth in surprise. What is wrong with me? *I'm losing it.*

"We need to go back into the shop to finish a few things." He takes a step toward me. "Can I trust you to come without fighting?"

My shoulders slump. What choice do I have? I nod my head yes. Moving around me, his hand on the small of my back guides me farther down the alley and then left into a second, smaller alley. The path between buildings winds left and right, stretching on far longer than I've seen an alley stretch before. We walk for nearly a full city block—right to the back of Brull's shop. The orc in question squeezes around us to open his back door.

The room we enter is large and dimly lit. It's bigger back here than in the front, though there's also a small forge in one corner, so I get it. I'm led over to a desk that has small tools strewn about, the wood shavings and sawdust telling me they're for woodworking. There's also a pretty comfortable looking chair, which I am ushered into.

"Do you have a—?" Ironstorm turns around to ask for something.

Brull makes a clicking noise with his tongue and holds out a chain and lock in his outstretched hand. "I gotcha."

My collar is pulled up through my shirt and the chain is looped through it and then down around one of the desk's legs.

"Be right back, puppy." A hand is run gently through my hair, and with a sad smile, he steps away. I half expect Brull to make some crack about not screwing up his office, but he gives me the same look as the two of them head through the door to the front of the shop.

Fuck. He's going to punish me for running away again. My ass is still throbbing from the last one. It's go*nna* be even worse this time, isn't it? Will it be another spanking? Or... There were other things in the shop, things we hadn't looked at. Things like paddles and canes and...whips. I hoped that was on purpose. I was too scared to ask and risk drawing attention to them. *I am so fucked.*

I can hear voices talking through the door, but I wouldn't have been able to understand them anyway. I really need to learn some Orcish if I'm gonna have any hope of surviving here. For a moment, I think about escaping, breaking the desk or maybe using one of the tools in reach to pick the lock. But my heart just isn't in it. What if he catches me again and things get even *worse?* How many times will I be able to push my luck?

So... I'll wait. Just sit here with my hands in my lap and wait for whatever fucked up punishment he has in mind. *Just like a good puppy, fuck.* I sink back into the chair and sigh.

I'm not kept waiting for long. Ironstorm re-enters the room with Brull right behind him, though the other orc ignores me, walking farther into the room and picking up a wooden bench. He takes it out to the front as Ironstorm approaches me.

"Business has been taken care of." Ironstorm speaks to me softly as he unlocks the chain from my collar. "Now we just need to deal with the matter of your punishment."

I sigh. *Told ya.* "When we get home, are you go—"

"Oh, no," the orc cuts me off. "We will be taking care of your punishment *here.*"

"What?" My stomach sinks. "Why do we have to do that?!"

"If you are going to misbehave in public, you can be punished in public," he reasons with me.

"You wouldn't." I narrow my eyes, calling his bluff. He's got to be fucking with me, right?

"I fucked you in front of a crowd of people not thirty hours ago," the orc *helpfully* points out. He thinks for a moment. "Would you trust me if I told you that it will not be as bad as you are expecting?"

"Would you really expect me to believe that?" I can be helpful too.

"Fair enough." He sighs and stands up straight, holding his hand out to help me from the chair. With a sigh, I take it.

I'm marched back to the front of the store. There are three other orcs here now, including Brull and the orc that came in during the underwear show. He must have wanted to stick around and watch the human get punished. The third orc is another customer, paying me no mind while she peruses the shelves. I am led to a corner where Brull is bent over the piece of furniture he grabbed earlier, making adjustments.

It's about as tall as my waist and all wood, except for a few spots that look covered in padded leather. I see a number of cuffs attached to its various posts, which is starting to give me some idea of its intended purpose. Pretty sure I'm gonna end up tied to this thing one way or another.

"Alright, she's all set up." Brull dusts off his hands and turns to the two of us.

"Please remove your shirt, David," Ironstorm requests.

I swallow my argument. Ironstorm is standing between me and the rest of the store, thankfully blocking most of the other occupants from my view. I know they can still see me, but whatever—let me have this. I unbutton and pull the shirt over my head, which he takes before I can drop it to the ground.

"Thank you. Now please turn around." He throws my shirt over his shoulder, twirling his fingers to get me to rotate.

I comply, coming face to face with a wall that is half underwear and half...paddles. *Shit.* Ironstorm walks to my side, his hand on my upper back pushing me to bend over the bench in front of me. I don't resist, resigned to my fate. My arms are drawn up and placed into cuffs which are closed and tightened around my wrists. The same is then done to my ankles with a set on the bench's feet. At least he's letting me keep my pants.

I jump when the orc bends over my body, both hands going under my waist. I spoke too soon. The hands feel around for my belt, untying it and loosening my pants. Then, after hooking his fingers into my underwear, everything is slid down to my ankles, exposing my ass to the air. A sudden wolf whistle behind me has my cheeks burn with embarrassment—both sets.

"Breathe, David." I feel a familiar hand on my back as Khazak walks back around to my left side and kneels down so I can see him. "How are you feeling?"

I can't hold back the laugh before I answer. "Seriously? Why do you care?"

"I told you I would take care of you, David." He looks thoughtful but serious. "I meant that."

"Then how about you untie me and let me go?" That at least earns me a chuckle. Can't blame me for trying.

"Have I been feeding you well?" I nod my head yes. "Other than a sore and slightly bruised rump, have you been injured?" I shake my head no. "Then what exactly is the problem?"

"I dunno, maybe that I'm naked and tied over this bench with three strange orcs behind me *probably* staring at my ass," I deadpan over my stretched arm.

"Oh, they are *definitely* staring at your ass." A hand rubs my butt appreciatively. "I cannot say I blame them. It is a very nice ass. Why is that a problem?"

Is he serious? "Because in human cities we don't strip naked in public!" Among other things we don't do in public!

"We are not *in* a human city," he points out. "You spent all day walking around on a leash. Other than deferring to me, did anyone treat you differently or poorly?"

I mean, I guess he's not wrong. I haven't exactly had a ton of chances to talk to anyone by myself, but the people I have met haven't been shitty. Most have acted as if there isn't anything out of the ordinary at all. I even remember seeing those other slaves on leashes in the market...but so what? The city treats slaves well. Not sure that's something I'd put in the travel brochure.

"I still don't want to do this." Nothing could make me *want* to be here, tied up and exposed like this.

"I know." There's that sad smile again. "But you are going to." And then he's standing and moving back behind me. "I think you may actually enjoy some of this."

I snort. *Fat chance.* I close my eyes, tensing as I wait for the first blow. So when a cold, wet finger suddenly prods at my ass, I yelp. I try to swivel my head around and see what's going on, but with my arms stretched like this, I can only see part of his upper body. After finding my hole, what I'm guessing is a finger breaches me slowly, something cold and slick helping to ease the entry. I hiss, the soreness bringing back the memories of yesterday I'd been trying hard to forget.

"What are you doing!?" Is he going to fuck me? Is that the punishment?!

"Hush," the orc shushes me as he continues to push his finger into me.

I whimper when I feel his bottom knuckle against my hole. Once it's inserted to the hilt, he slowly pumps his finger in and out. That whimper turns into a groan at the burn of finger #2 joining the first, *fuck.* Not sure I prefer this over a spanking. Sure, there's less pain, but there's also three strangers behind me watching me get fingered. I've also only known the orc doing the fingering for less than a day and a half, which doesn't exactly make him any less of a stranger.

At some point after the second finger, things start to feel good. My cock starts to fatten up, pointing straight down and trapped against the bench. If I didn't know how big his dick was, I'd tell him to just shove it in and get it over with. Fuck, I'm trying to tell myself to be thankful for this, but when he scissors his fingers apart like *that,* it makes me wanna climb off the table. In a good or bad way, I'm not sure.

The fingers are pulled from me, and I brace myself for what comes next. So I yelp for a second time when instead of an orc cock, something cold and blunt is poking at my hole. Not that I want an orc cock poking at me!

"What is that!?" I futilely try to crane my neck again and receive another shush and a light smack on the ass.

"I can get you a gag if you need one." The threat has me keeping my grumbling to myself.

The object is pushed deeper inside me, growing wider as it does. I do my best to suppress a groan once it starts to stretch me more than his fingers, the rest of it suddenly sliding in, my hole closing around the other end. For a moment I'm worried I'm about to lose whatever it is up there, but there's something wide and solid preventing whatever it is from going any deeper. Damn, do I feel full though.

"This is a plug. We looked at them earlier," Ironstorm explains as he taps on it, knocking it against something sensitive inside me and sending small jolts through my body. "They are made to help keep you stretched, among other things."

I remember what he's talking about now, next to all the fake dicks. It feels weird to be, well, plugged. Once the burn of the stretch is gone, I mostly just feel...stuffed. I think about trying to push it out of me, but not only do I get the feeling that the orc wouldn't like that, I'm also not sure pushing something out of my ass is the defiant gesture I want it to be.

"How are you feeling?" My captor walks around so I can see him again.

"I don't know." Why is he asking me this? "Fine, I guess? Full?"

"How does your ass feel?" Is he fishing for something?

"Sore." I narrow my eyes as best I can like this.

"Inside, or out?" The question makes me blush before I can answer.

"...Both," I mumble into my arm.

"Thank you for telling me." He gives me a warm smile. "We will put some more of the salve on when we get home. You will likely need it."

I don't like the sound of that, and I can already feel my body tensing up again when he leaves my line of vision. My hole clenches around the plug, which sends a signal to my brain that is half-pleasure, half-pain, and not at all confusing. Will he just hurry up and *get this over with already?!*

The first *smack* of what feels like leather against my ass isn't a total surprise, but the way it hits the base of the plug is, and it forces a noise from my mouth I'm not sure I've made before. Somewhere halfway between a moan and a yell. I'm assuming it's a paddle; the smack wasn't that hard, barely even hurt. But that plug is sure making me pay attention. The second and third blows are delivered the same way, not a lot of bite but sure to hit me dead center on my ass and the plug.

When I expect to feel the smack of strike number four, I'm surprised again when a hand delves between my legs to grab ahold of my cock. I'm not fully hard, but still hard enough that I'm gonna have a difficult time explaining this away. The hand grips me firmly, a thumb running over the head of my dick and making me shudder, spreading the slick precum I didn't realize I was leaking.

"Good," is the only word spoken before the hand is pulled away, and I'm getting paddled again. The blows never quite increase in intensity, though the angle and areas hit do change. Still always seems to knock against the plug somehow, and when the hand returns to my now fully hard cock, I realize that's by design. He wants me to enjoy this, even though it's supposed to be punishment for trying to escape.

I do *not* understand orcs.

After another round with the paddle, I feel the hand once more, this time slick with lube. It holds me firmly, slowly pumping up and down my shaft, making me groan involuntarily. Another memory, this time from this morning, having my cock stroked in bed but rolling out before I finished. The sudden smack on my ass with his other hand makes me clench around the plug again. I rock forward slightly, which drags his hand down my dick. Gods, what is he doing to me?

I turn back to look at him as best I can. He's not quite facing me, bent over with his body turned half to me and half to the shop behind us. That's all I can see. After the next spank, the hand doesn't leave my skin, instead sliding across it to the plug. He presses against it, pushing it in farther and pulling a low moan from my lips. All the while, his other hand continues to stroke me.

"You look good like this, puppy," he tells me, his voice low and husky. "Tied up, helpless, and spread open. Plug in your hole, ass a nice bright pink. I have half a mind to take you right now." The filthy words make my stomach flip, and I have to bite back a whimper.

He pauses on the spanking, content to toy with the plug instead. His fingers hook under the base and it is slowly dragged out of me. Before the widest part exits, the plug is released and slides back into place on its own. He pulls it out an inch or two once more, and this time I can feel him push it back in himself, forcing it deeper than it would go naturally. He repeats this, slowly fucking me open on the object.

Unable to help myself, I start rocking back into his hand. Small whimpers and moans fall from my open mouth, and my body heats with embarrassment when I realize that the other orcs are watching my reactions. But still, I don't stop.

"They are watching you," the orc holding my cock reads my mind. "They want you. The only reason they are not approaching is that they know you are mine." He gives my dick a firm stroke for emphasis.

"I like that you are mine, pup," he continues, adding a couple of spanks. "Mine to play with. Mine to show off. Mine to take apart."

The plug is pulled from my hole again, this time completely. I only feel empty for a second, his fingers quickly pressing in to replace it and delve even deeper. They don't stay there, as my Captain quickly pulls them back before settling into a steady rhythm as he fingerfucks me once more. He matches his strokes to the hand on my dick, and I am soon rocking back into his hands once again.

He keeps his pace steady for a minute, but I can feel things speeding up. The fingers inside me are pressing down as they move, each stroke passing over a spot that has me trying to hump down into his other hand. He has no trouble keeping his hold on me, the massive green fist encasing more than three-quarters of my length.

As things move faster, his tactics change. His hand stops stroking my full length, instead focusing his attention around the head. Similarly, his fingers no longer push into the knuckles, nor are they pulled out more than an inch or two. The pads of his fingertips continue to rub back and forth over that strange little button of pleasure, pushing me closer and closer to the edge. *Fuck, I think I'm gonna—*

"Cum for me, puppy."

I explode at the order, the muttered curse on my lips drowned out by a moan. The hand around the top half of my cock continues to steadily stroke as I shoot my load all over the floor and bench. My hole clenches tightly around the fingers inside me, fingers that are still pressing and rubbing, forcing even more sounds from my mouth. I don't even try to count as each rope of cum is shot, too exhausted to do anything more than slump against the bench when I finish.

As I come down from my orgasm, the hand around my cock leaves me, a sticky strand of cum landing against my thigh as it moves. The fingers still inside me are removed gently, and I feel my empty hole clenching around the cool air. Damn, I almost want the plug back in. There's a hand on my back before I'm left on my own, senses slowly coming back to my body.

A towel is run along my thighs and ass, even carefully wiping the lubricant from my hole. The cuffs around my ankles are removed, then Ironstorm is at my side again, bending over to release my wrists. Once they are both free, I use my hands to push myself up and stand, legs shaky after our little performance.

"You took your punishment very well," the orc tells me while wiping his hands with the same towel. "You may get redressed."

I nod silently. I'm not exactly sure how that was a punishment, but I'm not going to disagree. I bend over to pull up my underwear and pants, pleased to see that they aren't covered in the load I just shot. The majority of it seems to have landed on the bench, most of it already wiped up. I turn as I'm tightening my belt and meet the gazes of every orc in the shop, including two new ones who must have come in while... *Oh god.*

I try not to let the humiliation show on my face as I am handed my shirt. I pull it over my head maybe a little too quickly, staring at the floor while I fasten the buttons. Ironstorm steps over to the counter where Brull has moved, stuffing something into his pack. I notice the orc who walked in on me in the thong is also making some purchases. The other three are all badly pretending to browse the shelves while trying not to stare at me. Ignoring that, I move to join the group at the counter.

"You boys just made me a sale," Brull tells us while taking the man's money. Looking down, I can see that he has purchased...a paddle and plug. *Oh boy.*

"Happy to help, brother." Ironstorm smiles a little cockily.

After exchanging a few words with Brull, the man takes hold of his purchases. Then after giving Ironstorm a nod and me an appreciative onceover, he exits the shop.

"I should have the boots ready next week." Brull turns to us after pocketing the money. "And if there's a problem with anything fitting, you let me know and I'll fix it."

"I am sure your craftsmanship is as stellar as always." The two of them do their orc-wrist-handshake thing again. "Thank you for allowing me the use of your equipment."

"Pleasure was all mine, Khaz," Brull responds with a smirk. "Thanks for letting me meet him." Then he turns to me. "It was nice to meet you, David. When I watched you get taken down in the arena yesterday, I wasn't sure you'd take to all this so well. I can certainly understand all the interest in the captain's new puppy."

Great, so he was in the crowd of people who got to witness my very public humiliation yesterday. *And what does he mean by interest?* "I... Thanks. It was nice to meet you too." What else do you say to that?

Ironstorm already has my leash at the ready, and he clips it on before throwing his pack over his shoulder. With a nod to me, he turns and together we leave the shop. The streets are even more packed than they were before, and I'm almost worried the leash might turn into a liability by the time we're clear of the crowds and onto quieter roads.

"What did he mean by 'interest'?" I can't help it. The question has been nagging me since Brull said it.

"It would seem that word of our match yesterday has spread throughout the city." The orc turns his head to answer me. "The ritual is not a common occurrence. After one takes place, it is usually the subject of town gossip for at least a few weeks."

I sigh to myself. Of course everyone would be talking about that. I only hope it hasn't gotten back to my friends in the jail yet. The rest of our walk home is in silence, the glow of the streetlights illuminating our way. Away from the bars, the rest of the city seems to have gone to sleep with the sun. Just me, the captain, and my thoughts.

When we get home, Ironstorm leads me to the bedroom, turning on some lanterns on the way.

"Go ahead and undress," he tells me while moving to his chests and removing the items from his bag. "You may leave your underclothes on."

I guess that's an improvement over being naked. In this set of underwear at least. I pull off my shirt and lay it on the bed before sitting to remove my boots and pants. After folding the two, Ironstorm picks them up and brings them to one of the chests.

"Your clothes will be kept in here," he instructs. "I expect you to keep them neat and organized."

"Yessir." I respond without really thinking, having been told similar orders so many times by so many people at this point.

"Good boy." He gives me a sly smile and I roll my eyes. "Come. We need to eat and maybe a little reading before bed."

I follow him to the kitchen, opting to stand rather than sit on the damned pillow. I watch as he moves about gathering ingredients. Looks like fish tonight. The orc grabs a skillet and lights the stove, setting some vegetables to the side before he slices into the fish. My stomach growls. I really wish it would stop doing that.

"There is something on your mind," Ironstorm informs me over his shoulder.

He's not wrong. There're a million things on my mind. One thing in particular is still bothering me though.

"What was with that punishment?" I blurt out. *Smooth, David.*

The orc considers me for a moment before continuing to clean the fish. "Despite what you may think, I am not a monster, David. I was not *happy* that you ran, but I understood why. I know a panic attack when I see one. You were overwhelmed after a long day of being forced into unknown situations. Situations you have been handling well, given the circumstances. I do not want you to be afraid of me or to hate the things we do. Even if you are not ready to admit you like them." I stutter a protest, but he cuts me off. "Regardless of that, my intention was to show you that not everything we will do is something to be endured."

"So you decided to tie me down and strip me in front of total strangers?" I cock an eyebrow at his reasoning.

"Bit of a simplification," he smirks. "You still needed to be punished, and given the public nature of your transgression, a public punishment seemed appropriate. All day I noted your aversion to public nudity, among other things, which, given how we met, struck me as a *little* humorous."

"I told you I didn't know—"

"These are not concerns shared by the rest of the city," he continues over my protest. "Public nudity—and in certain situations more than that—are not uncommon. And I am sorry to inform you that they will not be vanishing from your life anytime in the near future. The best way to get you over that was to..." He pauses, thinking. "...'Throw you in the deep end,' is how Brull put it. I wanted to teach you that being on display like that in front of others is not always bad. And you were perfect for me, puppy."

"Why do you call me that?" I ask absent-mindedly, still processing the psychoanalysis he just dropped on me and ignoring the compliment even if it gives me a warm feeling in my stomach.

"You remind me of the dog I had as a child." He moves and lays the cleaned fish in the skillet. "Loud and impulsive, always getting into trouble, and frequently found where he was not supposed to be."

I narrow my eyes at the obvious insult.

"He was also very smart, and with a little training became the most loyal companion I could have ever asked for." He smiles warmly and moves on to chopping carrots. "He was my best friend. He was with my family for more than a decade and a half—to the very end."

I don't have any more questions after that, or at least I'm too preoccupied to vocalize them now. I lean against the counter, thinking about his words, his actions. It's clear that he's training me. He even compared me to his old dog. But what we've been doing isn't what you do with a pet. So what exactly is he training me for?

Chapter Nine

"We gotta slay the dragon!" I scream as I run up the hill, holding my sword high.

"Wait! My sword broke," the small voice calls from behind me.

"Oh." I stop, looking around on the ground for a suitable replacement. "Here y'go, Mikey." I hand the sturdy looking stick to my brother.

"Thanks, D." He gives it a few practice swings.

"Now c'mon!" I turn to start my run back up the hill. "He's gettin' away!"

I wake up slowly to the sounds of chirping morning birds muffled behind a thick curtain. My eyes adjust to the sunlight bleeding through the edges, and whatever the blurry green thing in my vision is comes into focus. Once the fact that it's a *person* crosses my mind, the rest of my brain finally kicks into gear, and the memories of the last two days come flooding back. I stop myself from jerking away in surprise, not wanting to risk waking the sleeping orc.

At least he's not spooning me this time. We went to bed on separate sides of the bed last night but once again migrated back to the center. This time I'm curled up in the crook of my bedmate's arm, my head on his shoulder and my arm thrown over his chest. Being this close to his armpit, it's hard not to smell the man. Considerably better than the locker rooms back home.

Home... My mind drifts back to the dream I was having. *Why was I dreaming about Mike?* I mean, besides the whole "leaving home two months ago without telling anyone including your twin brother" thing. I've gotten pretty good at burying the guilt from that under all the stress and fighting. I can't remember ever having any dreams about him before. Or anyone else from home. I don't usually remember my dreams at all.

I can't say I've been missing home or even my family much up until now, but knowing that I might not see them again for months or even longer is drawing out a small pang of homesickness. Maybe I could send Mike a letter? I drop that line of thinking quickly. Telling Mike would most likely mean telling everyone else, and I am *not* ready to do that. Gods know how pissed off Dad probably is, or what he'd do to get me back there. I wonder how long the academy took to tell him I was gone. Can't imagine they'd even want me back at this point. What would I even say? Especially given my current situation.

A situation that at present includes my dick pressing firmly against an orc's thigh, my leg thrown over his. Something I have been pointedly ignoring until now because... Family. *Gross.* But that is proving hard now that I also *really* need to pee. Which is the only reason I'm hard at all. That's... That's what I'm gonna keep telling myself. Just like how the only reason I haven't untangled myself is so I don't wake him.

It's not like I've been getting some of the best sleep I've had in months. Maybe even longer.

Ironstorm suddenly shifts, forcing me to move enough that I finally feel the urge to stretch my limbs. I hiss, not realizing my mistake until it's too late when my erection grinds into his flank. *Fuck.* The noise and my movements are enough to rouse him, his head turning slowly to meet my gaze, his own eyes still bleary with sleep. He lifts his head and takes in the rest of the scene before him.

"Morning," his chest rumbles, his unused voice rough like gravel. "Seems as though you are an early riser."

I nod my head, still too asleep myself to get the intended double entendre. I've always gotten up pretty early. Habit, I guess.

"Here." He reaches over to unlock the chains I forgot were attached. "So you may take care of that."

His nod downward finally makes the joke click in my head, and I can feel the first of what I'm sure will be many times I blush today. I carefully lift myself off his chest, pulling away from his body and ignoring the sticky trail I've left on his thigh as I move off the bed and into the bathroom. After some aiming and a little concentration, I manage to relieve my very full bladder. While I'm washing my hands, Ironstorm slides in behind me to take care of the same needs.

"I feel like bacon for breakfast. Do you like bacon?" he asks me while drying his hands.

"Sure." Who doesn't? Besides vegetarians.

"Good." He joins me in the hallway outside the bathroom. "I left you something to change into on the bed. See you in the kitchen." He passes me with a wink.

"Something" turns out to be a thong. It's green at least, not pink. And I *guess* it's better than being naked. *Heavy* emphasis on the guess. I take a moment to adjust myself, making sure all my bits and pieces are in the pouch. Not sure how anyone gets used to wearing a string up their ass. I look at myself in the bathroom mirror before walking out to the kitchen. I mean, I don't want to be wearing it, but I am definitely pulling it off. We'll have to see if Brull was right about my ass and jockstraps.

When I finally enter the front part of the house, I can already hear the pork sizzling in the pan. Gods, that smells amazing. Ironstorm is in front of the stove with an apron wrapped around his chest, ass still visible in the back. I stand at the counter for a minute before tentatively walking into the kitchen.

"Can I... I mean, do you need any help?" Standing around doing nothing makes me feel weird.

"Afraid there is not much else needed for bacon, pup." Good point. "Is cooking something you enjoy doing?"

"I liked helping out in the kitchens back home." I downplay my culinary habits.

"That is good to know." He gives me an appreciative nod over his shoulder. "Is coffee something you drink?"

"You have coffee here?" Oh shit, I haven't had a cup of coffee in *ages*. They ration that stuff like water in a desert at the academy.

"Red jar on that shelf." He points to the shelves against the wall to our right. "Sugar should be up there as well." He bends over to grab a kettle to fill with water.

I spot the red jar he's talking about immediately, the smell of ground coffee hitting me when I lift off the ceramic lid. The sugar takes me a little longer as I sort through some of the other jars. The first few are nothing special, salt, pepper, even cinnamon, but after that, I have a hard time naming them. I recognize one as shockvine and I think another might be grass of Hypnos—also known as hypnograss. These are potion ingredients.

I know this because Mike got *really* into potion brewing during our last few years of school. There was this week I was having trouble sleeping, and I had a really big test the next day, so he convinced me to try one of his "sleeping potions." I asked him what was in it and he told me that "it's mostly just a lot of hypnograss." And it worked: I could barely keep my eyes open for the next two days. I failed the test but learned to never let my brother use me as a lab rat again.

Now, you don't have to be magical to brew potions, but it helps. So what exactly is this orc doing wi—

"Everything okay?" I freeze at the question, replacing the lid on the jar and turning.

"Can't find the sugar." I think about asking about what's in the jars, but...it's like the more I learn, the less I understand who he is. That's enough reason to keep it to myself.

"I need to organize that shelf." He takes the coffee from me and finds the sugar. "I am almost finished; you may wait on the couch if you would like."

I make my way to the couch, settling quietly in one corner. My ass still feels slightly bruised from the last few days, but after applying another coat of that salve last night, it's really only a dull ache now. The fireplace in front of me is silent. Has it really only been two days? Barely even that. But it feels like I've been here a lot longer. This was not what I had in mind when I left home.

I'm pulled from my thoughts when I feel weight on the couch next to me. I look over to see Ironstorm with a large mug in one hand and a plate in the other. I didn't hear the bacon stop sizzling. He squeezes in next to me, ignoring the other empty end of the couch as he sets the mug on the floor. Then he hooks his arm behind my knees, lifting and turning me so my legs are over his lap. Before I can react, he drops the plate of bacon onto my thighs and picks up the mug to press into my hands.

I don't say anything about the manhandling—again, what would be the point?—but I give the mug a tentative sniff.

Mmm, coffee. I can see the steam rising from the mug, so I give it a small blow before taking a sip. Still *way* too hot, but fuck is that good. It's black, not how I usually take it, but there's just enough sugar that I don't mind.

"It's good. Thank you." I hand the mug back, at least until it cools off some.

"You are welcome." Ironstorm nods and grabs a piece of bacon in his free hand, bringing it to my mouth.

"Seriously?" I sigh at being fed like a child again. "My hands aren't even tied this time."

"Humor me." There's the hint of a smile on his lips as he holds the piece to my lips.

I sigh again but lean forward and take the piece nonetheless. It's still bacon. I swear I can feel the stress leaving my body with each crispy crunch. Damn, have I missed bacon. And steak. And bread that isn't a week old. And cheese you don't have to scrape the mold off of.

I open my eyes—they closed as soon as the bacon hit my tongue—to see I'm being watched, an amused look in the orc's eyes as he chews on his own piece. He says nothing, just leans over to grab a book from the table next to the couch.

"Why do you do that?" May as well ask questions at this point.

"Do what?" He puts the book down.

"Feed me." I cross my arms.

"I like it." He crosses his with a smirk.

"You like making me feel helpless?" I narrow my eyes.

"I have other ways to keep your mouth full if you would prefer," he responds with a leer.

"Fu—" Another piece of bacon is shoved in my mouth before I can retort. *Whatever.* I'll take bacon over his dick any day. Tastes way better. Probably.

I look up, happy to see he is once again engrossed in his reading and not watching me as I contemplate the flavor of his cock. What is *wrong* with me? I mean, given the events of the last 48ish hours, it's understandable, right? The ritual, the shower, the mornings in bed, the "punishment" last night... It's not like I've had a choice in any of it.

But why does that fact seem to make me like it even more? Being tied down, held in place, manhandled... Shit, I'm starting to get hard *right now.* I have to use my thighs to keep my cock trapped between them. Seriously, David, this is not normal. This is not like that time when you were sixteen and you got drunk at a party with Rich Fulbrush, and you thought he was going to kiss you, but all he ended up doing was puking all over your shoes. This is a stranger, a *monster*, holding you against your will. He's beaten you, humiliated you, practically raped you. So if you could *maybe* stop wondering what it would feel like for him to fuck you while chained to his bed *that would be great.*

A piece of bacon in my face refocuses my attention, right before a knock at the door draws away Ironstorm's. He slides my legs off his lap and places the mug on the table, walking around the couch to answer it still as naked as when we woke up. I know I shouldn't be, but I'm surprised when he opens the door without a second thought. There's a greeting and some words exchanged with the person on the other side, before Ironstorm is handed a *lot* of packages wrapped in brown paper. He takes a step back and gestures his head in my direction before the orc at the door pokes his head around the corner to stare at me. After bidding the delivery person farewell, Ironstorm then removes a paper seemingly stuck to the front door before closing it.

"What was that about?" I ask as he walks the packages to the kitchen.

"Butcher. I have a standing order delivered every other Ignisday." He drops the meat onto the counter so he can open the lid on the icebox. "Seeing your appetite these past few days, I told him I needed to start doubling it."

"...Sorry." A joke about having to feed your pets dies on my tongue.

"Nothing to apologize for." He starts loading the packages inside. "I take it you have not been eating very well on your travels?"

"No. Not really." I hope I'm not about to get a lecture on human nutrition. "I used to be a little bigger."

"I can tell by your frame." Satisfied with his organizational skills, he shuts the lid. "Hopefully while you are here, you can regain some of your mass." He rejoins me on the couch, lifting my legs to his lap once more.

"Why did he want to look at me?"

"He wanted to know if the ranger captain's new avakesh was as attractive as he had heard." He feeds me another piece of bacon before unfolding the paper he pulled off the door. "He agreed."

The compliment makes me feel a little warm, but like so many other times, I'm not sure what to say. I just chew my bacon. Ironstorm retrieves the mug and takes a few swallows before passing it to me. I do the same now that it is finally cool enough to enjoy.

"I have some news for you." The paper is refolded and placed to the side. "Your friends are to be brought before a council member in the morning."

"They ar—" A hand held in the air cuts me off.

"A proclamation of guilt has already been signed and submitted, so this is largely for determining any penalties or disciplinary action. As the ranger who made the arrest, I need to be there," he continues before putting his hand down. "I want to make a deal with you."

"What kind of deal?" I eye him suspiciously. Not sure I trust deals made around here.

"If you behave today, if you will *willingly* submit to some training—which includes following my instructions and not talking back—I will take you to see your friends tomorrow." He trains a stern look on me. "But you have to actually *try*, David. I do not want to spend the day fighting you."

I consider his offer in silence. Given what we've been doing, especially last night, it's not hard to figure out the kind of training he's *really* talking about. The kind of training I was just thinking about and risking my dick escaping its thigh prison. So it's not like I don't know I can do it. *But...it's getting* hard*er* to keep convincing him I don't like this. *Which I don't!*

Right?

"Will I be able to talk to them?" Staring at them across the room isn't gonna do much.

"I cannot promise that." He frowns a little. "If it is possible, I will do my best." Better than nothing, I suppose.

"Do you... Do you think they already know about what happened to me?" Like that I lost the match, but I'm not dead. Or that I belong to Ironstorm now and what exactly that entails.

"They are likely aware of your loss and also that you still live." He offers an apologetic look, probably knowing what I'm thinking about. "I cannot say what they may know beyond that."

I take a moment to think, but it's not a hard decision. I want to see my friends. "Okay," I answer after taking a deep breath. "I'll do it."

The smile reaches his eyes, and he feeds me another piece of bacon. "We will begin after breakfast."

I chew in quiet contemplation, the coffee passed back to me twice more before it and the bacon are finished. Ironstorm brings the dishes to the kitchen while I am sent off to the bathroom to clean up. After brushing the last of the bacon grease from my teeth, I rejoin the captain in the living room. He turns to me as I enter after laying something on the couch.

"What's that?" It's a...well, it's not a riding crop, but it's not *not* a riding crop.

"A tool that will help us later." Really don't like the sound of that. "Are you ready to begin?"

"I guess?" He cocks his eyebrow. "Okay, yes. Sorry."

"Am I mistaken in thinking you have had some form of military training?" He questions me as he looks me over.

"Kind of." The knight academy isn't exactly the military, but there are similarities. "The school I went to was sort of pre-military and trained a lot like one."

"I was not certain. I think I have heard the word 'Sir' from you a total of three times since you arrived." He crosses his arms, unimpressed. "So we will begin there. I expect that word to become a regular part of your vocabulary going forward."

"Okay." Eyebrow. "I mean yes, Sir."

"Better. This first exercise will hopefully feel familiar: posing and stances." *Uuuggghhh*, I hate position drills. The orc maneuvers me to stand in front of the couch facing away, about halfway between it and the fireplace.

"The first is simple: 'Attention.'" Probably different, but we used that one at the academy. "Heels together, toes pointed out. Back and head straight, eyes forward. Arms straight down, fingers curled into fists. Good."

Not too dissimilar. We'd get that word barked at us constantly so falling in line became second nature.

"Very good. Next is 'Rest.' Keep your back straight; move your feet slightly apart." I keep my posture straight while allowing my legs to take a more relaxed stance. "Good. Now move your hands to the small of your back, and grab your right wrist with your left hand."

I do as asked, turning to him for further instruction.

"Head straight, eyes forward." I correct myself, biting back a sigh. "This is the position you would take if we were stopped in public, and you were otherwise unoccupied, such as when I saw my friend in the market yesterday. Though I understand the urge your eyes have to roam can be strong." Was he watching me yesterday?

"Wait, like, *any* time we're in public?" Things weren't near that strict at the academy. "This is something everyone in the city expects?"

"No, most orcs in the city do not." He walks around me, looking over my posture. "But I am not most orcs. I am Captain Khazak Ironstorm of the Rangers of V'rok'sh Tah'lj. There are over two-hundred men under my command, so my expectations are higher than most, as are the expectations others have of me." He comes to a stop in front of me, finishing his explanation.

Wow. We're really not fucking around here. He's not going to make me run laps or drop and do a bunch of push-ups, is he? No, I suppose he'd prefer to just tan my ass. I swallow thickly even with nothing in my mouth. What the hell have I gotten into? Maybe sensing my feelings, Ironstorm walks over to me.

"I will not expect you to follow these protocols all of the time." He brushes some of my hair behind an ear. "But because of my position, there will be many times where it will be required of you. I have faith you will not disappoint me." No pressure there.

"Next is 'Inspection.' Your feet should be the same as when at Attention." I bring my feet back together. "Now move your arms up and clasp your hands behind your neck. Keep your elbows out, still standing with your back straight."

The name of the pose combined with the way Iron—*Sir*'s eyes my body as he walks around makes a warm feeling start to pool in my stomach. I feel the occasional tap of his hand as he corrects my posture to his liking. I jump when his palm ghosts over my ass, earning me a spank for breaking form. He comes to another stop in front of me.

"Good boy." The praise makes me shiver as his eyes rake down my body. "You will take this position when I want to look over your body or inspect your clothing. Or if I decided to allow someone else to." A vision of last night in Brull's shop flashes in my head and more heat pools in my core. "Now we will move on to kneeling."

I want to say the academy never taught us any kneeling positions, but I bite my tongue. Besides, maybe when I'm kneeling, the "problem" growing in the front of my underwear will be less visible. After his expectant look, I wordlessly sink to my knees on the floor.

"The next two positions are variations on what you have already learned." He takes a step back. "First is 'Kneeling Rest.'"

I think I can figure that one out at least a little on my own. I straighten my back and grab my wrist behind my back, eyes forward. Ironstorm walks around me, inspecting my progress.

"Good boy." His hand cards through my hair. "You are a quick learner. Next is 'Kneeling Inspection.'"

My hands move from my back to my neck. I spread my arms, elbows pointing out as I puff out my chest a little.

"Square your shoulders." A hand against my lower back helps correct me. "Keep your arms in line with your hips." When he circles around to my front, I can see he's picked up the not-riding crop.

"Good. Now arms down. The next position is 'Display.'" He walks around to my left side. "First, sit back on your heels." I feel the cool leather of the crop brushing against my ass, and I shiver, lowering my weight onto my feet. "Now, spread your thighs." A foot taps the inside of my thigh after I comply. "Wider."

I spread my legs even wider, almost uncomfortably so, but that seems to please him. There's a hum of appreciation, and the riding crop begins to slowly rub against the inside of my thigh, traveling up my leg and almost brushing against the pouch of my thong. My breath hitches, then it's gone and he's walking around me again.

"Lay your arms flat over your thighs, palms facing up." I move my arms, my hands stopping just above my knees. I shift the weight in my legs without thinking about it, earning a quick swat on the ass.

"Oww!" I move back into position.

"What was that?" He cocks his head.

"Oww, *Sir*," I grit out.

"Better." He walks around me slowly, lightly running the end of the crop over different sections of my body. I can feel goosebumps rising in its wake, and I have to hold back a shiver or risk another swat. I'm finding I don't really mind how the leather feels otherwise.

When he comes back around to face me, he kneels down on one knee so we're closer to eye level. "Normally, I would allow you to use my first name in private." He brings his hand to my chin, lifting so that I'm looking at him. "For now, it will still be 'Sir' until it becomes second nature. But soon enough..." He traces his thumb lightly across my lower lip before pulling back and standing, giving me one last long look.

"Beautiful," he mutters to himself and my ears go pink. "Only one more for today. 'Prostrate.'"

I stutter in my movement as I'm not actually sure what I need to do, so I look up for instruction.

"Still on your knees, bend all the way over, laying your arms straight out in front of you." I fold myself over, my hands running along the wood floor as I move forward. "Rest your forehead against the floor. Good." I can hear him walking around me again. "This isn't a position I would use often, certainly not in public. But it is a nice view." I hear the last part coming from behind me, and the warmth in my body spreads downward. "Okay, stand up."

"Is that all?" I dust off my knees. "Sir," I tag on to the end.

"No." He puts a hand on my shoulder, a grin growing on his face. "Now, we practice."

For the next hour, Ironstorm—or Sir, as he is intent on being called now—continues to pace around me, barking orders. At least I think it's an hour; the only clock in here is behind me. It starts simple enough: he says a position and I take it, with him giving nudges and light taps to perfect my pose. Then I have to hold each position for longer and longer periods of time. The standing ones are fine, but I can see why some of the kneeling ones would bother someone after a while, especially Display.

The longer I hold a position, the more my mind wanders to other thoughts, which results in me falling out of position. The nudges turn into love taps, which get progressively harder and harder until they're full-on swats. Every time the leather of the crop smacks against my skin, I bite back a whimper, and my annoyance grows into something angrier.

Once he's satisfied that I can humiliate myself in place long enough, we take things in the other direction. The orders to change poses start coming in faster and faster, as does the damn crop. Things are already moving rapid fire, then he starts to hit me for moving too *slowly*. I'm falling onto my knees when I see the crop coming in on my left, and I just fucking *snap*.

"AAAHHH!" I yell, catching the crop mid-swing and ripping it from the orc's hand. I fling it across the room, watching it smack into the wall and land with a thud. "No!" I lock eyes with Ironstorm and point sternly at the offending object like I'm scolding a pet. Apparently my skills in articulation went flying too.

He looks at me then the crop. I'm expecting a fight, some yelling—you know, *anger*—but all I get when he turns back is a deep belly laugh. *What?*

"That was..." He wipes a tear from his eye. "I mean, I will have to punish you for grabbing and throwing that, but you held your composure much longer than I anticipated."

"...What?" Was *all* of that just to fuck with me? "Did you just make all of that up?!"

"Oh no, the training was very real." He walks over to pick up the crop. "But toward the end, I was pushing you for a reaction. You lasted almost ten minutes longer than I expected. Now, more training or shall we break for lunch?"

Are you. Fucking. Kidding me?

"Aaahhh!" I yell again, throwing my hands up and falling backward onto the floor. "I quit."

"So lunch first then?" I hear the response coming from the kitchen.

"Nope. I quit everything." I sprawl my limbs out like a snow angel. "Just drop it on my face."

That gets me another laugh, though it seems he wasn't joking about lunch. I can hear him rooting around in the kitchen. That's fine with me. Bacon and coffee, while delicious, isn't much of a meal. Shit, I really *am* getting spoiled by the food here. Why is he even making me lunch? I just don't get any of this.

"I don't understand." I sit up to make my statement to the room.

"What, something with the training?" the orc asks over his shoulder. "We can go over—"

"No, *this*. Any of it. All of it." I stand and gesture between the two of us. "Being your, your...*avakesh*." The word feels strange on my tongue.

"Well, it is only your third day, I would not—"

"No, I mean why would *anyone* agree to this? Being tied up, molested, humiliated." The fact that I might have enjoyed some of what's happened over the last three days is purely incidental.

"I think you meant 'why would anyone agree to this, *Sir*.'" Good thing he can't see me rolling my eyes. "Most people who attempt the *Nagul*

Uzu'gor are less opposed to what awaits them should they fail." I feel like that's missing my point.

"Why would they even agree to it in the first place?" Assuming they actually knew what they were agreeing to if they lost. He turns to cock an eyebrow.

"Most people who attempt it are *also* not doing so to avoid only a few months in a jail cell." I can't see it, but I swear it sounds like he just rolled his eyes at me.

"Half a year is hardly a few." I stand as I argue.

"Just so we are clear," he starts, still focused on cutting whatever is in front of him with the knife he's holding, "the idea that someone would wager their freedom and risk becoming an avakesh is wrong, but killing someone or being killed for the same reason would be okay?"

"I didn't..." Glad he's not looking at me right now. "I didn't want to kill you."

"I know." He says it like it's the simplest thing in the world.

"What do you mean you 'know'?" I wasn't even sure what was going to happen!

"In the arena." He speaks over his shoulder while he works. "You had me beat. You sent me face first to the ground, and by all accounts your sword should have been at my neck." He puts down the knife and turns to me. "Why was it not?"

"...I told you. I didn't want to kill you." This is making me blush for some reason.

"My thoughts as well." He turns back to finish slicing whatever it was he was working on. "Do not misunderstand: I am happy you did not. Spirits know what might have happened if you had followed through."

People probably wouldn't have been too happy about me killing one of their own, especially someone so important, out in the open like that. Doubly so considering we weren't supposed to be killing each other at all. "What would have happened?"

"Honestly, I am not entirely sure." He seems to be using a different knife to cut into a loaf of bread now. "Killing is not explicitly against the rules. It is also not something that has happened previously, as far as I am aware. As I said, normally when someone issues a ritual challenge, they have already accepted the potential consequences of losing."

"Sure, but *why*?" Feels like he's still missing the bigger part of my question here.

"Because the intent of the relationships that result from the ritual is one of partnership. You were not strong enough on your own, so we will make you stronger *together*." He speaks without looking up. "Even if they lose, as an avakesh, the person knows they can count on a warm bed, a full belly, and protection. I think the benefits for the party on my end of things are a little more obvious." He turns his head and gives me a wink. "Again, it is not a risk usually taken to avoid only a few months of jail time."

That answer gives me pause, because yeah, *maybe* I wouldn't have rushed into things if I took a second to really think about it. Even when I was only thinking I might die, gambling my life against being locked up for a few months isn't an equal bet. I was just so freaked out, and angry, and worried that I rushed ahead anyway. Logically, I know I should just be glad I'm not dead, but the urge to keep mentally kicking myself is just too strong.

"We all act impulsively at times, pup." A hand holding a torn piece of sandwich is suddenly in front of my face, which apparently has my thoughts written all over it. I turn to see Khazak standing next to me, two sandwiches on a plate in his other hand. "I know you are not exactly thrilled with the circumstances you find yourself in, but I am glad our battle ended the way it did. For both our sakes. Ready for lunch?" He wiggles the sandwich piece in my face.

I guess things could be worse. I shrug and lean forward to grab it with my teeth, my lips and tongue brushing against his fingers as I do. *Damn, not bad.* Some type of ham? There's some leftover bacon from breakfast in there too. I chew and follow him back to the couch, resuming our earlier positions. We eat in relative silence, my brain working overtime to process the new info. The possibility of seeing my friends tomorrow stops me from complaining about being fed again. Though, the way I am basically licking his fingers now makes this feel a lot more intimate than the other times. I stop thinking about it too much, until at one point I lean forward and lick some sauce off his thumb without a second thought and freeze, feeling my face burn red.

It's early afternoon when we finish eating and move to the kitchen to clean up. There's not a lot, but Ironstorm still hands me a small towel to do the drying. It only takes us a few minutes together and then Sir is putting things away and drying his hands.

"I do not have much else planned for the day, but I thought we might go for a run." He throws the towel or a bar above the sink. "Is that something you would enjoy?"

"Running was never my *favorite* thing to do..." At the academy, if you pissed off your instructor, there was always a chance they'd make you run laps around the courtyard. "But it would be a nice way to get out of the house, Sir." The "Sir" gets me a smile.

"Then we will let our lunch settle and do just that."

Chapter Ten

We pull on our clothes about a half an hour after we finish lunch, shorts and a short-sleeved shirt for the both of us. We spent the last thirty minutes reading, or at least Ironstorm read while I stared at a bookshelf trying to figure out the titles. After watching me do that for ten minutes, he showed me which shelf held the books written in Common. *Ass.*

He has a decent selection. A lot of books on philosophy, war and peace, that type of thing. There are a few books on swordplay and technique that look like they might be interesting, but I cracked one open and the first ten pages were just this old dude recounting his childhood. Maybe it gets more interesting later on.

I finish tying my laces and do a little jog in place. I've actually been looking forward to the run since he asked about it. *What?* I'm used to either running drills five times a week or spending half the day on my feet traveling. Sitting around doing nothing for too long makes me antsy.

Just when I think we're leaving and heading for the front door, *Sir* (I'm doing my best to keep the title in mind) returns to the bedroom to retrieve some things: cuffs and a leash. The chain is long, at least twice as long as the others he's used, but it's still a fucking *leash*. I stare at it, the disdain on my face clear as day, but I don't protest when it's attached to my wrist. Better than my neck. Once we're *finally* ready and step outside, he locks the door behind us. We walk past the gate and go left before Ironstorm turns his face to me.

"Ready?" I nod in the affirmative and we're off.

Our pace starts at a brisk jog. I don't have any problems keeping up, but the leash does take some getting used to. I'm not worried about it getting caught on anything; it just keeps hitting me in the side, which is annoying. I also have to pay attention not to let someone or something get caught between us.

I inhale deeply as we run together. It really is nice to get outside in the fresh air and do something physical. I hate to admit it, but something I actually miss about the academy was how much stuff there was to do. You could always find a sparring partner, and there were pickup football games almost every weekend. I've been running around, climbing on, and hitting stuff since I was a little boy—it's just what I know.

The weather outside today is nice, the sky mostly clear with a few fluffy clouds. It's not too hot, though both of us are already working up a sweat. The streets aren't busy, a few orcs here and there. The houses and bodies that we pass fade into a blur as my brain starts to drift off during the run. I barely even register the leash after a while.

At some point, the sweat from my brow starts falling into my eyes. I wipe it off on my arm, and it's enough to make me aware of my surroundings again. I think the houses we pass look familiar, and my suspicions are confirmed when, after another turn, I recognize the park on our left from the previous day.

We slow down as we approach, coming to a stop under a tree to catch our breath. The park is as busy as it was when we first arrived yesterday, with plenty of orcs (and a few-non-orcs) around us playing games and eating their lunches. I lean back against the tree and wipe more sweat from my forehead while I look around. The park almost seems split down the middle: one half a mostly open field while the other is dotted with trees around a small pond in the center. The whole area is fairly flat, and I realize it's also the first place within the city that I've seen any grass. People seem pretty content with their dirt roads and yards. I see a few stone benches—and the meat-on-a-stick cart—but for the most part, everything in the park is natural. The trees here resemble the ones making up the outer city's tree line, though obviously much smaller. I watch a squirrel run down the trunk of one, only to climb up one of the statues lining the front of the tribal hall.

"Who are those statues of?" I point at the one with the squirrel atop it.

"The six members of the first tribal council." That makes sense. We've got something similar in our town square with Lutheria's founders. "Look, we can get some water before we start the run back." Sir nods his head in the direction of a well near the center of the park and leads us over.

There's a bucket, but no cups or anything so we just use our hands. The first mouthful of cold water after a workout always tastes amazing. Ironstorm fills a second bucket after we finish most of the first, and when I'm feeling rehydrated, I plop down on the grass to finish resting. Leaning back against the well, I see a group of a dozen or so orcs, men and women, playing a game of football. I mean, I guess it's probably not "football," but it's close enough. Everyone is trying to kick a round ball between two sets of goal posts made from tree branches stuck in the ground. I do notice some of the orcs tackling each other and even grabbing and running with the ball, which is different.

"Would you like to play?" The question comes from above, making me raise my head.

"...Could we?" I'm not sure they'd want some human forcing his way into their game.

He walks forward at my question, calling out to the group when they are between plays. Words are exchanged, and a thumb is swung back in my direction which gets me to stand. After what looks like a nod of agreement, Ironstorm turns back to me with a smile on his face. I meet him halfway, and he removes the cuff from my wrist.

"They are happy to have more players." He walks with me toward the group, who have paused the game for us. "The game is call *rug'bal.* The objective of the game is to—"

"Get the ball between the two sticks?" I mean I know it's *not* football, but it's still football. "One question: can we use hands?"

He gives me an amused look, hopefully because he finds my enthusiasm charming. "It can be grabbed, and you may run while holding it, but not pass it forward by throwing, only kicking. Also be aware: if you are in possession of the ball, you can expect close contact from the other team." He points at one of the goals. "That is your team's goal. They are the ones without shirts, so you will need to remove yours."

"We aren't on the same team?" I'm a little surprised, but that's fine with me. I'll kick his team's ass.

"I thought it might be more fun this way." He smirks before joining his team on their side of the makeshift field.

I pull the shirt over my head, tossing it under a tree where it looks like the others are keeping theirs. The women on my team seem to be wearing a thin wrap around their tops, which seem less for covering up and more for holding things in place. I've seen Liss using something similar. I make my way to the group of sweaty shirtless orcs, which is something else to repress, I guess. A few of the orcs give me a smile when I join them, but most give me a look that says "what is this human going to do?"

Things start up again quickly. Two players meet in the middle and fight for control of the ball when it is tossed in the air. I have no idea what the score is, but I don't really care; I just want to play. I hang back at first, watching the rhythm of the other players and seeing who to watch out for. It's not too difficult to pick up on who the best players are—they're the ones being passed to the most. Ironstorm is actually pretty good and seems to assimilate right into his team. I do not have the same luck. I can't really blame them. I probably wouldn't trust the scrawny looking new guy either.

So I'll just have to prove myself to them. I start moving more infield, keeping my eyes on the opposing players. No one from the other team is bothering to guard me, so when the ball is passed in my direction toward another orc, I use some of my newfound speed to sweep in and steal it. I start moving down the field immediately, hearing a grunt of confusion followed by some cheers behind me.

I don't take the ball all the way, too many bodies between me and the goal, but I do kick it right to one of my teammates who manages to score himself. I hear another cheer and get a clap on the shoulder. I keep this up, and after I manage to steal the ball for the third time, the other team *finally* starts to take me seriously. I stole that last one from Captain Ironstorm himself. I actually heard him laugh when I cut in front of him.

Following that, the rest of my team starts to actually pass to me, which also means there is an orc actually guarding me now, but it's nothing I can't handle. The size of some of these guys must make me look like a halfling in comparison, and I have to dodge more than a few tackles. I remember how well trying to tackle Sir in the ruins worked out for me, so I stick with dodging.

No idea what the score is still, but things have seemed pretty even between us so far. You can feel the competitive energy rolling off the players, and the little shoulder bumps I'm getting after I do something good are pretty nice. This is a lot of fun and something I'm not sure I realized I was missing before now.

I mean, I can and have sparred with Adam and Liss since leaving home, but sports? Football, racing, wrestling, all of those typically require more people, or at least people who are just as interested in doing them as you. I miss competing: the thrill of winning, the challenge of an unknown opponent, the satisfaction of being on a team you know has your back.

"This is the last round," Ironstorm calls to me from his side of the field. "Score is tied, so whichever team makes the next goal wins the game."

"We have this won," one of the orcs on my team says to me in Common, a confident smirk on her face. I give her a nod, because yeah, I think we do.

The ball is tossed up, and the two orcs at center immediately skirmish for control. It looks like the other team wins, just for a minute, before that player is tackled to the ground, and one of my other teammates sweeps in to take the ball. He starts moving up field with the rest of us fanning out behind him. The ball is passed back once, and then twice between my team, each of us guarded very closely by the others. Still, I can see the guy with the ball getting closer and think we might actually have a chance.

Of course, that's right when he gets tackled, and it's Ironstorm who manages to steal the ball back. I see him a few yards ahead of me, starting to move it back up the field toward their own goal. None of my teammates are close to him, but the confident orc from a minute ago is only a few feet away from me.

"Can you tackle him? I have an idea," I ask and she nods quickly. I give her a small head start before running straight at the captain. He sees me coming of course, another smirk on his face as he gets ready to side-step me.

And that's when the other orc slams into him.

It doesn't send him to the ground, but it does knock him off balance, the two of them evenly matched. It's more than enough for me. Distracted by the orc at his side, he barely has time to register me rapidly closing the distance between us. I drop into a slide at the last minute, aiming for the ball and shooting it straight between both their legs. The ball goes flying and with no one in the way to stop it, soars right between the goal posts, ricocheting off a tree behind it.

The whole field breaks out into shouting, and the second I pick myself up from the ground, I'm being pulled in for a hug by the friendly female orc, followed by the rest of my team. The orcs who earlier didn't want to take me seriously seem to enjoy taunting the other team with my presence. Even Sir looks impressed. I have no idea what any one is saying, but they're all happy, so I can't help but feel happy too.

"Good game," the orc who helped me with the final play tells me over water. "I am Glasha. You are a good player—for a human."

"Thanks, I think." I reach out to take her hand. "I'm David. It's nice to meet you."

"Nice to meet you as well, David." Then she turns to Ironstorm. "You managed to find a rather scrappy one, sir."

"Thank you, Glasha." I guess these two already know each other. "Everything going well in my absence?"

"Yessir," she nods. "Business as usual."

"Then I will see you and the rest of the station in four days." Sir returns her nod. "Thank you for letting us join."

"It was fun. You should play with us more often, Captain." She gives a small salute before she makes her exit. "See you in four days, sir."

"Sir? You got another slave or something, Captain?" I find myself teasing, still feeling the rush of my recent victory.

"She is one of my rangers," he answers with a smile.

"Why haven't you been at work, anyway?" It is a little weird how he's basically been home for the last three days.

"I was given the week off after winning our match to ensure you settled into things alright," he explains. "That was very impressive at the end there, pup. Did you play something like this at home?"

"A little. No hands or tackling but the same general idea." I flash a cocky smile. "Don't feel too bad. I was pretty great over there too."

"Is that so? Care for another challenge?" He hands me my shirt.

"What are you thinking?" I admit I am intrigued after my victory.

"A race back to the house." I turn to look in the general direction we came from. "Do you think you can remember how to get there?"

"I think so." I'm pretty good with directions, but hold on a minute... "Wait, like, no leash? You trust me enough now?"

"Between the running and the game, if you *did* decide to make another escape attempt, I think you would be too tired to get very far." He considers me for a moment. "*Can* I trust you?"

"Yes." I nod quickly. "Yes, Sir."

"Alright then." He turns to face the side of the park closer to the house. "First person to touch the front door wins."

"What does the winner get?" The question is out of my mouth before I even think about it.

"Oh, is this a wager now?" He smiles. "Winner gets to take the first shower."

"Sounds fair." That's a lot tamer than I was expecting. Not that I'm disappointed or anything.

"Okay." He crouches into a runner's stance. "Ready?"

"Ready." I copy him.

"GO!"

We both take off from the well with him in a slight lead. As we exit the park and make our first turn, I edge my way closer. I don't try to overtake him—not yet at least. I'm fairly confident I know my way back to the house, but just in case, I want to keep my eyes on him. It's also just common sense that you don't blow all your energy at the start of a race. Got to save it and then pour it all into the last leg.

We seem to be a pretty even match, or at least we're both good at pacing ourselves. At one point, I move behind him and start using his large form as a windshield. That only lasts a few minutes though, and when he realizes what I'm doing, he slows down and forces me to go around him. After that, we're pretty much neck and neck until we make one last turn onto the street I know the house is on.

When I see a familiar looking fence in the distance, I know we're in the home stretch and I book it, using all the energy I've been conserving until now to sprint forward. It looks like he had a similar idea, but it's not enough to keep me from pulling ahead. My feet skid against the dirt when I reach the edge of the yard, almost losing my balance as I try to pivot for the door. It's just another one, two, three strides, and my hand is on the wood.

"I WIN!" I shout to the sky and then immediately bend over, hands on my knees as I catch my breath.

"Good job, puppy," the equally out of breath orc congratulates a moment later, leaning against the fence. "Before we go inside, I want to show you something." He has me follow him around to the back of the house, where attached to one of the walls is a series of stone pipes. "There are a number of underground rivers running under the city. Thanks to them as well as some orc ingenuity, the enchantments on the pipes mean we are able to enjoy a nice hot shower without having to heat the water ourselves."

I stare at the crisscrossing pipes coming up from the ground and disappearing into the wall, a little in awe. I don't think have anything like that back home, not even the really rich people. Some places like the academy had plumbing to bring water inside, but all the bathrooms were still outside, and we had to heat our water the old-fashioned way, on a stove or over a fire. Imagine never running out of hot water for cooking or cleaning or whatever else you might need, not to mention being able to use the bathroom inside! I am already looking forward to that shower when we walk back around to the front. "If you had told me it was a *hot* shower, I would have run even faster. Do all your houses have this?"

"No, it was not until I was around ten that I lived in a home with plumbing." Yeah, I'm jealous. "It is a fairly recent invention. Maybe forty years old? At the time, there was a pair of orcs who had spent some time in an elven city with a similar system. After they returned, they devised a system of our own and began what I understand has since become a fairly lucrative business. Most public buildings have already been converted, and much of the rest of the city is on a waiting list."

"Wow." Who knew there was money in making toilets?

We start walking back around to the front while Sir fishes out his keys to unlock the door. Once we're inside, I can really feel the sweat-soaked clothes sticking to my skin. I start pulling my shirt off while being led to the bathroom, before we're even in the room. He pushes the door open and walks over to the tub, bending over and showing me how the knobs work.

"The left is hot and the right is cold. There is soap right there and towels under the wash basin." He turns and smiles at me before making his exit. "I will see you when you are finished."

I'm not sure why I do what I do next. Maybe it's because he's taking me to see my friends tomorrow, or maybe I'm worried that he won't. Maybe it's the day of training catching up with me, or because it feels like he might actually care sometimes. Maybe I've just lost my mind, but for whatever reason, I open my mouth and say...

"Together." The single word is blurted out, making him pause. *Let's try a full sentence now, David.* "We could shower together, I mean. To save water."

"To save water." A smirk spreads slowly across his face. "Are you certain?"

"I... Yes." I shift awkwardly but appreciate him going along with the flimsy excuse.

"Alright. Hand me your clothes and turn on the water." He begins removing his own shirt. "I will be right back."

I strip off the rest of my clothing as requested, which Khazak takes into the bedroom while I turn around and start the shower. I don't know how hot he likes it, but I think I remember what the water felt like the first time we showered...among other things. I'm testing the water with my hands when he rejoins me, body naked like mine. His skin is covered in a sheen of sweat, glistening in the light in contrast to his coarse, dark body hair.

Before I'm caught staring too much, I step into the wooden tub, leaving room for him to join me. It's a bit of a squeeze—this isn't nearly as big as our last shower—but we manage. Things are a little awkward at first, though it's more the "whoops, didn't mean to bump into you" kind of awkward. There's a lot more giggling than I would have expected for two grown men in a shower together.

Once we're both wet and settled into a comfortable position (which ends up being with his body blocking most of the spray), he reaches for a jar of what I figure is shampoo once he pours some onto my head. He does the same for himself, lathering up his own hair quickly before moving on to mine. He's not as fast, slower, sensual even, scratching my scalp gently with his fingers as he works. I close my eyes, both to avoid getting something in them and because it feels nice. He leans me forward when he's finished, rinsing the suds away so I can see again.

Next, he grabs the soap and a sponge. Just like last time, rather than hand them to me, he starts washing my chest himself, his other arm around my waist to steady me. I'm expecting him to move to the rest of my body like last time, but instead, he places the sponge in my hand, then lifts it to his own chest.

"I thought *I* won the race?" I joke as he "helps" me scrub his own chest.

"Your punishment for throwing the crop earlier," he reasons with me while wearing a lecherous smile, releasing my hand.

I don't complain, but I do give a knowing smirk when I take over the washing duties. I can do this. I run the sponge over the tattoo on his pec, the water dripping from over his shoulders and making the soap run down the lines of his muscles. I used to think I'd look like this one day, or at least close. Still might have if I had stayed at the academy. But it's a lot of work. And calories.

I have him lift his hands to my shoulder when I move onto his arms. This has the added effect of opening up his armpit, the scent of his musk taking me back to the old locker room. It's also having some other, newer effects on me that I'm really glad I didn't know about before. Of course, that only makes things worse when I have to lean forward to clean the armpits themselves. My cock is pointing almost straight out, the head occasionally brushing against his thighs. He doesn't mention it though.

I move down to his broad stomach. I can feel the muscles underneath the healthy layer of softness on top. I watch the soap run between the creases where his thigh meets his torso, to the left and right of his big green cock. It's not as hard as mine, but it's not fully soft either. I haven't actually gotten a good look at it before. It's thick, thicker than I am, and it certainly has a few inches on me in length too. He's uncircumcised like I am, his partial erection causing some of his cockhead to peek through the hood. I stare at it, still too unsure to just reach out and touch it when a green hand gently grabs my wrist and moves it forward.

The sponge presses against the side of his cock, and I see the appendage twitch in response. I tentatively scrub the sponge against his skin, dragging it over the top of his cock and through his pubic hair to bring it back down on the other side. *Okay David, stop pussyfooting around. It's just a dick.*

I take hold of his shaft with my free hand and hear a sharp intake of breath. I slowly spread the soap up and down before lifting it and swiping the sponge along his sack. That earns me a shudder, and I drop the sponge so I can use both hands to wash him more thoroughly. His balls are heavy as I spread the soap around, his cock only growing harder. I'm not trying to jerk him off, but I'm also not *not* trying to jerk him off.

Still, there's only so much I can do before it's obvious I'm not just washing him anymore, so once he's clean, I kneel down to pick up my discarded sponge. Looking up from there puts me face to face with his one-eyed monster and apparently that is finally enough for some of that good old-fashioned shame to kick in, forcing me to look away.

While I'm down here though, I start to scrub his legs. What? I want to do a good job. I steady myself against his leg, and I run the sponge up and down his thighs, even reaching around to wash the back for good measure. His calves are huge. By the time I'm finally done with his body, I feel like I've gotten a good workout.

"Good job," Sir tells me as he helps me to my feet. "Get my back?"

He turns around to present his muscled back to me, with his equally muscular ass right below it. It's covered in the same dark fur as the rest of him, his back less so. I set to work, scrubbing all the hard-to-reach places you can't get on your own. When I reach his lower back, I hesitate before going lower. I've never washed another man's ass before. I mean, I've never washed another man's dick before today either, but this feels different.

"Getting shy on me now, puppy?" the orc taunts me over his shoulder.

I'll show you shy.

I run the sponge *right* down his ass crack. That gets me a small jump and a chuckle, and now that I've jumped into the deep end, it feels like I can just wash him like a normal person. I scrub each of his cheeks, individually and in between, liking the way they bounce a little more than I would have anticipated. I think about delving my fingers in like I did on the other side, but that feels like it might be crossing a line, and I have no idea how I'd even ask about that. Thankfully, he starts to turn around when I pause, having deemed my work complete.

"Thank you for that, puppy." The timber of his voice sounds very relaxed. "Your turn."

Taking the sponge from me, he applies more soap before repeating the process on me. When he pulls my body against his, I am again reminded of our previous shower encounter, and I can't help but push into his hand a little when it reaches my crotch. He drops the sponge just as I did, wrapping his large green fingers around my cock, which is as hard as I've ever felt it. I gasp a little, but before I can make any more noises, his mouth is on mine.

I groan when his tongue swipes against my lips, opening them much more eagerly than I did then. He continues to slowly stroke me as he kisses me deeply, and I'm soon humping into him while pressing my tongue back into his mouth. His hand moves down to my sack, squeezing gently while the hand at my back moves down to my ass and does the same. After a few more minutes of kissing and groping—or seconds, or hours, I honestly have no idea—he retrieves the sponge and finishes washing my lower half. He shows none of the hesitation that I did, and I whimper when a finger brushes over my hole. He stands and kisses me again, switching our positions so the water can rinse the soap from our bodies. I whine into his mouth when he continues to tease my hole until he pulls away with a smirk.

"I believe I still owe you a reward for saving Mrs. Skycaller's daughter from that runaway cart." He brings a hand up to my face and traces his thumb along my chin.

"I... I guess you do." I think I get the implication here.

Still smiling, he reaches behind me to shut off the water before carefully stepping out of the tub and onto a fur mat. He grabs a large, fluffy towel from under the sink, turning to wrap it around my head and upper body, drying me as quickly and efficiently as he can. My hair is still wet, but I can sense the urgency in his motions.

"Bedroom" is the only word spoken when Sir helps me out of the tub before using the same towel on himself. I nod and make my way to the location requested with him right behind me. I pause when I reach the bed, turning around when I'm not sure what to do next.

"On your back." His hand pushes gently against my chest, and I fall back onto the bed. My cock hits my stomach with a wet *slap*. He leans down and grabs a hold of my wrists, pinning them by my sides. "You are to keep these here. Understood?"

"Yes, Sir." I nod quickly as he lowers himself to his knees, spreading my legs as he does. Just when I think I know what he's going to do, he hooks his hands under my legs and lifts them, pushing them toward my chest.

Wait, what is he about to—*oohhhmygods!*

"Fuck." I fist the sheets under my hands tightly when his warm tongue slide across my hole. I look down just to verify that he's doing what I think he is, that his mouth is on my ass. I can't stifle a moan when I feel the tongue a second time, my hands gripping even tighter. I didn't know this was a thing people did. I know I just got out of the shower, but this feels like it should be dirty. Not that I'm doing *anything* to stop him when the tongue returns for the third, fourth, or fifth times...

His oral technique changes before long, his mouth pressed more tightly to my skin. I feel his tongue prodding at my entrance at the same time as his tusks scratch gently against the backs of my thighs. They feel blunter than I would have guessed, though the way they scrape against my skin still makes me shudder. I look down, locking eyes with the orc, the hunger behind them evident. Appropriate too, given what he's doing.

He pushes more of his tongue into my hole, the wet appendage stretching me as it sinks in, leaving me feeling slightly empty when it pulls back out. I bite my lip and turn my head to the side, wishing I could just bury my face into the mattress and scream. This feels so fucking good. My dick is hard and leaking against my stomach, and without thinking, I reach my hand toward it, just to relieve some of the pressure.

"*No,*" a voice growls and the offending appendage is grabbed as he drops my legs to his shoulders. "What did I say?"

"Not to move them. Sir," I add on, hoping to get him to continue.

"Hold these." He pushes my thighs back to my chest, moving my own hands to grip them instead of his. "Move them again and I stop," he warns and lowers his face to my hole once more. "You are to let me know when you are close, but you may not cum without permission. Understood?"

"Yes, Sir!" I nod quickly. *Pleeeaaasse keep going, please.*

Satisfied, he begins to work again, pressing his tongue back into my hole. The warm wetness soothes my sore muscles, muscles I didn't even know could be sore before a couple of days ago.

Fuck.

I don't even try to suppress a moan when one of Sir's hands reaches up to wrap around my cock. Looking down, I see that his eyes are closed, the shoulder on his other arm moving as he works his own length.

If this is the reward for saving a kid's life, I need to do more of that. The rhythm of his hand working up and down my shaft soon matches the rhythm of his tongue fucking in and out of my ass. My body wants to push back onto his face and hump up into his hand at the same time, torn between the sensations. I met this man only two days ago, and he already knows how to play my body like an instrument. I'm not going to last much longer.

"I-I'm getting close," I announce, looking down for further instruction. I receive none, eyes still closed and the pace he's toying with my body at staying steady. "Sir? C-can I cum?"

"Not yet." The mouth is torn away from my hole for a second so he can answer and is then immediately replaced.

I look down with wide eyes at a face that is not looking back at me. *No*?! But if he keeps... If I... *What the hell am I supposed to do?!*

"Sir? Please?" I ask again, receiving no answer but seeing the corners of his eyes crinkle slightly. There's still no stopping, and I'm still getting closer to an edge I'm not sure I can stop myself from spilling over. "Sir? Captain? Please, I-I'm going to cum. Please, can I cum? Sir?! Please?!" The asking quickly turns to begging as the questions pour out of my mouth.

"Cum for me, puppy." The order comes after a few more seconds of jerking and tongue fucking and a split second before I blow my load all over my stomach and chest.

I moan, or at least try to when I start to cum. It's very high pitched and maybe comes out more like a squeal—I don't know. My brain's not working right now, having been shot out of my dick and sprayed all over my chest. The hand wrapped around me continues to stroke and the tongue in my hole continues to fuck, even as I clench around it uncontrollably. I think some of my cum hit my neck. All I can see is white, or black or...fuck I don't know.

What's happening?

Slowly, things come back into focus, and I see the blurry green form between my legs standing. He swipes some of the cum from my stomach, wrapping the slick hand around his own dick. I hear him curse in Orcish as he jerks himself over my body, chest and stomach sweaty and breathing deeply as he works. With a roar, his cock explodes, painting my body and adding his own sticky seed to mine. He stands over me, chest heaving and hard dick still bouncing, the both of us riding an endorphin high even greater than we got from all the running today. I look down at my body, covered from thigh to neck in white.

"I think I'm gonna need another shower," I say, too worn out to keep the stupid grin off my face as I look over my body and up to him. The same stupid grin on his tells me he agrees.

Chapter Eleven

I sleep soundly, at least until the very warm and very firm pillow I'm using decides it's time to get up. I grumble, reaching my arm out in an attempt to hold it in place. *Five more minutes.* I was dreaming about flying through a thunderstorm, narrowly dodge the lightning as it struck around me. It was a lot more relaxing than it sounds. A small huff of laughter at my act is what finally pulls me back to the land of the living.

"As much as I would like to continue sleeping, I believe we have an appointment to see your friends today, pup." His words are teasing, but the hand rubbing my back feels so good...

My eyes open and slowly adjust to the morning light. It's earlier than we've woken up the last few days. We're in the center of the bed with me on top of him, for once intentionally. After our run-and-fun yesterday, we had a pretty quiet evening. After I took another shower, *Sir* wanted to go over training positions again before dinner. Then after we had steak (fucking *steak!*), it was time for bed.

After what we'd just done on the bed (and the fact that we always seem to end up there anyway), keeping up my protests about the sleeping arrangements seemed dumb, so I just met him in the middle and didn't really think much about it. Or tried not to, at least. I roll onto my back and stretch my arms and legs. He's right; I get to see my friends today. Before they're sentenced to spend the next few months in a prison while I sleep in a warm bed and eat steak.

With a ruffle of my hair (I really need a haircut), Khazak stretches his own limbs and slides out of bed to walk to the bathroom. After I hear him finish peeing, I get up so I can do the same. While relieving myself, I look over to see him putting lather on his face in a few places while holding a small (for him) straight razor. He brings it up to his face, swiping it just above his cheek, removing the few days of accumulated stubble. He's cleaning up his beard.

"Everything alright?" He looks over to me. Didn't realize I was staring.

"Do you have another one of those, or can I use that when you're done?" I reach up to run my hand over my chin. I haven't shaved in over a week.

"Are you sure?" He reaches the razor-free hand over and runs his thumb along my chin. "I rather like you with a beard."

"I mean I... I guess I could keep it." Is it hot in here? It feels hot in here. "If you think it looks good."

"I will assist you when I finish." He smiles and finishes evening out his beard line while I watch. When he's done with that, he grabs a small pair of scissors and trims the rest of his beard. After washing his face and running a towel over it, he checks himself in the mirror before washing off the razor and turning to me. "Alright, your turn, pup."

I walk over to him, expecting to face the mirror. Instead, he turns me to face himself then lifts me to sit on the counter. I guess by "assist," he meant "do it for me." That's fine. I've never used a straight razor before and it is a little intimidating. He brushes the shaving cream onto my face and neck.

"It should go without saying, but you need to remain still while I do this," says the big scary orc holding the very sharp blade. I nod once stiffly before he brings it in close.

"As I told you yesterday, there will be situations in which I will need you to follow certain protocol." He starts with my cheeks as he speaks. "Today is one of those situations. You will not need to worry about kneeling, but we will be in a room with many of my peers and superiors. I would very much appreciate it if you were on your best behavior. It may even help your friends."

I give a questioning look with my eye as he moves to work on my neck.

"Do you remember what Brull said about word of you and I around town?" He's not looking for an actual response. "The council member presiding over the case today—Councilman Bloodfield—has an avakesh of his own and is known to have something of a soft-spot for them when they are involved in a case. Seeing you well-behaved next to me may tug at those heartstrings and do your friends some good." He finishes with my neck and steps back to look over his work. "Alright, wash your face and have a look."

I hop off the counter and wash up, drying my face with the towel handed to me. Not bad. I mean, it's only been a week, but after another I could actually have a half decent beard. Hopefully the judge-guy likes it too. Not sure I believe a guy with a name like "Bloodfield" has a soft-spot for anything.

"Thank you. It looks great." I admire myself in the mirror for a moment more before running my hand through the mop of hair on my head. "I need a haircut."

"We can certainly see about taking care of that soon." A green hand reaches out to smooth out my hair.

We finish taking care of our bathroom needs before we're back in the bedroom getting dressed. Ironstorm picks out a simple outfit for me while pulling out the leathers I remember seeing him wearing when I first met him. His uniform. Certain parts are emblazoned with an emblem that looks like an Orcish symbol surrounded by trees. It takes him a lot longer to get dressed than I do, but uh, I don't really mind watching. He certainly fills it out; everything about him in uniform screams "Sir."

You're learning new things about yourself every day, David.

When he's finished, he looks himself over in the mirror one final time before grabbing my leash. I mentally sigh but keep it to myself as we move to the living room. He grabs some jerky from the kitchen, handing me a piece and saying, "We will have an actual meal when we get home." I bite into it as we go outside, not minding the taste, but I have been pretty spoiled when it comes to food lately. I wonder what's for lunch.

We pass through the park for the third time this week, and walking past the statues as we enter the building feels a lot more intimidating than it did the first time. We pause before we walk up the steps, Ironstorm turning to me.

"Okay, pup. Behave." His look is only *slightly* pleading.

"I will, Sir." The idea that I could fuck something up worse for my friends is an effective deterrent from acting out right now.

We walk through the open doors of the tribal hall, the interior just as busy as it was last time. Our path isn't nearly as long this time. We take a right when we enter, and after a short distance down the hall, we walk through another set of double doors on our left into what I guess is the orc equivalent of a courtroom. There are a number of benches directly in front of us, and on the far side of the room, a set of large tables. Behind the largest one is a fairly old-looking orc in dark robes, currently engaged in conversation with the person next to him.

In the back left corner of the room, I see a cage containing my four friends. I also see that tall, red-headed orc from the jail, Redwish. The one that called himself our "advocate." The one that made it seem like the whole "Steel & Thunder" thing was a hell of a lot different than what

I actually went through. My hands clench into fists, but I fight the urge to walk over. Causing a scene will not help anyone right now. Instead, I turn to Ironstorm, hoping to get his attention while he silently scans the room.

"Hmm?" I look behind me at the cage, then back at him. "Ah, come with me."

He leads us over to the cage where I can see Redwish talking to Adam inside the cell. He sees us on our approach—it's hard to miss the Captain. My friends in the cell notice us too but don't say anything. I don't sense any animosity from the lawyer-orc, and I'm damn sure hiding my own. He smirks at me for a split-second before turning to Ironstorm.

"Captain Ironstorm." He holds his hand out and the two exchange what I am just gonna call the "orc handshake" from now on. "It is good to see you and your new human. I trust you have helped him settle in well?"

"Advocate Redwish." I can tell they know each other, but they don't seem overly friendly. Just work associates, I guess. "It has been an interesting week, to say the least. I was wondering if he might have a chance to speak with his friends?"

"I see no problem with letting them speak." I relax a little when he okays my visit. "I need to go confirm a few things with Councilman Bloodfield before we begin. I do not expect this to take very long."

When he steps away, I move for the cage, not bothering to ask Ironstorm for permission. The less these guys see about our "relationship," the better. Thankfully my leash is allowed to hang loosely without comment. I can already see Adam's got a million questions, and so do I.

"David," Adam says at my approach. The rest of the group sans-Nate crowds to one side of the cage, the dark-haired magician waving to me silently from a distance. He's the worst.

"David! Are you okay?! I've been so worried!" Corrine cries and tries to hug me through the bars, the anti-magic bracers around her wrists cutting her off.

"I've been worried about you guys too." I turn to Adam. "What about you? Are you and Liss still hurt?" I don't see any signs of injury on them.

"No, we're both okay," Liss answers from Adam's left. "You should see the other guys though."

"The other guys are also fine." Adam gives Elisabeth an exasperated look. "They took us all to a healer when we first got here. When they finally brought us back to the jail, you were already gone."

"Yeah, what the hell, man?" Liss says maybe a little too loudly. "I mean, sure we're in jail and that's not *great*, but we heard you tried to fight one of those orcs one on one, and he made you his bitch." Really hoping she meant that figuratively.

"That orc is standing right behind him, so maybe chill." Adam cocks his head at Liss, and I turn to look at Ironstorm, who is politely pretending to not be listening to any of this. "*Are* you okay, David? What happened exactly? They told us you tried to fight the guy that arrested us and now he...owns you." He looks somewhat nervously behind me and drops his voice to a whisper. "Is he hurting you or anything?"

"I'm okay, Adam. Really." Now I'm whispering. "It hasn't been that bad. He's...alright."

"What is he making you do?" Adam's *still* whispering.

"Just things like taking care of chores and stuff around his house. It's pretty boring." Now I'm whispering *and* lying through my teeth.

"Is that a leash?" Liss cuts in with an oh-so important question.

"Is that your natural hair color?" I nod to her extremely visible roots.

"I missed you too, David." She smiles.

"What's going to happen to you all now? Any chance of still fighting this thing?" I ask even though I know the answer.

"We don't really have a choice. We have to admit we did it and do our time." Adam shrugs his shoulders.

"Really? There's nothing else? Can't we just give them Nate or something?" I ignore the indignant "hey!" shot in my direction. "It was just an accident."

"An accident where people got hurt." I know he's right but *booooo.* "Even if they ignored that, the healer, repairing the damage to the temple, those things cost money. Money we don't have. There's nothing we can do." He doesn't sound dejected, but he's definitely come to terms with things.

No one says anything for a moment before Adam starts again. "Look, however long it takes us to get out of here, just hold on. We'll figure it out. We're still a team, right?"

"Right." It's hard not to smile when Adam's trying to cheer me up. I'm glad I'm in this with my best friend, but I wish I could be in there with them. Or that they could be in my place—never mind.

"Captain, we are about to begin, so you will need to take your seats." Redwish comes up looking apologetic, or at least feigns it convincingly.

"Thank you again, advocate." Ironstorm gives a short, polite bow, before turning to my friends in their cage. "Best of luck. *Rumk'r Avon.*"

"Bye guys." I give a sad wave goodbye as we turn to walk away. "I'll talk to you soon, somehow."

"You know they are going to find out about the nature of our relationship sooner or later," Ironstorm whispers softly as we walk away, so that only I can hear.

Yeah well, that's something I'll deal with later. We look at the long benches for an empty spot. For a moment, I hope we might be able to slip somewhere in the back, but of course the "Captain of the Rangers of V'rok'sh Tah'lj" (*are you impressed I remembered all that?*) sits us in the second row. The room isn't too full, but I don't know if that's unusual or not. A few more people find their seats and then an orc in a uniform similar to the one next to me reaches the center of the room and announces something in Orcish.

"He is saying that we are about to begin, as well as Councilman Bloodfield's full title." Ironstorm leans over to translate for me. "Then he will read out your friends' names as well as the crimes they are accused of."

I listen and watch as the guard orc does just that. It's funny hearing him try to pronounce "Elisabeth" and "Nathaniel," not to mention everyone's last names. I keep that to myself though. No smiles here. Just serious face. The orc turns to exchange a few words with the judge before taking his own seat. I know, he's a "councilman" over here, not a judge, but you know what I mean.

Next up is Mr. Redwish. "Councilman Bloodfield, would you permit to conduct today's proceedings in the Common language so that the people I represent may understand?" That will be handy.

"I see no problem with that, Advocate Redwish." The judge nods in understanding.

"Thank you." He takes a deep breath before continuing. "Three days ago, a group of five humans with no knowledge of our city or customs made the mistake of intruding onto our land. They entered the ruins of the Temple of Zeus intent on exploring, and when the rangers patrolling the area responded to the magical wards on the entrance being breached, they erred further in attacking them. Though I can say with confidence that what transpired that day was the result of a misunderstanding, they nonetheless understand the severity of their actions and do not fight the accusations."

"Hmm." Bloodfield sorts through some papers in front of him. "What were they doing in the temple? 'Exploring'?"

"From what I understand, there are humans in Holbrooke still sharing news of the temple's uncovering as if it were a more *recent* development." Remind me to send those dicks a postcard. "They were acting on outdated information."

"Even if it *were* recent, they would still be coming onto our lands uninvited, still attacking our citizens." *Uh oh.* "How many rangers were injured?"

"Four, sir. Two with minor burns and two others with more serious injuries." It's said with a sigh. He lays it on good—I'll give him that. "Three of the accused were also injured, two serious enough to require the services of a healer while the third was knocked unconscious. After an examination, he was placed in holding with the unharmed members of their group." I don't remember any of that.

"Glad we still give as good as we get." He flips through a few more papers. "I want to speak with one of them. Advocate Redwish, please retrieve Mr. Adam Bauer."

I watch Redwish and the guard walk a path on the other side of the benches to the cage. I see the guard place his wrist above the handle on the door, opening it a second later. I remember that wrist thing from the jail. Adam is already waiting on the other side, hands in shackles, and walks back side by side with Redwish to stand in front of the judge.

"Mr. Bauer, I understand you hail from Lutheria." Bloodfield leans forward. "I have not been there myself, but is this how I would be expected to act if I were to visit?"

"No, your honor." *See?* Adam thinks he's a judge too. "I am very sorry. *We* are very sorry. We didn't know the temple belonged to you, and I swear we did not come here with the intention of hurting anyone."

"And yet you did." *Okay, we're fucked.* "How exactly did that happen, Mr. Bauer?"

"We became...defensive at the sudden appearance of the rangers." Adam has always been pretty good at choosing his words carefully. "In a panic, one of our group acted before he should have. However, as the leader, I accept full responsibility for my team."

"A noble and honorable intention." His voice softens a little. "But nobility and honor do not heal injuries. Someone could have been killed— on either side of the battle."

"We understand that, sir." Adam's voice remains steady and contrite. "We will accept whatever consequences you feel we deserve."

"I understand there was a fifth in your group who undertook the *Nagul Uzu'gor* and lost." I go still in my seat.

"...Yes, sir." Adam sounds like he doesn't know half of what was just said. I hope I can keep it that way.

"Captain Ironstorm, are you in attendance today?" Of course he is.

"Attention." The order is whispered to me a split second before he stands.

For two long seconds, my mind goes blank, but then I remember his words to me earlier. If I want to help my friends, I need this guy to like me. So I stand up straight, hoping I'm slipping my feet and arms into position casually enough for Adam to not notice. Because he is of course staring *right* at me.

"Councilman Bloodfield." Captain Ironstorm gives a small salute that I think about copying, but since that's not something he's told me to do, I keep my head up and wait for what's next.

"How has your new charge been adjusting?" Bloodfield is looking at me too.

"It has been a challenge at times, sir, but nothing I cannot handle." I can hear the smirk. Glad my fists are already clenched. "Given the circumstances, he has been doing quite well."

"Knowing him for a few days now, how do you feel about these other humans, his companions?" He gestures to the three caged in the back. "It was your men they injured."

"I think they are travelers who made a very unfortunate mistake, Councilman." It sounds like he's trying to talk us up at least. "I hold no grudges against them nor do my men. I believe they are willing to learn from and accept responsibility for their actions. David certainly is."

I think that was a compliment. The room is silent other than the judge rifling through more papers. So much rifling. Everyone not green is holding their breath. After what feels like an eternity, Bloodfield faces Adam once more.

"Though your crimes are great, I understand the confusion and anxiety that comes with being in an unknown place so far from your home." Maybe he does like us a little. "While you are here, I suggest you reflect on the idea that we are not the monsters your people make us out to be. The four of you are to spend two months in the Yash'ak Cr'hol Labor Camp, to begin tomorrow."

I can see Adam's mouth hanging open, but he's at a loss for words. So am I. *Labor camp?* Redwish walks over and starts talking to him while the guard returns him to the cell with the others. Bloodfield remains seated, but most of the other orcs in the room stand up and make their exit. The two of us are still standing, and I turn to Ironstorm, a question already on my lips.

"What happens now?" I try not to sound panicked.

"They will be taken back to the station for the night and then in the morning brought to the camp to be processed," he replies casually. "Redwish is likely explaining everything to them now."

"Can I talk to them again?" I ask hopefully.

"I am afraid not." He shakes his head, looking apologetic. "We can talk more on the way home."

I nod numbly, the leash suddenly feeling heavy hanging from my neck. By the time we're outside, it feels like the collar is choking me.

"I know it sounds bad, but all things considered, two months is..." Ironstorm starts talking, but I'm not really paying attention. My mind is stuck on my friends and their sentences.

Two months in a labor camp? Two months in a prison I would understand but a *labor camp*? Labor camps, also known as work camps, are where prisoners of war are sent to be *worked to death*. It doesn't matter how long your sentence is because there's never any intention of actually letting you go. They just work you until there's nothing left. They were discussed in detail in our history lessons at the academy, but more than that, my dad and granddad would talk about them all the time because my granddad spent *four months* in one. His brother, my great-uncle, died before they could be rescued. And now my friends are going to die in one too. I can't just...leave them in there. I have to—

"—avid. David?" Ironstorm nudges my shoulder to get my attention. "Are you alright?"

"Sorry." I look around and see we are almost home already. "Just preoccupied."

"I understand." He gives me a sympathetic smile. "You are concerned for them. Two months is still a long time."

"Yeah." That feels like an understatement. "I'm still not even sure I understand what exactly happened."

"It is a lot of new information to process." Just as we reach the front door, a voice behind us gives us pause.

"*Kritar Uzi'gar!*" I catch something being said from across the street and a few doors down. It's the woman whose kid I saved, Mrs. Skycaller I think is her name, and she is holding a cloth-covered basket.

The two orcs speak animatedly before the woman turns to me, saying something as she shoves the basket into my arms. Then she quickly pulls me in for a hug and kisses my forehead.

"Um, thank you?" I hope she knows I can't understand her.

"She wanted to thank you for saving her daughter. She baked you something." Ironstorm translates for me, then presumably does the same for her. After a few more words, a smile, and another hug, she leaves us.

"Come. We will make some lunch, you can ask me some questions, and then we can keep your mind focused on other things."

I nod and follow him inside. I leave the basket in the kitchen while we disrobe in the bedroom, both in our underwear, though his solid black briefs certainly cover more than my red jockstrap. Then we are in the kitchen. Starting to think this guy might specifically have a thing for cooking in his underwear.

"First, let us see what we have here." The cloth covering the top of the basket is lifted off, revealing the contents. "Ah, *dar-buk*." He smiles down.

In the basket are at least a few dozen of these small, round, cake-bun things. They look fluffy.

"These are delicious. They are made with two kinds of flour: wheat and corn." He takes one out of the basket, tearing it in half. "Sweetened with tree sap and then stuffed with a jam made from berries that grow in the forest."

He shows me the gooey red contents of one half, before moving it toward my mouth. I'm getting a little too used to being fed, but I still take a bite. Mmm. They *are* fluffy. And sweet, especially the jam. *Damn.*

"Those are good." He lets me finish the half I've bitten into. "What did you call them again?"

"Dar-buk." He recovers the baked goodies and sets the basket to the side. "We can have more after lunch."

I pout as he moves about the kitchen. She made those for me! Then I remember that while I'm sitting here basically eating cookies, my friends are waiting to begin what will likely be the roughest two months of their lives. *Fuck, what am I doing here?* I can't just stand by and let this happen. I have to think of something. Anything.

...Right after lunch.

Chapter Twelve

"I am making soup for lunch—a family recipe." Ironstorm is already grabbing a cutting board and vegetables. "My father says that a good soup can heal wounds of the heart."

"Did your father do a lot of cooking?" I don't think my dad was ever in the kitchen.

"Still does. Insists on it. This is his stock, in fact." He holds up a jar of brown liquid retrieved from over the stove. Then he pauses, giving me a faux-serious look. "If I give you a knife for cutting vegetables, can I trust you not to try and kill me when my back is turned?"

Oh, he's got jokes. "I dunno. Got any ancient ruins around here I can raid first? It'll help sate my bloodlust."

With a chuckle, he retrieves a knife, handing it to me handle-first. "Go ahead and wash those and then you can start." He gestures to the vegetables on the counter as he moves to light the stove. "Seeing as you managed to tune out everything I said on the walk home, do you have questions about what happened today?"

We're using some vegetables I actually know this time. I grab a carrot to start with while I think, not really knowing where to begin. "Was that a normal... Is trial the right word?"

"Trial is accurate." He retrieves some meat from the icebox, some kind of poultry. "Other than the arrested parties being from so far away, that was fairly standard."

"How come Redwish was the only one who talked to the ju—coun-cilman?" I thought it was weird that no one else did any talking.

"Because your friends did not contest the accusations, another advo-cate was not needed." He joins me on the counter where we both begin to cut our respective ingredients. "Had they fought against it, or if I or any of the other rangers involved had sought any personal reparations, there would have been someone there to represent us or the city."

"What makes the councilman a councilman?" That sounded dumb.

"He is a member of the Tribal Council." Finished with his cutting, Ironstorm moves over to light a pan on the stove. "Six orcs who form our head of government. In addition to making decisions for the city as a group, they also oversee trials like the one today individually."

"How did they land that job?" I've finished with the carrots and move on to some potatoes.

"It is an elected position, held for three years." I hear the sizzle of the meat hitting the pan to my right. "At the end of each year, two of the seats are made vacant and new council members are voted in."

"Are those six responsible for every trial?" Doesn't seem enough to go around.

"No, there are other officials who also oversee trials, usually related to the position they were appointed to." He looks over to see me finishing with the vegetables. "Add those to the pot when you are finished."

"I didn't even realize potatoes and carrots grew over here." I do as requested, gathering all the chopped veggies onto the cutting board and walking it over to the pot, scraping them in with my knife.

"Originally they did not. Potatoes originated somewhere south of here." Ironstorm removes the pan from the fire. "They were imported to your part of the world some time ago. Same as carrots were brought here."

I didn't know any of that. I step away from the pot so he can do what he needs. "What kind of meat is that?"

"A large bird found in the forests. We call it a *lum'tik'bra*, but I believe I have heard an elf call it a 'turkey.'" I stand back as he adds the seared meat to the pot now.

Never heard of it. "What's the direct translation of the word you used?" Can't be better than *sad wood*.

"Large gargling bird." I was wrong. I can't hold in the snort of laughter, which Ironstorm copies as he turns to the shelf with the spices and begins pulling things down. "Any more questions about this morning?"

"Not really, I guess." I don't know if I was hoping for a loophole, but I've got nothing. "They'll be taken to the work camp in the morning?"

"Yes, first thing, I am afraid." He gives me a sad smile.

"Then what? They start working?"

"More or less." He shrugs, looking apologetic. "Though I cannot say I know exactly what they will be put to work doing."

"Great." I try not to sound bitter.

"They will be alright." He tries to look hopeful. "You seem like a resilient group."

"Thanks." Being resilient in a labor camp isn't exactly something any of us trained for, so forgive me if I don't hold my breath. Adam and Liss might stand a chance, but Nate and Corrine won't make it a week. Any hope I had when I woke up this morning is slowly fading into nothingness. Even if I had a plan, how would I possibly get to them? In the morning, they'll be taken from that crappy little cell outside and taken away. I spent maybe an hour or two there, but I can still remember the anxiety I felt while I waited to see if I would even be given the chance to get out of there. Silently praying that the guard would return to unlock the cell. They don't even have normal locks on all the doors. "What was up with the door on the cell during the trial? When Adam was being pulled from the cell, the guard touched his wrist to it and it opened. I think I remember that happening at the jail too. No visible lock. What was that?"

"Hmm?" I get a confused look for a moment as he puts the spices back on the shelf. Then I see something click. "Ah, *that* is a recent and *very* helpful magical invention. Let me show you."

After washing his hands, Ironstorm moves into the living room with me following behind him. He opens the drawer in the table by the front door, pulling out a leather wristband. "What does this look like to you?"

"A wristband?" It looks like what I'd seen the guards wearing.

"Correct. It is also a key." He wraps and buckles the strap to his arm. He's smiling like a kid with a new toy. "They are enchanted so that when they are worn and touched to a corresponding lock, it opens. The magic in each one is tied to only function when worn by the person it was created for. If someone else were to wear this and use it, nothing would happen. A very effective way of preventing break-ins and theft."

"Sounds really secure." I don't think I've heard of anything like that. Certainly not back home.

"We are in the process of converting all the locks in the ranger head-quarters and the tribal hall to use them." He begins taking off the "key" strap. "Which I am very much looking forward to having completed, because then I can stop carrying *these* around." He deposits the wrist strap back into the drawer and pulls out an almost comically large ring of keys.

I can see how that might be annoying and impractical. I can only imagine the number of doors and locks you'd have to keep track of, all the offices and equipment rooms and cells. Like the outdoor cells we were kept in. That orc guard used a key when he let me out. I guess those haven't been converted yet.

"Would you mind watching the soup while I use the restroom?" He starts down the hall to the bathroom.

"On it." I nod. I can watch soup.

I stand by the stove, stirring the pot slowly while my mind wanders. I know I should just let it go, but I now can't stop thinking about those keys. The key to our cell is on that ring. It might take some time to figure out which one, but it could be done, right? I sigh. I don't know why I'm even thinking about this. Even if I could do that, how exactly would I manage to steal the keys *and* sneak out without Ironstorm noticing I'm gone?

I shake the thoughts of a jailbreak from my mind. I'm here to watch soup. I pull the wooden spoon from the pot and bring it to my lips for a small taste. Not bad. Other than the veggies and the "turkey," I didn't really pay attention to what else he added. I look down and see two jars of spices that haven't been put back yet. I open the lids to see that one is pepper, and the other is... Shit, I know this one. We had it in the kitchen at the academy. It looks like short dried blades of grass. Maybe I should just ask.

I pick up the jars to return them to their shelf, trying to remember which side was spices and which side was potion ingredients. He really does need to organize this. I end up sticking them wherever they fit for now, and as I do, a familiar looking jar catches my eye. The potion ingredients. Specifically, the one I know contains hypnograss. I look over at the door and the table holding the ring of keys. *Could I...?*

No, I mean, how would I even give it to him? I look at the pot of soup. We're going to share that, possibly down to the same spoon and bowl. That wouldn't work.

Stop it, David. Let it go.

But I *can't.*

Quickly and without thinking about it too hard, I open the jar and grab a few leaves. Putting it back, I look around quickly for some place to hide them. My eyes settle on one of the bookcases, and I quickly sprint over. I pull out the book I read yesterday on sword technique and drop the flat leaves between two pages, closing it before returning it to the shelf. I then move quickly back to my station in front of the stove, stirring the soup like I didn't just do any of that.

Why did I do that, exactly? I still don't even know how I'd give it to him. Don't even know how much it would take to knock him out. But there's this voice in the back of my head, telling me that if I don't do *something,* my friends are in trouble. Ironstorm rejoins me a minute later, taking over soup duty for me. I don't really have anything else on my mind, at least not that I'm going to ask him about.

It only takes a few more minutes until lunch is ready. To my surprise, I actually get my own bowl and spoon. I even get to sit in a chair at the table. I want to ask why, but I'm worried he'll take it back. I think I might know, though. He feels bad. He knows I'm still thinking about my friends and is doing what he said and keeping my mind occupied.

Which he continues to do after lunch when we go for a run an hour later, and then when he insists I take a long, hot bath afterward. He's really going out of his way to make me feel better, which just makes me feel all the worse about what I've been thinking about. I'm a little glad I don't have the opportunity to do it.

At least until dinner.

"Do you like beer?" The question catches me off guard, and I look up from the book in my lap. I've been reading the same paragraph over and over for nearly half an hour, my mind constantly pulled to other things. I'm not even sure what this book is about, something about people living in the mountains.

"I like it." I mean, I never really drank it for the taste, but who doesn't like beer?

"A friend gifted me a batch he brewed himself. I have been looking for a reason to try it." He smiles. "Perhaps we can have it with dinner."

"This the kind of thing orcs usually toast to?" I make sure my tone sounds more playful than my words.

He rolls his eyes and stands, walking down the hall. I hear a door open, some rustling, and a door closing, then he's back with a small barrel in hand. It's like a mini keg, complete with a small spout. He places it on the counter before retrieving two mugs from a shelf. And there it is: my opportunity. My eyes drift from the mugs to the bookcase and back. I might actually be able to pull this off.

Maybe.

If I wanted to, that is.

Dinner is steak again. This is the second time we've had it since I got here, and I still haven't seen or heard a single cow in the area, or any other farm animals for that matter. He made it to cheer me up. And it works—food is a very easy way to get on my good side. And yet, I still feel like shit.

We both drink our beer with dinner, though I'm slower to down mine than he is. He refills both mugs after we finish eating, bringing them into the living room with us where he lights a fire. Really pulling out all the stops. He settles me on the couch, handing me my beer and putting his on the small table next to us before stepping over to the bookcase. The hairs on my neck stand up when I see his hand drift to the book I stashed the hypnograss in, but he passes over it, pulling a red book from the same shelf.

"I thought I might read aloud tonight," he announces as he walks back over to the couch. "Would you like that?"

"Sure." That does sound kinda nice.

It's the story of an old orc hero named Steelrun. The tale takes place four hundred years ago, though I'm not really clear if the story is real or made up. During that time, there were many different orcs tribes all fighting for dominance. Except Steelrun. He was a warrior, but he fought only to defend, not seeing the point in the senseless violence around him. A little cliché if you ask me, but I can get into it. The story begins in the camp Steelrun called home as they were preparing for another tribe to attack.

The two of us drink our beers as he reads. I sip mine slowly, not wanting even a small buzz. Just in case. Ironstorm, however, finishes his second glass just as the story is getting to the big battle scene. He gets up for another refill, and I let him top off my mug again. If things were just a little bit different, this could be really nice.

Before he gets back to reading, the two glasses of beer catch up with him, and he needs to use the bathroom again. And I have a split-second decision to make. If I go through with this, I'm not sure he'll be able to forgive me for it, and if I get caught, I sure as hell am gonna have a lot more than just a spanking to worry about. But if I don't do this and something happens to Adam, or Liss, or Corrine, I won't be able to forgive myself.

My glass is down, and I'm out of my seat as soon as I hear the door close, eyes already on the book. I tear it open, dropping the contents into my hand before quickly shoving it back in place. Then I'm back at the couch, crushing the dried leaves in my hand while standing over his mug. It crumbles easily enough with my fingers, but I really should've used a mortar to grind this down. No time, though. I take a breath. This is it. No turning back if I do this.

The sound of the toilet flushing makes the decision for me, and I turn my hand, dropping the bits of magical herb into the mug. I stir the liquid quickly with a finger, trying to get what's still floating on top to sink to the bottom. I hope that dissolves enough and the beer covers any weird taste. I have to remember not to lick my finger clean, wiping it on the couch as I hop back in my seat, doing my best to look like none of that just happened.

It works. I get a warm smile on his return, and he's got the book back in his hand, picking up where he left off. He sips his beer a second later, and I watch his face for any changes. But there's none; he just continues reading. I relax a little after that, ignoring the growing ball of guilt in my stomach. I'm no longer drinking my beer, only pretending, but Ironstorm downs about half of his before I start noticing the tell-tale signs of drowsiness. His eyes get a little droopy. Words are said slower. A few more sips in, he's practically slurring, and he even nods off once. Until finally...

"He held his sword aloft...ready to...strike..." The book falls gently into his lap as his form slumps back onto the couch, followed by the sound of light snoring.

I wait a moment, worried that any movement might wake him up. But the second I'm confident he's really out, I'm out of my seat and moving. I sprint to the bedroom, throwing open the chest with my clothes. I really wish I had something in black, but I end up going with dark brown pants and a dark blue shirt. I throw on some socks and my shoes (*damn, not gonna get those new boots now*) and look around for anything else that might be useful. I think about a sword but trekking through town with one of those on my back might look a little suspicious. I kinda wish he bought that bundle of rope at Brull's now because I don't see anything else that might be useful.

I've got a small window of time, so I move back out into the living room. Next is grabbing the ring of keys. I don't have a good place to hide them, so I end up sticking them down my waistband for now. After that, I put out the fire in the fireplace. I'm not a monster. I wouldn't let the house burn to the ground.

Just...drug its owner so I can steal his keys and break into the local jail.

I watch Ironstorm still passed out on the couch, and the guilt weighing on me feels even heavier. I think back to everything he's done to me the past week, the anger I've felt, the pain, the humiliation, trying to tell myself that I'm doing the right thing here. But looking at him also makes me remember things like cooking together, going on runs, waking up in bed together...

...The other stuff we've done in bed together.

I shake the thoughts from my head. *What are you doing, David?* None of this mattered before you got here, and none of it is going to matter after. The things you've had to do this past week aren't really you. Don't forget that the only reason you've gone along with any of it is because you didn't have a choice. This is what you've been waiting for: a chance to escape with all your friends.

I look around the room one last time. To see if I'm forgetting something, not for anything sentimental. I think about grabbing some food but not sure how practical that would be, especially when getting in and out of the jail. We can figure all that once we're out of this place. No turning back now. I'm doing this. I blow out the lanterns and walk out the front door.

It's dark outside and fairly quiet. The streets are mostly empty, and the people I see out pay me no mind. I keep my eyes to myself, one arm slightly stiff at my side as I try to minimize the sounds of the keys jangling under my waistband. I'm just a man out for a nice quiet stroll outside.

It's about a fifteen-minute walk to the jail, and I slow down once I see it a block in the distance. Time to try to find a way in. The walls outside are tall and made of solid, smooth stone. I walk on the opposite side of the street around the building, unsure of which wall is hiding the yard with the cells behind it. I think back to being led out of the building and figure it out easily enough, but finding a way to get over it is a lot harder.

It's the only building on the block and the streets are all so wide that jumping from another building isn't a possibility. There's a pole with a light atop on one corner, but it is also smooth so climbing it isn't an option either. At least not without getting noticed, probably. But other than putting on a disguise and going through the front door, that might be my only option. Paranoid about being on the street for this long, I duck into an alley to think things over.

The walls are too high for me to reach with a jump, though thankfully there's nothing along the top preventing entry. You'd figure some barbed wire or something, right? But that's a point in my favor. If I could jump from high enough on the pole with enough momentum, that might do it. I'm not a gymnast or anything, but when I was little, I climbed a *lot* of trees. Spending the last month in and out of the forest *after* all my skills in strength moved over into speed, some of that has come back to me. I think I have an idea.

I duck my head out onto the street, looking around for signs of anyone else. It seems I'm alone and that means showtime. I walk across the street and the only thing between me and the cell holding my friends is the wall in front of me. I turn so I face the light pole, putting the jail on my right. After one last look around, I take off running. As I move to the lamp pole, I bank left slightly so that I'm partially in the street.

This will be risky, but no riskier than saving a little girl from being run over, right?

I turn slightly, aiming for the edge of the wall on the corner with the light. I leap, connecting my right foot with the wall and pushing off to jump higher toward the pole. I grab on with both hands, swinging around the smooth surface once before kicking my legs up and vaulting myself at the wall. I just barely catch the edge as I come down, my feet dangling three or four feet from the ground.

Holy shit. I can't believe I pulled that off. I almost wish someone else was here to see that.

I quickly pull myself up, listening for the sounds of footsteps and making sure I'm alone before dropping to the ground. *Oof.* Alright, I *gotta* get new shoes after this. I creep silently through the rows, carefully peering down each alley to make sure I'm not seen. These first few structures don't look like cells, no wall of bars, just a single large door. Storage maybe?

After a couple more rows of that, I finally see the jail cells. There are twelve cells in each row, six on either side grouped together in twos with more alleys in between. They're all empty so far. I don't remember seeing or hearing anyone else out here during my very brief stay, but it still seems weird. I look at the main building, trying to suss out the location of my friends' cell. It's dark out here, the only light on this side of the fence coming from the building itself. After passing a few more rows, I finally see a familiar looking door at the end, the one I know leads inside. This is the row our cell was in!

Excited but still quiet, I pull the giant ring of keys from my waistband. I hold them steady in my hands, not wanting to risk a noise drawing any attention. Not sure from who, seeing as every cell I've passed has been completely empty, but better safe than sorry. I can see the cell the guys are in just up ahead. I can't *wait* to see the look on their—

Their cell is empty.

I look around, making sure I have the right one. I look in the cell behind me, I look in the cells next to me, then I start running up and down the rows of cells looking for *anyone*. They're *all* empty. I go back to the cell they're supposed to be in.

They're already gone. They haven't been here since this morning. They probably took them to the camp right after—

I jump at the sound of a door opening to my right. *Fuck*, somebody's coming. I try to run around to the side of the cell as fast as I can, praying the darkness gives me enough cover to hide from whoever just came out here. I mold my body to the wall, afraid to even breathe. Things are silent so I think I might be in the clear.

"*Ati gat?*" Shit. I hear footsteps move toward me before they stop abruptly. Then they seem to go in the other direction, and I hear the door being opened again. Phew, he's going back inside.

"*Jiak dez, giz Kritar Ghun'zuf!*"

Shitshitshitshitshit. I don't know what he just said, but it couldn't have been good. He's not moving, and the door is still open.

I quietly make my way back to the far side of the cells, tucking the ring of keys back into my waistband to free up my hands. As I do, I hear a second voice start talking to the first and another set of feet stepping outside. Great. I need to get out of here *now*. I make my way into the far corner, staring at the wall as if that will do anything to it. *How* do I get out of here? I may not have thought this all the way through.

I peer around the corner down the row, and I can see a flicker of a light at the other end moving closer. I have to get to the other side of the yard, put more distance between us so I can think of something. I peer around the next row only to be met with a second light, and I can see the orc attached to this one. I can hear the first one getting closer. I don't have a choice.

"*Ayah!*" The orc shouts at me as I sprint across. I hear both sets of feet break into runs as they give chase. *Think David...*

The walls are still too high for me to climb, but the cells are shorter. No time to hesitate, I repeat my wall-jumping trick from outside, this time managing to catch the edge of the top of the cell. *Ha!* I pull myself up as fast as I can. I'm in the clear!

Then a hand wraps around my ankle and yanks me backward.

I shout as I fall and land on my ass, but I'm up in a flash. I take off again and duck down another row of cells when a *massive* body tackles me to the ground from behind. Hands grab my wrists as I struggle to get free, the weight on top of me not making it easy to do anything, even breathe. The body kneels up, pulling my hands behind my back, and as I hear the two voices talking again, I feel manacles being locked around my wrists. *Dammit!*

No longer being held to the ground, I'm pulled up and turned around to face my new captors. I don't recognize them, but they sure seem to recognize me. Actually, scratch that, one of them—the one that didn't tackle me to the ground—is the same orc I talked to when I was in the cell here, with the bald head, big beard, and huge tusks. The one who took me to the arena. The other guy I don't know. He's taller than the orc holding me, a little thinner too but still way bigger than I am. He's got dark brown hair in nearly the same style as Ironstorm, and his bright blue eyes flicker in the light of the torch in his hand.

"*Avakesh va Kritar Uzi'gar.*" The orc holding me sighs once he gets a good look at my face. I think I actually recognized some of those words.

"Where are my friends?" I'm not in any position to be making demands, but that hasn't stopped me so far.

The orc says nothing, only narrows his eyes, looking me up and down. His eyes lock onto my right hip and the metal key ring poking out from it. I try to swing out of his reach, but it's no use; he pulls the keys from my waistband. His face looks even more displeased than it did a second ago. But rather than say anything, he turns to the orc behind me.

"*Kaj'ik Avakesh katu, mibaj va Kritar.*" The orc turns and jogs away, the sound of the door signaling his full exit. I don't know where he's going, but I have some ideas.

I'm fucked.

I'm marched inside the building and led into an office with a desk. My jailor walks me to the side of it and forces me to my knees, making it clear that I am to remain there while he takes a seat and we wait. It's at least twenty minutes before I hear the sounds of someone approaching. The orc in a chair stands just as Captain Ironstorm bursts into the room, looking furious. I want to stand, but his gaze pins me to the floor.

"*What is going on here?!*" Yeah, he's pissed. I open my mouth to again demand for my friend's location, but the new orc enters the room behind him and cuts me off.

"Orim went out back to grab some equipment and saw something. Called me out to help him look, and we caught this one making his escape." He crosses his arms. "Not sure how he got in, but he nearly made it back out. I found *these* on him when we grabbed him." He holds out the ring of keys, hanging from his two fingers.

Ironstorm takes the keys in hand, looking from them to me, his face souring even further. The hand holding the keys clenches into a fist, and I half expect a solid ball of metal to be sitting there when he reopens it. "Why would you do this, David?"

"Where are my friends?" I demand again through gritted teeth.

"In their cells." Ironstorm's eyes narrow.

"Bullshit." I spit back. "Every cell out there is completely empty."

"Their cells are *inside*." He looks incredulous. "We don't keep people locked up outside overnight."

"You kept us out there when we first got here!" I shout from my spot on the floor.

"Because we are in the middle of changing the locks on the cells, as I told you *earlier today*!" he shouts back at me.

"I tell him cells being fixed." Great, the third orc wants to pile on too.

"Prove it!" People can say whatever the fuck they want. Doesn't mean I believe them.

With a huff, Ironstorm yanks me to stand before roughly pushing me out the office door and across the hall.

"Remain silent," he warns with a growl before pressing his wristband to the lock and opening the door.

This new room is more of a long hallway with barred cells on either side. We walk silently down the hall, and I see most of the cells are empty. There's one that holds a snoring orc, but it's the next two that contain all four of my friends, Nate and Adam on one side and Liss and Corrine on the other. They're all asleep, but Adam stirs as we approach.

"Nnng, David?" he asks groggily. "Ev'ry thing okay?"

"Yes, go back to sleep," Ironstorm tells him, quickly turning me around and leading me back into the office.

"Satisfied?" he sneers, pushing me into the center of the room.

I don't have a response. He wasn't lying about my friends being inside, and I guess "Orim," or whoever that other orc is, wasn't lying on that first day either.

But so what? That doesn't change anything that is about to happen to them. A work camp is a work camp. I couldn't just do nothing!

Clearly unsatisfied with my lack of an answer, Ironstorm turns to orc #2. "Thank you for coming to get me. The evening is a little fuzzy, but I can help fill out your arrest report with what I can remember—"

"Actually, I'm not sure an arrest is really necessary," the more well-spoken orc cuts him off. It's not? "Orim and I are the only ones to see him. Perhaps it would be better if you took him home and handled this yourself, sir."

The two of them share a look that I can't quite read before Ironstorm gives him a nod, straightening his posture. "Yes, I think you may be correct. Deputy Rockfang, Officer Broadedge, thank you again. I shall see you back here in a few days." Both orcs salute him before he turns to me.

What just happened?

"*Come.*" He grabs me by the shoulder and turns me around to remove the manacles. Then after grabbing me by the collar like a dog scruffing a pup, I am led out of the room and out of the building. The few orcs I see on our way out don't seem to notice us. As we start the walk home, I can't help myself, needing to know what exactly is going to happen.

"Wha—" I am yanked to a stop and turned, an angry orc in my face.

"Not one *word*, David," Ironstorm growls at me before pushing me down the road.

Getting arrested might have been the safer option.

Chapter Thirteen

The walk back to the house is icy. With his hand still tight on my shirt, I can feel the rage radiating off of Ironstorm in waves. My mind scrambles to think of an excuse, a way out of this, an escape route, but I know anything I come up with is only going to make things worse. I'm as good as dead.

When we arrive, he opens the door and roughly pushes me inside. I find my balance before I land flat on my face, standing against the back of the couch, unsure of what to do or where to go. Ironstorm slams the door behind him, angrily stomping his way past me. He paces, running his hand down his face before finally turning his gaze to me.

"I—"

"Why would you do this, David? How could you possibly think that—" He cuts himself off, going silent for a moment. "Wrong question. *How* did you do this?"

"Uh, I uh..." *Thinkthinkthink.*

His eyes wander around the room, the fireplace, the bookcases, the couch, before finally landing on the half-full mug on the side table. His eyes go wide, flitting back and forth between me and the beer as he walks over to pick it up. He brings it to his face, inspecting the amber liquid still inside. Wordlessly, he walks it to the kitchen and grabs a small white towel. Standing over the sink, he holds the towel in one hand and slowly pours the remaining beer into it. When it's empty, he stretches the fabric of the towel as he inspects it closely. I know exactly what he's looking for. I really should have looked for a mortar...

"You *drugged* me?!" he roars, throwing the wet towel into the sink and quickly crossing the room to me.

"I'm sorry!" I cry out, panicking. "I wasn't—"

"Speak again and I will gag you." He clamps his hand over my mouth, staring me down menacingly. "There is *nothing* I want to hear from you."

Grabbing me by the shirt collar, Ironstorm walks me down the hallway, opening the spare room on the left. He pushes me inside and shoves me at the empty bed onto my stomach. With my arms still cuffed behind me, I have no chance of fighting back. I turn onto my side so I can look at him. The room is dark, the light from the doorway blocked by the silhouette of his body.

"You will remain here until I decide what to do with you." He sounds disgusted with me, and for some reason, that knowledge makes me feel even worse. He shuts the door without another word, the sound of the lock clicking signaling I won't be going anywhere.

I look at the door, but there's no point in checking. I roll onto my stomach and climb the rest of the way onto the bed. Might as well get comfortable since I don't think I'll be leaving anytime soon. Not that it's easy with steel manacles cuffed tightly to my wrists. I lay there in the dark room alone. My mind can't help but compare my current situation with that of my friends, though from what I remember their sleeping arrangements were a lot more comfortable than mine are tonight.

Eventually, my thoughts turn to Ironstorm. What exactly did he mean by "decide what to do with" me? My stomach starts to twist itself into knots thinking about what he might be planning. The last time he punished me, he went out of his way to take it easy on me. Can't imagine that will be the case this time. No way is he just spanking me for this. Maybe he'll whip me, or just beat me to a pulp. What if he breaks my leg because I keep trying to run? At some point, before I start hyperventilating, I pass out.

It's dark in the forest, the leaves on the trees rustling in the wind. From the ground, I can see the moon, large and full in the sky. A twig snaps in the distance, and I watch as a large black wolf slinks through the trees. It looks featureless in the darkness, all except its red eyes: two hot points of light surrounded by an inky, canine-shaped void. As it approaches, it feels like those eyes are burning a hole straight through to my soul. Hungry.

I wake up from the strange dream to more darkness. Whatever sleep I did manage to get was fitful. My arms are sore, still cuffed behind my back and kept in this weird position all night. I also need to pee. I have no idea what time it is, but the thin strip of light coming from under the door tells me that it's at least the next day. I hear the faint sounds of movement on the other side of the door, but it's too far for me to pick out anything specific.

I'm just about to try passing out again when I hear the sound of the lock being opened, the shadows of two feet visible under the door. I squint when the door opens, my eyes not used to the bright daylight. Ironstorm stands in the doorway, a plate in one hand and a cup in the other. He moves near the bed, placing both items on the small table next to me before reaching for me on the bed. He walks me to the bathroom, standing me in front of the toilet. After I relieve myself and he pulls my pants back up, he walks me back to the room, pushing me back on the bed before turning to leave again.

"Could you uncuff my hands?" My voice is rough from not being used. I'm not sure he hears me until I see him stop. "Please."

He sighs but turns around and walks back to me. He doesn't look happy, but I'm not sensing any specific annoyance over my request. I roll onto my stomach to give him access to my wrists, the sound of keys jangling followed by the lock on the manacles clicking. I roll onto my back and sit up so that I can face him.

"Thank you," I respond softly, the threat of being gagged still hanging in the air. He says nothing as he turns and exits the room, locking the door behind him.

It's difficult in the dark, but I manage to carefully feel for the plate and cup in the dark without spilling anything. Nothing more than bread and water. Wonderful. At least he's still feeding me, for now. I finish eating fairly quickly and push the empty cup and dish back onto the table. Without anything else to do, I lay back, trying to think about anything other than my impending doom or the fact that Adam and everyone else have probably already been taken to the work camp. I wonder what Mike's up to? I don't even remember what day it is. *Terraday?* He's probably in class right now, studying his spell books or something.

At some point, I doze off again, reawakening when I hear the door being opened again. I sit up a little faster than I need to, the both of us staring at each other silently for a few moments. He steps back, crooking two fingers at me and moving back down the hall, expecting me to follow.

"Sit." He points at the couch when I enter the living room and I take my seat.

He paces back and forth in front of me, occasionally running his fingers through his hair. He's obviously still angry, but a lot of the rage from last night seems to have settled. He's fully dressed, we both are, but he's at least not wearing the same thing he was last night. I don't dare open my mouth to complain. Finally, he comes to a stop and turns to me.

"I want to know why you did it, David." He locks his eyes on mine. "What possible reasoning do you have to justify your actions?"

"Because you sent my friends to a work camp." My voice is steadier than I would have expected, but I am nothing if not confident in my convictions. "I know what those are and what really happens there."

"What are you talk—"

"Don't play dumb!" He doesn't look happy that I cut him off, but he lets me continue. "Those places are where you send prisoners to work themselves to death. Where you use them until there's nothing left. We both know two months there is as good as a death sentence."

"Spirits, I swear this boy is going to drive me insane." Ironstorm sighs at my outburst, pinching the bridge of his nose. "David, I can assure you that your friends are safe and will continue to be safe as they serve out the terms of their incarceration."

"Bullshit. Tell that to my dead great-uncle." He cocks an eyebrow at that, so I continue. "He and my grandfather were captured after a battle and sent to a 'labor camp.' For months they were forced to do things like mining or logging or hunting dangerous fucking monsters. Barely fed, made to work until they wasted away to nothing." I speak bitterly to the floor. I was told this story so many times growing up. "My grandfather barely made it out alive."

"The term 'labor camp' only refers to the fact that your friends will be *laboring* while incarcerated." He sounds frustrated. "It is different from a normal prison because they will actually be leaving the site most days to do things like farming, or construction, or sewing. The administrators at the camp will determine what their skills will be best used for. They will even earn a wage for their work, which will go to paying whatever fines or damages are owed, and they will receive anything leftover upon their release. Your friends were lucky to be sent there at all; it is normally out of the question for anyone convicted of a violent crime."

Ironstorm stands in front of me, arms crossing his chest, waiting for a response I don't have. I sit there silently, staring at my hands. If what he's saying is true, that doesn't sound so bad... But how do I know it's true? Aside from the fact that he hasn't actually lied to me yet.

"I tried to explain all of this to you yesterday when we were walking home. I can only assume that the ideas in your head are a result of whatever *fucked* up system you humans use." I think that might be the first time I've heard him curse. "I can tell you with confidence that here *things do not work that way*. What would be the point in punishing someone if they are not given the chance to survive afterward? As a general rule, we try not to starve or maim our prisoners, let alone allow them to *die*."

"Well, I didn't know that okay!?" How could I have?

"You *never* know, David. You never even try to learn! You just *act*." He's not having any of my excuses. "You never think your actions all the way through. What exactly was your plan here? Say you did manage to break your friends out of their cells and get out of the jail without anyone noticing. Then what? The five of you would make the two-and-a-half-mile trek to the edge of the city unnoticed? Somehow sneak past the guards posted at the gates *and* the ranger patrols in the forest outside?"

"Let us say that somehow, the five of you manage to pull all of that off. *Then what?*" He continues to dismantle my plan. "You have no money, no food, and no weapons. The nearest human settlement is a three-day hike. Every last person you know is either in a jail cell or half a world away. So again, I find myself asking: what was your plan, David? What has been your plan for *any* of your escape attempts?"

"I would have figured it out!" I snap, standing so I can yell in his face. "Why does it even matter now? It didn't work and my friends are gone. Nothing happened. Your buddy was happy to let me go."

"He did not do that for *you*, David," he grits out, punctuating his sentence by pushing me back onto the couch, venom dripping off his tongue. "He did that for *me*. How do you think it would look if it got out that four days after taking you in, you managed to subdue me, rob me, and break into our jail? How do you think my superiors would react to that news?"

His career would be as good as over, probably.

"That is not to say you do not have anything to thank him for. You sincerely do not seem to grasp the seriousness of what you did tonight." His voice is starting to sound a little like my dad's now. *Yikes.* "You drugged me, a captain, a high-ranking government official. You then stole my keys, keys to a building in which we house alleged criminals. You then proceeded to break into that building intent on releasing four *convicted* criminals. Individually those are all already grievous crimes, but together? Even I would not be able to protect you." His voice shakes a little as he finishes. "David, they could *execute* you for something like this."

I let his words sink in. It's not like I didn't know that what I was doing was serious. I'm still not sure I would have done anything differently. "Look, I'm sorry, but I don't know what else you expect from me. As far as I know, you're keeping me here for the rest of my life. Being a slave was never very high on the list of things I wanted to do."

"I have seen how humans treat their slaves." The fuck he has! Outlawing slavery was one of the first things Lutheria did when it was founded. "You have slept in a warm bed every night and eaten better than you have in weeks. I even bought you a new wardrobe."

"Oh good, so I'm a slave with extra benefits." I roll my eyes. "Except things like feeding myself, or wearing clothes when I want to, or sleeping in my own bed."

"Just because in human cities you—"

"*Ohmygod*, I don't know if this has somehow escaped your notice, but *I am a human*. One who has spent the last twenty years living in *human* cities surrounded by other *humans* and generally being immersed in *human* culture. You know, because I'm a *fucking human!*" I stand from the couch again to shout in his face. "I'm sorry that I don't always get how things work around here, but the way you explain something and then just expect me to accept it and ignore *everything I've ever known* isn't as helpful as you seem to think it is!"

I continue because why not? I'm on a roll. "I get it. You live in this perfect city with its perfect people and your perfect job, and then me and my friends come in and start blasting fire everywhere and fuck it all up. I am well aware of just how much I *don't* have my shit together. If I did, I wouldn't have left everyone and everything I know behind two months ago just to end up stuck here turned into your fucktoy!"

"You would not be here as my *fucktoy* if you had not chosen to challenge me in the first place!" I can tell my comments have him bristled. His fists are clenched. "You are not here because you were 'blasting fire everywhere.' You are here because you broke onto our land intent on ransacking a temple and then attacked my group when we tried to stop you! This was not a simple skirmish. One of my men had almost all of the skin on his arm burned off. Another broke his leg in two places! And after you were arrested for all of that, rather than accept your punishment, you decided to take things further and challenged me personally to a fight to the death!"

"We both know I wasn't going to kill you." I roll my eyes again. "You even said it yourself: I could have if I wanted to. You were face first on the ground, and all it would have taken was a quick jab to the neck. But

I didn't, because—and this may come as a shock to you—*I'm not a shitty person*. Killing someone, even for my own freedom, is about as high on the list of shit I wanna do as being a slave. So when I had the chance to finish you off, even when I thought it meant me and my friends going free, I couldn't do it. So could you maybe stop being *pissed off* at me for it?"

"Just because you hesitated does not mean you would not have done it." He crosses his arms and puffs out his chest. "No one forced you to challenge me. You still walked into that arena fully intent on killing me."

"Yeah, and when you accepted my challenge, I thought you were doing the same thing. I thought that maybe knowing that the other person was also trying to kill me would make things easier." If only out of self-preservation, I figured. "Surprise! It didn't. I'd like to see you wake up in a jail cell thousands of miles from home to find two of your *best* friends are missing. You might find it a little difficult to not freak out and make some rash decisions."

"Rash decisions? You nearly killed me!" he shouts in my face.

"*And you made me your fucking slave!*" I scream the words and he winces. "From the second I met you, you have beaten, molested, and humiliated me. You can dress it up however you want, tell yourself that I deserve it, even make me *scream* and beg for it, but none of that changes the fact that at the end of the day, I never asked for any of it. You *forced* it on me."

"I hardly think that—"

"No!" I am so tired of him justifying this shit. "You keep acting like I'm crazy for not just rolling over and smiling about the fact that I'm your slave. Like there's something *wrong* with me. Everything I've done has been out of survival because as you have so helpfully pointed out, I don't have any other options. I had a life before all this, a life I plan on getting back to!"

Ironstorm goes quiet at that, his chest significantly less puffed up, not looking me in the eye. "I was never going to keep you here permanently, David."

"Great, so you keep me here a few years until—"

"A few months," he cuts me off, looking at me again. "I only intended to keep you until your friends were released."

Things are silent between us for a moment. "Why didn't you tell me that?"

"What reason did I have to?" He stares me down. "From the *moment* I met you, you have been nothing short of an unrepentant antagonistic *prick*. For all the indignities you have suffered, you seem to forget that the only person you have to blame for being in this situation is yourself."

"I told you the guy who cast the fire——"

"We are not talking about your friend, David. We are talking about *you*." He starts to close the distance between us. "Or did the blow to your head make you forget about how the rest of your group charged us right after the fire was thrown? How you came at me personally? No one forced you to do that. Just like no one forced you to trespass on our land and no one forced you to challenge me. *You* made all those choices, David, and all you have done since is try to shirk any responsibility to avoid the consequences!"

"Because if I knew that *this*," I gesture back and forth between us, "was one of the consequences, I never would have challenged you in the first place!" We're just yelling at each other now.

Ironstorm rolls his eyes and shakes his head at that. "So you keep saying. What *exactly* were you told about the ritual? How did you even know about its existence to begin with?"

"Redwish told me about it." Only after I really pressed him for it though. "He said that if I challenged you and won, me and my friends would go free. If I lost... Well, he didn't actually say anything there, just let me assume the worst and my mind went to death. There was no mention of sex or being a slave. Not to mention that if I knew what the actual rules were, I never would have hesitated and won. But instead, here we are." I sink onto the couch, crossing my own arms. "I wish you had just fucking killed me."

He winces again. Okay, maybe I said that just to be hurtful, but this is one of the first times it feels like I have any power between us. "When Redwish came to issue your challenge, I was going to say no. I saw no reason to accept. But before I could answer, he launched into a frustrated tirade. Said that from the moment you woke up, he found you to be rude, demanding, and possibly even prejudiced against orcs." I bristle at the description but find myself unable to deny it. "He told me that while he did not think you would be a threat, I still needed to be cautious because you would do or say anything if it meant sparing yourself. That I should not trust you. He did not say anything about you being unaware of what would happen if you lost. He *certainly* did not tell me you thought it to be a fight to the death."

"Well, he's the only reason I did." Even if he didn't like me, I don't understand why he would do that. I really could have killed someone.

"I believe you." Ironstorm sighs and crosses his arms. "While possible, I find it difficult to believe that Advocate Redwish would make an error of omission of this magnitude. Twice: a different one for each of us. Something is not right here."

I sit there in silence while he stands for two, three, four minutes. He's thinking, but I don't know what to do. I'm not really sure what I expect from him now after saying all that. I don't think we can go back to the way things were.

"Come with me." He gestures for me to get off the couch. I follow him down the hall to the guest room door again.

"Oh, come on!" He's going to lock me in there again.

"It is only temporary," he assures me, though his voice doesn't sound very convincing. "There are some things I need to discuss with others, things I need to think on. I will return in a few hours."

"You can't just lock me in a dark room when you don't want to deal with me." If this is going to be my new existence, I'd like to at least be able to see. "Can you give me a light or something?"

"One moment." Ironstorm goes back into the living room and returns holding an already lit lantern in one hand and a book in the other. He hands them both to me. "I will be back before dinner."

"Thanks." The sarcasm drips from my voice as I take the objects.

I walk in the room of my own accord, placing the lantern on the table and hopping onto the bed, book in hand. I open and pretend to start reading, not looking up when I hear the door being closed. As soon I hear the lock click, I throw the book down in a huff. I'm feeling a little like a bratty teenager, but whatever. I needed to say all of that. I just wish I had some idea of what he's going to do now.

Eventually my boredom gets the better of me, and I pick the book back up. It's the one I started the other day on sword technique, the one written by the old soldier. Ironstorm must have been remembered. It's also the one I hid the hypnograss in. I ignore the guilty feeling nagging at me and start reading again. After the old man finishes talking about his childhood, it's actually not half bad. He starts to talk about some of his adventures and battles when he was older. He'll describe a particular fight and what he did during it and then the next couple of pages have diagrams demonstrating his techniques.

I wish I had a sword or something to practice with. Would certainly make the time go faster. I put the book down and look around the room for anything suitable, spotting a broom in one corner. *Hmm...*

A minute later, and I'm standing in the center of the room, book in one hand and broom in the other.

"Okay, so first I raise it up and to the right." I lift my "sword" over my head, grabbing it just above the bristles. "And then I'm supposed to bring it down and spin..." I try to follow the diagrams, still looking at the book while I do. When I swing downward, I manage to catch my hip on the other end of the broom, which combined with already trying to twist my body around sends me tumbling right to the floor. "Oww."

The door handle jiggles, drawing my attention. The lock clicks and the door opens, Ironstorm's eyes scanning the room for a moment before settling on me on the floor. "Are you alright?"

"Yeah." I close the book and toss the broom to the side. "Just screwing around."

"I think you and I need to have one more talk." He offers me his hand to help me up.

"Okay." I follow out into the kitchen. I see two small, wrapped packages on the table.

"I got dinner while I was out. Have a seat." He gestures at the table.

"Wait, like, at the table?" My question is entirely genuine.

"Yes." A wry smile crosses his face when we take our seats.

I tear open the paper wrapping on what turns out to be a sandwich. A big one. I eagerly take a bite. It's some kind of bird. Tastes like the soup we had the other day. I see green hands opening the other sandwich, but no bite is taken.

"First, I want to apologize." I slow my chewing when he starts talking again.

"Why are you being so nice all of a sudden?" I blurt out, unable to help feeling a little paranoid that this might be a trick.

"Because I think it is possible that over the past few days, I have been taking a little more glee in your distress than necessary. Especially given that the circumstances surrounding the ritual challenge seem murky." He sets his uneaten sandwich down. "I would like to make you an offer."

"An offer?" I put mine down too.

"Stay with me for two months until your friends have completed their sentences and are released."

"So, be your slave for the next two months, and if I behave myself enough you—"

"No." He shakes his head, cutting me off. "It is not a test. There are no conditions. You stay with me for two months, and then I will release you."

"I... Why not just release me now?" It sounds like a nice offer, but I'm not sure I understand.

"I could, but you would most likely be deported immediately afterward," he admits somewhat sheepishly.

"What! Why?" That seems harsh!

"Because in the eyes of the city you are a criminal." Okay, that's fair. "One from a foreign country with no identification and no money. Every other person you know here is in jail. It is only your tether to me that overrides all of that."

"So I'm pretty much stuck here then." Just another thing I don't really have a choice in.

"It would be in name only." His voice sounds reassuring. "You would sleep in the guest room. There would be no more cuffs, no more leashes, no more eating from my lap or the floor. You would not have to make any public appearances with me or go out at all. Just live here until you and your friends are able to leave together."

It sounds like a great offer, really, but... "Why?"

"Because it is the right thing to do," he answers somberly. "The events that led to our current situation were already troubling, but to find out the extent in which you were misled... As a result, I have hurt you in ways I could not possibly begin to make up for, and for that I am truly, truly sorry. Letting you stay here is the least I can do."

"I... Thank you." Oh boy, that got heavy. My words earlier really got to him. I'm not sure what else to say.

"Does that sound agreeable to you?" He sounds less somber now.

"Yes. I accept." I guess he needs to hear it. I reach across the table to shake his hand.

"Excellent." With a smile, he shakes my hand before he finally picks up his sandwich and takes a bite.

The two of us eat in silence, both of our minds too occupied with processing all the information to talk. I'm happy. Right? This is a good thing. I can hang out here, and when the guys get out in two months, we'll be on our way. It'll be like none of this ever happened. Still a long time to be stuck in jail but at least they'll be earning some money while they're in there. Actually...

"What am I gonna do all day?" I'm about three-quarters done with my sandwich when I ask.

"It may be possible to find you a job in town." Then I could earn some money of my own. "The language barrier might make things difficult, but I could ask around if anyone is looking for some help."

"Thank you. I'd appreciate that." He's really serious about letting me go, isn't he?

With a smile and a nod, he tucks back into his food and the two of us finish in the next few minutes. After standing and throwing away our trash, Ironstorm washes his hands before turning to me.

"I know we did not do too much today, but I am still feeling rather drained, so if you will excuse me, I will be heading to bed." He crooks his fingers at me. "Just one last thing."

I step over to him, unsure of what he wants. He closes the distance and reaches into my shirt, pulling out my collar. He holds the padlock in his hand, and after producing the key from his pocket, unlocks it.

Oh.

He slips the chain from around my neck, gathering it in his hand with the key.

"I thought I had to wear one of those?" Isn't it the law?

"I can find you one that is a little more subtle, I think." He smiles, though I can sense some sadness behind it. "Have a good night, David. There should be some pillows and blankets in the closet in your room. Please remember to put out the lanterns before you go to bed."

I nod and watch him turn away and walk down the hall, bedroom door shutting behind him. *Without me. Wow.*

I mean, great, right?

I look around the living room, expecting things to look different in light of my newfound freedom. My eyes are drawn to the front door. I could leave right now, but there wouldn't be much of a point. I wander into the kitchen, spotting the basket full of *dar-buk* and grabbing a few. I've barely eaten today.

I sit on the couch and snack, not really sure what to do with myself now. He's really going to let me go, just like that. I mean, not "just like that." It's not like I've been at a tea party the last five days. Part of me almost feels bad for my friends. They're imprisoned while I still get a warm bed and good food. Of course, none of them lost their virginity in front of a crowd of people and were then enslaved, so it's a pretty small part.

Khazak—and I guess I can really call him that now—is basically letting me off the hook for everything. Wallowing in my own misery and self-pity the last few days, it was easy to forget that I attacked him and his men...

And almost tried to kill him in the arena...

And then drugged him and almost destroyed his career.

Fuck, is that why I feel guilty? I'm not saying I deserved all the...rough handling, but I guess I'm not sure what I'd do or how I'd feel if I were in his position.

After about fifteen minutes of sitting on the couch and staring at the empty fireplace while burying my feelings in pastries, I give up trying to do anything else and call it a night. I blow out the lanterns in the living room and kitchen and head to my new bedroom. It is extremely bare-bones: blank walls, a bed, a table, and some boxes in the corner. I remove the clothing that I realize I've been wearing since last night and grab the bedding from the closet to make up the bed. Maybe I can ask about putting up some pictures or something tomorrow.

I grab the book from the floor and crack it open, but it just doesn't hold my interest right now. I know I slept like shit last night, but I'm not feeling very tired either. After a few more minutes of trying to get into it, I put the book down, rolling over to blow out the light. I lay in the dark staring at the ceiling, trying not to continuously run the conversations and revelations of the day through in my head, or examine any of the weird feelings I'm having too closely.

In the end, I just close my eyes until eventually, sleep takes me.

Chapter Fourteen

I wake up the next morning in bed, alone. Which was supposed to happen. I slept like shit. No nightmares or dreams, just a lot of tossing and turning. I can't remember ever dreaming as much as I have since arriving here. Or at least I usually forget them by the time I'm awake. I wish I was surprised that part of me misses sleeping in bed with Khazak. It was nice waking up with someone right there. At least once we started getting along, if that's what you can call it. I'd never done that before.

Of course, there were other benefits to sharing a bed in the mornings. Though we never really took advantage of that, unless you count the first morning where I kinda...freaked out about it. I freaked out about a lot of things. Then they started to seem not so freaky. I reach down and give my morning wood a squeeze. It has been a couple of days since I last got off. Not since he did that thing with his tongue...

My cock throbs at the memory. It's not like I have anywhere to be. I grip myself more firmly and begin to stroke. Haven't done this in a while, not since Holbrooke, I think. Kinda hard when I was sharing a tent with Adam. Not to mention any masturbation material had to be pulled from memory. My go-tos were stories I'd hear from classmates, crude drawings from some very strange books in the library, and this one time I walked in on Lieutenant Smith fucking his girlfriend on a desk in one of the empty classrooms.

I've never really thought too much about what I was focusing on in those memories but... I don't think it was the women. When I first got here, it was easy to say I didn't like any of this, to dismiss my enjoyment as nothing more than a physical reaction. Then at some point, I stopped fighting it. Would that have still happened if I hadn't met Ironstorm? Did he turn me into this, or is this who I've been all along? Thinking about the way I stared at the lieutenant's muscled ass while he fucked his girlfriend, it was probably the latter.

But now I have my own experiences to draw from. I think back to that first morning, waking up to someone spooned behind me. The way I could feel him hard against my ass, his hand snaking around and grasping me gently, almost ghosting his fingers over my shaft. I copy the movement with my own hand, biting my lip at the ticklish sensation. I had no real idea who he was at that point or what he was going to do with me, only that he currently owned me...which somehow made it hotter.

Gods, what is wrong with me? Getting off on being forced like that when I have much nicer things to think about. Like in the shower. Both times. I never knew kissing was supposed to feel that good. I've kissed plenty of girls. Soft, warm, kinda wet. I thought that's just what it feels like. But with him? His beard rough against my face, his teeth biting at my lips, his tongue probing my mouth. Nothing like kissing a girl. I remember standing under the hot water, his lips on mine, his hand moving along my body... I run my free hand over my chest and stomach, pretending that it belongs to someone else. Then I move it lower and give my balls a little squeeze.

Tongues are useful for a lot more than kissing too. I remember after the football game, right out of the shower when he threw my legs back and... I didn't even know that was a thing people did. I spread my thighs slightly and move my hand lower, behind my balls. I tentatively run a finger along my hole, shuddering at the sensation as I stroke myself. I rub my finger around the rim, all soreness from earlier in the week gone.

We haven't actually fucked since that first day, unless you count his fingers in the shop. Both were pretty hot in retrospect. And maybe a little in the moment too. But I guess if I *had* to choose...I'd take the dick over the fingers, easily. Well not easily, because that thing is huge, but the way it stretched me open and just kept hitting that one spot inside me felt amazing. I didn't know you could cum without, you know, cumming. It felt like my entire body was having an orgasm. Comparing the way I came on his fingers at Brull's shop to cumming on his dick in the arena (twice) is like comparing the shot from a rifle to the blast from a cannon. I definitely would like for that to happen again.

I hate to admit this, but everything that happened that day was hot. Throwing me down and using his knife to strip me... I bring my hand back up and scrape a fingernail down my chest. Then he tied my hands above my head with the scraps and started stretching me open... My hand moves back to my hole, this time pressing in slightly, all while the hand on my dick moves faster and faster. Then he threw my legs back and pushed inside me, fucking me over and over. Everyone in the stands watching, literally unable to control myself and cumming dry on his cock, his tongue in my mouth at the same time he shot his load inside of me.

Fuck! My cock explodes, spraying cum all over my chest and stomach.

...Yeah, you're pretty fucked up, David. And now also sticky.

I frown, not feeling the usual blissed out aftermath that comes with a nice self-induced orgasm. It usually lasts a minute or two, but right now I just feel kinda...sad. I guess I shouldn't be surprised. Maybe jerking off to the thoughts and memories of the guy you have very confusing feelings for isn't the smartest thing to do. Do I miss him? I mean, he's probably just in the kitchen right now or something.

It's impossible to tell in the dark, but I really hope I managed to miss the sheets and mattress with my load. No one likes laying in a wet spot. I turn my head and see light coming from under the door. It's morning: time to clean up. I gingerly slide myself off the bed, hoping that none of the mess lands on the floor and also that I can get into the bathroom without issue or a certain orc noticing. With my sticky hand still wrapped around my dick, I slowly open the door and peek my head out.

Both of the other doors are open which hopefully means they're also empty. A look down the hall reveals nothing, though I do hear some noises coming from the kitchen. Perfect. I tiptoe my way into the bathroom so I can clean up and relieve myself, then it's back into the bedroom to put on some pants. I almost grab the thong from yesterday to wear before I remember that no one is making me do that anymore. I'll have to get the rest of my clothes out of the bedroom today. Freeballing for now it is!

I pad my way out to the living room, the familiar scent of bacon wafting in my direction. I spot Khazak in the kitchen over the stove dressed in pants and a shirt. That's a lot more modest than I'm used to, but he probably has to worry about fewer grease burns this way. His butt doesn't look bad in those pants eith—

"Good morning, David." My eyes shoot from his ass to his head, turned slightly to greet me. I don't think he noticed.

"Morning. Smells good." I'm great at small talk.

"It is almost ready. Go ahead and take a seat." He gestures to the table, and I remember he means in a *chair*. I get to sit at the table, just like a real boy! I move to sit down, maybe a little too quickly, but if Khazak notices, he doesn't say anything. *Oh fuck, I'm gonna get to feed myself again too.* I am way more excited about this than I should be.

A few minutes later, a mug of coffee and a plate of bacon is pushed in front of me, complete with fork. Khazak takes the seat next to me, and I eagerly dig in, skipping the fork entirely and stuffing a piece in my mouth. I moan a little. So good. A chuckle to my left has me reigning in my antics, but I still work through it pretty fast.

"How did you sleep?" He's eating his own plate a lot more slowly.

"Okay," I lie. "Took a while to fall asleep, but I didn't wake up tired."
Just horny.

"Good. I hope the room will suit you for the next two months." He smiles. "If you need anything at all, please let me know."

I nod and grab another piece of bacon. He made *a lot*. That isn't a complaint, but it occurs to me that this meal, his concessions to my behavior, his offer for "anything at all"—it's a peace offering. He's working overtime; I can feel the guilt coming off him in waves. I really got to him yesterday.

Again, not complaining, but it's not making me feel any better about my *own* guilt. For everything he's done to me, I know I'm not blameless here. If anything, I've only tried to make things worse for him. That plus all the residual feelings I'm having for the nicer parts of my stay is making for a very confusing morning. By the time we're finishing off the last of the bacon, I find myself remembering just a couple of days ago when we sat on the couch and he was feeding it to me. I actually miss sitting in his lap. Just a little!

I know, I know: get your shit together, David.

"I wanted to apologize again." His demeanor changes as he grabs my plate, refusing my help as he starts to clean up. "I feel terrible for letting things go so far."

"I can tell." I try to joke and lighten the mood. "Thank you."

"When I originally told you I was going to take care of you, I *meant* it." He's washing the dishes and not looking at me. "And then failed to do that, quite spectacularly."

"You didn't—"

"I did," he cuts me off. "This whole time there was a part of me that knew something was not quite right. That you were telling the truth about the ritual and I ignored it. Ignored my instincts. Worse than that, there was a part of me that actually felt you *deserved* it. That this was your punishment." His tone gets even more somber. "I do not like that you were tricked, but I like even less that I hurt you. That I forced myself on you."

"I didn't hate everything." I don't like hearing him talk like that because of me. "I don't think I can even say I hated *most* of it."

"That doesn't matt—"

"No, listen." I move to stand next to him. If I'm gonna try to deal with some of this repressed shit I really need him to hear me out. "Where I come from, two men being together is just...not allowed. Or at least not talked about in a positive way. And when you grow up like that and you start to notice that maybe you might be...different, it's easier—*safer*—to ignore those feelings, or hide them, or bury them deep down. You know what you're *supposed* to do, so you just do it."

"But then I get here," I continue, no longer speaking in hypotheticals and working through some of this on the fly, "and not only can I not ignore them, I'm confronted with them over and over, on a daily basis. And it's not just 'Hey David, you like men.' It's 'Hey David, you like men, and also when those men are rough, and tie you down, and strip you in public, and spank you, and force you to—'" I bite my lip because that little trip down memory lane isn't doing me any favors. He gets the point. "It's just a lot, and I don't know if you've noticed, but I don't really handle high pressure situations with a ton of grace. Because I didn't have the option of ignoring it anymore, it just got easier to focus on things like getting out of here. I couldn't run away from it which just made me want to run even more. I just wanted to get back to the way my life used to be, before I met you."

"...I am sorry you have had to go through life like that, David." I can tell he's sincere.

"I don't think I can go back to the way things were. Not anymore," I offer, feeling raw after saying all of those things. "It's hard to go back to lying to yourself once you've finally said it all out loud, but I'm sort of glad I don't have to."

"This still is not how you should have been forced to confront it." I see him lift a hand, but he aborts whatever touch he was going to give me. "Nor does it excuse what I did to you."

"Khazak... I was harsher than I meant to be yesterday on purpose." It got my point across, but I didn't want to make him feel like *this*. "I said those things to hurt you."

"True as that may be, I still forced all of this on you." He looks so disappointed with himself.

"Look, I'm not saying it wasn't messed up—*especially* at the beginning—but we both know I'm not a damsel in distress. I wanted you that day in the arena before we ever started fighting. Even if I wasn't ready to admit it yet." I remember the sight of his chocolate-brown eyes as he stood across from me. "If I had really tried to fight you, I don't think you could go through with it. You told me yourself: you're not a cruel man."

"That may be up for debate." He doesn't sound very convinced.

"I know I can't make you, but I wish you'd stop beating yourself up over it." So that I can stop beating myself up over it too.

"I will try," he says with a sad smile.

The rest of the morning and afternoon is awkward at best. I can tell he's giving me a lot of space. Forget sitting on the couch together—he barely wants to be in the same room as me. By the time we're eating again, I'm starting to feel antsy.

"Do you think I could go for a run?" I ask after we stumble through an awkward lunch. I need some air.

"Certainly." He looks up from his book. "I had not planned on going anywhere today, so I will be here when you get back."

"Sounds good." I head back to the bedroom to change into a loose shirt and some shorts. Once I'm dressed, I head for the door. "Are you sure you're cool with me going out all un-collared?" *Did that sound like I was disappointed?*

"I have a solution for that. One moment." Khazak walks to the bedroom, returning a minute later holding a metal chain which he hands to me. "This should satisfy the requirements."

It's a simple chain, thin with no real lock, just a clasp. I don't even have to undo it to slip it over my head. It feels light as it settles against my chest.

"David..." Khazak looks hesitant to finish what he's about to say. "If you decided to leave, I would not chase you down. I do not want you to feel like a prisoner here."

I nod to him as I turn to the door. Is that what he's expecting? I step outside, shaking the thoughts from my mind as I pick a direction and start running. Time to clear my head. The last few days have just been so fucking crazy. This whole week has been nuts. One day I'm camping in the woods and the next I belonged to an orc.

An orc who makes me feel some very confusing things.

What does he make me feel, exactly? I guess I've accepted that I'm attracted to him, attracted to men, but it feels like more than that. I like talking to him. Doing things with him. And not just in the bedroom, though I certainly like plenty of that too. I wish I had a past relationship to use as a model, but nothing I had with my ex-girlfriends ever came close to this.

I think about what we've been doing together the past week. Not the sex but the quieter times, the times I'd forget I was supposed to hate him. Meals, reading, lying in bed. Even playing that football game yesterday. My mind wanders, and I lose track of how long I've been running when

I come face to face with a huge wooden gate. I guess I made it to the edge of the city.

This must be the gate Khazak mentioned yesterday. The wooden wall surrounding the city is tall, made up of smooth round posts packed tightly next to each other. Short of digging into the wood and climbing over, I don't really see another way past other than using the gate. Not entirely sure how it opens but there's a pair of guards posted out front. They don't look particularly menacing.

I could probably convince them to open up for me. Khazak said it himself: I could just leave if I wanted to, and he wouldn't chase me. It wouldn't even have to be *right* now. I bet I could go back and pack a few things first. Head off for Holbrooke, take some work out there, save up some money, and then in two months when my friends are released, we can meet back up and pretend like this was all just a bad dream. I could totally do that.

But I don't think I want to.

So what do you want, David?

I turn my back on the gate. Time to head home. I start the run back, my mind now preoccupied with other things. Like when exactly did I start thinking of it as home? Just a few days ago, I was trying everything I could think of to get away.

Then a few days after that, I was happily waking up next to him. Among other things. That's not exactly an excuse to stay with him. It's not a reason *not* to either. Probably could have started things off a little slower than being his slave. Like a *date*, maybe? I wonder what people do for dates around here. *Fuck, are you really considering going on a date with a guy?*

Would that have even worked? Can't imagine that a week ago that I'd be receptive to a man asking me out, let alone an orc. Before I got here, I would have been shocked to learn that an orc that was capable of stringing two words together, let alone that there was an entire orc society arguably more advanced than my own. It's not just about being with a guy or an orc either. I liked the roughness, I liked giving up control. I liked the idea that I *belonged* to somebody, somebody who wanted to take care of me. Maybe it's all the years of training, but I even liked following his orders. There's a part of me that gets all warm and fuzzy when he tells me I did good.

That doesn't seem normal, those aren't things I'm supposed to want… except everything I've seen and experienced in the last few days says the opposite. Not even just my own feelings and reactions; we went to an entire shop dedicated to selling gear and equipment for these kinds of…

relationships. That fact that there even *is* gear and equipment for this stuff blows my mind, and I haven't even been doing it for a week! I can only imagine what else is out there.

When you think about *everything* we've already done together, it seems kinda silly to go backwards. I don't want to pretend like none of it happened. I also don't typically like to do *anything* the slow way, if I can help it. I once tried to have Mike "magic" me older so I could try and enter the academy early. Good thing he didn't. *Or couldn't, whatever.* Point is, I'm not sure trying things the slow route would have worked any better. But there has to be some middle ground between "complete freedom" and "forced bondage."

Even though I kinda like the forced part.

Seeing as we're actually talking about things now, maybe we can figure it out together.

If he is even still interested.

If I haven't already completely fucked this up.

Why am I even considering this? I got exactly what I wanted: my freedom. Why am I debating giving some of that back? I go back and forth like this for I don't know how long but eventually realize I'm back at the house. Well, that run really helped clear things up. I groan to myself and open the door, Khazak looking up from his spot on the couch as I enter.

"Hey." I give an awkward little wave. Are we roommates now?

"No problems, I trust?" He's asking if anyone bothered me.

"Nope. Just going to grab a shower." I point my thumb down the hall as I walk backward.

He nods, returning to his book while I get cleaned up. I grab my clothing out of his bedroom, taking a fresh pair of shorts to the bathroom with me. Of course, being in the shower brings back an entirely different set of memories. *Very* good ones. I sigh under the spray. I need to talk to Khazak.

When I'm finished cleaning up, I re-enter the living room, clothes dry but hair still damp. I join Khazak on the couch, bringing up one of my knees so I can turn to face him. Seeing my movements, he copies me, putting his book down so we are facing each other.

"Everything alright?" He eyes me curiously.

"Yeah, I just wanted to know if we could talk some more?" I ask hesitantly.

"Of course." He gives me his full attention.

"Well, I've been thinking about what we talked about earlier." Pretty much nonstop. "About what we've been doing together."

"David, again I am so—"

"No, it's not that." I don't need another apology to make me feel worse and more confused. "I more meant about how I was saying I liked it."

"What... What are you getting at, David?" What *am* I getting at?

"I just thought that if I'm going to be here with you for two months anyway, doesn't it seem silly to ignore the attraction we have to each other?" I feel like appealing to his logical side might work.

"Are you asking to sleep together?" He raises an eyebrow, not saying no but missing the point a little.

"I mean, yeah I guess, but I was more getting at the other stuff." Probably should've thought this through more first. "Like you taking charge, ordering me around, tying me up, calling you Sir. I'm going to be here with you for two months no matter what, right? And like I told you, I liked a lot of...*most* of what we've been doing. I didn't know what I was getting into at first, or even want to admit that I liked it, but now that I do—"

"David, are you seriously *asking* to be my slave for the next two months?" He sounds incredulous.

"Your *avakesh*, technically," I correct him. "There's a difference, right?"

Khazak laughs out loud at that, shaking his head. "How do I even *begin* to explain why that is a terrible idea?"

"Why?" I turn to face him more fully on the couch. "I mean as far as anyone else is concerned, I never stopped being your avakesh in the first place. I know that I like it now. I promise not to run away anymore."

"David, that is not..." He grunts a little in frustration, running his hands down his face. "You were not even interested in men before last week."

"*No*, I wasn't aware of or willing to *admit* that I was interested in men before last week," I correct him again, maybe a little more flippantly that I need to. "Cat's out of the bag now. Only thing left to do is move forward."

"Moving forward with your return to enslavement." He looks bewildered. "Do *all* humans where you are from make decisions this rashly?"

"Not really. This is pretty much 100% me." I shrug. "I know things between us started off really rough," *Literally, I might add,* "but they don't have to continue to be, right?"

He sighs, partially in frustration. "How could you even forgive me? Because the more I think about everything that was said yesterday, about everything I have done to you in the past week, the more I am unsure I can forgive myself."

Fuck, he's really shaken about this. "I told you, I only said those—"

"I am not upset because of the things you said, David," he stops me before I can finish. "I am upset because they were true. I never wanted to..." He trails off. "That is not the man I thought I was. Not the man I wanted to be."

"So then don't be that man." I can tell he's struggling not to roll his eyes at that. "No, I mean things are *already* different between us. We already understand each other more. We're actually talking. So as long as we keep doing all of that, why can't we try again?"

"David, yesterday you wanted nothing more than to be free of me forever." I don't seem to be doing a great job of convincing him. "Why would you want this now?"

"Because for whatever fucking reason, I like you. I like this," I gesture between us again, "and I know you do too. I'm not asking you to go steady, I'm just saying that it seems really fucking stupid to spend the next two months living together and pretending like that's not true. Also, let's not forget that the only reason we're even in this weird situation is that *both* of us were lied to. You have to stop blaming yourself."

"Believe me, I will be speaking with Advocate Redwish in the coming days about the way he conducts business." He crosses his arms for a moment before dropping them and turning to me, a shy smile growing on his face. "It would be untrue to say I have not enjoyed my time with you, but I just..."

"What are you afraid of happening?" I ask when he doesn't finish his sentence.

"Seriously?" He looks at me like I've grown an extra head. "Hurting you, abusing you, forcing you to do things you do not want to do?"

"So then don't do that?" He's no more impressed with the answer the second time I use it. "I'm not saying I loved *everything we did*, but...even when I *didn't* want it, there was this part of me that liked being made to do it anyway. Liked that *you* made me do it." I can feel my face start to turn red at the admission, and I'm just glad I'm still capable of shame at this point. "Can't we just...figure out what works and what doesn't?"

He considers this for a minute before frowning. "I am not sure I can be trusted to make that distinction."

"Okay, then I'll start." I roll my eyes. "You feeding me. I really a wasn't fan at first. It was more than a little awkward for multiple reasons—and for the record I'm glad you didn't insist on it when we had soup—but I still found myself liking it a lot more than I expected. I'm not saying I want to stop doing it completely, just that maybe I can feed myself a little more often so I don't forget how to use a fork and knife."

"Yes, it was very hard on you." He's being sarcastic but at least he's smiling. "What... What is something else you would want to change?"

"Well... What about your name?" I'm happy he's at least talking about it with me now. "I'd like to be able to use it sometime."

His eyes go wide at my request. "David, I am so sorry. I just...enjoyed hearing you call me Sir, and after that started, it never occurred to have you do anything different." He hesitates before continuing. "I never should have had you do that. Of course you no longer have to call me Sir—"

"Woah, I never said *that*. I just want to be able to use your *actual* name too." *Honestly, given the number of men I've called "sir" on a regular basis over the course of my life, there's probably something to unpack there.* "I like calling you Sir sometimes. It suits you. It just might be nice to cry out a 'Khazak' now and again." I bite my lip and wiggle my eyebrows. For the record, I've always been great at flirting—I just wasn't trying to before.

He reaches a hand out and runs it through my hair affectionately. "I like hearing you say it."

"Good." I lean into his hand a bit. "So... Where did we stand on me calling you 'Zak' again?"

He narrows his eyes. "You need discipline."

"So, there *is* something you'll talk about." *Ha, he fell right into my nonexistent trap!* "What's going to happen when you want to punish me?"

"I am not sure that will be necessary." He shifts uncomfortably.

"What do you mean not necessary? We've met, right?" I'm not saying I'm gonna cause trouble on purpose but *come on.* "What happened to the hard-ass that just said I needed discipline?" I can't believe I'm *asking* for this.

"I am not a hard-ass," he grumbles. "I just find that some *boys* require a certain amount of structure in order to be properly looked after." He looks at me, making sure I know what "boy" he's talking about. "Besides, you clearly do not mind it as much as you protest."

"Did your parents spank you as a kid or something?" That earns me a cocked eyebrow. "It would explain a lot."

"No. My parents did not believe in spanking children. Neither do I." He's smirking. "Only adults who insist on acting like them."

"I don't act like a child. I just have an adventurous spirit." I cross my arms. "But uh, maybe when I do screw up, you can take it easy on me?" Note that I said *when*, not *if.*

"That depends. Will this be a 'walk out of a store' screw up or a 'drug me and steal my keys before breaking into the jail' screw up?" The joke is said with a hint of anger, but then his face softens and he reaches a hand over to my thigh. "I understand that this is only temporary, but are you sure this is something you really want, David?"

"You mean the thing where I don't have to pay rent or feed myself for the next two months?" I give him an overly-cheesy smile.

I can see his eyes wrinkle, holding back a smile as he huffs. "David."

"Okay, the thing is, I've never really been in a relationship before, not a real one. I had girlfriends in school, but it was never serious. They never made me feel like...this. This *thing* between us is so unlike anything I have ever done that I have no idea what I'm doing. Before I met you, I didn't just not know that I liked this stuff, I didn't even know it existed. I don't even know what to call it." *There's only so many times you can say "stuff" and "thing" before you start to feel dumb.*

"I know they may seem more common in our city, but relationships of this type are not unheard of in other parts of the world. Even yours," he starts explaining. "I have known since I was younger where my interests lie. Not just in regards to men, but also in things like bondage and discipline, power exchange, submission and *dominance.*" *Okay, the way he just said that was kinda hot.* "But being dominant also means taking care of my submissive's well-being. Something I failed to do with you at every turn."

"That's a little harsh." Things got a little humiliating at times, maybe, but it turns out that's not something I mind all that much either. "Doesn't the fact that I want to talk to you about it count for something?"

"I am not sure I can agree with that logic." He shakes his head.

"Look, I'm only going to be here for two months, right?" He nods that I am correct. "So, if it doesn't work out, then it doesn't work out. I can go back to sleeping in the guest room until I leave, and we can just be friends. Right?"

"Right." The sad look he's wearing tells me he doesn't think it'll be that easy.

"So can't we just give it a shot?" I have yet to hear a compelling argument against. "Take it slow, ease back into things?"

He watches me for a few moments, his face unreadable, before he nods. "Okay, David. We can try." I get just the barest hint of a smile. "But my offer to live here with no strings attached still stands, and the guest room is still yours. As much as I liked having you in my bed, I think it is more import—"

"I like sleeping with you." I can tell he'll be tiptoeing around things for a while. "In bed, I mean."

"If you insist." He huffs a small laugh, but I can tell he's happy about it.

"So... Does that mean this discussion is no longer hypothetical?" I try my best not to let my stupid grin engulf my *entire* face.

"I suppose it does." His face is more guarded.

"Good." I sit up and lean over, trying to pull him in for a hug but instead get pulled onto his lap. *Works for me.* "So, you wanna go fool around, Sir?"

I'm almost offended by how hard he laughs. Almost.

Chapter Fifteen

I wake up from a deep, dreamless sleep in a familiar bed, half sprawled atop a familiar body. I let myself enjoy the warmth of being pressed against someone for a moment, eyes still closed. Memories of the previous evening begin to slowly drift back to me, all the talking, the frustration, the emotions. By the time Khazak and I went to bed, we were exhausted.

Part of me was hoping that getting in bed would lead to some things happening, but Khazak decided not to take me up on my offer to fool around. He was a perfect gentleman. He didn't make me sleep on the other side of the mattress or anything, but he wouldn't even take off his underwear. If I had to guess, I'd say he's still having some hang-ups, which I appreciate—a lot—but the hard cock I am currently grinding into his thigh does not.

Look, apparently it only takes a little trauma and a few good orgasms for me to get over years of deep-seated denial and self-deception. I'm not trying to argue the merits of that. I'm just horny and would like the guy who's been going out of his way to *make* me horny to do something about it. I may have to take things into my own hands. Hopefully not literally.

I finally open my eyes, the amount light behind the curtains letting me know how late it is. Seems like we decided to sleep in today. I run my hand lightly down his furry chest and stomach. Yeah, this is nice. Khazak doesn't stir at my movement, so I keep running my hand along his body slowly, until I bump into his tented briefs and my earlier thought of taking things into my own hands comes floating back to me.

Carefully extracting myself from his side, I move onto my knees and crawl backward until I'm kneeling by his hips. There's something we haven't done yet that I think I'm finally ready to admit I've been curious about. I reach a hand out, brushing lightly over his trapped erection, watching it twitch while its owner remains still. I reach for his waistband

and hook my fingers inside, carefully stretching it up and over the thick green slab of meat and tucking it under his balls.

Now that it's free, I can actually wrap my hand around this thing. Just barely though. I think this is the first time I've actually touched it, the first time I've touched another man's dick at all other than when it's been pressed against my leg or say, *inside me*. The memory makes me shudder slightly. It's thick, the head looking slightly thicker as it peeks out from behind his foreskin. There's the slightest curve upward in the middle while the base ends in a dark forest of pubic hair, a thick trail leading up to his stomach. I stroke my hand up and down the shaft, uncovering more of the head and feeling the heat in my hand. The organ gives another twitch, but there's no other movement from the still-sleeping orc and I continue my exploration.

I wouldn't really mind if he woke up—I don't *think* he'd stop me— but I feel a little like a newborn deer right now, just with dicks instead of walking. I'd like to get my first look and feel of one without any potential-ly-mocking eyes. I know I'm being paranoid, but I can already hear the jokes Mike would make. *Okay David, maybe not the time to start thinking about your brother.* Shaking off that thought, I kneel up slightly, ready to begin phase two of my plan.

I have no idea if I'm doing this right, but here goes nothing. I lean forward, one hand holding him steady and the other on the mattress as I lower my face to his crotch. Immediately the scent of his musk hits me, which is kinda nice now that I'm actually receptive to it. I open my mouth as I near the head of his dick, where a small bead of precum has gath-ered at the tip. A salty, slightly bitter taste hits my tongue as I close my lips around him. It's not bad, helped by the knowledge of who it comes from. I run my tongue along his foreskin, even daring to poke underneath. I'm not saying it's delicious, but it's a lot less unpleasant than I have been led to believe.

Feeling more confident, I sink my head lower, taking in a few more inches before I feel the head poking at the back of my throat. I stop before I make myself gag, but I'm barely getting a third of this thing in my mouth. Pretty sure I could wrap both my hands around what's left of the shaft. Still only using one at the moment, holding it in place while I try pulling my head back a little before sinking down again. That's what you're supposed to do, right? I've never actually seen or received a blowjob before.

See? This is why I'm glad he's asleep. This feels like something I should already know how to do, and *who would I even ask*? Trial and error works for now. I slowly bob up and down, a little more confident but still worried about gagging. It's weird trying to figure out how much suction I'm supposed to use, and suddenly I become very aware of my teeth and how I would not want to feel them on my own dick, and I can't stop thinking about how sore my jaw already is from trying to avoid it. I need to relax. This is supposed to be fun.

Not that my dick has gone down at all. I reach down and give myself a squeeze as I work my way up and down his length. Yeah, I'm definitely into this. I start to stroke myself in time with the movement of my mouth. I'm still going a little slow, but the hand on my dick is encouraging me to pick up the pace. I settle into a nice rhythm, but get too cocky and wind up going a little too deep and choking myself. Just for a second, but it's enough for my gag reflex to kick in, and I pull back before I start coughing. I don't want to wake him up yet.

I catch my breath, shifting around the mattress to kneel between his legs. His cock is shiny with my spit, even more so thanks to the gagging. I run my hand along the slick skin, enjoying the way it glides a little easier. Once I have regained my bearings, I lean over to take him back in my mouth, still using my hand to hold him steady. As I resume my oral endeavor, I realize I can use the saliva to my advantage, allowing some of the excess that builds in my mouth to drip down and lubricate the way for my hand to stroke the remaining five or so inches of his shaft. I think I'm starting to get the hang of this.

I look up at Khazak's sleeping form, a big smile plastered on his face. I relax into things again, confident that I now know what I'm doing and the limits of my gag reflex. I close my eyes, enjoying the way the darkness makes his scent that much more powerful. Yeah, okay, I get why people like doing this. I'm not really sure how long I've been at this, I lost track of time a while ago, when for a split second it feels like his dick is getting bigger in my mouth.

I shouldn't be that surprised when the first shot of cum hits the roof of my mouth, but I am. I mean, I know this is the end result of a blowjob, but I hadn't really gotten that far in my thinking. The second and third shots are less surprising but still manage to catch me off guard when they hit the back of my throat. I immediately start to choke and pull back, but that leaves shots four, five, and six to all splatter across my face.

By the time I've finished coughing, I'm not sure how much cum ended up down my gullet and how much is splattered across Khazak's groin and belly. I'm leaning up on one hand, the other used to cover my mouth during my coughing fit, leaving me with a jizz-covered palm.

Oh, how far you've come, David.

So that's how giving my first blowjob went.

"I am so sorry, David." I look up, only just realizing Khazak is awake. "I should have warned you when that was about to happen." The attempt he's making to hold in his laughter doesn't quite reach his eyes.

I give him a "Ya think?" look as I continue to cough.

He moves to the edge of the mattress, reaching under the bedside table for a towel. I (or any other guy who's gone through puberty) don't have to think very hard about why there's one of those nearby. He uses it to wipe my face and hand before moving on to his own body. Once he's satisfied, he tosses it to the side, sliding back up the bed and bringing me with him.

"Was that your first time?" He settles us on our sides, his arm going around my shoulders.

"Uh huh." I nod, moving my still sore jaw around, the taste of him still on my tongue.

"Well, you performed admirably." He cups my chin gently before leaning in to kiss me. "The soreness will lessen with practice."

"How long were you awake?" And how much of my performance did he catch?

"I woke up a little before the first time you gagged," he admits. "It seemed like you were enjoying yourself, and I did not want to disturb you." He's *still* grinning.

"How kind of you." I roll my eyes. "You better warn me next time."

"There will be a next time?" he asks playfully.

"If you play your cards right, Sir." I wiggle my eyebrows.

After chuckling and pulling me in for another kiss, we roll out of bed. It's strange how easy it is to slip into this...thing between us, how domestic it already feels. I'm not fighting against it, not anymore. I get the feeling that would just leave me with a sore ass.

It's late enough that we skip breakfast and go straight to lunch, just some grilled fish. We eat in relative silence, still waking up, when Khazak puts his fork down to tell me something.

"My family is having a dinner tonight. We normally have them once a month," he starts explaining. "Given the events of the past few days, I thought it would be best to skip. It is not normally *too* difficult to get out of attending, but my sister is home for the first time in over a year and my father is insisting. An invite has also been extended to you of course, but I would understand if you would prefer to stay here instead."

"They invited me?" *Maybe it's normal around here to invite your child's slave to dinner?*

"My family is nothing if not hospitable." Khazak nods.

"When did you find that out?" It sounds like it's new information to him too.

"Yesterday. It was one of the stops I made while I was out." He toys with his fork a little while he talks, like he's nervous.

My first thought is to take his offer of not attending because I think he's right. Meeting his family right now after everything that's happened seems like it would be more than just awkward. But so far almost everyone he's introduced me to has been pretty nice. Jury's still out on Brull. His family though, if they're related to him, they've gotta be decent people, right?

"Actually, I think I'd like to go." There's also a part of me that's interested in seeing what an orc family dinner is like.

"Are you sure?" He looks surprised at my answer. "It really would not be a problem to make an excuse for your absence." Aww, is he nervous about me meeting his family?

"No really. It sounds like it might be fun." His smile still looks a little stiff at my answer. "Besides, your dad is the one who taught you how to cook, right? I bet the food's gonna be great." That gets me a chuckle. "Your sister moved away?"

"In a way. She travels a lot, all over the world." He stabs a piece of fish with his fork. "This is the second longest she has been away from home. Right after our twenty-fifth birthday, she left on a journey south for almost a year and a half."

"Wow." She sounds awesome. "Wait, you have the same birthday?"

"I should hope so. She is my twin." He brings another bite to his mouth.

"No fucking way. You're a twin too?" How did I not know? *Don't answer that.*

"You have a twin sister?" He looks surprised, swallowing his food and dabbing his mouth.

"Brother." I wonder what he's doing right now.

"So there are two of you? Oh no." There's that dry sense of humor.

"You wish. We're not identical." That's usually one of the first things people ask when they find out I have a twin brother.

"It is quite the coincidence that we would both be twins." He looks genuinely intrigued.

"Yeah, that's crazy." Seriously, what are the odds? "What's her name?"

"Ayla." Simple enough. "Yours?"

"Michael." Or Mike. Or Mikey. "Are you two close?"

"When we were younger. As we got older, our paths in life diverged." Sounds like he's probably said that before. "She and I still talk, but it is not like when we were children."

"I know what you mean." It's not an unfamiliar story. "Mike and I were practically inseparable as kids, but then about two years ago, he went off to fancy wizard college and now we don't talk as much." Even less now that I no longer have a mailing address.

"But up until then you two had similar interests?" He takes another bite of his fish.

"Not even a little." I shake my head, smiling when I think about Mike and me back in school together. "We have the same eyes, same nose, same sense of humor, but we're different in just about every other way."

"How so?" He leans back in his chair as he listens.

"He's a nerd." I mean that in the nicest way possible. Do orcs have a word for nerd? "When we were little, he was always reading a book or getting excited about something he learned in school while I was busy running around trying to climb trees and hit things with sticks. He was always awkward around girls—"

"Whereas you were awkward around boys?" He is way too pleased with himself for that one. This is my own fault.

I narrow my eyes but continue. "We still wanted to do *everything* together. We'd lose our shit if someone tried to separate us. It wasn't until we were older that we finally started wanting a little space. Still shared a bedroom for eighteen years though."

"That is a long time to share a bedroom." He's a little taken aback. Probably didn't have to share with his sister. "Did that not get awkward?"

"Not really. I mean, it wasn't always easy to get some privacy when you wanted it, but we told each other everything anyway." Still did up until recently. "Even when we started getting older and doing different things, we still looked out for each other. He got picked on in school a lot. I didn't like that—I don't like bullies in general. So I kinda made it my job to be his protector. Taught him how to defend himself."

"I can just picture a tiny you making threats on the playground." That's actually pretty accurate.

"He's my brother. That's what you do for each other." There really isn't a whole lot I wouldn't do for Mike if he needed it. "It wasn't one sided either. I was a *terrible* student, but he was always there to help me. He used to stay up all night with me studying, or helping me with home-work, or going over a paper I had to write. He'd explain things over and over until I finally got it. He wanted to make sure I didn't fuck anything up too badly."

"He sounds like a good brother." Yeah, Mikey's the best. *Usually.*

"He also once told me, 'I refuse to have a dumb jock for a twin,' so I'm not sure he was being entirely selfless." Khazak's smiling, a hint of something else behind his eyes. "What?"

"You get excited when you talk about your brother." His head tilts, like he's figuring me out. "It is rather endearing."

That has me blushing. Time to shift the focus off of me. "What about you and your sister? Are you a lot alike?"

"When we were younger. We also liked to do everything together. Fishing, hunting, fighting—we were *very* competitive. Something our parents did their best not to encourage. I think they believed we were trying to outdo one another, but it was really more about pushing each other further. If we made a bet, there was never a sore loser. Although we still managed to find ways to get on each other's nerves."

"I figured that was a given with all siblings." His chuckle that tells me he knows what I mean. "Do you have any others?"

"Two younger brothers and a younger sister. Yogik, Ignatz, and Ursza." He holds up three fingers as he names them. "You?"

"Older brother and younger sister. Joseph and Kira." So we both come from big families.

"Are you also close with them?" He pushes his plate to the side, our lunch forgotten as we share our stories.

"Not really. I looked up to my brother a lot when I was little, but I grew out of it. My little sister is...a little sister. I could be anywhere from completely annoyed to super overprotective with her. Shit, her birthday is next month." She will not be happy I missed it. Or that I didn't get her a present.

"It may take a while to reach her, but you could always write to her," Khazak offers a perfectly reasonable solution.

"I'll think about it." I already know I'm not going to take him up on it, but there is something else I need. "So, since our fish is cold, and I'm meeting your family tonight... Do you think I could finally get the haircut I've been asking about?"

"Yes, David, we can get you a haircut." With a huff of laughter, Khazak stands and grabs our plates. Time to get cleaned up.

The sun has already started to set by the time we start our journey to Khazak's parent's house. We just left the barber after giving my hair a fresh trim. Nothing fancy: short on the sides and evened out top, same as I've gotten for years. I prefer my haircuts low maintenance, especially when I'm not sure when my next one might be. Khazak paid of course, but I'm thinking I may need to take him up on that offer to find a job so I can pull my own weight a little for the next two months and start saving up.

"We have arrived." We come to a stop in front of a home that looks like a large version of our own, all stone and wood. "Ready?"

"I think so." It's just dinner, right?

With a nod, Khazak leans forward to knock, and a few moments later, the door swings inward.

"Khazak" is the only intelligible thing I make out when the orc on the other side starts speaking, but hey, kind of impressive I even got that.

As we walk inside for a second, I think that the orc greeting us is Khazak's doppelganger. Same height, same hair, same build. But when he turns to me, I notice the small differences. His hair and beard are more salt-and-pepper than black, and the lines on his face run deeper. This must be his father.

It's my turn to be spoken to, but I don't understand any of it because it's in Orcish. "No, father, he cannot speak—"

"Well, I hope you are taking care of that," he tells his son before turning back to me, hand outstretched. "Orlun Ironstorm."

"David Ceranooooff—" I'm pulled into a hug when I reach my hand out.

"A little on the scrawny side." The comment is spoken over my shoulder as I'm placed back on the ground. "Nothing we cannot fix. It is nice to meet you, David."

"Nice to meet you too..." *Shit*, what am I supposed to call him? Orlun? Mr. Ironstorm? *That's* gonna get confusing. "Sir." *Aaaaand that was even worse.*

"Word around the city is that you and my son have been *quite* busy." He looks between the two of us expectantly and my face heats. Of course, everyone here has probably heard about...everything.

"Orda, I wanted to ask—"

"Sorry, I am still needed in the kitchen." Orlun cuts off his son again as he walks backward through an open doorway, pointing to his left. "Your sister and brother are in the den. Go introduce David."

"Yes, sir," Khazak tells the empty room with a sigh. "This way, David."

We walk through the doorway into a large but cozy looking room. A lot of chairs, a couple of couches, and an already lit fireplace in the corner. There are two orcs talking animatedly, who pause at our arrival.

"Brother!" they shout in unison before turning into a three-orc pile-up.

"David, this is my sister Ayla and my brother Yogik." I'm pulled in for two more hugs. Are all orcs this huggy or is it just his family?

"About time you brought him over." Yogik crosses arms while he looks me up and down. "You did not even let anyone know you received the challenge. Some of us could have been there."

"Don't be weird, Yog." Ayla slugs her brother in the shoulder. "It's nice to meet you, David."

"Nice to meet you too." I like her. She's another big one, just like her twin and dad, with the same brown eyes and jet-black hair pulled into a short ponytail. I notice a number of different piercings adorning both her ears. Yogik, a few inches shorter and much leaner, lets me know that not everyone in this family is a giant. In this light, his eyes have a slight green tinge to them and his dark brown hair almost reaches his shoulders. All of us are dressed pretty casually—cloth shirts and pants—except Ayla, who looks like she's ready for or just came in from a hike that included some mountain climbing.

"When did you get in, Ayla?" Khazak asks his sister across our four-person circle.

"Right before lunch." Arguably one of the best times to arrive.

"Why are you still dressed like that?" He sounds oddly accusatory, nodding down at her leathers.

"What do you mean? These are the only clothes I have," she defends. Sounds fair to me. Does he not remember my own clothing situation?

"You did not bring a change? Are you sure this is not just an excuse to launch into some long-winded tale about where you have been?" *Okaaayyy*, did not see that coming.

"Are you *seriously* going to—"

"**So Dave**, what do you think of the city so far?" Yogik cuts in with the force and precision of a guy who's had to break up his fair share of sibling arguments.

"Oh, uh, it's really nice. Not what I expected." Wait, that isn't a compliment. "In a good way."

"Has Khaz taken you to the Shadrok Springs yet?" Ayla turns to ask me.

I knew that nickname was a thing. "No, he hasn—"

"He has only been here for a *week*, Ayla," Khazak cuts me off.

"Spirits help me," Yogik mutters so quietly I almost don't catch it before turning behind him to shout for backup. "Ursza! Ignatz! Come out here and meet Dave." I wince when the unwanted nickname is used again.

Two more orcs enter the room, a male and a female, closer in build to Yogik than his larger siblings. The first thing I notice on the girl is her hair—it's short, shaved on the sides, and *bright purple*. So are her eyes, which I'm positive isn't a natural thing, even for orcs. The brother has similarly altered his appearance, though his color of choice is blue. Between their ears and noses, I count more piercings than I've seen on every other orc combined. They look the same age, or at least close to it. And that's when I realize what they are.

Teenagers. Oh no.

Our circle widens to accommodate the new additions, who immediately look at me before turning to each other to speak in Orcish.

"Come on. You know he doesn't speak *Atasi*." Yeah, I don't speak that word she just said.

"Ursza, Ignatz, this is Dave." Yogik makes the introductions while both teens stare at me silently.

"It's David, actually," I correct him. I *really* do not like being called Dave. I can tell Yogik wants to ask me about it but gets distracted by something behind me. I turn and see *another* orc entering the room.

"Khazak, it is so good to see you." The new guy embraces Khazak. Wait, I thought there were only two brothers. *Have I miscounted the men?* "This must be David. I am Jarek." Oof, another hug. Upon closer inspection, no, this guy looks a little older. Short black hair, medium build, small goatee and mustache.

"It is nice to meet you." He doesn't give me the chance to respond before turning to the rest of the group. "Dinner will be ready in a few minutes." And then he's gone.

"I'm sorry, but who was that?" I ask after the orc's speedy exit.

"That was Jarek, our father," Yogik answers. *Wait, what?*

"He is really more of a stepfather to myself and Ayla," Khazak explains. "But we do not think of him any differently."

Ayla is quick to correct him. "Please, you *hated* him when we were little."

"I did not *hate* him. He was new and I was having a hard time adjusting to him being here," Khazak growls through his gritted teeth. Okay, I think I understand what's going on now.

"Sorry, I thought Orlun was everyone's father." I guess the family stayed close after Khazak's mom and dad split.

"He is." Ursza speaks her first words to me, rolling her eyes in the process. Now I'm lost again.

"So why don't you like being called *Dave*, Dave?" Okay, now Yogik's doing it just to piss me off.

"I just don't." Five pairs of eyes stare at me in silence, expecting more of an answer. *Dammit.* I sigh. "My dad goes by Dave, so I just prefer David." Let's leave it at that, please.

"You were named after your father?" Khazak's voice questions from my left.

"Yeah. I'm *technically* David Cerano Jr.," I answer then turn my head back to everyone else. "Sorry, can we go back to Orlun and Jarek both being your father? You have two fathers?"

"*No*," Ignatz scoffs, even more exasperated than his sister, but there's an odd look on his face. He knows something. "We have three."

Wait, *what?*

"You have *three* fathers?" I look between the five of them, confused.

"Yes, Orlun, Rurig, and Jarek." Yogik lists them off like it's the simplest thing he's ever done. Which it probably is.

"I feel like I'm missing something." Like how many times their mom got remarried.

"Why did you not tell me you were named after your father?" Khazak asks before anyone can clarify things for me.

I'm sorry, I'm standing here struggling to remember half-a-dozen new names and faces, getting bombarded with both piles of new information *and* personal questions, all while his two youngest siblings treat me like the world's dumbest foreign exchange student, and *that's* what he's focused on? *Are you fucking kidding me?*

"I don't know. Why didn't you tell me you had *three fucking dads?*" I spit out in frustration.

The room goes silent. Everyone's staring at me. And also kind of behind me. Ursza and Ignatz look like they're trying to hold in their laughter. I turn and am greeted by the sight of Orlun, Jarek, and a shorter, stouter orc—I'm guessing Rurig—who have just entered the room. Probably to tell us dinner is ready. *Great.*

"I'm sorry. That was very rude," I say to them as calmly and politely as I can before slowly turning to face Khazak. "Can we talk somewhere in private?"

"So that was..."

"A shitshow?" I finish Khazak's thought.

"I was going to say interesting." He frowns.

"I agree. It was a very interesting shitshow." The two of us are standing in his childhood bedroom. It's not as exciting as I would have hoped. A bed, a bookshelf, a couple of bows on the wall. He was a real party animal.

"You may have overreacted to the news about my parentage," he offers, taking a seat on his bed.

"My mistake. I must have been distracted by how close you and your sister are." I stand in the center of the room facing him, arms crossed.

"Our relationship may be a little more...strained than I let on." He rubs the back of his neck.

"And you don't think having three fathers was something worth mentioning?" Just a heads up would have been nice, really.

"It did not seem important." I give him a look. *Really?* "Honestly. It is not that uncommon here to have a family arrangement like ours."

"How come you never mentioned it?" I *really* feel like this should have come up before. "I distinctly remember you saying 'father,' not 'fathers.'"

"I truly never thought about it." He looks a *little* sheepish at least. "It has always been normal for me."

"Doesn't calling three different people "father" get confusing?" Maybe someone goes by dad or pops or something.

He shakes his head no. "In our language the word for mother or father changes based on the person. Orlun is Orda, Rurig is Ruda. Jarek is—"

"Jarda?" Yay, pattern games. I have more pressing questions. "Okay, so, how did it happen? Do you have a mother? Wait, can male orcs get pregnant?" My eyes go wide and my hands shoot to my stomach in shock. "Can they get other men pregnant?!"

"You are not pregnant, David." Khazak laughs deep from his belly. "My fathers, Orlun and Rurig, met when they were serving on our militia. After their service ended, they wanted to start a family. I have... You might call them aunts? Not blood related, but they were friends of my fathers, women who also desired a family. So arrangements were made to help each other. Ayla and I were the first born, then my cousin Korra, then Yogik... You get the idea. When Ayla and I were eight and Yogik was three, my fathers met Jarek, and he became part of the family as well. Ursza and Ignatz were each born a few years after that."

"And you hated him." I remember his sister teasing him about it.

"I did not hate him. I was eight years old, and it was a difficult period in my life," he grumbles before standing and walking over to me. "I am sorry for not explain things to you earlier."

"It's okay." I close the distance between us, tugging on his shirt a little. "I'm sorry for freaking out like that in front of your family."

He smiles. "Are you ready to go back out there?"

"Oh no. We're not going back out there." I shake my head and step back.

"What do you mean?" He tilts his head.

"See that window?" I point to the wall behind him. "We're climbing out that, going home, and pretending like none of this ever happened."

"David." I know that tone.

"What? You can*not* expect me to go back there after all that." I wave my hand at the room we just left.

"It will be fine, David. Maybe a little embarrassing, but I have seen you survive worse." That might be up for debate. "You just needed a moment in private to collect yourself."

"And for you to explain yourself." I grumble and recross my arms. "Besides it's not like this is *that* private."

"What, you think my family is eavesdropping on us?" He sarcastically waves around the room at all the nothing.

I look at him like he's dumb. "*Of course* they're eavesdropping on us."

"Why would you think that?" *Oh you sweet simple man.*

"Because that's what you do when your brother brings home a complete stranger who freaks out in your living room about how many dads you have!" I'm panting a little when I finish my short rant. "Why are you looking at me like that?" He's wearing a really goofy smile.

"You are cute when you are frustrated." He brushes a thumb along my beard.

"...I'm going out the window." I start walking towards it.

"David." He grabs my wrist, laughing as he pulls me into him. "I am sorry."

I sigh. "I still think we should at least *consider* the window."

He doesn't answer, but he does give me a soft kiss. "Are you ready for dinner?"

"I guess." We separate and turn to the door, but I pause. "Hold on."

I motion for Khazak to stay where he is and remain quiet as I tiptoe to the door. Once I'm in position, I carefully reach for the knob, quickly grabbing it and flinging it open. Immediately the sounds of two adolescent bodies tripping over themselves echo in from the hallway as they scramble to get away from the door.

I give Khazak my best "told-ya-so" look. Time to get the rest of this shitshow on the road.

Chapter Sixteen

_L_ ess rattled after our talk, I exit the bedroom with Khazak. He leads the way to the dining room where everyone else is already seated around a large table. The room goes silent when we enter, all eyes watching as we take our seats. The only two open and next to each other are to the left of Ayla. Khazak pulls out my chair for me, placing me in the center, probably to act as a buffer. Yogik is seated to our left, the younger set of siblings to our right, and his fathers are on the other side of the table facing us.

Each seat has an empty plate in front of it and the rest of the table is covered in food, most of it meat: fish, pork, some kind of bird. They pulled out all the stops to welcome their daughter home. It all smells great. Khazak reaches for a pitcher and pours us some water, but no one is eating yet.

"So," Rurig starts, seated directly across from me. "How did you two meet?"

The men seated on either side of him groan, Orlun covering his face with his and Jarek turning his up to the ceiling. To my left, I hear Khazak choking on his water while I sit there wide eyed and slack jawed, unsure of what I'm supposed to say.

"I begged you not to make that joke," Jarek pleads with the heavens, defeated.

Rurig is too busy laughing at himself to respond, and there are snorts of laughter from the rest of the table.

"What my husband means to say," Orlun speaks to me directly, "is welcome to our home, David. We hope you enjoy the meal."

"You laughed when I said it in the kitchen." Rurig seems unbothered by his husbands' exasperation. "Hope you boys are hungry because I have been cooking all day. Shit, forgot the gravy, hold on." When Rurig stands from the table, I notice that one of his feet is missing, replaced by what looks like an upside-down cane handle in its place. Then I remember it's rude to stare and go back to looking at my plate.

"I have to admit, I am curious," Jarek starts next. "What brought you and your friends to this part of the world?"

"A boat?" I joke, desperately trying to lighten the mood. "I just wanted to get out and see the world, I guess." And leave certain people and organizations behind. "I, uh, promise we didn't mean to cause any trouble," I tag on sheepishly.

A hand squeezes my thigh under the table. Thankfully Rurig returns before I have to go into any more detail, bowl of gravy in hand. Placing it down with the rest of the food, he looks around the table, smiling. He claps his hands together and I half expect him to start saying an orc version of grace, but all that comes out is, "Let's eat!"

I'm used to big family dinners so it's no surprise when arms shoot out and begin grabbing at plates. Everything gets passed around, but I'm still feeling a little more timid than usual so I'm happy when Khazak notices and makes a point of making sure I get a little of everything that comes his way. I don't even know where to start; I just tuck a napkin into my shirt and dig in.

The number of times I hear a food-muffled "thank you" directed at Rurig tells me he's the main cook here, which probably means he's also the one who taught Khazak—which checks out because the food is amazing. I couldn't tell you what half this stuff is, only that it tastes delicious. Everyone else seems to agree because all around me are the sounds of chewing and swallowing. I want to eat until my stomach hurts.

After the initial rush, things slow down and conversations pick up. I'm content to just sit and listen even though the fact they're all speaking in Common is solely for my benefit. Jarek finishes saying something about work when I burp loudly, groaning happily as the pressure is released from my stomach. Then I realize what I did and quickly move to cover my mouth. "Excuse me."

"Thank you," Rurig takes it as a compliment. I notice everyone else seems to be winding down their food intake too. "That reminds me." Rurig clasps Orlun on the shoulder. "Gonna grab that ale we were saving for a special occasion. Get the mugs."

Orlun stands as his husband exits the room, walking to a cabinet and removing a set of carved wooden mugs that are passed around the table. When Ursza and Ignatz see that they aren't being given their own, they roll their eyes and scoff, pushing back and leaving the table.

"Ungrateful little..." Orlun retakes his seat. "Ayla, you have not told us anything about your trip yet."

"Aw, come on, Dad. No one really wants to hear about that," she says with all the bravado of someone who has a story ready to go.

"It is literally the reason they are having this dinner," Yogik deadpans from across the table.

Ayla huffs in response but doesn't let that deter her. "I was gone for 14 months. Where would I even start?"

"Hopefully not at the beginning," Khazak mumbles on my left.

"What was your favorite stop?" Jarek asks as Rurig re-enters the room carrying two large pitchers of amber liquid. Mugs are filled, but I notice Khazak eyeing his warily and not drinking. *Great job, David. You made the man afraid of beer.*

"Well, one of my first stops was to Shiveria," Ayla begins her tale. "I wanted to climb through the mountains and see the crystal waterfalls. They were breathtaking."

"Sounds cold," Jarek gripes, taking a swig of his drink.

"Freezing. We had to use magical torches to keep warm. The magic kept them lit—even if we dropped them in the snow—and also kept our body temperature at a safe level as long as we stayed near enough." That sounds dangerous…and kinda fun. "After that, I bounced around a little until I ended up on the Fangbei Plains. I took a job helping a team of researchers tracking the migration patterns of cyclosauri herds. I was sort of like their bodyguard. It was my responsibility to scout for places to set up camp, close enough to watch the herd but far enough away that we wouldn't disturb them. I had to get pretty creative when there weren't enough trees for cover. We were out there for over a month, but we never stayed in the same place for more than a couple of days. If anything went wrong, my only concern was getting everyone out safely."

"You always were a resourceful child." Jarek sips his ale, impressed with his daughter.

"That sounds like work, when you're supposed to be traveling," Jarek adds. "Please tell me you did some relaxing too."

"Well, the last boat ride I took was also the longest, but we stopped at *many* different islands. A lot of beaches, fishing, and a surprising amount of alcohol. They all had their charm, but for two days we were docked at this one chain... During the day the water looked like any other, but at night, it would *glow*. Not just the water, the animals living in it too. You could look down and see schools of brightly colored fish swimming by. I loved watching the sea turtles float by with their shimmering green shells before bedtime." I'm in awe at her descriptions. I've heard the names, read descriptions, but never so much as seen a picture. "Actually, that reminds me. One of the last islands we visited was run by these gnomes who were trying to start some sort of zoo, only all the animals would be mechanical. I only saw some prototypes but… that place is going to be *crazy*."

"Waterfalls and gnomes are well and good, but where was the best *food*?" Rurig has his priorities in order.

"Oh, that's easy. There was this halfling village in south Bhuvarsha. They called themselves the Gana." Ayla sips her beer before she continues. "They had an outdoor food market with dozens of carts, each one serving something different. I ended up spending two extra days there just so I could try everything. They used spices I'd never heard of before. Their cooking was almost as good as yours, Ruda."

"Almost, huh?" Rurig grins at the compliment as he downs more ale.

"What about you, David? Have you traveled much?" Ayla suddenly turns her attention to me, as does the rest of the table. *Crap*.

"Uh, not really. I'd like to." Things haven't exactly gotten according to plan, but that was the goal. "The trip here was my first. I came over here because it's the place I knew the least about. I wanted to experience it for the first time myself." It was also the cheapest and farthest away.

"Is there a place you'd like to visit next?" Ayla seems genuinely excited when she asks.

"Unless getting arrested and ending up here was on your list of experiences," Rurig adds wryly from his seat.

"Well, I figure I can squeeze in a few more jail cells before the end of the year." You have to fight jokes with jokes, even if they're at your own expense.

Rurig chuckles into his mug. "I like him."

"I honestly have no idea." I turn back to Ayla to finish answering her question. "I didn't really think that far ahead. …Any recommendations?"

Ayla's face brightens even more at my question. "Well, if you ever travel west, tucked away out in the Hayaki Desert is an oasis where crystals grow out of the ground like plants. Every color you could imagine: some even change throughout the day. You know how when light passes through something transparent, it leaves a colored shadow?" I nod. "There is something about the crystals, or maybe the land itself, but anything bathed in those shadows is dyed that color. It lasts maybe half a minute, but it affects everything. Rocks, plants, animals, people. There are rainbows all over the sand. It's truly amazing." She stops. "There is a group of people living there, a commune. I think they've been there a long time. They have these beautiful ceremonies at sunset."

"Wow." I'm whispering, completely drawn in by her story. "What's it called?"

"Li'akwa. I think you'd like it there." Ayla leans back in her seat. "Maybe you can convince my brother to loosen up and take you one day."

Or I could just go by myself in two months. I look to my left and notice Khazak sitting stiffly beside me. *How long has he been like that?* Wait, is he *jealous* that I'm talking to his sister? At least he finished his beer, as he is now pouring himself a second one.

"How has work been, son?" Orlun senses the tension and redirects the conversation.

"Good, Orda." I see Khazak's shoulders relax, back on familiar ground. "We have almost finished the security upgrades I told you about. The old holding cells will be torn down next week."

"Good riddance. I hardly ever remember using them." That would have been good information to have two nights ago, but ignoring that, it sounds like Orlun used to be a ranger himself. "Are you due back in yet?"

"Tomorrow." He is? Has it been a week already? "It will also be David's first day."

"It will? I mean, you're taking me with you?" I do not remember talking about this. Did I space out again?

"Well, we talked about finding you something to do," he reasons. "It seemed better than the alternative of leaving you home alone all day."

"No, that's okay. I just didn't know that was a possibility. Or that it was happening tomorrow." Or what they do exactly aside from arresting trespassers. Can't imagine they would even want me there.

"You would be acting as my assis—" he starts to explain.

"Ooo, is Khazak making plans without telling the other person about it until the last minute again?" Ayla cuts in, leaning forward on her elbow to look at her twin.

"That is not what I—" he tries again.

"Khazak, come help me and your fathers clean up." It's Rurig's turn to prevent an argument, standing and starting to gather up dishes. "Your siblings helped us cook, after all."

"Yes, Ruda." Khazak sighs and sends me an apologetic look.

Ayla pulls me to the side as the table is cleared and plates are brought into the kitchen. She leads me to a backdoor, and we head outside into the cool night air. There's no grass (I haven't seen much grass outside of the park now that I think about it), just a small fire pit with a few chairs around it. There's also what looks like a vegetable garden off to the side. Stepping away from the door, Ayla leans back against the house.

"Easier to talk out here." She offers me a smile. "Sorry about that. I love my brother, but it is just so easy to get under his skin sometimes. I can't help it. He is such a control freak."

"Who, the guy that would only let me call him 'Sir' for the first five days? Never would have guessed." She laughs and I relax, copying her stance against the wall. "Has he always been like that?"

"Honestly? Yes, ever since we were children." She shakes her head a little. "He was the responsible one while I was always getting into trouble. My parents would put him in charge of watching me and Yogik even though we're the same age. I'm technically older by two minutes!"

"We would do things together but in completely different ways," she continues, her hands moving animatedly as she speaks. "I have never met a more prepared person. He'd have a plan, a backup plan, and a backup-backup plan. I'm the type to just roll the dice and jump in, but he always knew *exactly* what he wanted. He was so stubborn. Once he set his mind on something, he'd make it happen."

"I think I know what you mean." Sounds a little familiar. Maybe that's why we get along sometimes.

"Problem is, when he can't be in control of a situation, or worse, when he *loses* control, he tends to..." She points her finger down and makes a twirling motion. "Spiral. I really shouldn't provoke him like that. He normally handles it better."

I can't bring myself to tell her that I'm probably the reason for that. It would explain why he's seemed so off. Our fight and the "renegotiating" of our...relationship probably left him feeling all kinds of shaky. Hell, not even just that, but the way I drugged him, robbed him, and nearly got him fired...he's probably feeling completely thrown off. "I think I understand that too."

She nods to herself. "So, is he treating you well?"

"Oh. Yeah. He... We're good." I don't think anyone's actually asked me that before, and I'm not sure how to answer. This whole night has felt like it's just a step away from something normal, then I get asked something about how my owner treats me, and I'm thrown off again.

"Good. We all knew he would, but you know, gotta ask." She smiles and shrugs. I really wish I knew what she meant, but I don't think Khazak would appreciate it if I told her about our recent issues.

"Can I ask you something that might sound rude?" It's at least something that won't get me in trouble. "Why is the way you speak Common so different from the rest of your family?" She's a lot less formal than most of the other orcs I've met.

"I've spent most of the last ten years away from them. You travel the world, you pick up a few things." She grins. "I speak eight different languages, but the one that pops up the most is Common. Especially the cursing. So versatile."

"I feel a strange amount of pride in my people for introducing the word 'fuck' to world." Can't wait to tell Khazak about our amazing accomplishments.

We both laugh, standing there looking into the night sky a little longer before I feel the need to use the little human's room. I only drank the one, but that ale has already worked its way through me. "Where's the bathroom?"

"Go left when you go inside and it's the last door on the right," she directs me as I head in.

"Thanks." The "for more than just the directions to the bathroom" goes unsaid.

I walk back inside, and you'd never guess that nine people just had dinner in here. The table has been cleared and looks spotless. I hear noises coming from the kitchen, but I don't see anyone. Nature is still calling, so I make my way to the bathroom, spotting Yogik coming at me when I turn into the hallway.

"David." He meets me halfway and stops.

"You remembered." Let's hope he keeps it that way.

"Just having a little fun." He winks at me before leaning in closer. "So tell me, has my brother started sharing you yet?"

"Uh, what?" What does he mean by "sharing" me?

"I will take that as a no. Pity." He frowns, still standing way too close.

"Um. I gotta...use the bathroom." I awkwardly walk around him,

Peeing is more difficult than it should be after that weird encounter but somehow I manage. When I finish and head back to the dining room, I see Khazak and Ayla talking together. Hopefully making up. I step over to join them.

"I missed you, Khaz." She leans in to hug him.

"I missed you too, Lala." Aww, he has a nickname for her. "How long are you in town?"

"Not sure yet." Ayla shrugs. "No real plans, so it looks like I'll be crashing here for a while."

"You are staying?" *Did his voice just crack?*

"Don't sound too disappointed." She scoffs but she's still smiling.

"I am not— I did not mean—"

"Calm down." She hugs him again. "You're still too easy to work up."

"And you are still a pain in my ass." He returns the hug nonetheless. They finally notice my presence when they separate. "David."

"He's a sneaky one." Ayla takes notice of me as well. "Might want to tie a bell on him."

"It was great meeting you *Lala*," I grumble. I thought we were friends!

"Low blow, David." She shakes her head.

"I think we are just about ready to go home, eh David?" His hand lightly squeezes my neck.

"Sounds good to me." I am feeling a little overstimulated.

I hug Ayla before Khazak leads me into a very large kitchen. Orlun is bent over a sink washing dishes while Rurig and Jarek are off to the side dealing with leftovers. Everyone pauses when they see us, Rurig approaching first with a stack of wrapped dishes in his arms and both husbands right behind him.

"He is too skinny. Make sure he eats these." He pushes the food toward his son before turning to me. "I expect to see some meat on these bones the next time I see you." He pinches my arm for effect.

"Yes, sir." I nod my head, not even considering there might be a next time. "I swear I'm working on it."

"Good." He gives me a toothy smile. *Are all orc smiles technically toothy?*

"It was nice to meet you, David." Jarek steps around his larger husband.

"Try to stay out of trouble." Orlun joins him.

"Yes, sir." The more I say it, the more I feel like I'm back in school.

When it's time to speak to their son however, they switch into their own language, the conversation between them flowing so much faster than it did in Common. God, they must feel like they're dumbing themselves down so much when they have to talk to me. I should have asked Ayla if she had any tricks for learning new languages. The three of them walk us to the front door where Yogik waves his goodbye from a distance. Good. Ayla is there, but the other two are nowhere in sight, and after more hugs and goodbyes, we are outside, walking home in the moonlight.

Things are silent for a little too long, and I have to break it. "So."

"So," comes the oddly neutral response.

"That was..."

"A very interesting shitshow?" He turns to me and I can make out a wry smile.

"Something like that." I'm glad to see he's in good spirits. "I dunno. It could have gone worse."

"It also could have gone much better," he grumbles. "Or preferably not at all."

"Oh my gods, *that's* why you didn't want me to come." And here I thought he was trying to look out for me. "You were worried your family was going to embarrass you."

"I may have considered that as a possibility." I remember his sister's words on the patio. Always a plan. "I sometimes find it difficult to be around my family but...you enjoyed your evening?"

"Yeah. I like them." For the most part. "Your dads seem nice. Your sister is pretty cool, your younger siblings are weird, and uh, I think your brother hit on me."

"He *what?*" Khazak freezes in his tracks.

"When I passed him in the hall, he asked me..." I really hope this isn't something a brother usually asks. "He asked me if you had started sharing me yet."

In the dim light I can just make out Khazak's hands tensing as they grip the leftovers. "I am going to strangle that little rodent." He turns on his heel and starts walking back toward his parent's house.

"Wait, wait!" I pull on his arm to stop. "Next time. I'd honestly rather just go home tonight." I'm not sure I'm up for any more family confrontations.

"I am very sorry, David," he apologizes with a sigh. "That is not something he should have asked you. That is not something even within the realm of possibility, and he knows that. I think he may have done it to get a rise out of you, or more likely me, but I do not understand why."

"It's okay. My brother can be a dick too." And a smug one at that. "I understand what you mean by difficult to be around."

"Would that have anything to do with the *real* reason you traveled here all the way from home?" My body goes still. "Like say, a father you do not seem to like being named after?"

I can only stare, mouth agape like I want to say something but haven't figured out what.

"You do not have to tell me unless you want to," he offers softly, encouraging me to continue walking with him, "but I would be happy to listen."

We walk in silence for a few minutes before I finally speak up. "He's not the reason I left, but he is one of the reasons I didn't stay."

Khazak turns his face to me, not saying anything but still walking.

"I wasn't happy with where it looked like my life was headed. A lot of other people seemed to be, but I wasn't." I stare at the ground as I walk.

"What direction was that?" It sounds like he's actually curious.

A very boring one. "Finish the academy, join the military, find some girl to settle down with, and have some kids." I shrug. "Same as my grandfather did. Same as my father did. And same as my older brother is in the middle of doing."

"What did *you* want to do?" Good question.

"I don't know." I shrug. "I just knew I didn't want that."

"Forgive me for asking, but...your older brother." Joseph. "Why is he not named after your father instead of you? Is that not more traditional?"

"Because he was named after my grandfather. You could say sons seeking their father's approval is a running theme in our family." Dad was always trying to get Granddad to respect him. I'm not sure he ever did. "You'd think that not being the first born I might get a break from all that pressure, but because he named me after himself, my dad expected even more. It wasn't enough for me to be *as good* as my brother. I couldn't just come close. I had to be better. Had to be stronger, win more games, date more girls."

"I know what it is like to do things to earn your fathers' admiration." Three times over, in fact.

"Yeah, but I get the feeling your dads actually tell you they're proud of you sometimes." I swear that sounded a lot less sad in my head.

"I am sure your father is proud of you, David." That sounded even sadder.

"That makes one of us." Okay, let's wrap this up. "It felt like I was turning into him, doing the same things he did with Granddad, fighting for every scrap of approval. And I didn't want to be like him. I *don't* want to be like him."

"So you left." He comes to the conclusion, and I'm happy to leave it at that.

"Like I said, in the end it was more about not staying than it was leaving." I am eager to get out of this spotlight. "So, what about you and your sister? What's going on there?"

"I am not sure what you mean." He stands a little straighter as he walks.

"One of the first things you did after not seeing her for over a year was insult the clothes she was wearing," I helpfully point out.

"I did not *insult* her clothing," he huffs.

"And that wasn't you getting jealous when I was talking to her about traveling either?" I don't know if he can see my side-eye in the moonlight.

"Why would I get jealous of you talking to my sister?" His tone gives away his annoyance.

"Cool, so you won't mind if I head back and ask her to take me to that place in the desert?" I ask, hooking my thumb behind me.

That gets him to turn and look at me, eyes narrow. "No. We are almost home."

Sure, *that's* why.

"Well maybe tomorrow I could go back and—"

"*Okay*, David." He takes a deep breath before continuing. "I love my sister." There's definitely a "but" coming. "But it is difficult to feel like you still know a person when you almost never see them. The first time my sister left home was when we were your age. That was just for the summer. Then she was barely home two weeks before she was gone for *three months*. Every time she left, it would be even longer before she came home."

"We got used to her missing birthdays and holidays," he continues. "It was not a big deal. In the beginning she would write to us frequently. I got postcards from nearly every place she visited. But eventually that slowed down to every other place until one day it stopped entirely. We would go months without hearing anything. My fathers only got the letter announcing her return here yesterday."

"Your dad made all that food in a day?" He managed to feed *nine* people like that on short notice?

"He is very good at what he does." Khazak lifts the leftover food. "At some point, it started to feel like what she was doing was collecting stories to impress us with. None of us have had any idea where she has been this past year. That is why my fathers were asking her about it at dinner."

"And why you were so eager to shut it down." It came off as rude when he did it, but I sort of understand now.

"My sister has never been the most responsible." It doesn't sound like he means it as an insult. "That is okay. It is who she is. I just wish that she would put more effort in where family was concerned."

"Have you ever talked to her about any of that?" I'm willing to bet he hasn't.

"Have you ever talked to your father about *your* issues?" he shoots back, unimpressed.

"Oh look, we're home." I notice the house coming up on our left. Perfect timing.

He snorts a laugh, fumbling for his keys while awkwardly holding the stack of food in one arm. Stubborn. But I am glad to be home.

"You know, where I come from, meeting your parents like that would be considered a pretty good evening." Honestly, that went better than most of the times I met a girlfriend's family back home, even if it's not quite the same thing. "We should celebrate."

"Celebrate? Are you somehow still hungry?" Khazak piles everything onto the kitchen counter. "I think Ruda gave us enough food to last a week."

"Okay, two things." I walk over, crowding him just a little bit. "One, who is this 'we?' I was given very specific instructions from your father to eat all of that food myself, Sir. And two... I wasn't talking about celebrating with food. Sir." Really hope he's picking up what I'm putting down.

"Oh." I see a flash of desire on his face before it's back to neutral as he starts to pack the containers into the icebox. "Are you certain?"

"Uh, yeah?" I laugh a little. "That's why I brought it up. You okay?"

"Yes, I am just still feeling a little...cautious in regard to that aspect of our arrangement." It's the same hesitation I've felt since we talked things out yesterday. I was kinda hoping I took care of that this morning, but I guess I need more practice.

"I appreciate you wanting to take it easy on me," I reach out and take a hold of the bottom of his shirt, "but you know, part of what I like about our 'arrangement' is you calling the shots."

That gets me a smile, but I can tell he's still thinking about it. "I am not sure it is a good idea."

"Why not?" All my ideas are good. Usually. "I thought we figured this out yesterday."

"We also said we were going to take things slow, did we not?" Not *this* slow.

"There's a difference between slow and celibate." And I don't plan on being the latter.

"I am not suggesting we be celibate." He rolls his eyes.

"Okay, well, I just asked if you wanted to go fool around—something I have never done with anyone before, by the way—and you had to ask if I was sure." The rejection might have stung a little.

"I am only being cautious, David." He's starting to sound annoyed.

"What are you afraid of happening?" He's making it sound like he might accidentally fuck me to death or something. "I trust you, Khazak."

"Well, *I do not*, David." For a second I think he's talking about me, but then I understand. He doesn't trust himself. He really is afraid he might take things too far and push me to do something I don't want. *Fuck.* It's at least partially my fault he's feeling this way. I don't want him to be afraid to touch me. How do I fix this?

"Khazak. Sir. You're not going to hurt me, or scare me, or—"

"I think our recent history and your own words have already proved you wrong." It's like he's not even willing to listen to me.

"Look, we both said and did some shitty things, but are you seriously letting that dictate everything else that happens between us?" I know I'm oversimplifying but come on.

"Yes. I am." Oh my *god* this man is so fucking stubborn.

"Your sister was right about you," I mutter without thinking.

"What is *that* supposed to mean?" He slams the lid of the icebox shut a little too hard. "What did my sister say about me?"

"Nothing, just..." Hold on, I think I'm getting an idea. "Just that you have control issues."

He scoffs. "And I suppose she thinks herself an expert on my 'control issues?'"

"I think her exact words were 'control freak.'" I tell myself that snitching is alright if it's for the greater good.

His nostrils flare as soon as the words leave my mouth. "What the hell would someone who has not been home for over a year know about my life?"

"I think I'm inclined to agree with her. You are *definitely* a control freak," I snark.

"What, *exactly*, makes me a control freak?" He takes a few steps toward me in the living room.

"I dunno, maybe the way you need to be in constant control of every aspect of any given situation, and when you can't, you just wash your hands of the whole thing?" Now I *know* I'm oversimplifying things.

"That is *not* what is happening here!" he shouts at the ceiling in frustration.

"Really? So you're not still feeling bothered by everything we yelled about two days ago and are now trying to take things in the complete opposite direction?" I'm great at sounding confident when I'm pulling things out of my ass.

"No." The single word is growled and I can see his fist clench.

"Great. Thanks for clearing that up." I roll my eyes much harder than I need to before I turn around. "Anyway, I'm just gonna go hit up a bar or something. Catch you later."

"You are not going out, David," he growls and steps toward me.

"Or what? We've already established that you're too afraid to touch me." Time to lay it on thick. "Not sure I have much reason to listen to you now."

"Do not test me, David." The threat is growled low.

"Oh no. The things you sister told me really helped paint a full picture." I don't shy away as he enters my space. "You're not actually serious about any of this."

"Keep pushing me, and I will show you just how serious I can be." He's right in my face.

"Yeah?" Okay, time to go for broke. If what I say next doesn't go over the way I want, Khazak may honestly never want to speak to me again. "You mean like how you showed me after I drugged, robbed, and humiliated you in front of your men?"

Before I even realize it, the front of my shirt is grabbed as Khazak pulls me forward.

"I know when I am being provoked, David," he growls in my face. "If you are going to insist on acting like an insolent brat, then I will be happy to correct you like one."

"What the hell are you—HEY!" I'm half pulled, half dragged around to the front of the couch where Khazak sits and yanks me over his lap.

"Disciplining an infant, apparently." Khazak grabs my arms to pin them behind my back before yanking my pants down unceremoniously, just under my ass. I struggle because despite having asked for exactly what's about to happen, I still wish it wasn't. "This is what you wanted, is it not?"

And then he spanks me. He starts with quick, steady smacks from his hand, just warming up. Each slap of his palm stings, but I can handle it for now. He's alternating sides, back and forth, but around twenty, things get uncomfortable. My breath starts to hitch, and I focus to keep it even.

"Honestly, David, I tell you one time that I do not want to have sex, and you throw a *temper tantrum*?" He speaks calmly while I'm fighting to hold back my whimpers. "Then, when that does not work, you decide to *intentionally* piss me off so I will punish you?"

To be fair, I didn't know for a fact that punishment was how he'd react. Just kinda hoped. His hand is moving slower, but the blows are raining down harder. I struggle futilely, and for a moment, he stops, running his hand over the abused flesh and even kneading it slightly, which finally gets me to whimper out loud. Then his hand leaves me, and I brace myself.

"Ignoring the fact that we *literally* had sex this morning, ignoring *everything* that happened not even *two days ago*." I cry out at the first blow and each one that follows. His arm isn't even getting tired. "Did you not consider for a moment that *maybe* after navigating an incredibly stressful dinner this evening with my *entire* family, I might simply *not be in the fucking mood?!*"

"I'm sorry!" I cry because no, I didn't actually consider that. Not that I get him to slow down.

"Then you bring up my sister *and* use what you did the night of your break in all in an attempt to make me angry?" I'm sobbing into the couch each time his hand hits me. "So I would react like *this*? I am once again *astounded* by your ability to commit to a half-baked plan."

"Fuck, please! I'm sorry!" I'm not just saying it either. The only reason I brought up the night of the "incident" is because of how shitty I still feel about that night. I remember the way I hesitated, the way the guilt I felt grew the further I went with my plan. The way I had to push down every good feeling he gave me. Then I bring it up and throw it in his face just to get him to do what I want. He really *might* hate me after this.

I'm not sure when he stops exactly, before I start blubbering or after. I remember crying into the couch, another "I'm sorry" on my lips. Then I'm gathered up, turned and made to straddle his lap, my head brought to his chest. Instinctively, I squeeze myself into the crook of his neck, his chin resting atop my head. One arm is around my neck and the other thrown over my waist, the hand stroking small circles onto the sweaty skin of my back.

As I come down from the endorphin high, I feel his chest hair poking out from his shirt, tickling my face as I mumble another apology against his skin. I can feel his rounder stomach against my flat one, my legs on either side of his meaty thighs. Once my heart is no longer pounding in my ears, I can hear him mumbling something above me, needing to focus to make it out.

"...Good boy." It's said so softly I'm almost not sure I'm hearing it. I press forward again, almost dozing in and out as the warm darkness envelops me.

"That hurt," I croak out once I find my words again.

"You took it very well," is the response. Then there is a hand on the back of my shirt collar, pulling us apart so that I can look him in the eye. "I do not like being manipulated, David."

"I'm sorry," I repeat for the umpteenth time. If my face could get any redder, it would. "I was only trying to——"

"I know." He strokes the side of my face. "I can appreciate that you wanted to get me out of a perceived rut, but this is not going to work if we do not communicate."

"Not just that." I shake my head a little. "I'm sorry for all of it. All the times I've insulted you or acted like an ass, for everything I did to you that night. I'm just so sorry."

"The purpose of punishment is to give you the opportunity to be for-given for your infractions, and to allow for both of us to move on." He's still stroking my back as he pulls me back into his chest. "Think of it as absolution for your sins. A blank slate is the expression, I think."

"You're not still angry at me for any of it?" My voice comes out as a whine when I ask.

"Blank slate, puppy." I feel a kiss on my head.

"Are *all* future punishments going to hurt that much?" I grumble into his chest.

"Are you planning on a repeat performance anytime soon?" he asks wryly. "I do not *want* to punish you like that, David."

"Yeah, you seem real torn up about it." I nudge the back of my hand against the base of his very prominent erection, as if this man didn't just light my damn ass on fire.

"And I suppose that half-hard lump I feel poking into me is where all that guilt you were feeling went?" He grabs my sore ass and grinds me forward into his crotch for emphasis.

"Shut up." ***spank*** "Oww."

Chapter Seventeen

A low bell chime is what pulls me up from the inky blackness of sleep. I'm lying on my stomach over Khazak's chest, my ass too sore for any other position. His body shifts underneath me, and I grumble a complaint as my very comfortable pillow moves out from under me. *Five more minutes.*

Whatever he's doing, the bell chimes stop. He moves back to the center of the bed, and I throw my arm over his waist to keep him in place. His arm slips over mine, his hand stroking its way down my back. I'm *just* about to fall back asleep when that hand drifts farther south and strokes over the inflamed skin on my ass. I hiss when it makes contact.

"I hope a certain puppy has learned not to provoke me, lest he end up with a sore rump." He chuckles and gives me a squeeze, making me try to move forward away from his hand.

"Didn't learn nothin'," I mumble against his chest, eyes still closed. "What was that noise?"

"My alarm." I make a grumbling noise. *Alarms are stupid.* "As much as I would love another lazy morning in bed with you, we have a busy day ahead of us." The hand goes back to stroking my back. "You need to make a good impression on your first day."

I whine into his skin. Whose idea was it for me to work again?

"I was also considering a repeat performance of yesterday's morning activities."

That gets my attention. I squeeze myself against his body for a moment, making sure to grind my hard length against him before I pull away, stretching and finally opening my eyes.

"Morning, Sir." I rub the sleep from my eyes as they adjust to the dimly lit room.

"Good morning, pup." He looks down at my erection. "Is that all it takes to get you moving?"

"I am a simple man, Sir," I respond. "Now what was this I heard about a repeat?"

With another chuckle, he sits up and moves to the edge of the bed. He snaps his fingers and points between his spread legs. "Kneeling rest."

It takes me a moment to register the order—that it even is an order—but once it does, I move from the bed and sink to my knees between his legs, hands behind my back. Right in front of me is his cock, lying hard against his thigh, green head peeking through the hood of his foreskin. I look up to await my next order.

"Seeing as we have a time limit, I am going to be more 'hands on' this time," he says with a smirk that tells me that is definitely not the only reason. I am okay with that. His hand moves to the back of my head, pulling me near my target.

"I think you have already figured out the most important objective: being mindful of your teeth." He grips his dick in one hand, pointing it at my approaching face. "We will start working to reduce your gag reflex next."

The already-wet head of his cock bumps against my lips, and I open them automatically. A familiar taste hits my tongue as the hand on my head beckons me farther down his shaft, more guiding than pushing. Once I feel his cock nearly reach the back of my throat, he changes his grip and begins pulling me back.

We move a little faster the next time, and then again on the next, and the next, until I'm steadily bobbing up and down on the first few inches of his cock. Each time he pulls me back, I try to swirl my tongue around his cockhead, making the appendage twitch nicely before I sink back down it. My jaw is already starting to feel the burn of being stretched open, but I don't let it show.

"Good boy." My eyes go up, my belly warm at the praise. "We are going to work on taking me deeper now, alright?"

He doesn't wait for an answer before pulling me down farther on the next stroke. I can feel his cock tickling my throat, and I tense up when I know what's coming. On the next round, he drags my head down even more and pushes his cock into my throat—and holds me there. I gag almost immediately, but I've got nowhere to go.

"Fight against the urge to gag and remember to breathe through your nose." He finally releases me, allowing me to pull off completely. The hand that was in my hair moves to cup my chin, his thumb stroking over my lips. "I know it is difficult, but unfortunately, the only real way to take care of your gag reflex is to *fuck* it out of you."

I whimper, the dirty talk going straight to my dick. Then his hand is back in my hair, and he's once again filling my mouth and throat. He repeats the same process as before, each time holding himself in my throat a little longer. He never quite lets me pull all the way off, instead having me nurse on his head when I need to catch my breath. My cock is so hard it *aches*, but I don't dare remove my hands from behind my back to touch it. I'm so focused on what I'm doing, I barely even register the pain coming from my spanked ass.

Once I am able to hold him in my throat long enough for his liking, he changes back to his earlier tactic of moving me up and down his length at a steady pace. Only now he's got the added benefit of being able to pull me down a few extra inches. I'm still only taking just over half his length, but if the muttered litany of praises and what I assume are Orcish curses coming from above me are any indication, he doesn't mind. Each time I make out a "good boy," my cock jumps a little.

My jaw is really getting sore, but I wouldn't complain even if I could, and things are starting to get messy. I can feel the drool that's been pooling leaking down the sides of my mouth, even dripping onto my chest. The hand in my hair is gripping me tightly, and I don't even attempt to move on my own, content for my owner to move me how he pleases.

My jaw and throat get a rest when I am pulled off of his cock completely, only to be shoved face first into his balls. I groan as the scent of his musk overwhelms me.

"Lick," comes the single-word command.

I press my face farther into him, testing these new waters with small, tentative licks. His skin tastes salty but not unpleasant, and combined with his natural scent, it doesn't take long to drive me crazy. Soon I'm practically bathing his testicles with my tongue, eagerly lapping at one and then the other, his hair lightly scratching at my face. Above me, I can hear the steady *schlick* of his hand stroking up and down his cock, lubricated with my saliva. I manage to suck one his balls into my mouth entirely, clumsily attempting to run my tongue along it in my overstuffed mouth. I repeat this on his other side, before the hand is back in my hair, and I am pulled away once more.

Khazak stuffs his cock back into my mouth and resumes the pace of our earlier face-fucking like it never ceased. It only takes me a second to adjust, then I'm right back in it with him, his cock stretching my mouth and throat each time I'm plunged down. Just about the only other thing I can think of is how hard I am. I bet it'll only take a few strokes before I explode everywhere.

I suddenly hear a growl from above me, and the hand in my hair slows my movements. Then I feel his dick getting even bigger, and I'm pulled back until only a couple of inches remain inside. A green hand reaches down to wrap around the rest of the appendage, and as the first salty shot hits my tongue, I realize he's cumming.

The hand in my hair tenses with each shot, holding me in place as my mouth fills up rapidly. The salty taste is familiar, and I try to swallow as fast as I can, but there's just too much, and some winds up leaking out of the side of my mouth—and he's still not done shooting. There are more growls and shudders as he finishes before he releases my head and allows me to pull all the way off and catch my breath. *Hey, no choking this time!*

I'm quickly pulled up from my knees and onto his lap, his mouth finding mine as my arms wrap around his neck. No way he can't taste himself after that. His hands find my ass and squeeze the sore flesh, making me whimper into the kiss. My dick is rock hard and the added pain coming from my butt being manipulated only seems to make it harder. I am so fucked up, and I so don't care.

"Does my puppy want to cum?" His voice is low and hot in my ear. One of the hands on my ass moves around to grasp my dick, making me hump up into it.

"Yes pleaaaaase, Sir." I try to grind against his stomach.

"Then it is a shame he is still being punished." *He's what now?* The hand leaves my dick as fast as it came in.

"What?" My eyes shoot open and I'm met with a smirk. *What!?*

"I do not believe I stuttered." Both hands are back on my ass, making me squirm.

Without thinking, I bring one of my own down to my dick. "Touch that and you will regret it." I freeze.

"But... But—!" I look from his face to my dick and then back. "You can't be serious!"

He leans into my ear again. "I told you I do not enjoy being manipulated, David." He pulls back to speak to me in a normal voice. "I think this will serve as a good reminder. Besides, you did say you enjoyed when I was the one 'calling the shots,' correct?"

My hand is only inches from my dick, and it would be *so easy* to grab it and finish myself off. Especially since everything he's saying is *still* turning me on. I want to cum *so badly*, but being told I can't is only making me harder. *Fuck.* With a frustrated huff, I let my hand drop to the side.

"Good boy." He leans forward to give me a gentle kiss. "If you can manage to behave yourself today, there will be a reward waiting for you when we get home."

That perks my interest. I (and my ass) remember the last time he rewarded me with his tongue. I bite my lip and nod. "Yes, Sir."

"Then it is time to get ready for your first day." He slides me off his lap and stands, grabbing his alarm and putting it back in its drawer. He showed me it before bed last night. It looks like a sundial on one side, and you just turn the ridge in the center to point to your desired wake up time, and that's it. The sound it makes is a lot more pleasant than any alarm I've used in the past.

Khazak leads the way to the bathroom, making us shower separately so there aren't any distractions, and I pout while taking the first one. He takes care of trimming his beard and brushing his teeth, and when I'm done showering, we swap.

We move back to the bedroom to get dressed. I don't really think anything of Khazak pulling out a simple blue shirt and brown pants for me, but the flash of nervousness I catch on his face when he adds a blue thong to the pile clues me in that something is up. He's not testing me, but he doesn't know if this is something I'm okay with. We didn't talk about it yesterday.

Lucky for him these things kinda grew on me. *He kinda grew on me.* I reach forward and grab the thong, slipping it on wordlessly with a shy smile, and making him relax while he pulls on the leather armor that makes up his uniform. The big contrast between our outfits makes me remember how we met. I suddenly find myself wondering if I need to be better equipped for the day.

After making a joke about how I've already been fed, we have a *really* quick breakfast of grilled fish (again). When we're finished, we grab some of Rurig's leftovers for lunch and make our way to the station. The walk there is busy; everyone we pass seems to want to greet Khazak now that he's in his full uniform. Most don't pay me any mind.

I can see the station off in the distance, and as we approach the building, I get a sinking feeling in the pit of my stomach. The last two times I was here weren't for anything good. I can only imagine what the orcs inside have been saying about me in the time since. The idea that I'll be working here is also bringing back some choice memories of the academy I'd rather just stay buried.

Sensing my discomfort, Khazak leans over and puts a hand on my shoulder reassuringly. "It will be alright, David. Clean slate, remember?"

I nod. I remember. I'm just not sure his co-workers will be as forgiving as he is.

When we walk inside, everyone seems to freeze, all eyes turning to Captain Ironstorm. They all stand, eager to greet their leader as he returns to work. I try to hang back silently, but it's not long before the attention is turned to me. I'm introduced to orc after orc: Officer Boldhammer, Ranger Bronzeaxe, Officer Frostsong. I really try to remember everyone's names, but there's just no way I'm going to get them all.

Everything goes pretty well until I'm face to face with two rangers that look oddly familiar, and I realize it's because they're the two orcs I fought back in the ruins. Rangers Deepfist and Firedrum don't look terribly impressed to see me, but both seem to accept my stammered-out apology, probably because their boss is right behind me. Eventually we reach the back of the building, and the new faces stop appearing. Khazak pokes his head into an open office and waves while I stand back.

"Ragnar." Khazak turns to look at me. "I think you will remember Deputy Captain Rockfang."

"Khazak, good to have you back." I poke my head around Khazak's torso to see the brown-haired orc responsible for my capture the other night. "There is a pile of paperwork on your desk."

"Of course there is." He sighs. "Just wanted to say good morning and introduce my new assistant." He reaches for me, pulling me into Ragnar's line of vision.

"Good to see you, David." He leans back in his chair a little. "I trust we will not have any issues with keys while you are here?"

There's a smart-ass comment on the tip of my tongue, but I hold it in, knowing it'll only get me in trouble. I want that reward. "No, sir."

He smiles at that. Khazak nods a goodbye and leads us across the hall to a closed door which opens to another office: his. It's pretty much just like the other one, a large desk in the center with chairs on either side and a couch against one wall. One of the walls has a sword in its scabbard and a longbow hanging from it while another has a large animal skin. There's a small lantern and something framed on the desk, as well as a stack of papers in the center.

Khazak takes a seat in the big chair behind the desk while I grab one in front. He flips through the top of the stack and sighs. "This may take a while."

"Do you have to fill all those out?" Seems a little beneath him, assuming their ranks are similar to ours.

"Most just need a signature." He opens a drawer to pull out a pen and ink. "Though I am certain Ragnar did not make things any easier for me. The man hates paperwork."

"Who *likes* it?" No one I'd trust. "So... What is it I will be doing here, exactly?"

"Oh, yes." He reaches over his desk to grab a mug. "Would you mind getting me some coffee?" He holds it out for me, smirking.

I stare at the proffered mug, offended. "Are you kid—"

"I promise I did not bring you here just to get my coffee, David." He sets the mug down on the edge of the desk with a chuckle and starts signing some of the papers. "Seeing as I am the one who arrested you, you already know that I am the head of the city's law enforcement. Our forces are split between two stations, this one and another about a mile east of here. Between them, we have approximately one-hundred officers and fifty rangers, and I am in charge of them all."

"That's a lot of people." Not as many as we had at the academy, but still.

"Indeed. Thankfully, there are two deputy captains to assist me, one based at each station. Deputy Captain Rockfang here and Deputy Captain Keenguard at the other. I sometimes work out of the other station, but as this one is closer to home, I am usually here. That will also apply to you. The officers handle most of the smaller day-to-day problems in the city, but more specialized issues are dealt with by the rangers." He's almost robotically signing the papers one after the other while he explains. "About half of what I do is administration, things like coordinating officers and signing paperwork. The other half is handling some of the more serious and high-profile crimes reported. When we are not here, you will be accompanying me on most of my assignments."

"I'm actually going to be going out with you?" I look down at the mug. I was hoping he'd just have me doing busy work around here. "Is that allowed?"

"It is a bit of a grey area." He pauses his signing to look at me. "You are technically considered an extension of myself, but you have no actual authority. You do not have the power to interrogate or arrest anyone."

"What exactly *will* I be able to do?" Still not any clearer on what I'm here for.

"Plenty, which I will be happy to go over with you as soon as I finish with these." He looks at the stack and sighs. "I *would* actually appreciate some coffee. Please." He looks apologetic at least.

"Yes, Sir," I say with a *little* bit of a grumble. "Where is it?"

"Take a left from my office and then left again down the next hallway." He points with his finger. "You will see an open door on the right. That is the breakroom."

"Be right back." I pick up the mug and make my exit. I guess we'll see if this place is anything like home. I hope not.

The breakroom isn't difficult to find, and on the counter, I spot a large metal coffee kettle, steam rising from the tip. There's no oven or hot plate, but I actually know the reason this time: an enchanted kettle. The ones we used at the academy looked different, but I'm sure these function the same. You fill it with water, add in the grounds (or tea leaves, *blech*), shut the lid, and five minutes later, you've got a hot pot of coffee. I hope the gods blessed the enchanter who came up with that one. I fill the mug and manage to find the sugar when I hear someone enter the room behind me.

I turn to look and see an elf standing in the doorway. "There you are," he says, walking toward me.

"Here I am?" I back into the counter behind me.

"Nice to finally meet you, David." He holds out his hand. "I'm Nylan." He does look *kind* of familiar.

"How do you know my—ah!" I'm pulled in for a hug. *Who the hell is this guy? Wait!* "You're the elf I saw in the marketplace the other day!"

"Wow, okay. One, I saw *you* first, and two, I'm only *half*-elf, thank you very much." He cocks a hip as he corrects me.

Way to go, David, offending someone right after they introduce themselves. "I'm sorry. I didn't mean to—"

"Woah, just kidding." His tone sobers and he straightens up. "I mean I am half-elf, but… Hit a little close to home?"

"…Let's just say that part of the reason I'm here is because I might have had some assumptions about certain groups of people and where they lived." I sheepishly admit. "Wait, you never told me how you know my name."

"Oh, Ragnar and I have heard *all* about you." He quirks his eyebrows at me.

"You know Ragnar?" That means he probably knows a lot more than the general public.

"You could say that." He reaches into his shirt to pull out a thin gold chain. With a lock. A collar. I take a moment to look him over. He's about as tall as I am with naturally tanned skin. His black hair is shaved on the sides while the middle is longer and brushed back. His right ear is pierced with a single gold loop and his body is lithe, though I guess all elves are. *Wait, was that racist?*

"So, you're his avakesh." I shouldn't be surprised, he is friends with Khazak after all.

"For three years now. Four in two months." He's talking about the date of his enslavement like it's an anniversary.

"Wow and I only just finished my first week." And will be gone in two months.

"A very interesting first week from what I've heard." He's smirking.

"...What do you know?"

"Pretty much everything. Khazak and Ragnar are best friends—have been their whole lives." That would explain why Ragnar was so willing to cover for him. "The first thing he did after accepting your challenge was stop by our place to let us know. He wanted us to get good seats."

"You guys were there?" So far, other than Brull, I've been pretty lucky in not meeting anyone who saw me. Or at least no one else has brought it up yet.

"Front row." He looks pleased.

"Oh gods." I bury my face in my hands.

"Hey, I don't think you have anything to be ashamed of." He manages to sound supportive and suggestive at the same time. "That was an amazing match. Both the fight and the after-battle show."

"Thanks." You'd think I'd be over getting embarrassed by this by now, but nope.

"I wanted to hire a choreographer for me and Ragnar's, but he wouldn't let me." He pouts. "Said it all had to be real."

"That sounds..." *Hold on.* "Wait, you *planned* your fight?"

His eyebrows furrow. "Well yeah, we'd been talking about it for like, two years at that point—"

"You were *already* together?" His *boyfriend* enslaved him?!

There's more confusion, then a look of realization, and finally a sigh. "Shit, he still hasn't told you?"

"*Who* hasn't told me *what*?" I grit out.

"David I'm not sure I should—"

"Uh-uh. This whole week people have been making it seem like there's something different or weird about what happened that day, and I *know* I've heard something about Khazak and having plans." I specifically remember Brull saying they had talked about "plans for this" right after meeting him. "You need to tell me what the hell is going. *Now*."

"It's not what you're thinking, I swear." He holds his hands out in surrender. "Look, I only hesitate because I think someone else should be telling you."

"Telling me *what?*" I'm starting to get frustrated.

"About the *Nagul Uzu'gor.*" He bites his lip. "The battle between you and Captain Ironstorm is the first real invocation of the ritual in something like over a hundred years."

"What? What do you mean by 'real'?" How exactly do you *fake* something like that?

"Hundreds and hundreds of years ago, before there was ever a city, there were different tribes of orcs fighting for control of the area in the forests," he starts his explanation, leaning against a table. "The ritual wasn't a ritual at all. It was more like a game. I don't know what it was called then. Captured enemies—prisoners of war—would be forced to fight against their captors. If they won, they would be freed and allowed to return to their own tribes. But if they lost, they were forcibly conscripted into the army of whoever had captured them. Usually with added subjugation and humiliation."

"Yeah, that part sounds familiar," I grumble. "Remember? You were there."

He ignores my comment, pressing on. "Over time, there was less fighting and warring over land, and the ritual changed into what it is today. It turned into something done between couples of a certain *persuasion.* It's almost like getting engaged, but with more sex and tying people up."

"Wait, did we get engaged?" *What exactly was that paper I signed with my blood?!* "Am I *married?*"

"Poor choice of words," he says it mostly to himself. "I just mean that for couples who have been together for a while, couples who like to do the sorts of things we do, it's like a commitment ceremony."

"How do you know I actually like any of this stuff?" He's making some bold assumptions.

"Remember? I was there," he mocks. "There's plenty of people who like to 'play' at these sorts of relationships and keep things much more casual, but these days, the ritual of Steel and Thunder is only ever used by couples, not criminals."

"Until me." The more I learn, the less things make sense.

"Until you," he agrees. "When word got out that the ritual was being invoked by an outsider, a human who had been arrested in the forest, news spread fast."

That would also be why everyone has been talking about it. "Did he plan all this? Did he walk in there knowing what was going to happen?"

"I'm afraid I don't know what was going through the man's head when he accepted the challenge, David. You'll have to talk to him about that." He sighs and shrugs. "But—and I really hope I don't get in trouble for telling you this—I think Khazak has always...*admired* the idea of one day having an avakesh of his own. He's talked about it with Ragnar and me before. So if he did have any 'plans,' I think that's all they were."

"And I served myself to him on a silver platter," I grumble and sip from the coffee cup I've been holding in my hands.

"Isn't that Khazak's mug?" He nods at my hands.

"Khazak can wait." And maybe get his own damn coffee, too.

He laughs at that. "For what it's worth, I don't think that's what's going on."

"What makes you say that?" I guess he *has* known the man longer than I have.

"Him showing up at our house two nights ago." The night of our big fight. The night after the "incident." That must have been where he went before he came back with dinner. "He was really upset. Didn't give us all the details, but he told us that he'd learned that you weren't told the truth about certain things surrounding the ritual. He said he'd made a lot of mistakes, that he was worried he's already wrecked whatever was developing between the two of you. He was just so *sad*, David. Which was weird because I remembered him being so angry the day before. He said he had to let you go."

"That was the gist of it, more or less," Khazak's voice cuts in and Nylan spins around, both of us staring as he stands in the doorway. He approaches holding a stack of papers in one hand that he hands to Nylan. "Would you please ask your *kavan* to stop slipping his paperwork in with mine?"

"Yes, sir! I will get right on that." Nylan nods, eyes wide as he eagerly takes the papers and the opportunity to exit.

That just leaves me and Khazak. I sip from the mug again, like I'm making a point.

"I was wondering what happened to my coffee," he jokes, trying to break through the tension.

I stare at him in silence for a moment. "Why didn't you tell me about the truth about the ritual? Why didn't anyone?"

There's a look of regret on his face before he answers. "I did not mean to keep it from you. Not for this long, at least. There never seemed to be a good time to bring it up, and the longer it went on, the more difficult it became to say anything."

"You specifically told me that it was something criminals did, that normally someone would only choose it for a crime more serious than mine." He made it sound like a common occurrence around here.

"That was not a lie. For centuries that really is how the ritual worked," he continues to explain, though he doesn't sound very confident. "Even today people still issue challenges when arrested for actual crimes... They are just never accepted."

"Why did you say yes?" I put the mug down on the counter. "You told me you were going to say no until Redwish talked to you. What made you change your mind?"

"At first? Anger. I had just come from checking on the injured and the attack was still fresh in my mind. When Redwish described the way you were behaving, the way you demanded the opportunity to do battle... All I could think about was how *arrogant* you were." He scratches the back of his head. "I only planned on going in, defeating you, and sending you back to your cell. But when you were lying there, telling me you were trying to kill me, I saw red. That and well..."

"Well what?" What is he getting at here?

He stifles a laugh and looks away, suddenly bashful. "You are an attractive man, David." My cheeks flush at the unexpected compliment. "That is not an excuse. If anything, it is worse. I allowed my desire to cloud my judgment. I ignored warning signs, ignored my own instincts that something was wrong. I convinced myself that even if you were telling the truth, you deserved what was coming to you." His form curls in on itself as he continues. "Holding on to that resentment and not being honest with you... It completely drove us apart. I thought that would be the end of it, but then for some reason, despite everything, you still wanted...this. Wanted me. After that, I was worried that telling you might disrupt the small bit of peace we had managed to carve out and then... Here we are." He struggles to meet my gaze. "I am sorry, David. Are you upset?"

"Yes. No. Maybe." I cross my arms and lean back against the counter. "I wish you had told me."

"Do you think knowing what you do now would have changed how you feel?" He asks like he's afraid of what the answer will be.

"I don't know." Maybe not. Or maybe it would have freaked me out even more. "A lot of things make more sense now, I guess. Like why the women at the arena before our fight were so nice." All the perfumes and oils seem less out of place too. "Or why your family acted like they were meeting your boyfriend the other night makes more sense now. Or how Brull's shop exists at all."

"I understand if this causes you to rethink things between us." He says it so matter-of-factly I think that's what he expects me to do. This probably contributed to his hesitation over the last few days.

I don't know what to say. I'm not angry, but it would be really nice if the rug would stop getting pulled out from under me. It's always right when I feel like I'm finally starting to understand what's going on. "Is there anything else you haven't told me?" I'm almost afraid to ask.

"No, that is everything. I promise." He gives me a hopeful smile. "On that topic, I have requested Advocate Redwish to stop by this afternoon so that he may explain the...inconsistencies in conducting the ritual."

"That's a nice way of saying he lied to us." I really don't trust that guy.

"I know." He sighs. "There is a part of me that still hopes this was all a misunderstanding but...I feel you may be right."

"At least we'll know." I don't like when information is kept from me.

A knock on the doorframe behind Khazak draws our attention. "Excuse me, sir." It's Nylan. "As an apology, my *kavan* would like to buy lunch for you and your avakesh."

"That sounds nice." Khazak turns to face him fully. "Would this *also* be to make up for your revealing aspects of my private life?"

There's a pause as Nylan's eyes go just a little wide in panic. "No, sir. That is what lunch *tomorrow* is for."

Khazak laughs at that. "That will not be necessary, Nylan. Lunch today will be fine, thank you."

"Of course, sir." Nylan sighs in relief as he makes his exit and Khazak turns back to me.

"What does that word mean?" They both used it to refer to Ragnar, I think.

"*Kavan?*" I nod. "It is the term for the owner of an avakesh. I am your *kavan*."

"Is this the part where you tell me it means more than just 'owner' or 'master'?" After all, I'm a slave-pet-servant.

"Correct. It also means protector or guardian," Khazak responds with a sly grin. "So..." He seems hesitant but hopeful.

"So..." I pick up the mug and stare down at the lukewarm coffee in my hands. "...Coffee?"

Khazak shakes his head with a chuckle and accepts the offering. "There is something else I wanted to show you. Come with me."

I follow him down the hall to a set of double doors that opens into a... gym. Like a *real* gym, with weights, and bars, and padded mats. There's even a punching bag in one corner. For someone who's been forced to do pushups in the dirt and pullups on tree branches until recently, it's heaven.

"I thought you might enjoy using the gymnasium while you waited for me to finish signing things." I follow him inside to look at the equipment.

"You mean to tell me that you've had access to a gym this *whole time*, and I've just been running around the city like some kind of idiot?" I make sure I sound exasperated.

"David, I did not—" Khazak catches my cheesy smile and huffs, realizing I'm only joking. He watches as I scan the room. "I trust you know how to use these? And which things are unsafe to do on your own?"

"Yes, Sir. Lift the weights, punch the bag, and don't do anything that requires a spotter." I point out the various objects. The details are different, but the equipment is essentially the same. The dumbbells, barbells, and other weights are made from stone rather than metal, and the mats and bags are covered in dark leathers.

"The officers and rangers make frequent use of this room." I would too if I worked here. *Wait.* "Should you encounter any of them, I expect you to show the proper amount of respect."

"Yes, Sir." I smile innocently. "Anything else?"

"Just be careful." He smiles. I think he can tell I'm excited. "You know where my office is."

"Come get me when it's lunch time!" I call after he leaves before turning back to the gym equipment, excitedly rubbing my hands together.

Let's get to work.

Chapter Eighteen

Once I start working out, it's easy to lose track of time. It's just been so long since I've been in an actual gym. The first thing I do is strip off my shirt because unless I feel like running home I don't want to be stuck wearing a sweat-soaked one for the rest of the day. I'd like to do the same thing with my pants, but I'm not sure the blue thong Khazak picked out for me today is really work appropriate. Or maybe it's totally normal around here? Either way, I don't feel like getting walked in on working out while wearing nothing *but* that.

It's an hour at least, maybe a little longer, before Khazak comes to get me for lunch. He shows me where the showers are, sticking around to watch me strip down and clean up. I catch him in the corner of my eye grabbing my thong and sniffing the pouch and tease him. *Pervert.* Once I'm finished, I throw on my dry shirt and slightly sweaty pants, and the two of us head to the breakroom.

There are a few orcs seated at different tables when we enter, Ragnar and Nylan at one in a corner with a mound of wrapped square packages in the center—sandwiches! We move to join them, and Ragnar happily doles one out to each of us. They're warm, and I eagerly open mine to see what I'm dealing with, the scent of something sweet and tangy hitting my nostrils. I take a bite and taste what may be some of the juiciest and most tender pork I've ever tasted. I moan a little.

"I see you spared no expense." Khazak speaks up after swallowing his first bite. "Thank you for lunch, Ragnar."

"Of course. Consider it a welcome back gift." He smiles broadly.

"I thought it was an apology?" Three heads turn to look at me, Khazak smirking and Nylan trying not to.

"Right." Ragnar levels his gaze at me. "I'm not sure how those papers ended up in the stack on your desk."

"Yes. Very mysterious," Khazak deadpans before taking another bite.

"Your father says hi, sir," Nylan speaks up from his seat.

"That would explain the obscene amount of food." Khazak looks over the small pile still in the center of the table before gazing over at me. "We still have those leftovers as well."

"What do you mean?" Did they pick these up from Khazak's parents?

"His father runs this *really* great restaurant in town," Nylan answers. That makes sense. I'd do that too if I could cook like Rurig.

"'Runs' is being generous," Khazak downplays. "He sold part of it years ago. These days he only goes in and works when he feels like it."

"I can't wait until you and I can do that around here one day," Ragnar speaks a little wistfully, and I can't tell if he's serious.

"Remind me to start looking for your replacement." Khazak shakes his head and takes another bite.

Ragnar ignores the threat, instead turning to me. "So David, how is your first day going?"

"Good, I think. I haven't really done anything yet." I shrug. "So far I've gotten coffee and gone to the gym."

"Enjoy the quiet days around here," Nylan recommends. "You will miss them."

"Do you work here too?" It would be nice not being the only orc-pet in the office.

"Oh, no." Nylan shakes his head. "I work part time at a bookstore. I just like to come in a lot, usually for lunch."

"He's really more of a house-elf." Ragnar smiles warmly at his avakesh, who leans over to kiss him.

"Ragnar and Nylan have been together for almost eight years," Khazak explains as we watch the display.

"How did you meet?" I point at Nylan and Ragnar.

"That is a very long and complicated story," Ragnar answers for them both. "The short answer is in school when we were children."

"My parents moved to the city for work, and we stuck around," Nylan recounts. "My dad only just moved away a few years ago."

"Is your mom still here?" I wonder if they split up or something.

"Ah, no. She died a long time ago." Shit, this time he's not just messing with me. *Great job, David.*

"I met Nylan at the same time Ragnar did." Khazak steps in to distract from the awkwardness. "He and I have been friends our entire lives."

Sitting next to each other, I can see that Ragnar looks a lot like Khazak. He has a slightly slimmer build, and he looks to be at least five years younger, but his brown hair and beard are cropped in the same style. His facial hair looks like it might be trimmed a little more closely than Khazak's, though it might also be his slimmer jaw and shorter tusks. His ears are a little longer, and he actually has them pierced. Most of the other facial details are of course different, but from a distance, I might think the two of them were brothers. Except for his bright blue eyes. I didn't know orcs could have blue eyes.

"You met in school too?" I point at Khazak and Ragnar. "Was he like your mentor? Like a big brother or something?"

"What? No, we were classmates." Ragnar looks confused. "I knew him even before that. We grew up next door to each other."

"...How old are you? How old is everyone?" Because now I'm confused.

At that, Nylan suddenly starts laughing which makes Ragnar roll his eyes before looking back to me. "I am *also* half-elf."

"Oh!" That explains some of the physical differences, like the eyes and ears. "Were your parents—"

"No, we're not related," Nylan cuts me off, sounding offended.

My eyes go wide. You'd think I'd at least try to keep my foot out of my fucking mouth by now. "Oh god, no, I'm sorry. I was just gonna ask if they were friends, I wasn't trying to—"

"Are you both done torturing my puppy?" Khazak steps in to defend me, and I realize Nylan is fucking with me again, awkwardness forgotten. Between making me think I said something racist and implying I accused them of incest, he's got a fucked-up sense of humor.

I like him.

"Why, jealous?" Ragnar snarks at Khazak before turning to me. "I've always wondered: is he this stuffy at home? Like when it's just the two of you?"

"Uhhhhh..." My eyes go wide at the question.

"I am not stuffy," Khazak growls on my left.

"He refuses to use contractions, David," Ragnar offers his compelling evidence.

"I just do not understand why it is necessary to mash every word together," Khazak fires back. "We do not even *have* contractions in our language!" I notice Nylan's smirk, but he stays conspicuously silent, probably glad the attention isn't on him.

"It's not even that." Ragnar crumbles the sauce-covered paper from his finished sandwich. "I swear, somehow you always manage to pick the strangest and most specific words to use."

"I like to be precise with my language." Khazak rolls his eyes.

"Come on, you know what I'm talking about, David, right?" All eyes turn to me at Ragnar's question, each hopeful in their own way.

"...I think the first time he brought me home he called his bathroom a lavatory." I can't help myself.

The look of betrayal on Khazak's face says I may pay for that later, but the way I get Ragnar and Nylan to laugh is worth it. What? I want his friends to like me.

"Insult me all you want, but I remember your mother asking me to tutor you two nights a week when you nearly did not graduate." Khazak opens a second sandwich.

"...I'm a slow learner," Ragnar grumbles to himself as Nylan reaches over to give him a half-hearted pat on the wrist.

"As well as a slow reader, a slow writer, a slow test taker..." Khazak trails off before taking a bite of his sandwich as Nylan starts laughing, and Ragnar responds with what I assume is a curse word that I am definitely asking Nylan to teach me later.

It's fun to watch the three of them interact during lunch, Khazak laughing and playing around with his friends. When the jokes start flying, I am a little worried he might react like he did with his sister but no, he's happily smiling while they fling barbs at each other. When we're finished eating, Nylan says his goodbyes—he's got an afternoon shift at the bookstore—and Khazak brings me back to his office.

"Finished signing things?" I see that the stack of papers has been moved to the side.

"Just before lunch." He takes a seat behind his desk. "Ready to discuss your duties?"

"Yes, Sir." I grab a seat in front of the desk. No point in avoiding this.

"First, I assume that when we are here, and you have the free time, you will want to spend some time in the gymnasium?" He nods his head in the room's direction.

"Yes, please." I nod. I'm already excited to start bulking up again, especially considering how much I've been eating lately.

"Good. I look forward to seeing the results." He gives me a lecherous grin. "But when you are not exercising, I would like you to work on this." He slides a book from the left side of his desk to me.

I take a hold of it. The cover reads *Learning Atasi*. "What's this?"

"A language book." He leans back a little. "I think it would be beneficial for you to start learning some Atasi."

"Atasi? You don't want me to learn Orcish?" That seems like a weird request.

"No." He looks at me oddly. "We do not speak Orcish."

"You don't?" I'm really confused now. "Then what have you been... Isn't that what orcs speak?"

"Orcs in *your* part of the world." He leans forward on his forearms. "David, you are aware that we do not even *call* ourselves orcs, right?"

"What are you talking about?" *Is he high?* "Why wouldn't you call yourselves orcs?"

"Because that is not a word that exists in our language." He pauses for a moment. "Think about the humans who live in the area. Not those who have migrated from your part of the world, but the humans already here. It is likely that most of them have never heard a single word spoken in Common, so 'human' means nothing to them. Why would it?"

"I've...never thought about that before." Does that mean elves don't call themselves elves? "What *do* you call yourselves, then?"

"*A'tahsaya.*" At least that's easier to pronounce than the name of the city, barely. "It translates literally to 'the noble uniters.'"

"Huh." I sit in my seat a little dumbfounded. "So I've spent the last week thinking everyone was speaking a different language. Wait, does that mean it's wrong to call you orcs?"

"No, it is just a translation." He correctly takes my confused face to mean he should continue explaining. "Take my title, for example. In Atasi, we have no word for 'captain' or 'deputy,' but the positions we hold are close enough that it is simpler to use those terms when speaking in Common than force a direct translation. That has been the case with most of the names for things I have told you. Take our small bout of confusion with the term 'labor camp.'" My head shoots up at the mention, eyes wide. "Exactly. Though I think I will be petitioning the council about changing that particular phrase. A lighter example: what did I tell you our word for 'paperwork' meant?" I can't hold in the giggle as I recall 'sad wood.' "You can see why it makes more sense to simply call it 'paperwork.'"

"Yeah, I think I get it." I look down at the book in my lap. Languages are complicated. "Wait, how do I even know the orcs where I come from call themselves orcs?"

"I am not sure. The only other group of orcs I really have knowledge about live far west of here. They use a similar name and language as we do, but even those are not exactly the same." He pauses for a moment. "Do you know who we could ask?" I shake my head no. "Our favorite legal advocate."

"Well, we're definitely not doing that." I'd rather memorize this book front to back. "Why would he know?"

"He is originally from Grimmlaand." Grimmlaand is a country not that far from home, located on the mainland southeast of Inisfalia and Albion. Despite its name, it is by all accounts a beautiful country blanketed in forests and lakes with rivers that stretch for miles. I know there are orcs living there, but big cities of any kind are few and far between.

A lot of wonderful scenery but not a lot of centralized government means attempted invasions aren't uncommon, but all the rough and unkempt woodland terrain is the perfect defense. Their neighbors to the south, the Empire of Roma Alba, tried and failed more than once. Of course, that led to Roma Alba joining with Albion to form the Holy Albion Empire and start what feels like a perpetual holy land war, but that's exactly why my group went west across the ocean and far away from all that crap.

"He's not from here?" I *knew* I heard an accent on him.

"No, he moved to Tah'lj early last year. I assumed the red hair would have given it away." I guess I never considered that orcs in different parts of the world might vary in appearance the same way humans and other races do. "Most of us here have black or brown hair. There is also a *slight* blue tinge to his complexion."

"I had no idea. Still don't want to ask him for anything." I will admit it is mildly interesting. "So what's the word around here for humans?"

"That depends on who you ask. There are over a dozen languages spoken along the eastern coastline alone." I roll my eyes. *We get it—you're smart.* "In Atasi, the word is '*ni'pak.*' It means 'hairless one.'"

"We are not hairless," I scoff, dropping the book in my lap. "Are all your words for non-orcs just descriptive insults?"

"Only the ones for humans," he jokes, smirking. "Our language has a tendency to be oddly descriptive like that."

"And I suppose the fact that you use the borderline frightening direct translations of your last names is purely coincidental and not something you take advantage of to intimidate outsiders?" Not that I blame them; if my last name translated to something like 'Firesword' or 'Godkiller' in another language, I'd use it too.

"They do not *all* translate like that." He doesn't deny it though. "That is quite the charge coming from the people who *literally* named their language 'Common.'"

"Hey, I didn't get to pick out what it's called!" I definitely wouldn't have gone with 'Common' if I had. "Besides, elves speak it just as much as we do."

"Yet somehow elves manage to be much less obnoxious about expecting everyone else around them to *also* speak it." He smirks, and I stick my tongue out in response. I'll show him obnoxious. "Now, concerning your duties when in the field. As I said before you have no actual authority on your own, but during the course of an investigation, you will be able to help me with things like conducting searches or questioning a witness. Should the need arise, you will also help me to defend against any would-be attackers or subdue individuals being detained."

"Gotcha." I nod and stare at the book in my lap.

"Is it learning a new language that is bothering you, or are you nervous because you have not done work like this before?" Khazak asks, noticing my lack of enthusiasm.

"Actually...this is a lot like what I used to do." I scratch the back of my head. I guess it's time to talk about it. "Not all the time, but enough."

"You know, you have mentioned this academy you attended several times but not exactly what you did there." He sits back in his seat. "Enlighten me."

"I already told you that it was essentially a pre-military school. The Northlake Academy of Knighthood." I start thinking back to the years of training and drills. "The idea was that you'd go there for a few years, graduate and become a knight, then get shipped off to some outpost somewhere. You make a big name for yourself while you're out there, come back, and get treated like a hero."

"And that is what you were going to do?" he asks from across the desk.

"That was the plan." I shrug. "I was never crazy about it. When I was little, I was raised on these epic stories of knights and heroes, good versus evil. But the world isn't like that. I'm not sure it ever was."

"I imagine there would be a lot of pressure in having to live up to something like that," he sympathizes.

"No kidding." I sigh. "Most of what we did was practice drills and take *a lot* of history classes. But sometimes we would get called into town to act as guards or police, like if there was a public event or holiday. Our authority wasn't very well defined though. At any given time, we had exactly as much power as the people in charge of us decided we would have."

"That sounds...vague." He tilts his head in confusion.

"Yeah, you might even wonder if it wasn't set up that way intentionally," I gripe.

"Did something happen?" He sounds concerned.

"Sorta. There was a protest. I don't remember over what exactly, taxes or land rights or something." I regret not paying more attention to that stuff. "There were crowds of angry people gathered around city hall, and we were deployed to break them up. When we got out there, it was chaos. Everyone was yelling and throwing things: rocks, vegetables, whatever they could get their hands on. We got the orders to start arresting people almost immediately. I watched my classmates start grabbing people and throwing them to the ground, cuffing them without a second thought. It wasn't like these people were looking for a fight. These were families, mothers and fathers, children, old people, all just angry because no one was listening to them." I pause and take a deep breath. "I remember there was this boy who threw a rock at my commander. It was a fucking pebble, and the kid couldn't have been older than fourteen. What the hell was he going to do, really? He was a fucking *kid*. When I refused to arrest him, my commander threatened to throw *me* in a cell. I walked off the field right then."

"Is that why you left?" He's on the right track.

"It wasn't the first time something like that happened. I was never really happy there, you know? But it was that kind of stuff that always made me wonder what I was really doing, who I was really working for. Sometimes we'd be deployed to work security at some private function or maybe we would have to escort someone somewhere, but it was never anything that actually seemed important. After a while, it started to feel like we were only really helping one group of people—the ones with money." It's starting to feel like I'm rambling. "I started saving up a little money last year, even though I didn't have a plan yet. It wasn't until Adam came to my room that night that I actually decided to do something."

"What did he do?" *Do I detect some jealousy?*

"I was in my bunk still fuming when he knocked on the door." I have a pretty clear memory of that night. "He wanted to talk about what happened at the protest, and for a minute, I was worried he was there to tell me to get over what happened like everyone else. But he didn't. He didn't stay out there very long either. He was on my side. Then he asked me if I'd ever thought about leaving. So, I told him about the money I had saved."

"Were his motivations similar to yours?" Less jealousy.

"More or less, but he had his own reasons too." Like losing both of his parents in a fire last year. "The day after that, we talked to Elisabeth, who was as apathetic about that place as we were. A week later, we packed up and left in the middle of the night. Took a wagon out of town to the coast, bought a boat ticket, and here we are."

"Was it really necessary to leave in the middle of the night?" He sounds skeptical.

"Probably not." I shrug. "We didn't break the law or anything, but none of us really felt like explaining anything to anyone."

"Like your family?" He raises an eyebrow. *Bingo*.

"Like my family." I nod wearily.

"Well, as much as I wish I could to assure you that things are different here, recent events might—" A knock on the open door interrupts him.

"Good afternoon, Captain Ironstorm. *David*," Redwish sneers my name, appearing as if on cue.

"Advocate Redwish." Khazak rises, and I move to stand beside him on the other side of the desk. "Thank you for coming in."

"Of course, sir." He offers a small bow before taking a seat. "I was told you wished to speak regarding the day of Mr. Cerano's arrest."

"Yes." Khazak takes his own seat while I remain standing next to him. "It has been brought to my attention that you may not have been completely forthcoming with the objectives and consequences of the *Nagul Uzu'gor* that day."

"I am not sure I know what you mean." He plays dumb well. I'll give him that.

"You made it seem like I was supposed to try and kill him," I growl, unable to keep my composure. "You made it seem like he was trying to kill *me*."

"I did no such thing." He sounds completely unimpressed with my accusations.

"I must admit I *also* feel as though something is amiss." Khazak pushes forward, ignoring my outburst. "You implied to me that David would be lying about—"

"I am sorry, but have you known him to be particularly honest?" He eyes me suspiciously. "I understand he has made a *number* of escape attempts."

"That is not the reason I asked—"

"Then what did you ask me here for, sir? Are you accusing me of something?" Redwish snaps. "What I have done, Captain, is my job. You will have to forgive me for not paying mind to the incorrect assumptions of a common thug. Honestly, I am not sure why either of you are complaining to begin with. Given how *cozy* I understand the two of you have become, I would think you would want to thank me."

"I apologize, Advocate Redwish." Khazak's tone definitely does not suggest he apologizes. "I meant no offense."

"Yes well, unless there is anything else, I will be on my way." He stands and moves to the door. "Good day, gentlemen."

I break the silence after he's gone. "You don't believe him, do you?"

"Of course not." Khazak sighs. "But I cannot accuse him of professional impropriety without something to back it up. I am not actually sure what I could accuse him of at all."

I move back to my seat and slump down. I'm not sure that cleared anything up, but I think we can assume whatever he did, it was intentional. If he had told me the truth about what was going to happen in that arena, I'd probably be locked with my friends right now. Which is what I'm supposed to want, right?

I look up to see Khazak lost in thought like I am, a frown on his face.

"Earlier you asked me if knowing the real reason for the ritual would have made me feel differently." His eyes meet mine when I start talking. "And the truth is, it probably would have. If Redwish had told me what was actually going to happen if I lost, then I never would have considered challenging you. Hell, if my group had just decided not to explore the ruins to begin with, we wouldn't have ended up in jail at all. So as fucked up as it is... I'm kinda happy all those things happened because if they hadn't, I might not have met you."

"I am happy I met you too, David." I can see my words warming him, and I stand to walk around the desk again.

"So what I'm saying is: me making bad decisions is a good thing." I grin and bump into his shoulder.

With a laugh, he pulls me into his lap, bringing our mouths together for a kiss that feels a lot more romantic than I expect. I linger there just a little too long, scrambling to stand a moment later when I feel flustered.

"So, uh, was there anything else around here you wanted to show me?" I sheepishly mumble.

The rest of the afternoon is pretty boring. Khazak shows me around the station a little more, showing me where equipment is kept and introducing me to the people in charge of specific departments. Toward the end of the day, I wind up cracking the Atasi book open while on the couch in Khazak's office until I feel a hand on my shoulder shaking me awake. *Shit. Time to go home.*

"So how did I do on my first day?" I ask as we walk in the door after our short walk home.

"Your performance was adequate," he teases, walking in the kitchen to return our uneaten leftovers to the icebox.

"Was it *adequate* enough to have earned a reward?" I kick off my shoes and lean against the counter.

"Not sure. My coffee *was* cold..." He turns to see me glaring and laughs. "But I suppose you did well enough. Sit on the couch."

He doesn't have to tell me twice. I move to the living room and hop onto the center of the couch. He joins me a moment later, standing in front of me before dropping to his knees and rubbing his hands along my thighs. *Oh shit, that's* what my reward is? He locks eyes with me, reaching up to tug me down by my collar into a kiss.

"You are not to move these." He grabs my wrists as we break apart, placing them on the outsides of my lightly furred thighs. "*Or* to cum without permission."

"Yes, Sir." I nod eagerly. I can do that.

His hands move to my belt, removing it and unbuttoning my pants at the waist. Hooking his fingers into my waistband, he has me lift my hips so he can pull those and my thong down and off my legs in one smooth motion. He runs his hands over my thighs, the skin-on-skin contact making me shiver. Then he lowers his head.

He nuzzles at my half-hard cock, kissing the skin where the shaft meets my sack. His facial hair tickles and his tusks scrape at my skin, the dueling sensations making me fist my hands at my sides. His tongue lathes over one of my balls, and I moan as he takes his time, kissing and licking me until I'm fully hard.

He moves up, dragging his lips along my shaft until he reaches the head, taking it into this mouth and sucking gently. His tongue dips into my foreskin, swirling around the tip and making me squirm. Looking down, I can see a glint of playfulness in his eye.

Then he swallows me down to the hilt.

"*Fuck*," I groan, struggling not to grab onto his head. My hips are less successful at remaining still, the urge to hump up into his face hitting me instantly, but his hands on my thighs hold me in place. His mouth is so hot, and wet, and I know that is an obvious description, but I've never gotten a blowjob before so fuck off—*this is amazing.*

He pulls his head back, leaving just a few inches of me in his mouth before sinking back down like it's the easiest thing to do in the world. Which it might be for him? He bobs up and down, his forehead bumping into my stomach as he goes. *Fuck*, I can feel the flat of his tongue stroking along the bottom of my shaft. I'm going to need to remember how he's doing some of this. I can already feel myself starting to get close.

Then he pauses, pulling off completely and letting my dick hit my belly with a wet *slap*. He dives back into my crotch, once again working over my nutsack with his tongue and making me gasp. Only when the urge to cum has left me do his lips wrap around my flesh once again and swallow me down.

He repeats this two more times, each bringing me closer and closer to spilling over the edge, before backing off at the last moment and moving to tease me until I calm down. After the third time, the frustration finally gets to me, and I groan. His eyes catch mine, and I can see that they're filled with that same playfulness.

"Please," I whine. "Please let me cum, Sir."

"You may cum now, puppy." The words are spoken right before he sheathes my cock in his throat.

His movements are fast and practiced, taking every inch of me without gagging. His hands are no longer holding me down, my hips free to chase the warm, wet heat of his mouth. It only takes me seconds before I'm on the edge again, my legs tense until after one final bob of head, I explode. He sinks onto my lap as my cock pulses, shooting my cum directly into his throat. If I could think straight, I'd be impressed that he isn't gagging.

I'm not thinking straight.

When I finish, I'm nothing more than a David-shaped puddle on the couch. I feel sweaty, and hot, and kinda like I want a nap. Khazak stands in front of me, holding a hand out to pull me up and kisses me. I can only barely taste myself, most of my cum already in his stomach.

"I hope you enjoyed that." He strokes my sweaty back. "Because I am going to make you work hard to earn the next one."

"Yes, Sir," I respond, a little dazed but more than up for the challenge.

Chapter Nineteen

The forest is quiet. Calm. Khazak and are walking to... Where were we walking to again? I look over at him to ask, but when I speak, the words don't sound right. When he turns to answer me, I can't understand what he's saying either. Suddenly, something in the sky swoops down at our heads. Then another, and another. A large flock of birds circle us in the sky overhead, their feathers pitch black. They're huge. I've never seen so many. They dive at us again, attacking and driving us further into the woods. Their talons claw into my skin as I struggle to pull away. No matter where I turn, they just keep coming. I can't—

"—avid. David!" I freeze when I hear my name, opening my eyes a second later.

Khazak lays in front me, hand on my shoulder.

"You were struggling in your sleep." He runs his hand down my arm. "Are you alright?"

"Yeah." I nod, rubbing my hand over my face. "Just a nightmare."

"I gathered from the thrashing," he jokes. "What was it about?"

"Angry birds." I shake my head. "It's nothing."

"Do you have nightmares a lot?" He keeps stroking my arm.

"No, not really." Not until recently at least.

He seems happy to leave it at that. After allowing us to be lazy in bed a little longer, he gets us up and moving to get ready for the day. No time for morning sex today; it's just bathroom, clothes, and breakfast. We grab lunch and are off to the station, same as yesterday.

I'm a lot less anxious when we arrive this time. I even work up the nerve to say hello to some of the people I met yesterday. Ragnar pops his head into Khazak's office when he gets in, but the rest of the morning is pretty quiet, and I end up cracking open my language book sooner rather than later. I'm at Khazak's desk asking for his help in pronouncing something when someone walks into the room.

"Attention," Khazak whispers the order to me before standing and saluting his visitor. "*Krisur Mara'ok.*"

"*Kritar Uzigar.*" This new orc is older and gruffer looking than Khazak but wearing a similar uniform. Khazak relaxes his stance as the two speak while I continue to stand in place at his side. Whatever they're talking about seems important. When they finish, the new orc looks me over for a minute before turning to Khazak, who salutes him once more before he leaves.

"Who was that?" I ask when we're alone again.

"That was Commander Grandtooth, my superior." Khazak answers before moving around the desk. "He also oversees the city's militia forces."

"That was your boss?" Considering how high up Khazak is in the food chain, that guy must be *really* important.

"Correct." He starts to leave the office. "Come with me. I need to discuss this with Ragnar."

We walk across the hall to Ragnar's office where he is seated behind his desk looking bored out of his mind.

"Ragnar." Khazak pulls his friend's attention away from his paperwork.

"Khazak." He points at the door. "Was the commander just here?"

"Yes." Khazak nods "There has been a potential robbery he wants me to look into personally."

"A robbery?" Ragnar sounds skeptical. "Isn't that a little below our pay grade?"

"Normally I would agree with you," he admits wryly. "However, this was a shipment of supplies meant for the militia, including some dwarven-smithed weapons and armor."

"Shit." That seems to cement the seriousness for him. "Do you need backup?"

"Not yet." He shakes his head. "David and I are going down to the shipyard now to see what we can learn." That actually sounds kinda fun.

"Alright, I will be here." Ragnar turns back to his paperwork and sighs.

"So, we're looking for stolen weapons?" I ask as Khazak and I go back to his office.

"We do not know for certain they have been stolen yet," Khazak responds while grabbing his sword from the wall.

"Then is that really necessary?" I point at the weapon.

"Standard protocol." He shrugs. "We can stop by Brull's shop on the way. Your boots should be ready."

I perk up even more at that. I'd almost forgotten about those.

We leave the station and start walking south. I can see the arena in the distance on our left, but eventually it vanishes behind the bars and other buildings I remember from our last visit. The area is a lot different in the daylight, most establishments not yet open for business. A lot less people too. I almost don't recognize the building until Khazak is knocking on the closed door of Brull's shop. It opens a crack and a suspicious looking eye peers out.

"Khazak, David!" Brull opens the door wider. "Come on in!"

We enter the shop with Brull not quite closing the door behind us.

"Here for the boots?" He's already walking to the backroom.

"That is correct," Khazak answers as we move to the counter.

"Finished 'em yesterday. I'll grab 'em now." He heads into the back, returning a minute later with a pair of black leather boots in his hands.

"Here you go, pup." Brull holds them out for me.

"Thanks." I try not to mumble as the boots are handed over.

"Excellent work, Brull." Khazak looks over the shoes with me. I run my fingers over the leather. They're nice. Sturdy. "Try them on, David."

I nod, kneeling down and placing the new shoes on the ground while I untie the ratty pair on my feet. I pull on the new pair one at a time, lacing them up as I go. When I'm finished, I stand up and walk around a little. They need to be broken in some, but the fit is perfect.

"Thank you," I repeat a little louder. "They're great."

"Glad you appr—" Brull's teasing is interrupted by the sounds of shouting coming from outside.

The three of us move over to the front door, which Khazak pushes the rest of the way open to reveal a small crowd gathered outside. In the center are two orcs slowly circling each other, looking like they're ready to fight.

"Just a moment," Khazak sighs before stepping outside and calling out to the group. Most of the crowd disperses immediately at his appearance, but the two feuding orcs alternate between glaring at him and each other. They relax a little when Khazak starts speaking with them but still look pretty tense. Should I be out there helping him?

"He's got it handled," Brull says from my side, reading my thoughts. "Just a couple of idiots who started drinking *much* earlier than they should have."

"Does that happen a lot?" I guess this *is* where most of the bars in the city are.

"Around this part of town." Brull walks back around to the front counter, bending over to pick up my old boots. "Want me to get rid of these for ya?"

"Please, thank you." I've got no sentimental attachment to them.

Brull once again disappears into the back while I wait for Khazak to finish outside. I look around the shop at all the toys and implements, some of which I have gotten to know very intimately. Some of them make me think about that one thing we haven't done since that first day in the arena. The thing I'm not even sure how I would get ready for. But seeing all this, maybe Brull can help me with some of the logistics.

"Can I ask you something kind of weird?" I pose the question when Brull returns from tossing my shoes.

"Sure." Brull eyes me skeptically.

"Okay, well, when I first...*met* Khazak," I start, already feeling my face and chest getting hot. "We, uh, did something that was very *new* to me."

"I'm pretty sure everything you've done in the past week has been new to you," he taunts, and he's not wrong. "But I know what you're talking about."

"Right. Well, right before we went out, one of the attendants there did...something to me. Like, to my stomach. Something that made it easier to..." I full-on blush, unable to finish my explanation.

Confusion colors Brull's face before a wave of realization passes over. "Cleansing spell."

"What?" I wasn't expecting a two-word response.

"A cleansing spell," he repeats. "It's what they used on you. It empties out and lubes up the lower half of your body."

"I, uh, that—" Brull's description has me stammering.

He holds a finger up, reaching under the counter and placing an oval shaped stone on top.

"What's that?" Besides a rock.

"A cleansing charm," he explains like I know what that is. "Place that right below your belly button for about five seconds, you'll feel it start to warm up as the spell activates."

"Oh, wow." That is a lot handier than I was expecting. "I was just gonna ask if you had any ideas for what I could do on my own."

"There are certainly less magical solutions," he offers, "but they all require a lot of time and effort that is better spent on what comes *after* the cleaning."

Morbid curiosity almost has me asking about those alternate solutions, but I think better of it. "Do you sell a lot of these?"

"Oh yeah, one of my best sellers." He nods. "I've been trying to convince the head of the Healer's Guild to let me start selling some that will work as contraceptives, but they won't budge."

"They make them for that too?" I can think of a few girls back home who would have found a charm like that very useful.

"You'd be surprised what the mind comes up with when a person is dedicated and horny enough." He's joking, but given all the new things I've discovered in the last week—several of them in this very shop—there has to be some truth to that.

"How much are they?" I look down at the small and unassuming smooth stone.

"Four gral." My stomach sinks a little. That was almost as much as my entire wardrobe.

"Oh. I, uh, don't have any money." I frown, scratching the back of my head. I'll need to talk to Sir about how I'm getting paid. Or if I'm getting paid at all.

"Well, I'm sure we can come up with some way you can pay me back." He eyes me lecherously before sliding the stone towards me. "Kidding. Consider it a gift. Not just for you, but for Khazak."

"Really?" I know I shouldn't be surprised by the kindness by now, but I'm still not expecting it.

"Yeah. I know it's only been a week, but I think you're good for him." He smiles and waves off my concerns. "The charm holds fifty charges. When they've all been used, you can either find a healer who knows the spell to recharge it or just buy a new one."

"Got it." I nod and take the charm and slide it into my pocket. Fifty charges should be more than enough for the next two months. Who would even know that spell? Gods, I can just imagine trying to ask Corrine to recharge it. "Is there anything else I should know?" Using unknown magical items can be dangerous.

"Don't use it more than three times a week and never more than once a day. Good way to end up malnourished." My eyes go wide. I never considered that. "Other than that, just have fun."

"I will. Thanks." I smile at the horny orc.

"Yes, thank you, Brull." Khazak steps back inside at that exact moment. "The boots look wonderful. As much as I would love to stay and catch up, David and I need to get back to work." He turns to me. "Ready?"

"Yes, Sir." I nod and clutch the charm in my pocket. Can't wait to surprise him later. One that won't end with an arguably well-deserved spanking for once!

"Good to see you as always, brother." Brull walks us to the door. "Don't be a stranger. You either, David." With a wink, he shuts the door behind us.

We continue our march south, leaving most of the bars and shops behind us. I notice the buildings around us getting bigger, not taller but taking up more space. Off in the distance, I can see the wall surrounding the city getting closer, and I think I spot a section where it opens up entirely.

"This is the industrial section of the city," Khazak explains as we walk. "Mainly workshops and factories as well as a few storehouses."

That explains the size of the buildings. Manufacturing things takes space.

"See that building there?" He points to a lot on the right. "That is where Jarek works."

On our right is a set of smaller buildings surrounding a large open yard filled with young trees—a nursery. I see a pair of orcs surround one and use magic to remove it from the ground, almost like they're melting the earth away from its roots. They lift it and bring it to an open-air building, laying it onto a workbench. Then, still using magic, they begin to bend and shape the tree in tandem. It's fascinating to watch.

"That's what Jarek does?" As far as I know, we just have regular wood-workers and carpenters in Lutheria.

"He made much of the furniture in my home personally," he muses. "A housewarming gift."

As we continue walking, I think I hear the sound of running water. Not much farther ahead, I see where the wall ends and gives way to reveal the banks of a wide river on our right. Looking across to the other bank, I see a small cottage in front of an open clearing, one that is filled with live-stock—cows, goats, chickens. So *that's* where they've been keeping them.

"The area we use for farmland is an island." He gestures across the river. "The river forks about two kilometers east of here and then loops around to rejoin two kilometers in the west."

"And two kilometers is..." Am I going to have to relearn math while I'm here too?

"One and a quarter miles." He rolls his eyes. "The river is the main way shipments and deliveries are brought in and out of Tah'lj."

"Isn't that dangerous with the whole secret city thing?" What's to stop anyone from just floating down and waltzing in?

"We have a number of guard posts set up along the river." He points a finger both down and upstream. "Should someone manage to slip past them, there are a series of silent alarm spells set along the path. If one of them is tripped, or if a guard alerts us and we activate them, illusion spells designed to disguise the riverbanks are triggered."

"Sounds like a lot of work." Hiding a city in the forest seems exhausting.

"It is a very rare occurrence." Moving down the river bank, he points at a set of docks and small buildings coming up on our side of the river. "That is the shipyard."

It is indeed a shipyard, though much smaller than one you'd see on the coast. A series of docks extend into the river, a few with small boats tied to them. Small unassuming buildings stand in front, and I can see where the city wall and forest begin again just beyond them. Khazak leads the way inside the closest building.

"*Drepa lat.*" The person behind the counter greets us as we enter, doing a double take when he sees Khazak's uniform.

"Good morning," Khazak responds in Common for my benefit. "Captain Ironstorm with the rangers. We are here about the missing militia shipment."

"Oh yes! Let me just—"

"Captain Ironstorm." The voice catches all three of us by surprise, and we turn to see an older, very well-dressed orc emerging from a back room.

"Councilman Murbank." Khazak gives a little bow, and I wonder if I should copy him.

"I just learned what happened this morning." The man's voice is filled with concern. "The men and women who serve on the militia are nothing short of heroes, and the idea that someone would steal from them is unconscionable. I insisted on coming down personally to assist in any way I could."

"Thank you very much, sir. I agree about the militia." Khazak nods his head. "We were just about to begin the investigation, but I will personally make sure you are updated as we learn more."

"Excellent." He clasps Khazak on the shoulder, smiling. "Please let me know if there is anything I can do for you." He then turns to his employee before he returns to his backroom. "Help them with whatever they need."

"Yes, sir." The employee nods.

"Who was that?" Besides a politician?

"One of the members of the tribal council." I gathered that from the title. "He owns this shipyard."

"Wow. So he's rich?" Owning the city's shipyard must be *very* lucrative.

"Do you remember the story I told you about the orcs who invented our plumbing system?" I nod. "One of them was his father."

"Oh, so he's *rich*-rich." Should have figured when I realized he was a politician.

"Quite." He turns back to the man who has been waiting patiently behind the counter. "Good morning."

"Good morning, sir." He repeats. "I was just gathering the records on that delivery for you." He hands over a stack of papers. "The shipment from the city of Kiz'Urngor arrived yesterday evening. If you will follow me, I can take you to the storage unit it was held in."

Ironstorm starts to flip through the pages while the man walks us out of the building and across the street. He opens the gate to a series of small warehouses all lined up in rows, which feels a little familiar and not in a great way. We wind through them until we come to a stop in front of a specific unit as the orc leading us pulls out a key.

"Two members of the militia came this morning to pick up and transport the delivery to their headquarters, but when they were brought to retrieve the items..." The worker opens the large doors on the unit, revealing an empty interior. "Nothing was here."

"I can see that." Khazak steps inside and looks around. "What about the wards usually placed on the storage units?"

"All dispelled," the man says with a sigh. "Not a single alarm spell was triggered, and there is no sign of anyone having been in or out overnight."

"An officer will be down later to run a magical analysis and verify that." Khazak runs his fingers along the unit's inner wall. "This sheet says Thog Grimrock accepted the delivery. Is he here?"

"No sir, he is not working today." The employee shakes his head.

"Do you know him well?" I can see Sir switching into interrogation mode.

"We have worked together for a few years." He thinks for a moment. "I would not exactly say we are friends."

"Is he a hard worker? Difficult to work with at all?" He seems to think he might have a lead.

"He always gets his job done, and we get along fine." The man shrugs. "He's always seemed nice enough."

"Thank you for the answers. I am afraid I will need to speak with him next." Sir exits the unit. "Would it be possible to get his address?"

"Yes, sir. I can get you that back in the office." The man closes and locks the gate on the storage unit before leading us out.

"You think this Thog guy did it?" I ask under my breath.

"I do not know, but it is the only lead we have at the moment." He pauses. "If the ward spells were all removed from the unit, that means whoever did this is either an employee or working with a powerful magic user."

"Are there a lot of strong wizards in the area?" I wonder if that is something you can even keep track of.

"Not many that I know of." He sighs. "Hopefully the forensic mages will be able to pull traces of something."

Back inside, the employee walks back around the desk, grabbing a pen, ink, and a sheet of paper before pulling out a thick book. Must be some of the business's records. He's flipping through to find something in particular.

"Here we are." He spots it and begins jotting down words. "Here is the address I have on file, sir."

"Thank you very much, Mister..." I think he just realized we never got the guy's name.

"Kurdt Swiftrun." He hands over the paper. "I hope this helps. Please let us know if there is anything else we can do," he repeats his boss's line to us.

"Thank you. I hope the rest of your day is a pleasant one." He gives the man a quick bow of his head. "*Rumk'r avon.*"

"You as well. *Rumk'r avon.*" Kurdt returns the bow as we walk out of the building.

"Is that our next stop?" I indicate to the paper in Khazak's hand as we start walking north.

"Not yet. I want to go back to the station first." He looks bothered by something. "If they are the magic user we are looking for, this may be more dangerous than anticipated."

"So backup might be a good idea." Hadn't considered that. I might be fast and Khazak might be strong, but a wizard just needs one well-timed spell and we're finished.

"I am sure it is nothing we cannot handle." He turns to grin at me. "Much more exciting than your first day, eh?"

"Looking good so far." I have to agree, though I still haven't done anything except stand around gawking. Hopefully I'll be of more use when we meet Thog.

Chapter Twenty

𝕿he sun is high in the sky by the time we make it back to the station, and if we weren't in the middle of something important, I'd ask to stop for lunch. Searching for a shipment of missing and possibly stolen weapons is admittedly a pretty great reason for working through it though, so I keep it to myself. Our first stop is to the forensic lab, where Khazak asks the mages to inspect the storage unit. Then we walk straight into Ragnar's office.

"How did it go?" He looks up when we enter.

"We confirmed the items were delivered, but there was no sign of them when the militia attempted to retrieve them this morning." Khazak stands behind one of the chairs in front of the desk.

"So they were stolen?" Ragnar sighs.

"That is the assumption." Khazak nods, standing in front of his desk. "All the wards on the storage unit had been dispelled and not a single alarm triggered."

"Shit." Ragnar sits up straighter. "Any leads?"

"I have the address of the worker who signed for the shipment. We were going over there to interview him next." Khazak holds up the paper with Thog's information.

"You want backup?" Ragnar sounds hopeful to get out of the office.

"To be on the safe side." Khazak nods.

"You got it." Ragnar grabs his own sword from the wall behind him and we head out.

"Do you really think this guy is dangerous?" I'm feeling a little under-dressed walking between these two big...swords.

"No, not really." Khazak shakes his head. "But I would rather be pre-pared than caught by surprise."

We make our way to a section of town I haven't been in yet. The houses here are much smaller, though there are also some large buildings that look like they could be apartments. I see broken fences and a lot of sparse clotheslines, and I realize we are probably in a lower-income area of the city.

"This is it." Khazak stops us before we approach Thog's small home. "Okay, David. Deputy Rockfang and I will be asking Mr. Grimrock some questions, which will also keep him busy. While that is happening, I would like you to look around his home for anything suspicious."

"Are you sure that's okay?" Seems a little weird.

"This is one of those grey areas I mentioned." He shrugs.

"What am I looking for exactly?" Am I just supposed to search through all his stuff?

"Just anything that seems out of the ordinary." I give him a look. What does that even mean? "I understand your idea of 'ordinary' might differ from ours, but trust your instincts."

"Yes, Sir," I sigh. Nothing like vague instructions, a case that involves the city's military, and my own personal hang-ups to really pile on the pressure and stress. I'm sure there's no way I can screw this up. It's not like Khazak's high ranking job or professional reputation are on the line.

I keep my thoughts to myself as Khazak reaches out to knock on the door, which opens a crack a minute later.

"Hello?" The occupant is still mostly hidden by the door.

"Good morning, Mr. Grimrock? I am Captain Ironstorm, and this is Deputy Captain Rockfang, with the rangers." Khazak motions to the insignia on his shoulder. "I am here about the militia delivery you signed for yesterday. I was hoping you might have a moment to speak with us."

"I don't know nothing about weapons being stolen." Well, that is an interesting thing to say when we haven't mentioned anything being stolen yet.

"I understand, sir." Khazak definitely doesn't believe him. "However, I still need you to answer some questions. May we come in?"

There's a moment of hesitation, but then he nods, opening the door all the way and waving us inside. It's a small home, much smaller than Khazak's. The living room is barely bigger than our bedroom, and there's a small kitchen connected in the back of the room, separated only by a long counter. A lot of the furniture just seems less...nice. Thog himself is about my height, though stockier, with braided mid-length brown hair that passes his ears. His large tusks have been scowling at us since we entered.

"Who's he?" He stands stiffly behind his couch, eyeing me wearily.

"My avakesh and assistant," Sir responds as both orcs I came with move to partially block me from his view. Almost wish I had that collar now. "Could you walk us through what happened last night when you received the delivery?"

As Thog starts to recount things, Ragnar gives me a look that says it's time to start snooping. I start my search slowly, wandering around the room aimlessly while I watch for Thog to notice my movements. Aside from a brief glance, the two rangers hold most of his attention, and I slip down the hall unnoticed. There are only two doors: a bathroom and a bedroom.

I start with the bedroom. It's sparse; nothing on the walls and the only furniture is a set of shelves in one corner and a small bed in another. I'm not even sure *I* would fit very well in that bed, let alone an orc. I look under the bed and pick through the shelves but don't find much interesting. Just some folded clothing and the occasional random trinket. Seems Thog has a penchant for collecting wooden carvings of animals.

I move on to the bathroom, which is nothing to write home about either. I don't see faucets so I don't think there's plumbing. Not a lot to look inside of or under either, but I check the tub and lift the cover on the thankfully empty chamber pot. Nothing. As I turn around to leave, my foot bumps into something I missed—a metal waste basket on the floor. I peer down, suddenly interested in its contents.

Sitting at the bottom is a book, leather bound and slightly singed. There are also some half-burned matches, like someone tried to burn the book but did a shitty job. But what really catches my eye is what's on the cover: a large, black claw. A bird's claw, I think. I reach down to pick it up.

I open the book, flipping through a few of the pages and noticing the burned edges. Yeah, someone definitely tried to torch this, but for whatever reason it didn't take. I try to read a few pages in vain, unable to recognize any of the letters, but I do notice a lot of numbers. I think. It's only been like a day since I started learning, alright? The way these are arranged look like some sort of table, a different one on each page. Maybe it's nothing but...better safe than sorry, right?

I step back out into the living room with my findings, waiting for a moment to grab their attention.

"Sirs." All three orcs cease their conversation and turn to look at me. "I found this in the bathroom." I hold up the book in front of me, cover out.

At the sight of the book Thog's eyes go wide, and not a second later, he bolts out the front door.

"What the fuck?!" Ragnar exclaims as the three of us take off once the surprise of the sudden exit wears off, but he's got a good lead.

"Dammit, he is getting away." Khazak growls as we watch him down the road, fading in the distance.

"Like hell he is!" I shove the book at Ragnar and start running.

"David, wait!" I hear both orcs call out to me, but I ignore them. I am *not* letting this guy get away.

He's fast but I'm faster, and I gain a good amount of ground on him before he notices I'm following him. Once he looks back though, we lock eyes and I see him panic again and start moving faster. Of course, he won't make this easy. Why couldn't this have happened next week after I had the chance to break in these boots? My feet will be killing me later.

Thankfully, the streets here are mostly empty so it's not like I'll lose him. He makes a sudden turn down an alley on our right, but I'm right on his tail. It's devoid of people, but I have to jump over a few crates Thog knocks into my path. When we emerge on the other side, the roads are significantly busier. He goes left and darts into the crowd, or at least tries to while bumping into and knocking over a lot of people.

"Sorry!" I shout behind me after leaping over a prone body on the ground. I think he did that on purpose.

He makes another turn at the next road, leading us right into the middle of a street market, possibly the same one I went to on my first full day here. Even more people and new obstacles. I have to actually focus on keeping him in my sight now, though the chorus of unhappy grunts and yells does some of the work for me. The crowd makes it next to impossible to gain any ground, at least unless I start knocking people over myself. If I don't figure something out soon, I *will* lose him. I spot a fruit cart in the middle of the road ahead of me and get an idea.

"Sorry!" I apologize again, this time to the owner of the cart whose wheel I step onto, using the leverage to leap over a small section of booths and closing some distance between us. Thanks to all the people, I don't think he notices me catching up on him.

Until he looks back, sees me, and slows down to sideswipe me. He's not as big as Khazak, but he's still got plenty of muscle on me, and when he slams into my side, it's enough to throw me off balance. I stumble and thanks to my speed, I'm still moving forward, about to crash face-first into a fabrics stall. Wonderful.

"Excuse me!" At the last second, I turn my fall into a slide and slip right under the stall's table. I roll and jump back up once I'm on the other side, still running.

I need to end this chase already, and I think I see my chance coming up ahead. There's a big enough gap in the crowd that I might be able to bring him down if I hit him hard enough. But how? I weave left and right as I scan around for an idea. Then I spot one propped up against a wall next to a weapons booth.

"I'll bring this back! I promise!" I hear the dwarf working his weapon's stall shout something at me angrily when I grab one of his staves as I run past. Hopefully Sir can explain for me later. I really have to learn Atasi if I'm gonna pull shit like this.

I ready myself as we approach the clearing in the crowd. Just as he reaches the edge, I plant my pole in the ground in front of me, jumping and pushing off to propel me forward and onto Thog's back. I land with a loud thud, staff still in one hand as I wrap my free arm around his neck. It doesn't take much more to send us both tumbling to the ground. I roll free of his body as we hit the dirt, landing much more gracefully than he does.

He's up in seconds, glaring at me for daring to try and stop him. He roars with anger and leaps at me, ready for a fight. I'm too slow, and he knocks me into the stone wall of the building behind me. *Fuck, that hurt.* I manage not to fall this time, push myself off the wall, and strike his left flank before stabbing the staff into his stomach and pushing him back.

I knock the wind out of him, but it doesn't keep him at bay for long, and he charges at me. Dad always said you should never fight dirty, but honestly I always thought that was a stupid rule. If you're in a fight, like a real I-will-be-in-serious-danger-if-I-lose-this fight, then you should use every fucking trick at your disposal. Which is why my next hit is directly to his groin followed by a firm kick to the stomach. He doubles over, though he is still standing, and I'm honestly a little impressed by his resilience. Just when I ready myself for him to come at me again, he's tackled to the ground by a green and brown blur.

Takes a sec, but it registers that the forest-colored blur is Khazak when I see him wrestling Thog to the ground. He manages to pull both of Thog's arms behind his back and slaps on a pair of manacles just as Ragnar steps up on my right holding the book I basically threw at him earlier. Glad they didn't forget that.

"Should we be helping?" I indicate to the two men struggling in the dirt. Khazak is saying something to Thog I can't really make out.

"No, he's got it," Ragnar assures me. "Good job catching him."

"Thanks." I realize I'm still holding the stolen staff in my hands. "I, uh, kinda grabbed this without asking. Can you help me give it back?"

I point at the weapon stall several yards down, complete with unhappy weapon seller glaring daggers in our direction.

"Sure." He chuckles and takes the staff from me as we both walk over to the stall. Ragnar greets the unhappy owner, apologizing for and explaining my behavior. At least I hope that's what he's saying. The face on the shop owner does soften somewhat, though I won't say he's exactly happy by the time we leave to return to Khazak and Thog.

"That was dangerous, David." He's frowning at me. "You should have listened to me when I told you to stop."

"Oh come *on*. You can't be mad at me for catching the guy." My shoulders sink and I roll my eyes.

"You could have been hurt." He looks concerned.

"But I wasn't." Other than a few scratches and bruises, I'm fine.

"What if he had a weapon?" He scowls.

Okay, why is he acting like my mom?

"He didn't." Are we just playing a big *"what if"* game now? "And if he did, I would have handled it, or do you not remember how I took you and that big-ass longsword down?"

"That is not the point," he grumbles. "You disobeyed an order."

"Well it was a stupid order." I cross my arms. "Punish me if you want, but I'm not gonna feel bad about catching the bad guy." I'm getting frustrated. All I've done since yesterday is stand around, read, and dig through trash. "Why did you bring me if you weren't going to let me do anything? Did you just want me to stand around and look pretty?"

"No, David but—"

"Then maybe trust me a little more. At least when it comes to stuff like this." I nod my head at the bound Thog who has been pointedly silent this entire conversation. "You've seen me in action. You know that I'm more than capable of chasing down this idiot. Other than handing me a book and telling me to learn a new language, you haven't given me anything to do. Forgive me for taking some initiative."

He cocks an eyebrow at my last comment. Probably could've said that a little nicer, but the rest still stands!

"*I* thought it was pretty impressive, David," Ragnar injects, ignoring Khazak's look of exasperation as we start the walk back with Thog in tow. "All the jumping and diving, using the staff. Where'd you learn to do all that?"

"Huh." Where *did* I learn to do all that? "I don't really know. I just kinda...did it."

Ragnar looks at me funny then looks at Khazak.

"Trust me. I have just as many questions as you," Khazak says flatly. He sighs, his scowl softening. "I am sorry for underestimating you, David. I know you are very capable. Perhaps after we get you some armor, we can do some combat training to show me just how capable." I like the sound of that, especially the new armor! "However, when I give you an order, you need to listen to me, especially when we are in the field."

"Yes, Sir." I try not to sigh. I know what he's getting at: listening to your leader is important. Nate not doing that is why he and everyone are in jail. But I still don't regret chasing Thog.

Our prisoner has been quiet since he stood up, something that continues as we make our way back to the station. We get a good amount of looks and people pointing and whispering, probably speculating on what the guy did. Truth be told, I'm not really sure of that myself, but the fact that he ran has to mean something, right? I'll leave that for the captain and his deputy to worry about.

"Hold on." Ragnar pauses as we approach the building. "Something has been bothering me. How did you make it into the cell yard that night without anyone seeing you?"

I stiffen at the mention of my break-in. We never really did talk about that night in detail, at least not about how I pulled it off. I'm a little nervous to pick at old wounds when things have been going pretty well lately, my sore ass notwithstanding. I look over to Khazak, who gives me a nod of encouragement. Alright.

"I climbed over the wall." I point at the wall in question. "Well, more jumped."

"What?" Ragnar and Khazak both look from the wall to me. "How? Those walls are almost fifteen feet high." For once, someone doesn't make me convert measurements.

"I used that pole." I point to the streetlight on the corner." They both look at me skeptically. "I guess I could show you?"

"Please." This time it's Khazak speaking. "I am very curious now myself."

"Okay." I start to walk to my starting position but pause. "I'm not going to get in trouble for this, right?"

"No, David, you will not get in trouble," Khazak assures me as Ragnar laughs next to him.

"I need the sidewalk clear from here to the other corner." I stand with the wall on my right.

Ragnar does the work of moving away anyone between me and the light post while Khazak stands off to the side holding onto Thog's cuffs.

I crouch down and look at my goal. It's easier to see in the daylight, but the fact that I have an audience now is making me nervous. There are even more people gathering now that they noticed Ragnar trying to clear the area. It's alright. I can do this. I already did it once.

I run, charging down the sidewalk with everything I've got. I fan out as I near my mark, running back in at an angle and jumping at the wall. I kick off with my feet, aiming for and grabbing the pole. I swing around once to build up moment and then let myself fly, once again just barely grabbing the lip of the wall with my hands.

I hear people cheering as I pull myself up, and I carefully flip myself around to look down at my audience. I mostly ignore the people clapping, instead focusing on my slack-jawed owner and his deputy. Even Thog looks shocked.

"What in the hell..." Ragnar mutters loud enough for me to hear.

"*How?*" Khazak looks at me shocked but not like he expects a real answer.

I shrug. "*Tada?* Can someone help me down now?" The height is a little more intimidating in the daylight.

Khazak responds by pushing Thog at Ragnar and walking closer to the wall. "Jump." He holds out his arms. "I will catch you."

I raise an eyebrow at what seems like an overly-cheesy display, but that does sound better than ungracefully hitting the ground with my ass.

"Okay." I nod, inching toward the wall's edge. "Ready?"

"Ready."

After gathering my nerves, I let myself fall, and I'm caught by a pair of muscular arms. "Oof."

"Got you," Khazak tells me after I peek one eye open before he sets me down.

"Thanks." I try not to blush, but the audience isn't helping.

Ragnar finishes waving off the stragglers still hanging around before joining us with Thog in tow. "That was amazing, David." He then turns to Khazak. "What do we do about that? Make the walls taller?"

"They are already four and a half meters high," Khazak responds, the four of us walking around to enter the building. "I suppose we could add spikes?"

"Seems violent." Ragnar frowns. "We definitely need to do something after giving everyone a free demonstration."

"We can talk ideas after Mr. Grimrock finishes answering our questions." Khazak's tone shifts into what I'm calling interrogation mode.

"You take him first. I am going to ask the forensic mages to take a look at the journal."

"On it, sir." Ragnar's tone shifts the same way as he starts walking Thog through the building, talking to him. "This all could have been so much simpler."

After that, there isn't much for me to do. Khazak joins Ragnar in the interrogation but won't let me follow. He says something about regulations, but I think he's more worried that I'll throw off their rhythm. Which is fair—they've worked together for years, and I wouldn't even know what to ask.

It's just so boring sitting here in the breakroom and pretending to read my book when all I want to do is figure out this mystery. There's an entire shipment of weapons and armor missing, magical alarms and traps that were dispelled like they were nothing, and a mysteriously burned book that our suspect ran at the sight of. It's been over an hour already. I just wanna know what's going on!

"Hmm." Orim is in here with me, seemingly doing the same thing, though he's much further along in his book. He looks up from his table. "Can you help? Please."

"Sure." I'll do my best, but book-learning has never been my strong suit, so book-teaching isn't gonna be much better. I move over to his table. "What's wrong?"

"Just...confusion," he starts. "'I walk to work'" is right. 'I walk to work yesterday' is *not* right. Why?"

I reread both statements a few times because I'm not sure what he's talking about at first. "Oh! The second sentence isn't in past tense."

"How do I fix?" He looks at me intently.

"Well, I think you just need to change the verb." I hope I don't sound like I know what I'm talking about. "So you want to change 'walk' into 'walked.'"

"Add 'ed' to the end?" He scratches his beard.

"Yeah." *Yay, he gets it!*

"Do all past tense words end in 'ed'?" He looks hopeful when he asks.

"Err, no." I shake my head. "Sometimes you have to change a 'u' or an 'i' to an 'a.' Other times it's something else entirely. It depends on the word." He scowls at me. "Hey, don't get mad at me. I think it's stupid too."

"Thank you for help." The scowls fades into something happier, then he looks over at my book on the other table. "I can help you sometime?"

"That would be great." I'll take all the help I can get. "Actually, maybe you can explain to me the difference between these two letters because

I swear they sound exactly the same when Captain Ironstorm tries to show me."

I go to grab my book but don't get the chance because the man himself walks in. "David, we finished questioning Mr. Grimrock, if you would join us." Still in interrogation mode I see. *Woof.*

"Yes, Sir." I turn to Orim. "Next time?"

"Next time." He nods.

"Making friends already I see," Khazak comments as we walk to Ragnar's office.

"I'm very popular." *Not too shabby looking either.*

"Unfortunately, we were not able to get much information out of Thog." He starts to fill me in as we enter. "We have no idea where the shipment might be."

"What could he have done with it?" We're literally talking about supplies for a small army.

"He claims to have destroyed it," Khazak answers flatly. "Says he threw everything in the river. We have already sent officers to scour the riverbed, but we are fairly confident they are not going to find anything."

"Why would he do that? Or why would he say he did that, I guess?" Kind of bold to just confess after leading us on a chase like that.

"We're still trying to figure that out," Ragnar speaks up. "He was tight-lipped about everything else we asked him. The only other thing we could get out of him was when he denied that he was working with anyone else. So we know *that's* a lie."

That's really frustrating. He has to be protecting someone, right? "What about the book?"

"A schedule of deliveries, including the one that has gone missing." Khazak taps the book where it sits on Ragnar's desk. "The shipments themselves do not seem to have much of a connection. More weapons and armor, alchemy and medical supplies, even food. Some of are not expected for more than a month. We are not sure how he would have gotten the information."

"Couldn't he have stolen it from work?" He does work *at* the place people ship things to.

"Already considered that." Khazak takes a seat on the couch. "We need to check the shipyard's files, but it seems unlikely. I doubt some of these orders have even been placed yet. The shipyard would not have a record of those."

"The book *is* enchanted through." Ragnar holds up the book in question. "Specifically so it can't be burned. Which is fine when protecting your record keeping..."

"But is weird when it's evidence of a potential crime." Right?

"Our thoughts exactly." Ragnar nods before sighing. "The mages were not able to glean any other information from the book or anything about the wards on the storage unit either."

"What about the symbol on the front?" The eagle's claw. Okay, it's probably not an eagle, but it has me thinking about my nightmare this morning which might be creeping me out a little.

"Oh, get *this*." Ragnar looks excited. "He's got the *same* symbol tattooed on his arm. The captain noticed it when he rolled up his sleeves."

"What does it mean?" *Now I'm excited!*

"No idea!" Ragnar throws his hands in the air, a big fake smile on his face.

"Boo," I pout. "What happens now?"

"Well, we have enough to charge him for the theft." Khazak stands, walking over to the desk. "But we still do not know where the shipment is."

"We'll search his place, but you saw the size of it." Ragnar shrugs. "Not sure where he could hide that many sets of full plate mail and two dozen swords in there. Not to mention everything else."

"Councilman Murbank let us know they conducted a full search of the other units after we left this morning. No sign of the goods there either." Khazak sighs. "The good news is that we will now be able to alert the individuals in this book so steps can be taken to prevent anything from being stolen. David, you and I will take care of contacting everyone on the shipment list and hopefully that will help us gather some more information." Khazak sounds optimistic as he stands up.

"Yes, Sir." That sounds like it could be interesting.

"But do you know what comes next for *you*, my noble deputy?" He walks around the desk and places his hand on Ragnar's shoulder.

"...What?" Ragnar eyes his friend and superior suspiciously.

"Paperwork." Khazak grins wide.

"Aww. Sad wood." I pretend my finger is a tear rolling down my cheek as Ragnar curses at the both of us.

The rest of the day passes in a blur. We visit a few businesses around the city to talk to the owners, all who seem shocked when they learn they may have been targeted for a robbery. Khazak was right; the shipyard doesn't have even half of the orders on file yet, and the ones that are change their shipping plans immediately. None of them turn up any new info though, and Khazak still can't seem to find a connection between them.

Councilman Murbank is naturally surprised to learn of his employees' arrest and offers his apologies. He and Khazak discuss plans for increased security and what sounds like a potential stakeout for the next delivery, but they don't sound very confident. If the people behind this know we have Thog, they're probably already changing their plans.

By the time we get home at the end of the day, my feet are fucking sore. I probably have a blister or two, but I think I can say these boots have been officially broken in. Later, while we're sitting around the dinner table, I wonder what it might take to convince Khazak to give me a foot rub. That and why we seem to be eating fish...again.

"So, this isn't a complaint, but...is there a reason we've had fish at almost every meal for the last few days?" At least every meal that hasn't been prepared by someone else. It all tastes great, usually some kind of salmon I think, but it seems weird.

"I...may have used all my good cuts of meat last week in my attempts to impress you." Khazak looks sheepish as he toys with his meal.

Aww, he was trying to use meat to tell me he liked me. "That is... really sweet."

"I am glad you think so because we will be eating fish for at least a few more days." Khazak tilts his head toward the icebox, and I laugh. "What?"

"Just thinking about how things might have been different if we had just talked." I shake my head. I know if things happened differently, we probably wouldn't be sitting here together right now, but still, what a couple of idiots. "But I guess I'm happy things worked out the way they did," I tease.

"I guess I am too." Khazak's smiling but looks hesitant for some reason. "I had something I wanted to ask you."

"Everything okay?" I can't help but be a little anxious after the emotional whiplash over the past week. "I'm not in trouble for something, am I? You're not gonna actually punish me for running after that guy at work, are you?"

"No, nothing like that." He shakes his head as he stands to move next to me. "Things have been going rather well and I was wondering... I am not trying to get ahead of myself or make any assumptions, and it would

be completely fine if you said no to this, I would not be offended. I—"
He pauses, looking at my confused face before sighing to himself. I have
to admit—it's kinda cute seeing him as the flustered one for a change. "—
Am very much over thinking this. I just wanted to know how you would
feel about wearing this again."

He reaches into his pocket and pulls out a familiar chain collar. I feel
a twinge of regret, a few bad memories surfacing when I see it. But they
pass quickly now that I know a little more about what this means. Not
just the collar but the two of us. Which is a little intimidating on its own.
I'm not signing up for a commitment, I'm still leaving in two months, but
I know it's important to him.

"I'd be happy to wear your collar, Sir." I smile and lean forward, tilting
my neck so he can remove the thin chain replacement I've had on.

His fingertips tickle my neck as they pluck the chain away and replace
it with his personal collar. I shiver as the cool metal touches my skin. The
two ends of the collar hang down my shoulders, and I watch Khazak's
face as he joins them, pushing the lock closed. He stands there for a
moment, admiring me in silence.

"You look good." He strokes the side of my face.

"Thank you, Sir." I smile at the praise. This seems like a good time to
bring out my own surprise. "I have something for you, too."

"You do?" He looks at me questioningly as I reach into my pocket.

"Well, for both of us." I place my new cleansing charm on the table.

"Where did you get one of those?" Khazak looks at it on the table,
voice filled with amusement.

"A gift from Brull." I grin. "Not to get ahead of myself or anything, Sir."

It's hard to read his expression as he looks from the charm, to me,
then over to our mostly-eaten dinner, then back to me. "Go get cleaned
up. I will meet you in the bedroom."

"Yes, Sir!" I hop up and make to leave, though not before I'm pulled
in for a rough kiss and a slap on the ass.

I wash my hands and face in the bathroom before stripping down and
grabbing the charm. I'm just supposed to put it right here on my stomach,
right? The stone gets warm and *there* it goes... That's a familiar feeling, but
not one I'm sure I'll get used to. When I walk back to the bedroom, I see
Khazak coming down the hall, already stripping off his shirt.

I hop onto the bed, sitting up against the headboard when he enters
the room. He reaches over to grab one of my ankles, pulling me down
the mattress as he climbs on and stalks over me. He lowers himself to kiss
me, slotting our bodies together, his furry chest against my own. It's gentle

at the start, just leisurely pressing our lips together, but soon his tongue is demanding entrance to my mouth, and I feel his aggression building.

He grinds down into me, the roughness of his pants against my bare dick making me shudder. If he's not careful, I'm gonna leave a stain. I try to reach around to tug them off him, but he grabs my wrists the way he likes to, pressing them into the bed near my head. My whining response is muffled by his mouth.

"Patience, pup." He breaks the kiss to whisper into my ear before gently biting and licking his way down my neck.

He continues mouthing his way down my chest, nipping at each nipple before he reaches my stomach. He pauses, nuzzling my belly button before abruptly pushing himself up, grabbing me by the waist, and flipping me over. I squawk indignantly but don't struggle and am immediately rewarded when I feel his hands groping and squeezing my ass.

"Still sore?" He kneads my flesh a little rougher than he needs to.

"Only a little, Sir." I bite my lip, not really minding the small twinges of pain.

"Good." He spanks me lightly a few times before grabbing both cheeks, spreading me wide and lowering his mouth to my ass.

"Oh fuck," I groan into the sheets when I feel his wet tongue slide across my hole.

I grind my cock into the mattress as he slowly laps at me from bottom to top, his tongue pressing more firmly against my entrance on each pass. I can feel the flat of his tusks against my ass, spreading me even farther the more he pushes in. The lapping soon slows, and his tongue starts to focus on my hole, each time dipping inside a little deeper. I grab the pillow in front of me, holding onto it tightly as he toys with my ass.

Khazak settles himself on the bed, pulling back one last time to spread me wide before growling and forcing his tongue all the way into my hole. I cry out in surprise, but his hands stop me where he wants as he feasts on my ass. He fucks his tongue in and out of me, the wet sounds his mouth makes drive me crazy. All I can do to hold on is hug the pillow tighter.

With a final lick and a smack to my ass, Khazak climbs his way up my back, biting my shoulder lightly when he passes it. He reaches over to the nightstand and retrieves the lube (filing away where he keeps that for later) before sitting up, his weight on my legs. I can feel his hard dick pressing into me, especially when he uses his hand to slap it against my ass a few times.

I hear the cork on the lube as it's removed, the cool, slippery liquid spilling into the crack of my ass and making me shiver. Sir's warm fingers massage the slick into my hole as he pushes the first of them inside. He growls again from his spot perched right below my ass.

"Just as tight as the first time I felt you." I whine at the huskily spoken words. "Shhh, just need to make sure you are ready for me, puppy."

Even with the charm, he wants to make sure I'm prepared enough, which is sweet and probably necessary given how big he is. He presses more of his finger inside, and I whimper at the slow burn of my muscles being stretched. He hushes me again, his spare hand stroking my flank as he slowly fucks in and out of my hole.

Then one finger becomes two, and I cling to my comfort pillow at the added intrusion. He slows down but doesn't stop, giving me a little time to get used to the stretch before pressing them both in deeper. When he bottoms, he scissors them open, and I groan loudly as I try in vain to press myself farther onto his hand. By the time I'm up to three, he's got me writhing and begging for more.

"Pleeeeeease, Sir," I whine. "I'm ready. I swear I'm ready."

His fingers are pulled from me and my hole clenches around the empty air, but I bite back a whine because I know what comes next. I hear more rustling and feel him kneeling up, but it's not until I feel the slick, blunt head of his cock prodding at my hole that I go still. I can feel his hand gripping himself, aiming downward as lowers his weight onto me and pushes inside, breaching my hole. Even after all that stretching, it's almost too much, and my eyes squeeze shut at the full feeling.

When I open them again, I see one of his green arms stretched to the headboard above me, holding himself up while sinking himself deeper into my body. He pulls back a little, pressing down a little more on the next one, and the next one, until finally I feel the heat of his groin against my ass. He lets go of the bedframe and settles along my back, his weight pushing his cock inside me to the hilt.

He nuzzles and kisses my neck, ears, and shoulders while I shudder and whimper as my body gets used to the intrusion. I feel a gentle rumbling from his chest as one of his hands moves under my head, turning my face to the side and making it easier to breathe. I can feel his heart beating against my back, and his free hand reaches up to entangle his fingers with mine.

Slowly, Sir drags his hips back a couple of inches before relaxing and letting gravity do most of the work sliding him back into place. I let out a small moan on the return stroke, one that is repeated as the movement of his hips settles into a steady pattern of slow, lazy thrusts. The hand under my face strokes my cheek before turning me a little more, Khazak bending down to meet his lips to mine, awkward angle be damned.

I whimper into his mouth as his thrusts become more pronounced, sucking lightly on his tongue as it probes me. No longer content to let gravity take all the credit, he starts to pick up speed. His legs move to the inside of mine, pushing them apart and spreading me wide. I'm held in place as his cock drives into my body over and over, and I feel a pressure in my muscles growing that I haven't felt since that first day.

"W-what's happening?" I ask weakly, not explaining myself well at all. "Why is it d-different?"

There's no response at first, and I want to curse because I know that pretty soon, I'm barely going to be able to string together a coherent thought at all. I just want to know why cumming like *this* feels so different when I'm with him, when he's fucking me. Then I hear the low chuckle in my ear.

"Because you were made for this, pup." He bites my ear gently, his thrusts never stuttering. "Not everyone is capable, especially not their first time, but to be able to make you cum like this? Dry, hands free, on my cock?" He gives a few particularly deep thrusts. "I am so happy you are *mine*."

That's not much of an explanation, but it only takes a few more thrusts for things to finally spill over and my mind goes blank. As I cry out, my mouth is once again captured by his own, and he eagerly swallows the sounds of my pleasure. I can feel my hole spasm around him, struggling in vain to push him out.

Sir releases my head, letting it fall onto the pillow. He lifts himself with both arms, giving him more leverage and changing the angle for his cock. My eyes roll back in my head as things build once more. Sweat drips down his chest onto my back, and I can practically feel his ass bouncing up and down on top of mine as I cum again, crying out weakly.

I lay there and take my fucking, Sir's body moving faster and harder atop my own. I'm caught completely off guard when I cum for a third time, and it's not even a minute later before I can feel it starting to happen again.

Oh gods, he's going to kill me with his dick. The entire bed is shaking with the power of his thrusts.

My head lolls to the side, and I'm sure I'm drooling onto the pillow, my mind empty except for thoughts of how incredible everything feels. I don't even register when Sir's thrusts get more forceful or when I feel his dick grow thicker, right before he cums with a roar above me. His hips continue to slam me into the mattress, like his body is trying to make sure his seed is planted inside me as deep as possible. I cry out when he finishes and grinds his cock inside of me. Finally, he collapses on top of me, moving to the side just enough so that we can both breathe easily.

After a few minutes of lying in a sweaty heap, Khazak rolls us on our sides, making sure not to pull his cock from my hole. His arm wraps around my waist, and he pulls me back into his still heaving chest as we cool down. Our skins are slick with sweat, and to any outside observer, we probably look disgusting, but I feel amazing. I don't want to move from this spot for the rest of the night. Maybe the week. Once my consciousness has fully re-entered my body, I notice the hand lazily tracing patterns in the fur on my chest, and I reach my hand up to hold his.

"That was..." I start. "Don't make me wait another week and half before we do that again, Sir. Please."

I feel the rumble of his laugh, and he squeezes me against his body, which has the added effect of pressing his softening cock farther into my well-worn ass one last time before it finally slips out. My hole feels like a mess right now, but I don't care.

"It would seem as though I have been depriving myself." He kisses my neck before turning me over to face him, drawing me into him. "Thank you, David."

"I don't think you need to thank me when I enjoyed it as much as you did." Maybe even a little more when you compare our respective number of orgasms.

"Not for that. For giving this a chance, despite everything." He takes my hand, thumb ghosting over my knuckles. "Do you think you can handle this being your life for the next two months?"

I look up from my place on his chest, green eyes meeting chocolate brown, feeling warm and content for the first time in... *Fuck, maybe years.* It's an easy answer. "Yeah. I think I can do that." I lean in to kiss him, content to spend the rest of the night wrapped up in his arms.

About the Author

Dominic N. Ashen is an author and avid reader, with a heavy focus on gay, BDSM-themed erotica. After spending his youth in search of books with characters who were more like himself–queer ones, specifically–he decided to start creating some of his own. His stories star queer protagonists, most often gay and bisexual men, and feature heavy themes of dominance, submission, and all sorts of kink. Dominic loves the fantasy, sci-fi, and horror genres, with a penchant for writing longer stories where he is able to weave in the sex and kink right alongside the plot.

dominicashen.com

facebook.com/dom.n.ashen

instagram.com/dom.n.ashen

twitter.com/DomNAshen

MORE FROM DOMINIC N. ASHEN

Steel & Thunder
Storms & Sacrifice

4 Horsemen Publications

LGBT Erotica

Grayson Ace
How I Got Here
First Year Out of the Closet
You're Only a Top?
You're Only a Bottom?
I Think I'm a Serial Swiper
Lookin in All the Wrong Places
What Makes Me a Whore?
A Breach in Confidentiality
Back Door Pass

My European Adventure
An Unexpected Affair
Finding True Love

Leo Sparx
Before Alexander
Claiming Alexander
Taming Alexander
Saving Alexander

Erotica

Ali Whippe
Office Hours
Tutoring Center
Athletics
Extra Credit
Financial Aid
Bound for Release
Fetish Circuit
Now You See Him
Sexual Tourist
Swingers

Chastity Veldt
Molly in Milwaukee
Irene in Indianapolis
Lydia in Louisville
Natasha in Nashville
Alyssa in Atlanta
Betty in Birmingham
Carrie on Campus

Honey Cummings
Sleeping with Sasquatch
Cuddling with Chupacabra
Naked with New Jersey Devil
Laying with the Lady in Blue
Wanton Woman in White
Beating it with Bloody Mary
Beau and Professor Bestialora
The Goat's Gruff
Goldie and Her Three Beards
Pied Piper's Pipe
Princess Pea's Bed
Pinocchio and the Blow Up Doll
Jack's Beanstalk
Curses & Crushes

Dalia Lance
My Home on Whore Island
Slumming It on Slut Street
Training of the Tramp
The Imperfect Perfection
Spring Break
72% Match
It Was Meant To Be... Or Whatever

FANTASY/PARANORMAL ROMANCE

4HorsemenPublications.com